More titles from Kristopher Rufty

All Will Die
The Devoured and the Dead
Hell Departed: Pillowface Vs. The Lurkers
Anathema
Master of Pain
(Written with Wrath James White)
Something Violent
Seven Buried Hill
The Vampire of Plainfield
The Lurking Season
Bigfoot Beach
Desolation
Jagger
Prank Night
The Skin Show
Proud Parents
Oak Hollow
Pillowface
The Lurkers
Angel Board

Jackpot
(Written with Shane McKenzie, Adam Cesare, & David Bernstein)
Last One Alive
A Dark Autumn

Collections:
Bone Chimes
Bone Chimes 2
Escapement

PILLOWFACE

Kristopher Rufty

This book is a work of fiction. The names, characters, places, and incidents are products of the writer's imagination or have been used fictitiously and are not to be construed as real. Any resemblance to persons living or dead, actual events, locale or organizations is entirely coincidental.

For childhood friends.

CHAPTER ONE

(I)

Mother Nature enjoyed playing tricks. Dawn Cunningham would vouch her hiking expertise on it, but the heavy crunching she'd heard a few moments ago hadn't been caused by Mother Nature's peculiar sense of humor. She'd hiked this trail enough to know that deer never wandered out this far away from the streams. Those arcane footsteps were too heavy to have been a raccoon or bunny, anything small, so that didn't leave many other options. Anything that size that was not a deer wouldn't be friendly and could do physical harm to either her or Kevin. And, as an added bonus, they were probably infected with rabies.

She wondered if Kevin had heard the noises too. If he had, he wasn't saying anything about it. He'd just been sitting on the rock beside her and drinking an abundance of bottled water. She'd already warned him to take it easy. They still had two miles left to hike to the quarry. Up and down hill. He needed to savor what he could.

"About done?" she asked.

Kevin belched. "Just give me a minute to let my stomach settle, then I'll be A-okay." He smiled. His mouth was moist, and above his lip was a moustache of water beads.

She'd worried that bringing him along was a bad idea. Kevin was *not* the outdoorsman he liked to think he was. He could talk the talk,

1

but once she'd gotten him to the isolated wilderness, he'd turned into a girl. And this was bad, considering she was the girl, and had been acting more like a man than he had. But, after hearing those sounds on the other side of the grove, she'd gone into full girl mode.

Dawn couldn't shake the feeling that they were being watched.

"I'm ready to go, Kevin. This spot isn't good."

"It's better than any we've come across yet. It's got shade, rocks to sit on, and that level spot right over there would be perfect to spread out the blanket and get a little…"

"No!" He flinched at the loudness of her reaction. She smiled, taking it down a notch. "Not here."

"Why not?"

She'd probably regret it, but she decided to tell him about the noises. She explained how it could not have been a deer, and if it was big enough to be heard where she was sitting, then they definitely didn't want to meet it.

Taking it all in, he stared dumbly at the spot in the woods she'd mentioned. From his expression, one would think he had never seen trees before. "I don't hear anything."

Aggravated, she repeated herself, "Like I *said*, it followed us up from the path, then stopped over there. I could hear it pacing behind the trees, settling where it could see us, but we couldn't see it."

"If that's true, then what's it doing?"

"Measuring us out."

He shivered. "What does that mean?"

"It's seeing if we're a threat."

"Are we?"

"Highly doubtful."

"Fuck. I told you I should have brought my gun."

"We don't need the gun."

"Not right now, but we might later."

He was right. Why hadn't she let him bring it? She could have kept it in her backpack, far away from his trigger-happy hands. She supposed she didn't think they'd actually need it. Only a day long hike to camp at Murmur Lake, then another lengthy hike back to the car.

Just something fun for us to do as a team.

They hadn't been able to spend much time together lately, and she'd hoped this would be a good way of doing so.

"What do *you* think it is?" he asked, putting his water bottle in the side pocket of his backpack.

"I don't know, but if it's sizing us out, then it's big, probably either a bear or mountain lion. Bears aren't so aggressive unless they're threatened, but a mountain lion is."

Kevin put on his hat and shades. He stood up stretching, his ligaments popping and cracking. He held his right knee, rocking his leg back and forth until it popped good and loud. Dawn flinched at the awful sound. His old football injury had really been giving him some trouble in recent months. It had happened in college and continued to nag him sporadically. She wondered how it would hold up for the rest of the hike.

So far, so good.

But if they had to run …

Don't think about that.

Kevin absentmindedly rubbed his crotch. "I'll take a whiz, and then we'll head on."

Dawn groaned. "Do you have to do that here?"

"Why not?"

"Because." She pointed toward the trees.

"I won't go over *there*."

"Damn it, Kevin."

"Alright, jeez, I'll hold it." He grabbed his backpack, slid his arms through the straps, and hiked it up on his back. It tugged his sleeveless T-shirt up, exposing his burly abdomen. He grabbed the bottom of his dampened shirt and tugged it down.

Dawn glimpsed his sweaty skin. She felt a tingle inside her shorts and was beginning to wish she had taken him up on his offer to spread out the blanket. "Don't be mad."

"I'm not."

She stood up, lifted her backpack off the ground, and sat it on a rock. "Yes, you are. You think I'm being stupid."

"No," he said, smiling. "I think you're being *silly*, not stupid."

"That's just a nicer way of saying I'm being stupid." Dawn glanced at him over her shoulder. Her blond hair drooped down into her eyes, fluttering in the breeze. She figured she looked good. Skin sweaty and slick like she'd been oiled in butter. She propped her leg on the rock, and let the pack lean against it. She dug through its contents for her Chapstick. As she rubbed it across her lips she added, "You're just being nice."

She followed the path of Kevin's stare to her arched leg. Her hiking shoes were tied tight, a segment of white sock showed above her ankles. Her halter top stopped below her breasts, leaving a wide band bare around the navel. Her skin was dimpled at her ribs. Rising shorts rounded securely over her buttocks. The round curves peeked out from the bottom of her shorts. She could feel Kevin's eyes on her and wondered if he'd noticed she wasn't wearing any panties.

Probably.

He finally spoke. "You're just being sexy."

"I think the sun's getting to you."

"Maybe. But I still think you're hot."

"I *am* hot," she said. "I'm ready to take a swim in some mountain water. It's cold at first but feels *sooo* good after that."

He laughed, but then stopped. "Wait a second. Did we bring any swimsuits?"

"Nope." She hitched her pack over her shoulders, threw on her sunglasses, and kissed at him.

He should be ready to go now. Far away from those trees.

Just knowing that they'd be away from here put her at ease. She could feel the water slurping her skin like an arctic tongue, swooshing between her legs, through the valley of her buttocks. She wondered what Kevin's reaction would be in the water. Would he shrink up? Probably at first, but she'd make sure it didn't last.

They moved on.

Staying side by side when they could, Dawn would only take the lead when the trail narrowed. At times, she thought she heard something trailing them through the woods. But when she'd look over her shoulder, expecting to find a wild animal about to attack, she would find nothing.

They reached the lake just short of two hours. Within five minutes they were swimming. Kevin did not shrink up like she had feared. In fact, it took all she had to keep him off her until they reached the flat rocks on the other side. It was as if the icy water ignited a scorching spark inside of him. They made love three times and fell asleep under the sizzling sun.

When Dawn finally woke up, the sky was no longer blue, but orange and spilling a film of red over the clouds. There looked to be a couple red gashes in the violet canvas. The sun had nearly set. She cursed herself for falling asleep. They hadn't even set up the tent yet or gotten wood for the fire. Hell, they hadn't even made a makeshift fire pit to put the wood in.

And they still had to swim back across before they could even get started.

They'd really messed up by falling asleep.

Dawn sat up. Her skin felt dry and tight as she stretched. "Kevin. Wake up. We've gotta get back across. The sun's going down, and we need to get things set up."

Kevin lay on his side, his back to her. Deep in sleep, he didn't acknowledge her, so she shook him. But unlike her skin that was roasting and a little tight, his was cold. He felt sick. She hated to think he was coming down with something. They didn't bring any medicines with them, other than pain relievers and some antibiotic ointments.

"Kevin? Are you okay?" The shadow of the rocks above them cast a blue shade on his skin. She crouched, shaking him again. Then she realized the rocks weren't making his skin look blue. It actually was.

She grabbed his shoulder, rolled him over, and gasped. A scream brushed her throat.

An arrow was lodged between Kevin's eyes on the bridge of his nose. Blood had streamed into his eyes and was already drying.

He must have been dead around two hours.

Dead.

The realization punched that scream out of her. She dropped onto her rump. The rock jabbed her. How could she have not heard this? Kevin must have screamed or made some kind of noise at least. But she hadn't heard anything. She wasn't *that* heavy of a sleeper, was she?

No, she usually woke up when the garbage truck parked in front of her house. Surely she would have heard something happening to Kevin right next to her!

Unless, he'd been killed somewhere else, and then placed beside her. Or maybe someone had shot the arrow from across the lake.

Her body started convulsing. Trembling as an uncontrollable breakdown of grief shook her like a seizure. She could feel a part of her being ripped away. Kevin was dead, and she'd done nothing to prevent it. She'd slept like a baby next to him while he was *murdered!*

Dawn sprung to her feet. Her back throbbed from lying on the rocks for so long. She scanned the slopes above her. They appeared to be deserted. Just trees, grass, water, and rocks protruding from the ground like tombstones. She remembered she was naked and threw an arm over her breasts, squishing them against her chest. The other hand shielded the neatly trimmed tuft of hair between her legs. She'd never felt so exposed and vulnerable.

She scanned the rocks for her clothes but didn't find them.

Then she heard laughter.

Goosebumps pimpled her arms. The laughter was high-pitched, and indistinct. It sounded as if it had come from where they'd left their packs. With nowhere else to go, she had just one choice, one option for an escape.

The water.

She'd swim to the other side of the bank. It would be tough. Not only was it a lengthy swim to attempt, but the temperature had dropped. The water would be even colder than earlier, and it had been freezing then. After their first dip, she'd had the blazing sun to dry and warm her. All she'd have by the time she reached the other side, *if* she reached it, was the moon and night sky.

A long shot, but a shot regardless, at her survival.

Tensing up, preparing for the brutal cold splash of the water, she plunged.

(II)

Haley Olsen poured herself a hot cup of coffee. A dabble spilled onto her thumb. Before it could burn, she plopped her thumb in her mouth, and sucked. The rich taste of caffeine, hazelnut creamer, and sugar was wonderful on her tongue. She moaned. *Nothing like a great cup of coffee after an early jog and warm shower.* She took another sip from the mug as she walked to the counter. She sat the mug down and tore a paper towel from the roll hanging under the cabinet and wiped her hand.

"Joel! I made you something to eat!"

She wondered what his mood would be this morning. Last night had been awful. The last five months had been nothing short of vicious with each day like another low-blow, or sucker punch to their already crumbling moral fiber.

It began when their mom and dad were killed in a car accident back in the winter. Their father, trying to keep a dinner reservation on date night, had accidentally run a red light, and the eighteen-wheeler that hit them tore straight through the car like football players ripping through a flag on game day. Haley hoped the police would have discovered the accident was somehow the trucker's fault, like maybe he'd been drinking, texting while driving, or doped up on something, but no, that wasn't the case. The blame was all her father's. He'd been killed instantly, but Mom survived for two days on life support. She never came out of the coma and died peacefully when they pulled the plug.

After that, it wasn't long before they learned just how deceitful their own relatives could be. Distant kin, some they'd never even heard of, tried claiming a piece of their parents' fortune as if it were a twisted lottery. These *relatives* had assumed the money would be divided equally amongst the family, with all of them taking a healthy chunk of the *prize*.

It wasn't.

Mom and Dad had done what any parent would have in the same situation—left it all to their children.

Ruth Gimsby, someone who'd claimed to be a distant aunt of their dad's, offered to take Joel and raise him with her Mormon family in Utah for a generous lump of the inheritance.

Just to make things easier for Haley.

She'd thanked Ruth for the offer but declined. It was written in the will that until Joel was eighteen, Haley was to be his rightful guardian, and a judge agreed, granting her sole custody of him. That was what finally put an end to all the squabbling.

Haley was grateful their parents had put so much faith in her to raise Joel but was terrified of the obligations and responsibility. Truthfully, she felt so burdened that it was sometimes hard to breathe. Given the circumstances, she felt she'd done the best she could so far but understood there was much room for improvement. Only being twenty-three, her job and own life kept distracting her attention away from her twelve-year-old brother.

He'd need her now more than before, especially with school out for the summer.

The first weekend of summer vacation had started with the unexpected death of their dog, Rusky. A spotted, five-year-old hound dog. He went to sleep at the corner of the house, where the trees from the woods shaded a nice pool of comfort from the heat, and never woke up. Joel found him around nine last night when he'd failed to come home for his favorite meal of Gravy Train.

Joel had wanted to tramper into the woods and bury him right then, but Haley had refused. It quickly became a shouting match. She finally said they could go out there together to bury him, and that seemed to have angered him even more. He'd wanted to be alone to do it. She understood and even respected that, but she wasn't going to allow him to go into the woods by himself at night. He could get lost, hurt, maybe even worse. After hours of arguing, he'd finally agreed to wait until the morning. Then he'd stomped away to his bedroom and drifted off to sleep watching chainsaw murder movies.

Him wanting to bury Rusky was the only reason she'd attempted to get him up so early this morning.

Where's he at? He should've come down by now.

The phone rang, only once, but it was enough to ground her where she stood. She knew who it was.

Him.

The one who kept calling. He was just saying hello. Unlike last night, when he'd offered her the smacking sounds of him masturbating. Of course she'd hung up, but that hadn't discouraged him from calling back in time for her to hear a repulsing, whispery moan of ecstasy as he climaxed.

"On my way," Joel cried, jarring her from her thoughts. She could hear his clumsy, tired footsteps treading from the living room.

Haley took another sip of coffee, and suddenly felt nervous.

How did Mom and Dad do this?

Joel entered the kitchen, dressed still in what he'd been wearing last night. His hair was a rustled mess. Flat in the front, it pushed its way back on his head and stuck up in points.

"Good morning," she said.

"Hey." He squinted at the brightness of the kitchen.

"How are you feeling?" She stood by the island, tossing things in her purse as he sat at the table. He groaned his response. "That good, huh?"

"I've been better."

"Fell asleep watching chainsaw videos again?"

"It helps me relax."

Hearing him say that made her feel weird.

How can movies depicting scantily clad women being devoured with various gardening tools be relaxing?

She enjoyed reading something with scares and chills, but not blood and boobs. She'd never understand someone's love for gore, which also made her fear she'd never understand her own brother, either.

"Are you doing okay? I mean, after Rusky ..."

"Stop it," he said, cutting her off.

"If you want to talk about it ..."

"I don't.

This was already harder than she'd anticipated. "Sure?" He nodded. "Okay."

"What's to eat?"

Raising her shoulders, Haley lowered her head while warily grinning. "Well …" She grabbed a paper plate from the counter, and carried it to the table like a server, sitting it in front of him. He frowned at the two, rectangle-shaped pastries, burnt in the corners.

"Pop-Tarts?"

"Yeah. It's strawberry. Your favorite."

"You've got to be kidding."

"Uh no, I'm not. I figured I would bring pizza home for dinner or something else that you like. Haven't thought that far ahead, yet. I would have done more this morning, but … I just … ran out of time."

"Uh-huh." He clucked his tongue, staring hazily at her feeble breakfast attempt. "You woke me up at seven in the morning, on the first official day of summer vacation, just to feed me Pop-Tarts? Wow. You're the best big sister in the whole world!" He intentionally spoke to her as if he were five. Something he liked to do when he didn't get his way. He obviously hated the breakfast.

"I know it's not fantastic, but it's something, right?"

"Oh, it's something."

She sighed. "I just wanted to make sure you ate something. And this was all I had time to make."

"You're not adapting to this whole 'Mom' thing very well at all, are you?"

Ignoring his abuse, she sat an empty glass beside the plate, filling it to the brim with orange juice. "Is this okay or do you want to make me feel like shit because I didn't squeeze the oranges myself?" On her way to the fridge, she immediately regretted having said that.

"Wow," he said. "Ouch."

Putting the orange juice on the top shelf, she glanced back at him. He looked pitiful, sitting over the burnt tarts, poking them with his finger. "I'm trying my best here. This hasn't exactly been easy for me, either."

He flicked a tart. It spun off the plate and onto the table. "Whatever. You run off any chance you get and leave me here to fend for myself with Pop-Tarts and frozen dinners."

He was right. The freezer was overloaded with frozen meals. Haley felt a weight in her stomach. She thought he liked them.

Doesn't he get how hard this is for me?

How could he? He's only twelve. But he thinks he knows every goddamn thing about everyone.

Now she *really* sounded like Mom.

Haley could feel her eyes swelling. Her jaw seemed to be coming to life on its own, trembling and shaking. She was going to cry. But she wouldn't do it in front of Joel. He wouldn't get the benefit of seeing it. She slammed the fridge door so hard the magnets flew off. They spun across the floor. "I'm sorry about Rusky, but I'm also sick of you talking to me like I'm a piece of shit."

"Oh, boy." He looked to be tensing in preparation for the oncoming fight.

"After you bury Rusky, I want you to mow the yard!" She felt stupid even saying it, but it was the first thing that came to her.

"What?"

"Yep, weed-eat and all the other shit that makes a lawn look pretty. I've been doing it since the spring. It's your turn now, pal." The back of her head was going numb with anger. Her mouth moved, wanting to keep the lashing coming, but her mind didn't know what to say next. She allowed her instincts to speak on her behalf. "And if it's not done by the time I get home, I'm going to fucking burn your mask collection."

Gasping, he said, "You wouldn't dare."

"Try me."

He stared into her eyes, looking for the spot inside of her where she knew self-doubt lingered. He wouldn't find it this time. Her bright blue eyes had turned cold and callous.

Looking away, he buried his face in his hands and nodded. His voice was muffled when he said, "Fine, Haley. You can leave now. Have a good day at work."

Haley snatched her purse from the counter. Keeping her head aimed high, she marched out of the kitchen. On her way out, she glanced back and watched Joel as he folded his arms on the table and buried his face into them. She slammed the door to ring her point home.

In the garage, Haley sat in the idling car. She geared it into Reverse and thumbed the red button on the remote attached to her sun visor. The garage door slowly began to lift. By the time it was high enough for her to pass under it, she was crying too hysterically to leave.

Putting the car back into Park, she leaned her head against the steering wheel. It felt cool and hard under her wet cheek. She spent the next five minutes crying, screaming, and beating the seats with her fists.

CHAPTER TWO

(I)

A crow cawed, pulling Dawn from her slumber. It hurt to open her eyes, but when she did, she discovered that not only had morning replaced the night, but she was still naked. The sun sparkled off the dew-slick trees and her sweat-layered skin, casting a golden glow in the light mist. Pine needles carpeted the ground and felt soft and prickly under her feet.

She could vaguely remember diving into water so cold that it felt as if her body were being punched by icy fists and making it across the lake only to be ambushed by a rather attractive man who was probably in his thirties. He'd been waiting for her with a smile on his pleasant face. She'd thought he was there to help, but she couldn't have been more wrong.

A twig snapped somewhere in the distance. Dawn whipped her head around, expecting someone to be there.

Nobody was.

Her neck was tight and sore, and her head felt as if it had been pounded against concrete for hours. Her long hair, caked with mud and congealed blood, was glued to the sides of her pretty, yet bruised and scabbed face. Both eyes were blackened and swollen. The vision was blurred in the left. A trickle of blood slid down her head, down the nape of her neck.

She had no clue exactly where she was, but it was deep backwoods, where all she could see were thick walls of green and brown, choked with a calm miasma. It was almost beautiful.

A perfect morning.

The kind she usually enjoyed with Kevin and some coffee. The thought of Kevin brought a fresh batch of tears to her already stinging eyes. She was surprised there were tears left to shed.

She went to wipe her eyes, but found her arms felt jellied and artificial. Looking up, she saw both wrists had been bound to opposing trees by barbwire in a Jesus Christ pose, and then looped over two separate tree limbs. She scanned her body. Leads of barbwire had been wrapped around her naked chest and were pricking her breasts, fastening her to the tree behind her.

Tiny rivulets of blood tapered down the valley between her breasts.

It hadn't hurt until noticing it, but now she felt every puncture and poke to the slopes of her breasts and dark coins of her nipples. She tried pulling away, but it only made the sharp jabs even worse.

Dawn tugged at her wrists, feeling her flesh ripping through the numbness of her hands. She bit her lip to stop from screaming. She tried with the other hand this time, only to have the same result. The barbwire was just wrapped too tightly to wrench her hands free.

She let her weight drop into her knees. It wasn't the best position to be in, but she was exhausted, and her legs felt too weak and stringy to stand. Bending them at the knees felt much better, but the razor-sharp points of barbwire burrowed even deeper into her wrists and breasts. But right now, she didn't care.

When the burning from the penetrating points became too much, she stood up straight again.

Her eyes surveyed the area, searching for him. Turning right then left, she didn't find anybody. He'd stayed with her most of the night, watching her writhing against the tree, making her scream. She'd passed out after he'd used the machete to saw into her left calf muscle. She tried looking back to check on it but couldn't bend back that far.

Dawn looked for him again, but he still wasn't there.

Just be glad he's gone.

He must have hung her up while she was unconscious. If she'd been coherent, she sure couldn't remember him doing it, but it might be for the best that she couldn't.

How close to the lake was she? It felt like she was miles away from anywhere, a secluded planet where she'd been dumped. She wondered what they'd done with Kevin's body. One of them had to have done something with it. It was unlikely they'd just leave it there for someone to find. How many of *them* were there total? More than the man in the hat who'd left her there hanging. He was number two after the man at the lake, the handsome one with the gorgeous smile. He'd been there, filming with some old camera, while the one in the hat had tortured her.

And he was also wearing a mask.

Something scampered in the distance, but big enough that she heard it.

Now would be when I'd get attacked by a mountain lion.

She listened another moment and was finally unable to stand it any longer, so she called out, "Huh-hello?" She spoke barely above a whisper, but it hurt as if she'd been shrieking. Her throat had been screamed raw. She was parched and probably dehydrated. Her pores felt as if they were producing sweat, but her skin was dry, save all the blood. Patches of brown stains dappled over her breasts and stomach, the clear dried currents of sweat cutting paths through the redness. Her legs glistened with the combination, changing them from a bronze tint to a tacky burgundy.

There was an abundant snapping of twigs behind her somewhere. Heat racing, her skin went prickly. She expected any moment to see the Hat Man returning with more devices to harm her with.

But he never came.

She exhaled a measured breath. With her teeth clinched, the air made hissing sounds as it wafted out.

Why can't the animals out here be like the kind in Disney movies and help me get loose?

That wouldn't happen, and the men would come soon, she could feel it. She needed to be gone before they did.

Dawn checked her left wrist. A line of blood seeped down to her armpit, sparking an idea. An idea that would hurt. That didn't matter, though. She'd been hurt so much already that it didn't scare her.

She jerked her hand as hard as she could. The skin tore in skinny, serrated lines around her wrist. Blood deluged around the bracelet of barbwire. Twisting and turning, the thorny tips slashed and shredded her flesh away until there was enough blood to act as a lubricant.

As hard as she could, she yanked one more time, tearing her hand free, and leaving pieces of flesh dangling from the wire. Her arm sagged to her side like a useless appendage. Dawn gawked at her wrist, crying. There wasn't much left of it. It no longer resembled a part of her body, but only mangled meat. She was lucky she hadn't severed an artery and bled to death.

At the first hint of sensation returning to her arm, she raised it to the other and began unraveling it from the barbwire. The knot was tight, but she managed. After a struggle, and jabbing most of her fingers, she got it undone. Not giving it time to become useful again, she began working on her breasts.

Reaching behind her back, she found where the wire had been roughly rigged together. She needed to be incredibly careful here since the skin was much more sensitive. Finding two tips, she began uncoiling them as if they were a bread tie. It had been tethered sloppily, so it was not long before it became loose enough to drop. It fell to her ankles, slicing her all the way down. She collapsed onto her stomach, breathing heavily and not wanting to move. But after a moment, Dawn forced herself to stand.

Her legs wobbled, trying to give way as she looked around. The coast still seemed unbelievably clear. Gazing from right to left, she tried to decide the best way to go. Whatever she chose was a gamble. She'd never been a lucky person to begin with, so she decided to go with her gut, and charged to the right.

She nearly fell several times. But as she struggled to find her rhythm, a second wind gracefully kicked in. Soon, she was soaring, albeit with a slight limp. Leaping over fallen branches, roots that jutted up from under the ground, dodging jagged tree stumps, she raced on.

She ignored the pain in her feet. Low-hanging limbs whipped her as she ran, but she didn't let them slow her down. Their stinging lashes were nothing compared to what she'd already endured.

With her eyes focused forward, she slid on loose leaves dappled across the ground. Mother Nature was determined to make her fall, but through it all, she managed to stay upright. Her breasts bounced and swayed, slapping against her. Her blood pumped in a brisk surge.

Then her vision became hazy, slowing her to a trot. Every inch of her was vaulted with heat. Her forehead tingled. Mini sets of fireworks exploded in front of her eyes. A battering ring clamored in her ears.

Don't faint, damn it …

Dawn stumbled over each sloppy step. Unable to go any farther, she dropped to her knees, trying to regain her strength. Her damaged wrist screamed at her. She started to cry. All her abrasions and holes wrenched as her sweat seeped into them. If she ever got out of here, she'd have to bathe in a tub of disinfectant. She hugged her wrist to her chest. It seemed to help, holding it close like this.

Unbeknownst to her, someone wearing old camouflage pants and a work shirt with the sleeves ripped off at the shoulders, baring his thick muscular arms, had crept up behind her. Lines of strength cut through his biceps like thin valleys through concrete. His grimy boots were caked in dark colored filth. The clothes were horribly stained. Blood, food, bird shit, and sweat had left splotches across the fabric. His hands, black from blood and waste, ended in jagged fingernails.

Covering his face was a rough-hewn mask made from a white sack. Straps had been sewn on the sides and wrapped around the back of his head, disappearing under the short patches of hair projecting through the age-worn gaps. Three holes, two for the black eyes and one for the mouth had been sloppily cut out of the front. The mask, much like the rest of his attire, was tattered and torn.

Dawn sniffed. A revolting stench leached its way into her nose. Her scalp went crawly. Her nipples stiffened with her rising fear.

Someone was behind her.

She could smell him.

As the light breeze calmed, softening the rustling leaves, she began to hear his deep, heavy breaths. The lively woods halted, as if it were also waiting for his move.

Then the calm hush was disrupted with the explosive sound of a cranking chainsaw. It bellowed from behind her, revving several times. She couldn't hear her frantic screams over the boisterous motor.

She whipped around, catching him moving in on her, hunched over so his colossal height could step under the branches of a nearby tree. She didn't recognize this man. He wasn't either of the two men she'd already endured. He was all new.

How many are there?

The left corner of his mouth curved upward.

He's smirking at me.

He was convinced he was about to kill her, and she wasn't sure if there was a way of proving otherwise.

He's not getting me without a fight!

She sprung to her feet and bolted, trying to put distance between her and him. His stalk turned to a fanatical dash in pursuit. The chainsaw revved in front of him like a cannon.

(II)

oel stood over Rusky, tears flooding his eyes. He backhanded them away as he gaped at the dark sheet covering the remains of his departed friend.

A shell.

That was all that remained of him—an empty box, like a DVD case missing the disc.

The gentle morning was fading fast. The air was already becoming heavy on his skin. It would be scorching soon. He could smell just a hint of decay coming from under the sheet. Part of Rusky's left rear paw was poking out from under the blanket. Eager flies buzzed around it. Joel squatted, fanning them away and pushed the foot back underneath. There was some resistance, but he managed to do it. The paw no longer felt soft and warm, but dry and stiff like old, matted carpet. He needed to get the dog in the ground before it got much hotter, but he dreaded doing it. He had wanted to do it last night because the dark would have hidden Rusky's lifeless eyes and the blank frozen expression on his normally happy, enthusiastic furry face. If he couldn't see Rusky the way he was supposed to be, then he'd rather not see him at all.

Rusky was the kind of dog that always seemed to be smiling, especially when Joel came home from school. They lived deep in the country on Marble Lane, which was on the outskirts of every school district, so his school bus wasn't permitted to drive to his house. So, as a compromise, the driver would let him out at the end of the road, which left him having to tolerate a mile hike back to his house. He didn't mind it, really, and had told his mom she didn't have to wait for him out there with the car.

The true explanation behind that was he was tired of being picked on about it by the other kids on the bus, asking him if he was afraid to walk home alone, or claiming Mommy held his dick when he pissed. The quantity of humiliation he received from the guys on the bus also made talking to the girls that rode with them hopeless.

Ethan and Paul, who he considered to be his friends, would do little to defend him. They knew to keep their mouths shut or the abuse would turn on them. Joel didn't blame them for not getting involved, but still, it angered him.

But no matter how bad the bus rides were, he quickly forgot them thanks to Rusky. Somehow, which Joel could never figure, the dog knew the time Joel was set to come home as if he had a timer hidden somewhere to alert him. Didn't matter if it was sunny, raining, hot, cold, or if asteroids were pounding the earth, Rusky was programmed to the comings and goings of Joel. So when he'd be pretending to casually stride the mile-long walk, he'd come to a halfway point where the road curved at the Whitmore's house, and just on the other side was woods and an open field. It was kind of creepy, really. He often imagined werewolves lurking behind the trees, or trolls clambering through the high grass.

But all that was ever truly hiding in the bushes was a hound dog eager for a belly rub. He'd pounce on Joel, lapping his face with his warm, sloppy tongue. When he'd flop on his side and roll over, Joel knew it was time to kneel down and start scratching. He enjoyed those few moments where it was just the two of them reuniting after a long day.

"Why'd you have to die?" he asked, the tears returning. He quickly sniffed them back, trying to be tough. "You were all I had left in the world. The only real friend I've ever had." He could feel himself becoming angry with Rusky, as if it were the dog's fault he'd passed away.

A shimmer of guilt tugged at his heart. *Gotta do this. Get him buried before he starts to stink.*

Joel winced at the horrible truth. The hotter it became, the more repugnant he would be.

Joel wrapped the blanket snuggly around the dog, dug his hands under him, and scooped him up into his arms. Rusky felt as if he was ten pounds heavier. Joel strained to hold him. The dog's body was unyielding and remained firm, all four paws sticking straight out. With Rusky's body so close to him, the smell was much stronger and awful. Ignoring it the best he could, he headed for the edge of the backyard where it merged into the woods.

Joel spotted Rusky's rubber steak, his favorite chew toy. At one time it could have actually passed for a raw steak, and it also squeaked. But after three years of Rusky's chewing, his syrupy saliva, and constant burying, it had faded to a milky white and hadn't made a noise in a very long time.

Keeping his dog pressed tightly to his chest, he kneeled, flexing his fingers until he managed to pick it up. He planned to bury it with him. As he ventured on with his deceased pal trenched in his arms, Joel thought he heard something further out in the woods. He stopped, listened.

Was that a scream?

He turned his ear to the direction, trying to aim his ear where he thought it had come from. The wind drifted across him, making the thick green leaves on the branches sigh. He could hear, albeit faintly, the sputtering of a chainsaw.

He shrugged. As he entered the woods, he thought he heard it again, but this time he ignored it.

(III)

Dawn raced through the woods. She was saturated with sweat, her eyes burned from it. She slapped away low hanging branches that reached out like skeletal hands. Stealing a look over her shoulder, she saw the large man wasn't far behind, even though he moved much slower due to his bulky size. That meant she was traveling at a pace she needed to quicken. The tree limbs looked to be giving him the same trouble, but he was able to cut a path through them with his chainsaw.

Dawn wished she had something like that, or better yet, some wheels. She pictured her car sitting alone in the field where they'd left it. She had no idea how far away she was from it, so it was best to pretend it wasn't there at all. If she focused on the car, she'd just become depressed.

A thicker plot of woods came into view from up ahead. Bending forward, she charged through them, hanging an immediate left, and left him behind.

When he stomped down the hill, he realized that he'd lost her. He stopped running and scoped out the land. She couldn't have gone far. With dedicated patience, he'd find her. His dark eyes darted back and forth intuitively, as if watching a tennis match. His mouth was drooped open and panting. All he saw were hills and trees.

No girl.

Thankfully, he hadn't noticed Dawn looming behind him, holding a bulky rock above her head with both hands. The coughing motor of the chainsaw silenced her approach.

The wafting exhaust squeezed her throat, and the burning tang of gasoline and oil singed her nostrils, bringing tears to her eyes. She blinked to clear them. *Almost there. Just a few more steps.* His back was like a thick wall, a giant compared to her. Dawn had never been one who was known for her height, but this guy was ridiculously huge. *Like a bear.* Standing on the tips of her toes, and stretching her legs and arms, she brought the rock higher.

If he moves, I'm cooked. She held her breath.

What are you waiting for? She heard a voice say. It sounded like Kevin's. *He's going to catch you. Do it, now!!!*

Dawn lashed the rock back, and as she brought the rock forward, she aimed for the back of his neck…

He whipped around, the chainsaw roaring and struck the rock. Sparks showered as the rock was flung from Dawn's hands. She screamed. She'd walked straight into a trap! He revved the saw again, then lunged at her. The spinning chain was a blur. Dawn avoided its whirling points, just barely, but felt a blast of air knock the sweat beads off her sleek skin. She ran for the rock, scooping it up without slowing down. As she spun around, she swung the rock blindly, and managed to crack the rock against his jaw while he was moving in on her.

He staggered a couple of steps back.

Her moment had come.

Dawn charged, shrieking, and slammed the rock against his forehead. The solid blow resounded above the chainsaw's racket. His head tilted first, torso following, and then raising his left leg into the air, he fell on his back. A cloud of dust puffed out from under him. The chainsaw slammed the ground beside him, idling, with his hand still clutched around the handle.

Going for the saw would be risky, but she wanted—needed—to finish him off. She could bash his skull with the rock but would have to get right on top of him to try. Plus, it might take multiple hits to do the trick, but he could use that saw to put an end to her with one swing.

She needed something better.

Dawn scanned the length of his gargantuan body and spotted a machete strapped to his leg. In a provisional sheath, it quickly captured her attention as if heaven's light bore down from the clouds, illuminating it.

Thank you, God.

She smiled maniacally as she went for the blade.

She understood she was no longer in control of herself, and that somehow her body was acting without her mind's consent. She'd read about the ability to survive on animalistic instinct in books, or magazine articles featuring a mother who had lifted a bus to save her kid trapped underneath it. But she'd never believed in it, until now.

No matter what, she would survive this.

Dawn's fingers gripped the machete's handle and tugged, but it wouldn't rip free. She kept trying, yet it still remained in the same spot. By this point he was lethargically becoming alert to what she was doing and began to swat at her hands. His attempts were feeble, but it wouldn't be long before he'd regained his strength. Then she noticed a flap folded over the handle, a thin rope looped through the bottom and tied around the machete. A latch. Trying a different approach, she grabbed the holster with both hands and jerked with all she had. It snapped free from his belt. She stumbled back, falling flat on her rump. The coarse ground lacerated her buttocks, sweltering like a carpet burn sprinkled with salt.

Dawn fidgeted with the fastener, but from the intensity of her trembling hands, it was nearly impossible. Her attacker began to sit up. The chainsaw puttered steadily from the ground beside him. He adjusted his mask. Once it was precise, she could see the infuriated scowl through the torn notches in the white hood. His eyes narrowed, only showing dark black orbs inside. He snatched the chainsaw, holding it between his spread legs proudly like it was his massive penis. He revved the motor a few times, taunting.

Dawn jerked the machete free of the sheath. The lengthy blade looked as if it could slay a dragon, and she needed both hands to hold it. It was rusted from the countless blood stains of his multiple victims.

He'd managed to get to his knees. Bringing his right foot forward, he braced himself in a worshiping stance.

Screaming like a feral brute, she charged and attacked like one. She swung frantically, not caring what she hit as long it was a part of him.

And she managed to do this multiple times. Once or twice in the chest, slashing his arms, legs, whacking him across the head. The blade gouged deep into his chest, and she had to prop her foot against him to wrench it free.

Chunks of meat and swatches of clothing went flying around her.

Finally, he dropped onto his side. The chainsaw still remained clutched in his hand.

Was it glued there?

His clothes, drenched in his blood, were torn and shredded in various spots. Dawn's confidence had strengthened enough that she crossed over to him, one foot and then the next. She stepped on something sharp but ignored it. He rolled onto his back as she stood over his head, placing one foot next to each of his ears, giving him a good view between her legs. Although, he kept his right hand on the grip of the saw, she doubted he had the strength to lift it.

She had won.

Raising the machete into the air, she rolled it through her hands. With the tip pointed down, the handle gripped in her hands, she was prepped to finish him off like a druid administering a sacrifice. She gazed him over one last time. He coughed up a wad of blood. It trickled down the sides of his mouth.

She smiled.

Then she brought the machete down for the killing blow.

It stopped abruptly, veering her weight forward, and toppling her over him. When she hit the ground, she quickly rolled onto her stomach, checking to see if the machete was lodged in his chest.

It wasn't.

He held it by the blade in his left hand. The point had stopped a breadth above his chest. Somehow, he'd barehanded the blade before it could pierce him.

"*Nooo!*" She clasped handfuls of her tangled hair, screaming as all hope vacated her body. It was useless to continue this fight, pointless to think she had a chance to survive. All that was left was to run. Run as fast as she could to get away from him. She started to crawl but dropped onto her stomach when she felt a *whack* on her back. It didn't hurt right away, but the pressure made it difficult to move. Then all at once her back burned with a searing strain. Her arms became heavier, knees wobbling. She could hardly move.

Then the weight lifted with a wet rip. Glancing over her shoulder, she saw blood, her blood, seeping off the blade, dousing his hand in red.

His warped smile returned.

He'd stricken her with the machete diagonally across her back from shoulder blade to hip. A warm wetness oozed down her back, cascading her buttocks and thighs.

You will not die here on your knees. Get up you helpless bitch!

Finally, her mind took control of her body again. Though it hurt like hell, she forced herself to stand.

She bolted deeper into the woods. Soon, she could barely hear the putter of the chainsaw at all as the woods thickened, immersing her. She smiled, knowing she'd left him back there.

CHAPTER THREE

(I)

Joel gently patted the ground flat with the shovel. It had taken longer than he'd expected, but Rusky was at last buried. He'd finally quit crying when the process had become such a chore. But now it was done. Joel could recollect himself and remember just why he'd been working so hard. Plus, returning home didn't seem so nice. He'd rather remain in the woods as long as possible.

Nearby was an old tree stump. Using the shovel like a walking stick, he went over to it and sat. Some birds chirped, but other than that the woods were silent. For a moment, he thought he heard the chainsaw again, but it was soon forgotten.

He sighed, staring at the island of loose dirt at his feet.

(II)

Dawn needed to live, and not just for her, but for Kevin as well. Yes, he was dead, but she owed it to him to survive, to get the police, and make sure these sick fucks paid for what they had done.

Her ears caught wind of a dulcet sound. It took a moment to register, but slowly she began to realize someone else was out here. She could hear them, the tone was higher, young, and they were crying.

Had to be a kid.

What's a kid doing out here? Don't they have any idea what's in these woods?

Her bladder pushed against her back, announcing it was at a surplus level. She wondered how long she'd had to pee before just now noticing. Keeping her legs clenched tight, she walked toward the sobs. Hope overruled the dread of someone being out here; maybe they could help. *Or, God forbid, they could be hurt as well.* Maybe they'd had a run in with the psychopaths. Whatever the case, she needed to find out for sure.

Her footsteps barely produced a sound above a light scuttle. Her stomach was starting to cramp from holding in her pee. She wouldn't last much longer. Treading softly, she squatted behind a cluster of bushes. She could hear the soft weeping much clearer now.

Then her bladder released, hastily emptying a day's worth of urine on the ground below her. Spats of warm liquid splashed her ankles. It speckled across her wounds, infuriating them to sting, but the flaming commotion inside of her was even worse, scorching, as hot as the sun from the all-night abuse, bringing more tears to her eyes as her bladder continued to drain what she'd kept dammed up for so long. She wanted to scream but bit her lip to keep her mouth shut. A few faint whimpers managed to escape her tightly scrunched lips, but not enough that anyone should have heard her. She was more worried about the gushing splashes her urine was making as it rained on the dry ground.

Finally, the pee reduced to a trickle, then to a drip. She shook her hips from side to side, making sure there were no leftovers. Out of habit, she went to pull up her panties. She still was naked, had been since making love to Kevin for the last time. She'd never be with him again. Another snivel emerged, but she stopped it.

And noticed the sobbing had stopped.

Had they heard her peeing? Were they killed? She imagined another deformed maniac charging through the bushes to get her while she squatted.

That'd be a way to go out.

How Dawn's luck had been so far, it seemed absolutely feasible.

Dawn eased her face into the bushes. She could smell their sweet scent. She used her hands to part the bushes just enough to peek through. Movement caught her attention to her left. Shifting her body to see, she spotted a boy. Tall and slender, he looked to be much older than he'd sounded. The young man she saw had to be close to fourteen, maybe a little younger. His back was turned to her, and he was dragging something behind him.

A shovel?

His hair waved in the slight breeze, as if telling her goodbye. She couldn't let him go. He appeared too old to be lost and didn't look frightened. His posture suggested he was sad. Heartbroken.

Don't let him go!

When she stood up, the bushes were level with her chest, and her head poked above the shrubbery like an additional limb. As she opened her mouth to call out, a sticky thick hand covered it, choking off her cries. A sour stench filled her nostrils. She could feel warm saliva dripping along the back of her neck.

Her head was jerked back and all she could see was the brilliant blue sky above. She caught a quick glimpse of something metal as it passed over her face. A stiff coldness pressed against her throat. In a quick instant, it shot across her skin, leaving her throat smoldering. Thick currents of heat ran down, sloshing her breasts. The hand left her mouth. She tried screaming but could only generate a sopping burble.

When she attempted to run, her legs wouldn't cooperate. She fell through the bushes, landing on soft, freshly tilled dirt. A batter of red splattered the ground below her.

Blood?

She caressed her throat. Pulling her hand away, she found it swashed with red fluid the solidity of syrup and hot as soup.

Her vision distorted. When she checked for the boy, she glimpsed him just briefly as he disappeared over a hill. She tried calling for him, but again, nothing happened. She'd seen enough horror movies to know that her throat had been slit, and she'd always assumed it to be a terrible way to die. She'd been right. It was slow, agonizing, with her mind remaining sturdy enough to grasp the awful truth that she was bleeding to death.

Dawn looked for the man and found him hunched over, using a tree for support. His clothes were soaked as if he'd been caught in a heavy rain. *A heavy red rain.* She'd done a number on him, too. He'd probably die soon.

We can die together.

Whether she'd bleed out or not, she was going to try and catch up to the kid. If there was a chance he could help her, then by God Almighty she was going to take it.

On impulse alone, she got on her feet, and staggered after the boy.

He followed progressively behind the woman. So tired, he wanted to lie down and sleep. He'd butchered enough people to know that if you're cut up this bad and go to sleep you don't wake up.

He kept the distance short as he followed her but didn't know what to do once he caught her again. If that boy was there, he wasn't sure what to do with him, either. For some outlandish reason he couldn't quite fathom, he didn't want to kill the kid. He'd slain plenty his age before, even younger, but there was something unique about him that he had picked up on right away. He felt a bizarre attraction to him. Not that he wanted to use the boy for sexual immoralities, it was different.

He could feel a connection.

The boy was sad, and he felt that, also.

(III)

Dawn tottered through the woods, bumping into tree after tree. The kid had vanished from her sight, but she wasn't giving up. There was strength left in her legs and she was going to use all of it. Her vision was frosting over, blurring out of focus, but she could still somewhat see, so she was going to continue.

The woods started to thin out. As she approached the top of a small incline, she noticed there was a house up ahead. She'd nearly reached the end of the woods, and from where she stood, she could see where a yard began. She also located roofs of other houses scattered throughout the woods farther away. She'd been walking down the mountain all this time, slowly approaching a tiny community. If that was the case, she had a pretty good idea of where she was, and better yet, where her car was. If only she could get the boy, to a phone, she could put an end to all of this.

Her body tingled with excitement. Help was so close her stomach ached for it. She ran. Not a swift rate, but it was the best she could do. She felt a pinching pressure in her head as she reached the bottom of the small hill.

There he is!

The kid was exiting the woods ahead of her, but still so far away that she doubted he'd hear her if she tried calling for him. At least she had the visual confirmation he was still ahead of her, and she would follow him out. She pushed herself harder. She didn't have to worry about dodging the trees; for they were so spread out they barely seemed to be there at all.

She reached the edge of the woods, stopping at a tree to observe the location.

A thought swished through her head.

What if I'm already dead, and this kid is leading me to Heaven?

What if he wasn't leading her to Heaven, but somewhere else?

Now here's a very farfetched idea. What if he's just an ordinary kid who's just going about his business as he would any other day and is totally unaware of me?

That seemed the most likely.

She set her eyes on the backyard of the nice house. There was a wooden fence that separated it from the house next to it, but the kid was nowhere to be found. She began to feel a slight tremor of panic until hearing a ruckus inside the shed. It may be a good idea to check there.

She stepped into the yard. The ground here was much softer on her feet. The grass was high and grazed her shins as she pressed through. It felt like feathers compared to the rough terrain her feet had endured.

Another clang resonated from the shed. The door was open, and inside she could see the kid struggling with a push-mower. It was giving him some trouble as he tried pulling it out of the shed. Her heart pounded. He was there. She was so close. She was going to make it after all.

Then there was a tight grip around her stomach. Her feet lifted off the ground as she sailed backward. Everything was happening so fast. She grabbed at the air, hoping somehow, she'd latch onto something firm that could stop her recoil.

The hold loosened. She dropped roughly on her back. Trees bowed above her, lightly swaying in a soft summer breeze. Then she saw those grimed boots again.

He'd caught her.

She was so *close!*

Knowing she was defeated, she began to cry, and even if she thought she might be able to take him, she was too weak to try. The sun's reflection glinted off the machete, a gleaming line across the tree bark in front of her.

She braced herself for the end.

Then her body lit up with a series of sharp joggles as he continuously hacked her with the machete. Her release from the pain didn't come as fast as she'd have liked, but when it finally did, she was grateful.

(IV)

Joel let the lawnmower drop. It landed with a harsh clang. He wanted to kick it but knew doing that would only add the aggravation of a hurting foot to the already annoying lawnmower wedged under a bunch of junk.

He walked around the front and moved the fishing net first. It lay across the mower, its pole lodged between the handlebars. He tugged it out and made a face. He couldn't recall why they even owned this net. They'd never been fishing as far as he could remember. He chucked it over his shoulder. It landed somewhere amidst the rest of the debris. He didn't want to sort through the boxes that were piled on top of the mower and hoped with the net out of the way he could tug it out.

He could.

It wasn't easy. After another clash, he finally managed to dislodge it. Once it was in the grass, he decided to let it sit there for a moment. He was already tired of messing with this. His shirt was plastered to his back from sweat. His brow was sopping, so he used the bottom of his shirt to wipe it dry.

Joel walked around the side of the mower, planted a foot on top, and gripped the pulley. He jerked it with all he had. Expecting the engine to roar to life, it didn't. He adjusted the choke and tried again. Still nothing. Now, he was getting annoyed. All he wanted to do was mow the damn yard so Haley wouldn't be a bitch, but the piece of shit was being difficult.

He tried three more times before giving up. He had a good idea what the problem was, so he returned to the shed for a screwdriver and spark plug. Dad had a small toolbox full of little replacement parts. He was positive he could find what he was looking for in it. They'd had to change that plug quite often. Obviously, the mower was defective, but Dad had never thought it was important enough to get another one. He didn't like to throw money around and figured a little bit of grief was livable as long as you could afford it.

He smiled, thinking about Dad, just as he normally would. There were times when memories of his parents brought on a flood of emotions that would render him helpless with sobs, but this wasn't one of them. It was a good memory. But it still reminded him that Dad and Mom, just like Rusky, would never be coming back.

His chest felt heavy, so he forced the memories of his parents into the pit of his mind.

Joel found the toolbox on a provisional shelf Dad had added years back. There was one spark plug left inside. He took it, grabbed a screwdriver, then walked back to the lawnmower. He squatted beside it and used the screwdriver to pop the rubber cork out of the hole. The spark plug inside was corroded with oil and gas. He could smell it. It took some effort, but he managed to unscrew it. Finished with that, he replaced it with the new one, sealed it up, and was ready to give it another try.

Then he noticed a flicker of movement in the corner of his eye.

He turned around, faced the woods, and froze.

A large man stood at the edge of his yard. His head was covered with some kind of shroud. Although the distance between them wasn't great, it was far enough away that Joel shouldn't be able to see all the blood the man had been bathed in.

Their eyes locked, neither of them looking away.

Joel knew he should run, but he only stood there gawking at this horrible-looking man, becoming more infatuated with him by the second. It was like something out of a horror movie, something he would have dreamed up, but he hadn't. This was real.

Joel was raising his hand to wave at the man when he suddenly collapsed onto his side. He quickly rushed over to him. The man rolled onto his back. His mouth smacked, bubbles of blood popping between his lips.

Joel knelt down, placing a hand on the man's arm. It was the only spot that wasn't sodden from blood.

CHAPTER FOUR

(I)

Haley sat behind the laptop in her one windowed office, hammering away on the keys as if punishing them. The room was suffused in chattering clicks. She'd thought about Joel often today and felt guilt more than anger over how the morning had turned out. It had been her fault, really. He was probably feeling the shock of Mom and Dad all over again after finding Rusky dead.

She stopped typing.

Thoughts stampeded through her head. She didn't know what to do at this point, and even worse, dreaded going home. He'd have had the whole day to think about what to throw at her next. That was a lot of time to build up a surplus of malicious words. But that was all right. She would have plenty of words and punishments to give right back.

Not that that it would matter.

Her stomach growled. She checked the clock. It was almost time to take her lunch break, finally. The day had seemed to drag by with each minute excruciatingly longer than the last. She let her head drop flat on her desk with a thump. The wood was cold and soothing against her forehead.

The door to her office bumped shut. She didn't bother raising her head to see who had entered, because she already had a good idea who it was.

"Got your wakeup call right here."

She was right in her assumption. *Carlee*. Her assistant, and probably the best friend she'd ever known. Since getting hired at Jones and Jones Law Firm two years ago as Geoffrey Jones' paralegal, it had often felt like she'd bitten off more than she could chew.

But Carlee helped make things so much easier by assisting her every step of the way, going far beyond her call of duty to make sure Haley was not only comfortable, but able to handle the tricks to surviving the constant rotation of employees that came through the office. Haley was certain Carlee had saved her job more than once. A friendship had kindled, and she'd thanked God *every* day for blessing her with Carlee. Not just great to work with, Carlee was absolutely perfect as a human being, and an even better friend.

Haley raised her head, squinting. Carlee stood in front of her desk, brandishing two cups of coffee. Her tan-colored suit snuggled her curvy body. Today's skirt was much shorter than her usual choices. It draped an inch above her knees and showed the smooth gradients of her calves. Haley assumed she was trying to impress John Kilward, a recent client and victim of wrongful termination at some power plant. He was gorgeous from head to toe, with a rock-hard body and would come into a lot of money when his case settled. Haley worried Carlee might come across as desperate in an outfit like that.

"You're a life saver," said Haley, accepting the offered coffee.

Haley tilted the cup upward, gulping three big swallows before stopping. It left behind a moustache of creamy foam above her lip. Taking a tissue from the box on her desk, she wiped it.

"Wow," said Carlee. "I'm impressed."

Haley returned the cup to her mouth, guzzled down the rest, and tossed the empty cup over her head. It smacked the wall and dropped into the trash can.

"Now, I'm really impressed."

"Don't be. It's just one of my many useless talents."

"I don't know," said Carlee. "I think any guy would find the way you sucked that coffee down without flinching or gagging to be quite a *useful* talent indeed."

35

Haley smiled at her slyly. "I've never gotten any complaints before."

Altering her voice into a poor imitation of a man's, she said, "Why Haley, I've got something else you can suck down, but it's not coffee."

They laughed as Carlee sat in the chair across from her. "So, how's your day?"

Haley groaned.

"Sorry I couldn't get in here sooner. Jonesey had me at the meeting with Mr. Kilward. It ran over."

"I figured so." Haley smiled. "Did Mr. Kilward notice you'd waxed your legs?"

Carlee's face went scarlet. She tugged at the bottom of the skirt as if hoping to somehow lower the length of it. "That obvious, huh?"

"No," lied Haley. "Not, at all."

"You're full of shit." She sighed. "Why *did* I wear this? This isn't me."

"No, it's not. Looks hot, though."

"Damn it. John probably thinks I'm a floozy now."

"Why do you say that?"

"Well, I was wearing this, and …" She stopped talking, as if wary of telling Haley the rest.

"What'd you do?"

She grimaced, gnawing at her bottom lip.

"That bad?"

"I totally kept crossing my legs in front of him, and when he'd look at me, I'd bat my eyes." She repeated the choreography for Haley. Tilting her eyes up, her thin lashes flickered like butterfly wings. Haley exploded with laughter. Carlee stopped, making a face. "Too much?"

"Did he ask you out?" Haley asked, finally.

"Not yet."

"Wait. Isn't he *married*?"

"I don't know. Is he?"

"I think so."

Carlee rolled her eyes. "What the hell's wrong with me? Am I that desperate?"

"Look at what you're wearing."

Carlee looked down at the skimpy outfit and gasped.

"Answer your question?"

"No wonder Jonesey's eyes kept trailing down when he'd talk to me." She pointed at her top. It was a triangle-cut, low in the front, showing the small gorge between the slopes of her breasts.

"Jonesey's eyes *always* drift downward."

"Yeah, but this time he had plenty to see."

Haley winced looking at it. She was about to offer Carlee the chance to go home and change her clothes when the phone on her desk rang. It was a loud, beating pulse that hurt her ears. She raised a finger to Carlee before answering. "Haley Olsen."

The voice on the other line shot back at her fast and torn with static. "Haley? My God. You're not gonna believe this, but there's a psychopath in the yard!"

Sounded like Joel, his voice frightened and shaky. "Joel?" she asked, just to be sure.

"Who else would it be? There's a psycho in the backyard!"

"A what?"

"A psychopath!"

Carlee watched her, confused.

Haley rolled her eyes. Joel was up to his old tricks, so he must not be feeling *that* bad. "Oh really, and what's this psycho doing?"

Carlee's face crinkled, even more confused than moments before. She mouthed, "Is he okay?"

Haley nodded with a smirk while Joel fired more outrageous lies at her.

"He's just lying there, not moving...covered in blood...wearing some kind of mask!"

"Riiight."

"Just get home, now!"

"I'm not in the mood for your horror movie games. Am I going to come home and find one of your special effects in the backyard like on my birthday?"

"No!"

"Trying to scare me to get back at me for this morning?"

"What? No!"

"Uh-huh, suuuure."

"I'm not playing games, Haley! Now get home, damn it, and tell me what the hell I should do!" His voice was packed full of anger.

Haley could hear the sincerity in it. Could he actually be telling the truth? *Doubtful.*

"Did you call the police?" she asked.

"Well—no…I wanted to call you first…"

"Why?" If he was telling the truth, then the first call he made would have been to the police.

"Wuh-well…I-I-I…" He paused. "I didn't know what to do!"

"I'll tell you something you *can* do," she said.

"What? What?"

"Mow the fucking yard!!!" She slammed the phone down on its base.

Carlee jumped from the loud clatter. Still hyped up on her own anger, Haley slammed her fist on the desk.

Damn him, she thought. *Damn him.*

(ll)

Dial tone.

Joel stared at the phone, dumbly. She'd hung up on him. He couldn't believe she actually hung up on him, but at the same time wasn't surprised that she had. Haley could be such a bitch when she wanted to. The tone turned to a pulsing beat, and he pressed the button to hang up before the annoying recorded voice asked him if he'd like to make a call. He sat the phone down by the sink.

Looks like I'm on my own.

He was fine with that. It wouldn't be the first time. He returned to the window above the kitchen sink and peered out.

The yard was empty.

Where the psycho had collapsed, the grass was no longer green, but red and matted down to the contour of his immense body, but the *actual* body was no longer there.

Gone.

A shrill caught at the back of his throat. He felt as if spiders were crawling up his scalp. He rubbed the rising goose flesh on his arms. Their texture was rough and pimply.

Then he hauled ass to the nearest drawer, jerked it open, and sifted through its contents. All he found was a can opener, some tongs, and metal and plastic spatulas. None of these would make for a useful weapon. He slammed the drawer shut and turned around. Scanning the kitchen, he spotted the knife rack centered on the counter, and darted for it. His frantic hands crashed against the spinning rack, toppling it over. A gleaming flurry of knives crashed to the floor. Squatting, he searched the pile until he found the largest one: a chef's knife.

He stood and smiled.

Just like the one Michael Myers uses.

Then he remembered how terrible the remake was and felt another kind of anger building. He crossed through the kitchen, the blade held out in front of him.

In the sunroom, he discovered the double-glass doors standing open. They'd been closed before he got on the phone.

"No." He felt those bristles of adrenaline drain from his body. His eyes roamed down to the floor. In a smeared line were bloody footprints. A size sixteen, easily. "Oh, God."

He thought briefly about calling the police but decided not to. They probably wouldn't believe him, either. Plus, if they showed up and couldn't find anything, they'd think this was all some kind of joke, and he'd get in a lot of trouble. Again. Just like on Haley's birthday.

Screw that, he was going to find the guy himself, and show them all he wasn't lying.

The prints led Joel out of the kitchen, through the doorway, and into the living room. From there, they progressed to the stairs, becoming lighter with each track. By the time he reached the carpeted stairs, they had vanished completely. How could he track them now? He obviously went upstairs, but where should Joel look?

And what if *he* found Joel instead?

He shivered. His skin went bristly.

I'm going to find him first. Better believe it.

"Hello?"

Walking to the stairs, the knife aimed ahead, he continued talking into the air.

"Where'd you go?" He spotted his reflection in the elongated blade and hardly recognized the kid inside. Mussed hair, bags under the eyes. This person looked like a junkie. He angled the knife so he couldn't see himself any longer.

Joel began climbing the stairs, lightly placing each foot on the thick carpet. "You don't want to hurt me, *do* you? If you did, you would have done it already. Ruh-right?" He was trying to convince himself more than the intruder.

At the top of the stairway, he had a choice. Right or left. To the right was Haley's room, the bathroom, and at the end of the hall, his parent's room, and that door had remained locked and closed since the accident. Neither Joel nor Haley had worked up the nerve to try going inside.

Each door in that direction was closed. Centered in front of him was an extra closet that they used for keeping towels, washrags, and extra soaps or shampoos. It was too small and cramped for anyone to be hiding. That only left one room. The one located at the opposite end of the hall. As if to prove his wandering suspicion, a thump came from inside. Like the other rooms, this door was also shut. On the outside of the door, an *Evil Dead* poster was proudly displayed.

"My room," he whispered, swallowing so hard it made a wet sloshing noise. His legs felt weak and rubbery. The knife quavered in his hand.

Relax. He's not going to hurt you.

So, he hoped.

He'd felt so brave downstairs, but now he cowered as he traveled to his bedroom. He eased an ear to the door and listened. He couldn't hear anything on the other side. Joel pictured a beefy arm bursting through the thin wood and latching onto his hair and pulling him inside.

He quickly pulled his ear away.

He clenched his mouth shut to stop the rising soft squeals and folded his lips inward. The quick gasps shot out of his nostrils in rapid hisses.

Just do it. Go in there. Get it over with.

He began wondering if he really wanted to go through with this plan. Plan? Did he actually have one? There was a point to all of this, right?

Wrong.

It was stupid. He'd been more in love with the idea of it all than the actual reality of it. What was he thinking? He had no clue, and that would probably be why he'd die soon.

Yet, with that in mind, his hand rose to the doorknob. His fingers curled around it. The knob was cold in his sweaty palm. He removed his hand, then quickly wiped it dry on his shorts. The stale odor of wet metal had clung to it. He grabbed the knob again and slowly turned it.

The door popped loudly when it opened, thunderous in the still house. He recoiled. He could feel his heart pounding in his throat, could hear the wet clucking it made while doing so. The door stopped in mid sway, leaving only a small band for him to see through. It seemed to be darker than normal in there. He could partially see his table, littered with masks and molds he'd made himself. His walls were covered with posters, leaving no spot bare. His bed was empty and unkempt. If Haley would have known he hadn't made it this morning, she'd surely have added that to the list of his chores.

Shit. He had those to do yet. He had time.

If he was alive later to do them.

A musty odor drifted out of his room. It smelled sort of like the petting zoo at the county fair. It had to be the man who smelled like that. He was in here somewhere. Joel needed to figure out how to handle this.

An idea struck him that made even less sense than what he'd already been doing. So what could it hurt? He'd gone this far, might as well see what happened.

Plenty could happen, and none of it good.

He'd decided to kill the prowler.

With kindness.

"Excuse me?" His voice sounded higher than normal. And dry. Why was he so thirsty? "I know you're in there. Just make yourself at home. I don't want to hurt you."

Yeah, sure. Like he'll believe that. You're only armed with a Myers knife.

"Tell you what I'll do." *What am I doing?* "I'm going to put my knife down to prove to you that I don't want to hurt you."

Am I crazy?

Yes.

He released it, letting the shiny blade fall to the floor. It bounced on the carpet near his feet with a soft thump. "Did you hear that? That was the knife hitting the floor. I don't have it. Listen." He lightly clapped his hands to prove his point as he edged into his room. It was silent in here. Too much so for his liking. Felt like something was waiting.

For him.

Ignoring it, he said, "I'm coming in."

He cautiously entered all the way into his room. Psychos and madmen were everywhere, but they'd always been there and none of them was the one he was looking for. Toys, models, and statuettes of Jason, Freddy, Michael Myers, and Leatherface. Posters, lobby cards, and papers printed from the internet depicting scenes or cover art from various horror movies wallpapered his walls. Not only was his worktable dressed in grotesquery, but the tops of his dressers were as well. His closet was even worse.

But there was one missing though, and that was the psycho wearing the white hood. Was it a pillowcase?

Joel's bedroom usually felt so welcoming and familiar, but now it felt like a strange place, as if he'd never been in here before. A slow, distressing creak of the door being closed froze him where he stood. The drawn out, raspy huffs behind him sent an arctic blast through his body. His bowels felt heavy and cold, like they were being ringed by icy fingers.

He turned around like someone with a gun on them.

There he stood, hunched over and leaning against the wall, his right hand pressed firmly against his wounded chest. On the hardwood floor, a puddle of red had circled around his feet. The man's eyes were glossy, hazy. His breathing was deep and slow.

He was hurt.

Bad.

Joel forced himself to smile. Not with happiness, but the way one would smile as if trying to approach a stray dog with a bowl of food. "Hey there."

He didn't acknowledge the attempt.

"I'm Joel."

He raised his eyes at the introduction, looking at Joel from inside the holes in the sack.

"Uh—do you have a name?"

The maniac didn't respond to that one either, only continued wheezing, his shoulders rising and falling with each deep breath.

"What...are you doing here?"

He took a heavy step in Joel's direction. His figurines softly shook on their shelves. Joel quickly leaped back, and because of that the man shied back against the wall.

Joel felt stupid. "Sorry. I'm so sorry. I didn't mean to scare you. I'm not going to hurt you. I don't want to hurt you, at all." The maniac raised a cagey eye, tilting his head as if confused. The eyes pulled away from Joel and scanned the room. The posters, the horror merchandise, the masks, the toys—eyes getting wider as the stare took it all in. Joel watched with excitement and pride. "Do you like my room? Look around if you want to. I've got a lot of cool stuff. I'm pretty proud of it."

He pushed himself off the wall with his elbow, grunting as he shambled forward like a drunk man leaving a bar. With each staggering step he took, he left a dotted trail of blood behind him.

Joel couldn't peel his eyes away from the inflictions across the maniac's massive torso. Slashes, gashes, and gullies of gore drenched through the torn fabrics of his clothes. His arms were marked just as bad, but the penetrations seemed less severe.

"You're hurt really bad."

Ignoring him, the man clumsily hobbled to the desk of Joel's creations. Some were tributes to other iconic horror characters, but many were of his design. A burlap mask curtained a Styrofoam head. Two eye holes had been neatly trimmed and a small slit where the mouth should be. Joel watched him as he rubbed his thumb across it.

Now, Joel couldn't be sure, but it seemed he liked that mask. He vigilantly approached, keeping a good distance from him as he leaned closer. "Are you hurting?"

He glanced at Joel over his shoulder, hesitant like an untrusting animal. Finally, he gave him a single head nod.

"Do you need help?"

His eyes tapered.

"I mean, do you need me to fix you up?"

Slowly, he shook his head, pointing a thumb to himself.

"You can do it?"

Another nod.

"Okay, well, do you want some uh … supplies? Like bandages, stuff like that?" Nod. "We have all that. But you can't use them in here. I'm sure it'll get messy. So I'll show you the bathroom. Follow me!"

Joel darted to the door. Turning around, he noticed the man hadn't moved from the table. Nor, had he changed his stance. With his back turned, he continued observing over the shoulder with one eye. "It's all right, I promise."

He finally took Joel's word and put the mask back on the desk, then turned around, keeping an arm draped over his bloodied chest and stomach. Facing Joel, he still appeared uncertain to give him his trust.

"I swear. You can trust me. I won't hurt you, or even try to. It's not like I could do much if I wanted to. Look at me." He grabbed his shirt, tugged, and let it drop. "I'm skin and bones. You'd kick my ass." Joel nervously laughed. "I want to help you."

Why did he *want* to help this guy so much? He'd disagreed with his own words even as he'd heard them spoken. Nothing was right about this. He shouldn't be offering anything to this man. And so far, he'd given up his room, soon the bathroom, and the first aid supplies. What was next? Food, a bed, a place to stay?

Just have to see how the rest of the day goes.

The deep stomps of boots pulled Joel out of his conflicting thoughts. The man was tottering toward him. His tread reminded Joel of Frankenstein. Another classic movie, but this one had a scene where the monster accidentally drowned a child. More red flags that he should really pay attention to. Nothing good ever came to the children in horror films.

He already regretted what he'd done, but that didn't keep him from bracing the man, draping his arm over his shoulder, and helping him to the bathroom, making sure he didn't bleed all over the white carpet on their way.

(III)

The kid locked the door once they were inside.

Starting with the wide gash across his abdomen, the kid studied his wounds, following them to the two massive gorge-like wounds on his chest. Those were the ones that hurt the most. They were deep and burned like fire in his lungs. He wondered if that girl had busted one of them, but he doubted he'd be breathing if that were the case. The only trouble he'd had so far came when he took deep breaths. Those pulled against the wounds, triggering more jolts of pain in his chest.

He was in bad shape. Fortunately for him, the boy was more than willing to help. This was odd, too. Why was he?

Pointing to the toilet, the boy said, "Might be easier if you sit down."

He escorted him to the porcelain seat and helped him down. He could feel the coolness of the lid seeping through his pants. He leaned over, bracing his elbows on his knees, letting the burden fall against his arms. Taking the pressure off his chest helped the pain. His dog tags fell out from under his shirt, dangling against his thighs.

"Wow, dog tags? Were you a soldier?"

He grabbed the tags and tucked them back under his shirt. They marked a time he wished to forget but knew he never would, but he definitely didn't want them consuming him at the moment. Usually when that happened, people died. The boy was nice and seemed like a good kid. If he continued letting his mind drift, he wouldn't be able to help himself.

"Don't want to talk about it, huh?"

The kid responded better if he acknowledged him, so he shook his head.

"I understand. My dad was in the Gulf War. I hadn't been born yet, but my sister used to tell me stories about how he'd just get quiet on certain dates and times. She figured that was like an anniversary or something of one of his army buddies being killed. You know, a lot of people pick on the Gulf War, but from what I hear, it was pretty bad for the soldiers, too."

He'd heard the same stories. But much like the war in Iraq, civilians looked at the American soldiers as the bad guys. The way they'd been treated after nearly killing themselves to protect them—*he had to stop*—was something that he—*stop it*—

They'd just been doing what they were ordered.

Stop!

He took deep breaths to stagnate his rising heartbeat and blocked those images before they could surface. He could hear the screams; see the red, all of it, everywhere. When he looked at his hands, he found four short indentions from his fingernails across both palms. Thin layers of blood had risen to the surface. He wiped them on his pants. As his head cleared, the ringing in his ears slowly ceased, but the boy hadn't stopped talking the entire time, hadn't even noticed the rage that was taking him over.

Hadn't even noticed how close to dying he'd just come.

".... but my Dad was a great guy over all. I miss him, a lot. I'll tell you more about him later." He got quiet. Then he asked, "Can you talk? Or do you just choose not to? That's okay if you don't talk, I'll do the talking for both of us, even though I'm normally the quiet one. At school, I barely say a word, which is why I think I get picked on a lot. I'm glad it's summer vacation and I don't have to worry about those assholes for a couple of months."

At one time, he probably would have picked on someone like the boy. But now, he could relate to him. Hell, he could identify with someone like him more than most. They were similar.

Joel opened the mirrored cabinet, rummaging along the thin glass shelves. He took a tube of antibacterial ointment and placed it on the sink. He squatted in front of the cabinet underneath, then removed a large bottle of peroxide, a roll of gauze wrap, and some larger bandages. He reached up, dropped them in the sink, then he grabbed a white aluminum kit with a red cross on the front.

Joel stood up. "There's some stuff in here, I hope it's enough."

He handed the lunchbox-looking kit to the man. He opened it. Inside were plenty of items he could use. But there were two things missing that he would definitely need. He handed the kit back to the boy.

"What? What's wrong?"

He pinched his thumb and forefinger together and lowered them to his stomach. Doing an up and down motion, he pretended to tug at the something thin from the wound. Joel didn't grasp what he was saying. Lowering his pinched fingers down, he mimicked poking something through the flayed opening and repeated pulling up at it. Joel's face brightened, understanding the sewing act.

"Ah, you need a needle? Like you're gonna stitch yourself up?"

Nodding, he stopped performing the charade.

"No problem. I'll get that for you. But first you have to do something."

He walked over to the shower, leaned over, and cut it on. The water rained from the nozzle.

"You're all bloody and stink. If you're going to be hiding out here for a while, then you need to clean yourself up."

Tilting his head to the side, he couldn't believe what he'd just heard. Had the boy just told him he smelled bad? He didn't doubt that his body odor was pretty repulsive to a sensitive nose like Joel's. He'd grown used to the smell, himself.

Explaining, Joel said, "Look, it's my sister. She'll smell you a mile away. Then that'll be bad."

Joel pointed at the basket hanging from the spout. Inside was a bottle of shampoo, conditioner, liquid soap, and a loofah hung from the side. He grabbed the loofah and soap.

"Now, you take the soap and squirt it on here like this." *He mimed the procedure.* "Rub it on your body until it builds a good lather. Be sure to get all over."

He knew how to do it, but thought it was kind of funny how Joel spoke to him like he'd never heard of something as common as a shower. He must smell worse than he'd originally thought.

Joel barely stopped to breathe.

"Then rinse."

He sat them back on the rack and took the shampoo.

"This is the shampoo. I don't know how much hair you've got, so just put a decent amount in your hand. Lather it up real good in your hair and then rinse. It's got the conditioner mixed in, so it's a two for one deal. Then it'll be shining like mine. Understand?"

He shot him thumbs up.

"Well, I'm going to let you get in there and clean up. My dad has some old hunting clothes somewhere, camo-stuff, I'll find them. He was tall too. They should fit you. I hope so anyway. We haven't touched his stuff since the … well…"

Joel lowered his head. His bottom lip quivered a few strokes. He saw that the boy's eyes had gone watery. "Will you be all right alone?"

He nodded.

"Great. Hop on in. I'll get out of your way."

His voice sounded different now, not full of the excitement that had been there beforehand.

The door closed.

He was alone in the bathroom, and the air was growing heavier with steam. He could feel himself perspiring under the mask. He grabbed the back of his shirt and pulled. It had become plastered to his chest from the blood. With one good yank, he ripped it up the middle so he could peel it off like banana skin. As he tore away the pieces of his shirt, he tried his best to ignore the pain from the drying wounds he'd reopened while doing so.

Gashes went up the front of him like cracks. It was a wonder he was still living, let alone walking around on his own two legs. How'd he survive that attack? He must be becoming stronger. She had come at him with everything she had, using his own weapons. He'd have to get them back. They were still in the woods. She was too. Her body had to be disposed of. He'd get to it, eventually.

He unhooked his belt, pulled it through the loops, then tossed it on the floor. His boots came off next. The odor around him turned sour. He could smell an odd combination of rotten eggs and sweat. When he realized it was his own feet, he quickly removed the browned socks, his pants, and under garments and got in the shower.

The water slapped at his chest, stinging as it rained down. As much as it hurt, it felt so good at the same time. He turned around, letting it pound his shoulders and neck. His hood was getting drenched, cementing around his head and neck like when he'd get caught in a rainstorm. Made everything much more difficult with the flimsy cover obstructing his range of sight, but he had never dared to remove it. He knew what he looked like underneath. Plus, it had become part of his errand-boy uniform. How had he become the one who finished off what was left of the victims. He'd like to see Buddy or Carp do what he did while wearing this shit.

On that, he reached behind his head. Fingering through the doused fabric, he found the thin string of twine. The knot was small and had grown tighter through time. He doubted his chunky fingers could unhook it. Instead of trying to untie it, he tugged, pulling until the twine dug into the creases of his fingers, and slit them open. Then he pulled harder until the thread snapped. He tossed it over the shower curtain. The hood hung over his head like a wet towel. Some of it was engrossed in the scar tissue on his face. Pulling it loose would hurt, but he didn't care. He wanted to feel the water on his face.

It had been too long.

He tore the pillowcase from his head, like ripping a bandage off hair. It burned, but only briefly. His face felt free, as if it could breathe, welcoming the warm steam on his damaged skin. It'd been so long since he'd removed the mask that it had become a part of him. Literally. His wounds had healed into the fabric. Tearing it free like that had opened some of them up again. Some dead-skin chunks dropped off his face and into the tub. The blood turned the clear water pooling around his feet a pinkish shade, and with the added lumps of skin it looked like a grotesque mixed drink.

He was tempted to touch his face, to feel the damage that had been done to him all those years ago, but he didn't have the courage to do so. He'd only dared once to see and that had been enough for him to never want to acknowledge it again.

He resisted the urge.

Then, sticking his face into the water, he embraced the downpour. Though it burned like hell, he didn't turn away. It wasn't long before the stinging stopped.

Soon, it felt wonderful.

CHAPTER FIVE

(I)

Face never kept them waiting longer than an hour, and it had been damn near half a day since he'd left. Buddy was far beyond concerned as he stood outside the makeshift barracks, assembled from old wood and tarps shortly after they'd settled on this mountain. The location had been fine at first, but recent land developments had been moving in closer and closer. Buddy figured they probably had three months left, tops, before they had to find somewhere else to station.

Where the hell is he?

He could hear the crunching of leaves from approaching footsteps, their light density revealing the hiker to be Carp. Face sounded like a bear when he went tramping through the forests.

Though Carp wore full camouflage fatigues, he could always pinpoint him in the rough. His eyes were used to it.

"Did you find him?" he asked Carp.

Shaking his head, Carp stepped up the side, using the protruding rocks like stairs. "No, the girl's gone too."

"What?"

"Went back to where we left her. Found the barbwire hanging there, pieces of that bitch's skin stuck in the loops."

"But no girl?"

"No. No girl."

Placing his hands on his hips, Buddy stared at the ground. Carp could tell he was getting angry. Buddy wasn't a muscular man, barely six foot tall, and he stood with a slouch. If it came down to it, Carp could dice Buddy up without much effort. Yet, something about Buddy was scarier and more intense than Carp or Face put together. It was how he could talk to people and come across as perfectly normal, when in fact he was nowhere near it.

He ran a hand through his short, spiky hair. "Face doesn't just disappear like that without good reason."

"Well, he's done it before. I know you haven't forgotten."

Nodding, Buddy did remember.

Face had unloaded from the bus looking like the invisible man. Head bandaged up, all you could see was his eyes. It just so happened, a little girl no older than six or so, was also at the station and found it hysterical that he was dressed like that. She couldn't stop her high-pitched laughter. Buddy had said, "Just ignore her, Face." Then she pointed at him and called him *Pillowface*. Buddy guessed this because his face was white and fluffy from the gauze, like a pillow. No matter how much her parents tried to make her, she wouldn't shut up. Finally, the mother popped her on the mouth, and told her to stop being rude.

Buddy figured that was why Face had let the parents live, but the little brat hadn't stood a chance. When he found Face with her, it looked as if she had exploded. There was blood, skin, and innards scattered all over the forest. And none of it was his. Face had been missing for three days before Buddy found him with the little girl. Kimmy was her name. He'd taken her from her bedroom in the middle of night, even bringing her goddamn favorite pillow along. After he'd destroyed her, he'd begun to wear the pillowcase over his head to hide his scars, and to also use it as a symbol. That was when he'd demanded to be called *Pillowface*. Buddy never had, because he felt his name should remain what it was on his dog tags.

Face.

But he wasn't the same man he used to be.

Hell. None of us are.

That was why they'd come here. To start over, going after them one at time, showing them just how horrible their homeland could be. They'd been betrayed by their own country. Now, it was time for them to betray it right back.

"What do you want to do?" asked Carp. He removed his hat, scratched his sweaty head, flipping his hair all over.

"I guess we'll wait. If he's not back by sunrise, we'll go looking for him."

And find him one way or another.

(II)

Joel found the key to his parent's room hidden in Haley's jewelry box. He'd have to be sure he put it back when he was done. Didn't need her knowing he'd been snooping around in her room.

He unlocked the door and went inside. The closed curtains blocked most of the sunlight from outside. The dark red veneer hanging in front of the window illuminated the room like an inferno. Not wanting to be in there any longer than he had to, he rushed to the closet.

He sifted through clothes, eventually finding some camouflage pants. Then he found a paper bag packed full of what Dad called his grease monkey shirts. Those he'd wear while changing the oil in the cars or doing any other repair work that he could handle himself.

He took two; one was dark blue and the other gray.

He put the key back in Haley's jewelry box on his way back to his room. He marched straight to the worktable to find the mask he'd made out of burlap for a scarecrow prop he'd planned to build. Having started it several times, he had never actually finished it. Joel took it from the Styrofoam head and quickly left the room.

(III)

He rinsed the shampoo out of his hair. The pleasure from his tingling scalp was nearly orgasmic. It'd been too long since he'd gotten the chance to do this. After finishing, he took the loofah from under the basket.

He used his thumb to flick open the bottle of liquid soap, then squirted a large mound onto the sponge-like ball. He put the soap back and began scrubbing. This didn't feel as good as washing his hair. The wounds and open slashes screamed at him. He kept on though, knowing that he had to clean them before dressing them. Hopefully, he'd get rid of any type of infection before it was too late.

He heard the door creak, followed by a light knocking.

"It's me." He heard Joel say, through the water in his ears.

The gash on his chest throbbed when the soapy water filled it. He screwed his eyes shut and punched the wall it hurt so badly.

"I don't want to peek, just give me a thumbs up if you're okay."

Slowly, he raised a trembling fist above the shower curtain, lifting his thumb upward to tell him all was well. But all was not well. He was in some grisly pain.

"Okay, good. You scared me."

The kid was silent a moment.

"Hey, uh—I have something for you if you want it. It's the mask you were looking at earlier. The one you were wearing looked pretty bad off and I thought maybe you'd like this one. I made it myself."

He stood under the water, listening as Joel continued.

"Here's the stuff you needed." He heard footsteps toward the door. "I'll leave you alone to take care of all that; I'm going to toss these dirty clothes. Don't want my sister finding them."

There was some rustling, assumedly from a plastic trash bag.

"When you're done, just push that switch to turn off the shower, then twist the dial to cut off the water."

The door bumped as Joel exited.

After waiting another moment to make sure Joel wasn't coming back, he left the water running as he stepped out of the shower. He stood on the floor mat, dripping onto the carpeted square, and reached over the toilet, filling both hands with supplies Joel had left him on the sink.

Then he returned to the shower, keeping his back to the jetting streams.

He twisted the cap off the peroxide and raised the bottle above his head. He took a deep breath, then upturned the bottle. A peroxide shower ignited the openings in his body like liquid fire. He gritted his teeth against the pain. When it had subsided enough that he could move on, he chucked the empty bottle over the shower curtain.

Next, he took the spool of thread, pulled out a lengthy line, and used his teeth to snip it off. Then he carefully removed one of the small needles from the pack and fed the string through the tiny hole. After tying it into a knot, he was ready to begin.

Using his free hand, he pulled up a slab of skin. He pressed the needle's point to the skin and inserted it. Surprisingly, it barely hurt. Felt like nothing more than a briar prick until he tugged it through the other side. By doing that he felt more pain, but still not as much as he should. He assumed numbness was settling in, his body's natural sedative, and as he continued to sew himself up, the pain became less acute until it wasn't there at all.

CHAPTER SIX

(I)

With her feet propped on the desk, her bare legs exposed, Haley read from a paperback copy of Dean Koontz's *Demon Seed*. She'd seen the movie as a kid on TV and remembered loving it. However, reading the book made her not like the film adaptation as much as she had growing up. The computer system had so much more personality in the book. She pitied it. The way it wanted to live just so it could hold the woman it loved. God, she would almost sell her soul to have someone love her half as much as the computer loved the woman in the story.

She really didn't mean it. Because of the phone calls at home from whomever that pervert was, she found herself identifying more and more with Susan in the story. Actually, they had an awful lot in common. *Stalkers*. She wanted to laugh but couldn't since there was a possibility someone *was* obsessed with her. She'd called the cops more than once, but they'd done very little, and basically made it sound as if they wouldn't do anything unless he physically harmed her. The best hope for her was to try not to let him frighten her.

Yeah right.

She'd had guys in her life that had actually claimed to love her, but she'd turned them away. Haley could be quite the heartbreaker and couldn't justify why she was such a bitch to the ones that truly seemed to care. Was she a loner? Did she enjoy the sadness of solitude? God, she hoped not. Yet, she had never been able to come up with a better explanation. But no matter how desperate she became she would never dress the way Carlee had today just to impress a guy. That had been just way too much. Luckily, she'd convinced her to go home and change.

Haley felt sorry for her. She'd obviously been planning this, and knowing Carlee, she was probably sick with dread trying to decide what to wear, how she should style her hair, and what to say in hopes John Kilward would swoon over her, beg her to accompany him to dinner or a movie.

Poor girl. Poor, dumb, girl.

Someone knocked at her door, blunt and heavy.

Probably Carlee wanting to make sure I approve her new attire.

"Come in," she said, without taking her eyes away from the book. She wanted to finish the paragraph she was on before dog-earing the page.

"Is this how you greet everyone that comes into your office or am I just special?"

Oh, shit!!!! Quick to react, Haley slammed the book, cover down, on her desk. She jerked her feet off the top, swung the chair around, and put her legs underneath.

"Mr. Jones…? Wow…hello."

Geoffrey Jones, her boss, was adjusting his suit, as he flung the door closed behind him in one quick swoop. He'd been tugging at his tie when he'd noticed her velvety legs were angled up on the desk, shoes on the floor, and her bare feet were arched with twinkling toes. He had seen a lot more of her than she'd ever wanted him to.

Humiliated, her dusky skin flushed scarlet, liquid fire surged through her.

"Come on now, you know better than to call me Mr. Jones." He pulled at his tie again. Then he slid both hands over his thinning hair, weighed down by so much gel it glimmered in the fluorescent light. His sloping nose sniffed, his head bobbed as if moving to a beat. His facial structure had always reminded Haley of the rat from *Charlotte's*

Web. The way his nose crinkled, he looked as if he were sniffing for cheese.

"Right, I forgot, sorry. Geoffrey, this is unexpected."

"Close, but not quite."

"Geoff?"

"Bingo!" He chuckled, his arrogance shining almost as brightly as his hair.

"So, what brings you by?"

"Well, I was just on my way to lunch."

"Oh?"

"Yep."

She sat silently, wondering what his point was, or if he even had one. He rarely did. Normally when he peeked his head in, he'd say a few awkward comments about her neck, and be on his way.

Holding his arms out, he slowly rolled them over each other as if trying to persuade her understanding. "Come on Haley, I was on my way to lunch and..." He waited.

"And?" she asked back.

His smile oozed above his chin. "And I realized I didn't have a date."

Help me.

"Oh...?"

"That's right. *And* I was wondering if you would help me correct this problem?"

"Geoff, are you sure that would be appropriate?"

He scoffed, as if offended by the question. "Haley? This is just lunch, of course it would be, plus I am your boss, so I'm demanding that you come with me and make me a happy man." He picked at a piece of lint on the sleeve of his cheap suit, then flicked his fingers until the pesky flake was gone.

"Isn't that your wife's job?" As soon as the words left her mouth, she already wished she hadn't uttered them. She was well aware that she did not want to go with him to lunch, but damn it, she didn't want to get fired either. With the morning she'd had, getting fired halfway through the day would be a great way to top it off.

To her surprise—and relief—he laughed. Smirking, he stepped up to her desk, obviously taking her comment as a challenge. She eased her chair away from him as he leaned over, placing both hands on her desk. "If she was making me a happy man, would I be in this office right now?"

She sighed. "Touché." Haley knew that if she told him no, he'd keep bugging her until she eventually caved, and things at work would probably become awkward. But she was pretty certain that if she told him yes, then he'd make it a trend. What else would he try? What *wouldn't* he try seemed a better fit. Would he take this as her welcoming his advances? If she went to lunch, would he expect more? A special thank you, perhaps? "But just so you know, all this is, what we're doing, is lunch. Nothing else."

"Absolutely. What else *would* it be?" He was lying. She could read it through his bleached white teeth.

She felt trapped, cornered. "I'm a cheap companion, but I like to eat classy."

"And that's where I come in. You like to eat costly, and I can afford the cost. We make a perfect team."

She chose to ignore his last statement. "I'll meet you at the elevator."

"I'm happier already." He walked to the door, stole a glance of her from over his shoulder, then left.

The office was pummeled with stillness.

It's just lunch. He'll treat you to a nice meal, better than the pig-slop you've been feeding yourself and Joel for the last several weeks. It'll be okay. Just put up with him for an hour, maybe a little more, and get a good meal out of it. How bad could it be?

Plenty.

What had she done?

(II)

Joel sat at his desk, the search engines pulled up on his laptop, determined to find out all he could—if anything—about this man.

There had to be something online, a story or an article about either an eyewitness, or a...*murder.*

He typed into the search-bar: *Unsolved Murders in NC history.*
Enter.

The links filled nearly two hundred pages. Groaning, he didn't know where to begin. Some were dated as far back as the twenties. He decided to narrow it down the best he could. Trying again, this time he typed: *Recent Unsolved Murders in NC.*
Enter.

A slightly smaller list of websites with article links popped up. Scrolling through the pages, he found something on the third that caught his eye.

Missing Hikers in Danover.

A small town on the other side of the mountain. Sounded like it could be his guy.

It was dated April 29th, almost three months ago. He clicked it.

The article loaded immediately. He whispered it as he read. It helped him focus. Often when he read his mind would wander, thinking of things other than the words in front of him.

"Two bodies found near Oak Hollow. Has to be him." He scrolled the pointer down a few sentences to where the article began. "Early Wednesday morning, a group of water skiers discovered the bodies of Anthony Hern and Shannon Hammond floating in the waters of Canopy Creek. Amputated, mutilated, and covered with stab wounds, pieces of the body had been removed. Blah-blah-blah...." He skipped lower. "The pieces of meat looked as if they'd been removed by a butcher ..."

He sat back in the chair. "Cannibal? Could he be? Doesn't seem like him. That's more of the *Hills Have Eyes* type of killer. He doesn't come off like a people eater. But I guess anything's possible."

Scratching his head, he wondered if he should ask him about it.

The glass of soda sitting on his desk bobbled slightly. The Coke inside rippled.

STOMP! CREEAAK! STOMP!!

He was coming to the bedroom.

Joel quickly exited out of the website and closed the computer. He spun around in his chair as the door slowly opened.

His dad stepped into his room, dressed to change the oil in one of the cars. A rush of excitement cascaded through Joel, but it quickly died when the image dissolved to the maniac as being the one really dressed in the clothing. Joel remembered he'd left them out for him. Camo-pants, the dark blue mechanics shirt, and the burlap mask. It fit him fine around the face but looked a bit too large for his head. The top section draped each side like dangling ears. It didn't make the mask look ridiculous. It actually added more personality, more charm. He'd used the thread to loop the mask snug around his neck. The tattered tips of burlap draped his collar bone.

He looked as good, if not better, than any slasher-movie icon Joel adored. He seemed more massive, and menacing. He didn't know whether to be amazed or frightened by him.

So far, fright had little to do with it.

"Looks good," he said. "Do you feel better?"

Ignoring him, he walked to the upright mirror on the back of Joel's closet and stared at his appearance.

Joel leaned up in the chair, "Do you like the mask?"

He raised a hand to his chin, rubbing it along the burlap. It made a soft, coarse sound of friction. Then he nodded.

Unable to hide his beam, Joel allowed it to conquer his face. "I'm glad you like-"

His words were cut short by the man viciously ripping off the left sleeve of his dad's shirt. He tossed it aside like useless trash. The arm underneath was thickly layered with strength and raked with surface abrasions.

He'd ripped the sleeve as easily as paper.

"What's wrong … did you not …" Before he could finish, he tore the right sleeve away as well. Both arms were now exposed. Joel would have never thought it possible, but he looked even more intimidating than he had just moments ago. "Wow," he snickered. "Nice touch. You look … scary."

He turned around, nodding. Obviously agreeing with what Joel had said.

"I was thinking, if you want, you could hide out in the basement as

61

long as you'd like to. You know to recover or whatever. I'm no doctor or anything, but I can tell you got messed up pretty bad and could probably use a place to rest. My sister never goes down there because it's a shithole. Too much junk everywhere."

Haley.

He leaned his head back, groaning as he remembered. "Shit. My sister's going to be home in a few hours." The man tilted his head. "We had a fight earlier, and she told me I had to do all this yard work, or she was going to throw out a bunch of my stuff."

He exhaled a heavy breath through the mask.

"It's okay, I have to do it. I sort of egged her on, you know. If I don't get that yard looking good, I'm dead meat." Joel realized his choice of words might not have been best suited for the circumstances, especially after reading that article. "You wouldn't happen to know how to run a weed-eater would you?"

(III)

The tables inside the restaurant were full so they had been seated outside. It was a lovely day, and Haley didn't mind a sidewalk table. She scanned the menu like a detective searching for clues. Everything looked wonderful. *Wonderfully expensive.* But that didn't matter, she wasn't paying for it. Jonesey was.

She choked on the thought.

Jonesey. God, how'd I get here?

At least it was a chance to eat at a lovely place like Palmers. She'd driven by it many times, wondering what it would be like to eat here. She'd know soon enough, just have to put up with Jonesey for an hour.

Shouldn't be too bad, right?

She dreaded the next hour. And the car ride back. Her attempt to use him for a high dollar meal would undeniably backfire in her face.

As if able to sense her anxiety, he snickered.

Raising an eye over the laminated menu, she said, "What?"

"Oh, nothing." He snickered again, sucking in his top lip, hissing air through his nose and mouth like a vacuum hose losing pressure.

"You're making fun of me."

"Me? Noooo, not at all. I just wish you'd let me order for you. I know this menu back and forth."

"True. But you don't know my tastes back and forth. So, I'll order if you don't mind."

"Re-yawr!" He clinched his hand like a claw and pawed at her. "You're a feisty one. I like that."

Haley stopped herself from rolling her eyes.

She caught her smeared reflection in his menu. The smooth slant of her neck was bordered by gorgeous hair hanging perfectly around it, curving over her jawline, as if massaging it with the golden locks. She caught his gaze lowering to her breasts. Her shirt was low enough that he could see the top mounds of her cleavage. He cleared his throat. Sweat had beaded along his brow and hairline.

And I'd given Carlee a hard time...

Haley sat the menu down. Noticing Jonesey was having a hell of a time adjusting his pants, she was prepared to tell him to take her back to the office. She could no longer handle his eyes staring her up and down. But the appetizers being placed in front of her distracted her long enough to notice the waiter.

He looked very familiar. Just a year or two younger than her, his handsome face was smooth and clean. His hair, a little lengthy, hung just slightly in his eyes. He nervously combed his hand through it.

Alan Somerson. She hadn't recognized him in the uniform. She didn't know he worked here. Being so used to seeing him at the bookstore in regular clothes, the white buttoned shirt and black pants had deterred her. Not to mention the bowtie. It looked hideous around his neck. The red apron only added to the blandness. She realized she was ogling him, and quickly tried to hide it from her lunch companion, but judging his sneer, he'd already noticed.

Alan removed a small, white pad from his apron. Then searched the other pocket, his shirt pocket, pants pockets, and couldn't find whatever it was he was looking for.

Clearing his throat, Jonesey leaned forward. "Behind your ear, son."

He slowly raised a hand to his ear. A pen was nestled securely behind it. Laughing, he removed it and clicked it, ready to write. "Whoops, forgot it was back there."

She smiled at his cuteness. He hadn't even noticed her yet and she found that just as adorable. She was extremely nervous to talk to him. It was hard to deny she had a crush on him, but normally in the bookstore, she had no problem keeping the conversation going. Seeing him out somewhere else made it different somehow. Glancing at Jonesey, she could see the bubbles of jealousy clucking in his throat.

"Okay," continued Alan. "Let's get this show going. Sir, what will you be drinking today?"

"Oh, just the house wine and the same for the lady."

Nodding, Alan started to write it down.

"Actually," interrupted Haley, "I'd like sweet tea if you have it."

"Sweet tea?" Turning his attention to her, Alan's face lit up. "Haley?! This is quite a surprise."

Leaning closer, she said, "Surprise," keeping it quiet as if it were their little secret.

"It's good to see you. And yes, we do have sweet tea. The best in town. I've been sipping on it all day."

"Good, sign me up." She laughed. "I didn't know you worked here."

"Yeah, just a day here and there when I'm not at the bookstore."

"Wow, you keep yourself busy."

"Not much else to do." He said with a shrug.

If Jonesey weren't sitting across from her at the moment, she'd use this as her chance to offer him something to do, like taking her out on a date.

"Haley, aren't you going to introduce me to your friend?"

"Oh right, Mr. Jones...." The way he cringed at her reverting back to the *mister* label did not go unnoticed, but she couldn't care less. "This is Alan. Alan, this is my boss Jonesey—uh—Mr. Jones." She bashfully laughed.

Alan extended his hand to shake, "Nice to meet you Mr. Jones."

But it was ignored. Sitting with his hands in his lap, he clucked his tongue as if trying to fetch something from between his teeth. "The pleasure is all mine, I'm sure." He put on a hideous smile so bogus it could have been purchased from a store. If Haley would have already eaten, the food surely would have come up.

Alan devoted his attention back to Haley. "So, will you be coming to the weekly shindig tomorrow night?"

"I wouldn't miss it."

Jonesey intruded, "If you don't mind my curiosity, what's the weekly shindig?"

Haley wished he would just go away. "Alan owns Second Chance Books, a used bookstore, and on Tuesday nights, he keeps the store open later to serve coffee and pastries to the public. It's a lot of fun."

"I see."

"The books are fifteen percent off." Alan added, "It's a pretty big deal."

"It's gotten me so excited that my throat is parched. How about those drinks?"

Haley watched Alan's smile fade. "I'll make sure you get your drinks." Quickly, he walked away.

"Won't you be coming back?" she asked.

Alan didn't bother turning around, didn't even show if he had heard her. He just continued moving steadily through the tables.

Haley lowered her head and focused on the menu, but nothing looked as delicious as before. Jonesey had ruined it for her, hurt Alan's feelings too. That was the worst part of it. She could go without lunch, but knowing Alan was probably upset really bothered her.

"Hmmm. Nice kid, kind of goofy, but he seems like a lot of fun."

"Don't you think you were being...?"

"Being what?"

"Honestly?"

He nodded.

"An asshole?"

Gasping, he grasped his chest. "Was I? If I came off that way, I apologize. Honestly, I'm very interested in books and coffee."

"Yeah, sure you are." Her retort sounded snottier than she'd intended.

He placed a hand over his heart. "I am. Scout's honor." He chuckled. "So what time do you want me to pick you up?"

"I'm sorry?"

"For the shindig."

"Um, I don't think that would be such a good idea."

"Why not?"

"You're my boss, *and* you're married. You're my *married* boss."

"Listen, I just want to go to this thing and since you've been there before I figured we could go together and you could show me around, fill me in on the gossip and whatnot."

"There isn't any *gossip.*"

"Well, then we can just talk about us."

"Mr. Jones, please understand, I don't think it's a good idea."

"Of course. I understand. It was just a suggestion. But I am interested in checking it out, though. So I suppose I'll just meet you there." He raised the menu, disappearing behind it.

Haley wondered if he'd notice her leaping the fence next to them and running into oncoming traffic. Maybe jump on the back of a truck, letting them take her to whatever their destination might be.

"Maybe *I* should order some sweet tea." He added.

She groaned, not caring if he noticed or not. Her legs were too weak with shame to attempt an escape. She was stuck there with Jonesey for another hour, at least.

CHAPTER SEVEN

(I)

By the time Joel had finished mowing the front yard, the maniac had already taken care of everything else quickly and efficiently. Joel put the push mower back inside the shed. Then he returned the weed-eater to its rung on the wall. Finished, he stepped out, closing the door behind him. His clothes were drenched in sweat. His hair was soaked against his scalp. He hadn't eaten anything all day and felt very lightheaded.

He found the maniac standing at the edge of the yard, staring into the woods. Joel wanted to show him the basement. After a few tries, he was able to get his attention and lead him to the side door entrance.

"The basement's over here." He glanced behind him. The man followed sluggishly. Joel wondered if he was tired, worried about something, or distracted.

The basement was stocked full of oddments. Old boxes had been put down there, their contents forgotten. The smell was thick, a combination of mud, rust, and dirty water. Joel walked to a corner and sorted some boxes. Sifting through old clothes, camping gear, and the tent, he finally came across a brand-new air mattress still in the box. They'd bought it last summer with intentions of going on a family camping trip, but the summer had quickly gotten away from them.

He tore it out of the package and dropped it on the dirt-coated concrete floor. The included air pump was nothing more than a thin tube and footswitch. While the man stood over him, Joel inserted the tube into the air cylinder, fastened it, and dropped the switch on the floor. He stood up, stomping the pedal, and said, "I know it's not great, but it's the best I can do right now. I'll sneak you some blankets and let you use one of my pillows. Sometime, we'll sneak off to the store, and I'll get you some stuff. Can't cost much, because I don't have a lot of money. Sound good?"

He plodded a few more gusts of air into the mattress, removed the tube, and clamped the insertion tab into the cylinder to hold it in. He stood up with a groan. He was beat. Today had been the hardest he'd worked in a long time. Smiling admiringly at the mattress, he said, "What do you think?"

He turned around.

The man was gone.

"Hello?" He passed the water heater and stepped around a tower of boxes. The side door stood wide open. He gasped, "Oh shit, he's gone!" Then he ran out of the basement on legs that seemed to be working against him. In the yard, he spotted the maniac standing back at the launch of the forest where he was previously.

His arms hung limply by his sides as he stared motionless into the thicket of trees. Joel approached him carefully, so as not to startle him. He wanted to say the right thing. Obviously, there was something about the woods. Either somewhere he wanted to be, or something he'd left behind.

"Is everything okay?" He didn't respond, which worried Joel a little. He'd reverted back to the silent treatment. "Something out there that you want?"

A light shrug.

Well, that's a start. He noticed the dog tags were hanging outside of his shirt again. He took a step closer, hoping to read the name stenciled on the thin metal. Noticing his approach, the man grabbed them, and tucked them back into his shirt.

"Sorry," he said. "I was hoping to find out your name." Sighing, Joel adjusted his shorts that clung against his legs uncomfortably. "Do you *have* a name?"

He glanced down at Joel. He felt toddler-like compared to him.

"Care if I come up with one for you?"

The man nodded.

"You *do* care?"

Another nod.

"Oh… well…what's your name? I can't just call you 'Hey' or 'Man' all the time."

The maniac looked around the grass, then stooped to pick up a stick. He snapped it in half, and using the sharp end, began to carve something into the dirt.

Joel stepped closer, squinting his eyes as he tried to read what he was writing. "Pillow …" He focused on the last four letters the hardest, but no matter how hard he tried, he couldn't figure them out. "I can't tell what that says. Pillow what?"

The man tossed the stick away. He pointed at the word *pillow* again, then pointed at his face.

"Pillowface?"

He nodded.

"Your name's Pillowface?"

Standing up, Pillowface patted Joel on the back. He wanted to ask him more questions, like why he was called that, and where it came from, but decided not to pry any more than he already had.

Pillowface returned his attention to the woods.

"Are you homesick?"

He shook his head.

"Then why are we staring at the woods?"

He pointed into the trees.

"Oh jeez, all right. I'm not really sure what you're telling me here. Do you want to go out there? In the woods?" He nodded. "Okay, we're getting somewhere." He nervously chuckled. "Is there something out there that you want to see?"

Pillowface shoved him. Laughing, Joel staggered back, and lost his footing. He fell on his butt, hard. "Ow…" When he looked up, he saw Pillowface pointing to the woods again. "I don't get it…" His ass was throbbing. The fall had apparently jarred it up into his spine. Even his shoulders were hurting.

Pillowface scooped him up off the ground. Instead of setting him down on his feet, he threw him over his shoulder. Then they were heading for the woods.

"Whoa, easy." He didn't like this, the way he was being handled. It was scaring him, though he didn't want to admit it. He'd grown to enjoy the idea of the two of them being friends. The way he was tromping through the woods, with him dangling over his shoulder, he couldn't help fearing Pillowface wanted to add him to his list of victims. A few months from now, someone would find a link to his own headline that read: *Dumb Local boy Tries to Befriend Maniac!! Goes missing!!*

"Hey, put me down." He tried to sound playful, but knew his voice was too shrill for it to have been believable.

What's he doing with me? God, he's going to kill me. After all I've done for him and he's going to take me into the woods and butcher me. Why? I thought we were friends!

"Seriously, drop me, man." Pillowface stopped marching and tilted his head to the side to look at him. Their faces were close. Joel could feel gusts of warm breath on his cheek and smell the aroma of decaying teeth and stale food. "I don't like being up like this. I didn't do anything to you. Just helped you, that's all. Why are you doing this?" Joel's eyes flooded with tears. His voice became unsteady. He tried to sound tough but failed.

Pillowface slanted his shoulder, allowing Joel's weight to shift. He slid off. But, before striking the ground, he felt two meaty arms wrap around his stomach and chest, flipping him over and placing him on his feet. His legs wobbled, knees clamoring together. Joel felt dizzy. Around him, the trees looked as if they were swaying this way and that. The ground seemed to be doing the same.

Slowly, his eyesight began to clear. As it did, he noticed he was alone in the woods. All he saw were trees, and all he heard was the chirping of birds and buzzing of pesky insects.

Pillowface was gone. Vanished.

"Hey? Where'd you go?" He spun around. Looking from side to side, he found no trace of Pillowface.

Probably ran off because of how I was acting.

But what did he expect? Carrying him like that...what was he supposed to think?

Joel sighed, mortified over how he'd reacted.

Like a baby.

It seemed more logical that he was only hauling him because he'd been too dumb to understand what Pillowface was trying to tell him. He'd given up and was going to show him. Joel wanted to catch up to him, so he decided to continue heading in the direction that Pillowface had been carrying him in.

It wasn't long before he found him. He hesitated to call out for him. Not because of his embarrassment, but because of what he was carrying.

Draped over his shoulder was a body. A woman. Nude. There was a large gash across her throat and various others spread over her body, short and long. Her back was bent at his shoulder, and her face directed toward Joel. Her lifeless eyes seemed to be staring straight through him. He shivered, feeling as if someone was squeezing his stomach with icy hands. At one time, he figured she had probably been very pretty. But her hair was mussed with solid red clumps, and her face was swollen and bruised. Her mouth slacked open, yawning off to the side.

He'd never seen an actual corpse before. Other than Rusky, she was the first. He chose not to witness what was left of his parents lying in their coffins, so she'd been the one to pop his corpse cherry. Sure, he'd seen them in horror movies, but this was different. *Real.* As disgusting as they appeared on film, there was no comparison to how disturbing this woman looked.

What was he going to do with her?

Joel felt a quiver of excitement when he recalled she was naked. He wondered if he could get close enough to see her tits, possibly between her legs. Just as with the corpses, he'd seen naked women in the movies, but never in reality. Well, there was that one time with Tonya, and then another time, but he was so far away it was hard to tell what they looked like, so he never counted that.

But he'd never seen an actual … pussy. And he'd always been curious. Even at a younger age he was fascinated with women. The way they looked, smelled, and felt. What would it feel like to touch *her*? Squeeze her? Finger her? He'd heard the guys at school talk about doing those kinds of things with their girlfriends, or various other girls all year long. For the most part, he was pretty certain they were all lying. None of them had probably even kissed a girl, let alone done sexual things with them. But if given the chance to do some of those things with this woman he could go back to school and tell the guys what it was really like.

She's dead, he reminded himself. *That's gross. What's wrong with you? Getting hard over a dead body?*

He wasn't having any trouble ignoring the reality it was a dead body. Knowing she was open and vulnerable for his eyes to see and his hands to explore caused him to ache. His penis began to grow, becoming hard and stiff. He adjusted his shorts so it could have the room it needed to expand.

Pillowface gave Joel a quick glance before moving on, the dead woman's upper torso dangling behind him like a cape.

(II)

Joel kept a short distance behind Pillowface while they walked. After several minutes he stopped near a stream snaking through the woods. The current was heavy for the gulley's size. *Spirit Creek*. Joel had heard stories of people being sucked into it and dragged downstream to the waterfalls, and then they were never heard from again. He figured that was bullshit, but the fear it might happen was always there.

Approaching the rushing water, Pillowface pulled the cadaver off his shoulder and chucked her in without wavering and ending Joel's perverted fantasies of getting to fondle her. Joel's heart broke as she disappeared in the rivulet farther up the course. He briefly considered tracking the stream to find her, but knew it was pointless to try.

Then he noticed Pillowface was looking directly at him.

He didn't seem pleased.

With his arms folded across his chest, he titled his head, questioning him with his eyes. Did he have an idea of what he'd been thinking, or what he wanted to do with the woman?

Why *had* he wanted to do that so badly? Now that she was gone, so were those urges that had consumed him just minutes ago. In their place were deep feelings of guilt and shame.

Pillowface approached him, taking long strides with his steps. He was dark with the needle-like rays of sunlight backing him.

It would be a cool camera angle.

"Hey," said Joel.

Pillowface answered with a heavy exhale.

"I was just ... curious ... to see what you were doing."

Pillowface glanced behind him, then turned back to Joel.

"I saw her." Joel looked down, kicking at a broken stick. "I mean, I won't say anything. It didn't scare me." He was lying. It had terrified him, and even worse had been his own sadistic thoughts. "I've seen them before." *In movies.* "So I can handle it."

He truly doubted he could handle much more.

Pillowface placed a meaty hand on his shoulder, and lightly squeezed, assuring him everything would be fine. Then he turned and began walking. Keeping to the left, Joel trotted behind him like a puppy nipping at his heels.

"What are we doing now?"

Joel followed him through the woods. Though, he'd practically grown up having adventures out here, it all looked and felt different. They appeared to be darker, more mysterious, and maybe even more evil, as if something sinister lurked out here. It was a feeling he'd never experienced before, an overwhelming understanding that things weren't as innocent as people had led him to believe.

After his parents' death, he'd begun having suspicions, but now, trudging through the forest on a mission to God knew where, he was certain the bright armor he'd been promised was a happy life was actually a rusted illusion, cracked and littered with ill will and pain.

Pillowface halted ahead of Joel, squatted, and began feeling around the leaf-covered ground. After a quick search he retrieved an object from the debris.

A machete—thick, long, and massive.

The blade was blemished brown from what Joel figured was old blood since there were also splashes of a fresher red spattered across it. Joel cringed when Pillowface offered him the blade that had undoubtedly killed that pretty woman. At first, he didn't accept it, but Pillowface was persistent in nudging him.

So, he took the machete. It was heavy like a sword. Joel tried holding it with both hands, but just couldn't manage it. He let the tip drop to the ground. It stabbed two inches in.

Pillowface went back to sifting the ground. Joel looked around the ground and surrounding forestry, noting all the areas swashed in red. There was a lot more blood than he ever imagined could have come from one person, especially one the size of that girl.

He wondered what her name was.

"Is all of this that woman's blood?" Pillowface shook his head. "Is this *your* blood?" Nodded. "On the blade? This is what cut you up like that?" Pillowface found the sheath and stood up. Joel struggled to give him back the machete. After he took it, Joel's arms felt sore and useless.

It was funny to Joel how he was becoming more capable of understanding Pillowface. Even without words, he seemed to speak clearer than most people he knew. Joel liked him, and no matter how heavy things got, he had no plans of ditching him.

Pillowface led them deeper into the woods. After a while, Joel sat on a tree stump, allowing Pillowface to go on without him. He was exhausted, and his shins were screaming. Ten minutes passed before he finally returned, carrying the largest chainsaw Joel had ever seen. With Pillowface's toys all gathered, it was time for them to return to the house.

(III)

The kid looked parched and sore by the time they made it back to his house. Walking alongside him, Pillowface carried the chainsaw in one hand, and the machete in the other.

"Are you thirsty? I am. Want to get some water or something?"

Joel took the lead, marching to the side of the house where there was a water spigot with an attached hose. He turned it on, leaned over, and slurped the water as it dispensed. He stopped when the sudden blaring of rock music erupted from the other side of the wooden fence.

The chainsaw and machete clattered when they slapped the ground. Pillowface left them there on his way to the fence.

"Wait," Joel whispered, trying to shout without raising his voice. "Don't go over there. They might see you."

Pillowface ignored him and marched straight to the wooden barrier anyway.

Joel trotted after him, catching up as Pillowface pressed his bulk against the fence to peer over the top. What he found on the other side was a young woman with dirty blond hair, no older than eighteen, sunbathing. She sat on a towel with her legs extended in front of her, massaging glistening oil onto her skin, causing it to shine as if she'd been swimming in wax. He couldn't see her eyes behind her sunglasses. A thin, two-piece white bikini was tied around her hips with noodle-like straps. The top was nothing more than small triangles over her nipples that laced around her neck. Her breasts were nearly falling out of it.

He licked his lips, practically able to taste her.

Then he felt that familiar hatred rising from deep within. His hands trembled with pumping adrenaline. He wanted her. Not to hold her, or to caress, but to crush and disfigure. How could *she* be so beautiful? How was it allowable that his beauty could be so callously stolen yet this insipid girl could be so effortlessly beautiful?

She would laugh at him if he took the mask off. If she could see his face, she'd make fun of him, laugh at his scars.

They all would.

"That's Tonya," said Joel.

Pillowface jumped at the sound of his voice. Looking down, he saw his little buddy peeking through a small knot in the wood. If Joel had noticed his reaction, he gave no indication to it.

"She's the neighborhood hottie. And the neighborhood slut." Joel snickered. "She let me look at her tits before. I swear it. One time after my parents died, she let me play with them. It was her way of trying to make me feel better. It worked. But she made me swear not to tell anyone. So, you can't say anything. Promise?"

Even if he wanted to, he had no one to tell. And if he did, he wouldn't dare to anyway. In some way, he was honored Joel had shared that, and wouldn't betray him.

"Look," he said. "She's taking her top off. Shit, that's two sets in *one* day."

Tonya's hands were behind her back, tugging at the knot. The top came off easily. Her perky breasts slumped, but only slightly. Perfectly round in shape, the nipples were the size of raisins. She began lathering them in oil, cupping them in her hands, fondling them with the glaze. Her breasts looked wet and slippery under the yellow spread of sunlight.

"Aren't they huge? They felt so soft though …"

Pillowface felt warmth in his pants but willed it to remain limp.

Joel groaned. "She has a jerk boyfriend named Clay Ray. He's an asshole. Always picks on me. Makes fun of me."

Tonya stretched back, aiming her chest at the sky.

"You like her, huh?" Joel whispered.

He didn't know what it was about her that had him so interested, but he wouldn't say he *liked* her. Actually, he felt a strapping effect of loathing towards her.

"I think she's hot. I've always wanted to do *it* with her, you know? You should see her mom. She's hot too."

Pillowface wondered how she was able to lay outside topless without her parents doing something about it. They must not be at home, which was the only rational explanation.

"Come on. Let's get back in the basement. My sister will be home soon. We can get some water, and I'll sneak you some snacks down."

He turned his back on Tonya's exposed flesh and followed Joel to the side of the house. Before entering the basement, Joel turned to him and said, "I still have to clean up all your bloody footprints."

Pillowface hoped Joel could handle it without his help. He felt beyond tired, almost sickly he was so exhausted. The air mattress beckoned him. It would be the most comfortable bed he'd had in a long time.

CHAPTER EIGHT

(I)

Haley took her time cruising along Marble Lane, passing houses while neighbors she'd never met walked their dogs, or finished up yard duties before it got dark. Kids were playing, relishing the cooler temperatures of evening. Houses were spread out through the trees, scattered and secluded. She knew none of their owners by name. Sure, they would acknowledge each other with waves and smiles, but other than Joel's friend Ethan, she didn't really know anyone on this side of Marble Lane, including Ethan's family.

And she was just fine with it remaining that way.

As she neared her driveway on the other side of Marble Lane, she spotted her next-door neighbors' daughter Tonya, and about the only family she was friendly with, checking the mail. She wore cut-off jeans, the straps of her bikini bottoms curved above the waist band and over her hips. Instead of a shirt, a thin bikini top that was basically just nipple patches barely covered her breasts.

Haley felt embarrassed just looking at her.

Tonya waved, hand filled with mail. Haley was tempted to pretend she was messing with the radio and hadn't seen her. But as much as she wanted to avoid her, she couldn't even be rude to someone as obnoxious as Tonya.

She was already in the road before Haley had stopped the car.

Smiling, she rolled the window down and said, "Hey, Tonya. What's up, girl?"

Tonya leaned into the car, propping her elbows on the door. Her breasts squished against her forearms. Their pliant mounds were right in her face. The scent of coconut oil began seeping into the car. Tonya's lotion smelled good. It made Haley think of the beach. "Not much of anything. You just getting home from work?"

"Yeah. It was a rough day."

"Aw, that sucks. Maybe we should go hang out or something, help take your mind off of it all."

"I can't tonight."

"I can't either. Maybe another night this week?"

Not that Tonya was bad company, she just felt awkward going out with her in public. Haley was five years older than her, and Tonya had only been a high school graduate for the length of a weekend. When it came to opinions of a fun night, their tastes clashed heavily.

"Sounded like you had Joel doing some yard work today."

Haley couldn't stop her surprised reaction. "Really? He actually did it?"

Laughing, Tonya said, "Yeah, sounded like a massacre was going on over there with all the machines going."

"Are you sure he wasn't just watching one of his movies?"

They both laughed.

"Could've been," said Tonya. "But I didn't hear any screams."

Haley laughed. "How are things going with Mr. Clay Ray?"

"Not bad. He's actually pretty damn sweet when no one's around."

"Nah, he just wants in your panties. That's all that is."

"Probably. He's been kissing my ass pretty hardcore, so I'm eating it up while it lasts, making him wait for it."

"Good girl. All the stuff I've heard about him, making him wait sounds like the best plan."

"Yeah, I want him to realize there's more to me than these tits."

Haley doubted there was much more than her busty mounds. She sighed. She felt exhausted. Drained. Her body was achy. All she wanted was to go to bed, cover up with a blanket, and hide. That sounded fantastic. But unfortunately, it would have to wait. "Well, I better get home and see what Joel's getting into."

"I hear that. Call me later if you get a chance."

"I'll try." She wasn't going to call. Again, not because Tonya was a terrible person, but they had nothing in common, and it had been excruciatingly painful trying to keep even *this* conversation going.

Tonya pulled away from the window, her breasts clouting the door as she stood up. Haley wondered if there would be streaks left behind from the heavy oil residue varnishing her skin. Tonya wandered idly away. Haley could see the bottom cambers of her buttocks nudging out from the unraveled shorts and remembered when she used to dress the same way. She was thankful it hadn't taken her long to grow out of it, but she doubted Tonya would ever let it go. She'd probably dress like that for the rest of her life.

She put the car in drive and drove up one more driveway, and on to home.

Haley thumbed the button on the garage door remote. As she waited for it to rise, she took a moment to examine the front yard. Just from her initial glance, it appeared as if a lawn squad had completed an overhaul. It hardly resembled the same place she'd left earlier that morning.

Even the hedges looked to have been trimmed.

What a nice thing to come home to. Joel had gone above and beyond what she'd asked him to do. *Asked?* More like demanded. She felt horrible about it now, but if she hadn't, the yard would not be this fabulous.

Can't make an omelet without breaking some eggs, right?

That was one of Dad's lines.

Haley took her foot off the brake and eased the car into the garage.

She entered the kitchen from the garage and stood on the welcome mat admiring the unblemished floor. *He'd mopped too?* It looked so spectacular she was afraid to walk on it, so she kicked off her shoes, then sauntered barefoot across the linoleum. It felt cool and clean under her feet and squeaked with each step.

Dishes sat in the drainer, washed and drying. The entire kitchen had an aroma of fresh pine. Her eyes began to mist. Not from the smell, but from something else. Was she actually so touched that she was going to cry?

What a woman thing to do.

"Juh–Joel?" She could hardly bring her shaky voice above a murmur. She forged ahead, spinning a circle as she took it all in. It was the best thing he could have ever done for her.

When she entered the living room, she quickly found Joel, chest down on the couch. His right arm hung off the side and was bent at the elbow on the floor. One shoe was off, the other just barely clinging to his foot. It looked as if Joel had fallen asleep while kicking off his shoes. He must have been pretty tired after the day he'd had. Burying Rusky, doing all the yard work, and on top of it all, cleaning the kitchen.

She moved past him to the stairs. The carpet felt springy and soft. He'd also vacuumed. She wiped her eyes, but they quickly refilled with tears.

What's wrong with me?

Her throat clucked. Her body jerked as she quickly returned to the kitchen, took a paper towel from the roll, and blew her nose in it. Then she wiped her face with a fresh one. After tossing them in the trash, she went to the freezer and removed two frozen steaks. She filled a pot to the brim with hot water and dropped them inside to thaw.

Then she headed for her room.

(II)

Pillowface was sleeping when he heard movement upstairs. He'd assumed it was Joel stirring about until a woman's soft fragrance wafted into the damp room through the vents. It was a scent he could decipher from anything, and she smelled lovely.

Haley.

The soft patter of her footsteps traveled from one room to another and then back. Finally, they'd transcended to the stairs and faded. Joel had told him to stay put and he'd planned on complying. He was tired and felt like shit. However, it hadn't taken long to become anxious, to feel cooped up, and after smelling that wonderful scent, he couldn't sit still. He had to move around.

So he climbed the wooden stairs in silence except for the occasional squeak of wood. The fragrance became stronger at the top of the staircase, and when he nudged the basement door open, he was slapped with it.

He had to see who smelled so wonderful.

As if he was on a mission, he infiltrated the living room. Moving in total silence, he snuck past Joel without disturbing him. He followed the scent to the stairs and took them. At the top, he heard movement coming from the room straight ahead. There was a crack of opened space where the door hadn't latched. Stealth-like in his advance, he slipped to the opening. With his body pressed firmly against the wall, he adjusted his stance so he could peer in.

He spotted a bed, and a woman's tight back, arched in the middle, facing him from the other side of it. The points of her spine pressed delicately against her dress. Her hair, the color of sunlight, hung gently to her shoulder blades. Her fingers massaged her neck.

Pillowface's fingers tingled to rub her.

Her hand eased away from her neck, gripping the thin straps of her dress and slid them off her shoulders. Her dress dropped, disappearing somewhere on her side of the bed.

He ached as he gawked at her in the black-silk bra and matching thong panties. Freckles were peppered here and there across her downy flesh. Her buttocks were smooth, slanting tenderly and ample. He imagined they would squish like marshmallows if he were to squeeze them. The thin black line of her thong disappeared between the silky mounds. She hooked her thumbs under the straps and slid them down her legs. As she stepped out of them, she unhooked her bra and held it out before letting it drop.

He hadn't seen her face, but he already knew she was elegant, stunning. His heart sank just looking at her. He didn't deserve seeing someone so faultless. He was blessed, and if he had still believed in

God, he surely would have thanked him for allowing this gentle moment.

Faint music erupted from inside the room. She turned around. He saw her face, albeit briefly, before he ducked away from the door. She was *beautiful*. What constituted as perfection was standing just on the other side of the wall. He heard shuffling, then a zipper. The music became louder momentarily before she said, "Hello?"

A cell phone.

He edged his way back to his peeping spot.

"Hey, Carlee." A pause. "Hold on, I'm putting you on speaker." Pulling the phone away from her ear, she pressed a button, then situated it next to her. She sat on the edge of the bed, her left leg crossed over the right. Her hand gently rubbed her thigh as she talked. "Can you hear me?"

Another female voice, distorted, said "Yep."

"Good." She leaned back on the mattress. Her breasts pitched back on her chest. "You just caught me before I hopped in the shower."

"Hop in? Why don't you just step in? You might hurt yourself."

"Hardy har."

"Getting all dolled for something special?"

"Yeah, my pajamas, then I was going to fix Joel some dinner."

"Oh? Was he still screaming maniac in the house when you got home?"

Pillowface's throat tightened. How had she known that? Had Joel told her? "No, he was asleep on the couch But listen to this, I came home and not only had he mowed the yard, he'd cleaned the kitchen, vacuumed, and who knows what else. He worked really hard."

"Good for him. That's very nice."

"It is. I'm going to cry again just thinking about it."

"Again?"

Haley sighed. "Yeah, I cried right after I saw all the work he'd done."

Carlee sounded surprised. "You?"

"It was a rough day. I guess it was bound to come out sooner or later."

"Why?"

She placed a hand on her stomach and fingered her navel. "Well, for starters my assistant never came back to work."

"I know, and I'm sorry. I was just so mortified. I couldn't …"

"*You* were mortified? Do you have any idea what I went through after you left?"

"No, but from the sound of your voice, I'm guessing it was bad."

Haley laughed mockingly. Pillowface adored how the muscles in her neck constricted, the way her lips curved up and back. He squeezed the door paneling, wishing it was her flesh. This wasn't like him. Carp was the one that had to *feel* the girls, needed to be *inside* the girls. He'd never approved of Carp's methods. Neither had Buddy, but they'd allowed him to do what he wanted all the same. Since Amanda, he hadn't wanted to be with another woman.

But now?

He wasn't so sure.

"I went to lunch with Jonesey." She grimaced, as if even the act of saying it was difficult.

"Say that again?"

"I had to. It was one of those situations that I couldn't get out of."

"Oh my God. No wonder you're so pissed at me."

"I'm not pissed, but I could have used you there to have my back. I was waiting on you to get back so *we* could go to lunch."

"Haley, I'm so sorry. I should have called *you* instead of the front desk."

"I wish you would have. I got the message you took the rest of the day off when I got back from lunch. He took me to Palmers, and you'll never guess who has a part time job there."

"Who?"

"Alan."

"The cutie from the bookstore?"

"The one and only."

"Did you talk to him?"

Haley crossed her legs the other way. He could see the smooth gradient of her outer thigh. The soft light from the window reflected in her dusky flesh like a small moon on tanned water. "Yeah, but Jonesey had to open his big mouth and embarrass him pretty bad, I think he's mad at me now."

"Who? Jonesey or Alan?"

"Alan. I couldn't care less if Jonesey is mad."

"Well, that's just great. Are you still going to the bookstore tomorrow?"

"I planned on it. Wanna go with?"

"Sure. Want me to pick you up at seven?"

"Whoa, are you asking me out?"

Laughing, Carlee said, "I feel like I should after the day you had, but you know, once you get in my car it's either put out or get out."

"Ugh, don't say that. Reminds me of Jonesey. He might be there Wednesday night, by the way."

"You're kidding."

"I wish I was. Kept saying how he was interested in it, and he might have to check it out."

"Yep, he'll be there."

Haley sighed. "I know. Can't that be considered stalking your employee?"

"He's a lawyer, he'll just find a way around that."

Haley groaned. She looked near tears.

"Just ignore him. Focus on making things right with Alan. Then give him a big wet kiss."

Haley looked confused. "Kiss who? Alan or Jonesey?"

"Alan, duh!"

"God, I want to so bad. He's so cute it drives me crazy."

"I know he is. So you better do it, or I will. Then you'll have to live your fantasies through my reality."

"Girl, I'd kick your ass."

"Well, I'm issuing the challenge right now. Either you make your move, or I will. It's on bitch." Carlee laughed.

"Don't test me young lady. I will break you in half."

They talked a few more minutes before hanging up. Pillowface hated the phone call was done, because he enjoyed the sound of Haley's voice so much. It calmed him, putting him in a mood he thought he could no longer reach.

Haley tossed her cell phone behind her on the bed and lay back once again. She draped her arms above her head, fully extending her body.

Pillowface gripped the paneling even harder. He could hardly contain himself. His breathing had become a heavy pant. The thin-wood section of the doorway popped under his sturdy grip, lugging the nails back from the wall, and made a sound like a snapping pencil.

He quickly darted away just as Haley looked at the door. He hoped with all his might she hadn't seen him.

He retreated to Joel's room and could hear her footsteps soft and quick on the thick carpet behind him. "Joel?" He ducked inside, hiding behind the door. Through the opening between the hinges, he watched her head poke out like a curious prairie dog. She checked the paneling and frowned at its loose position. Her azure-colored eyes were round, confused. "Joel?" She turned from side to side, scoping out each direction of the hall. Using her left arm to shield her breasts, her right hand cupped the small triangle between her legs.

She stepped out into the hall.

He quivered. Every inch of him wanted to feel her pressed against him, writhing under him. He wanted to be inside her, between those silky thighs, encased in her hugging warmth.

She tiptoed to the stair railing and glanced over. "Who's there?" She waited another moment, then dropped her hands, opening her body up for him to see again. "Well, I guess you're just hearing things, kiddo." She shook her head, turned around, and disappeared back in her room. After she closed the door, he heard the lock engage with a *click*.

His erection pushed against the door so hard that it crackled under the pressure. He turned away, leaned back against the wall, and sunk down to a crouch. He took slow, deep breaths. Breathing exercises. The shrinks had recommended them to help control his rage. Now he used them in hopes of controlling the urge to burst through her door and take her for himself. Several minutes later, his heartbeat had nearly returned to its normal pace. He should get back to the basement where he couldn't see her. He'd still smell her down there, but that he would have to deal with.

He fled back down to his hole in the basement.

He crawled onto his cot, pulled his legs to his chest, and hugged them. If there was a next time, he feared he might not be able to control himself. Once he was set off, he couldn't be contained until everything around him had been destroyed.

Squeezing his legs tighter, he performed the breathing exercises until drifting off to sleep.

(III)

Joel woke to the smell of Worcestershire sauce and cooking meat. It was late afternoon, and the room was dim, enriched in orange and yellow shades. He hadn't moved since falling to sleep, so now his left arm felt useless and fake. He struggled to sit up.

How long had he been asleep?

Swinging his feet around in front of him, the remaining shoe dropped off his foot and rolled across the floor. He rubbed his eyes. Throbbing jolts of pain tingled through his left arm. Blood sloughed through, feeling like rice trying to be shoved through his veins.

He looked through the sliding doors to the backyard. Haley was at the grill. Gusts of smoke puffed around her while she sprayed water at lapping flames with a squirt bottle, using her free hand to fan it away from her face. It smelled like steak. She must have pulled the grill out of the basement. It'd been locked down there since the fall.

He suddenly felt as if he'd been kicked in the ass. Pillowface. Had she stumbled across his hidden guest? Surely, if she had, he would've heard about it by now.

Joel's mouth felt dry and brittle. His tongue seemed as if it were a dehydrated snake, flopping around between his teeth. He wondered if Haley had seen Pillowface's tools.

Tools? Weapons that he'd used to murder people. *Real* people. He had the slasher of many victims hidden below the floor, or he assumed so, at least. Far as he knew, Pillowface might have taken off. There was a part of him that hoped he had, but that part was muted, the thoughts barely registering inside of him.

His legs rejected the idea of standing, so he gave them some time to accept carrying his body outside. Finally, he was able to get on his feet. Then he waddled over to the glass doors.

He realized he was sneaking. *Stop being stupid.* It wasn't like he was trying to ambush her so why was he crouching? He tugged the handle on the glass doors. They sucked inward and popped when they opened. The loudness made him flinch. Haley heard it over the sizzling meat on the grill. She turned, smiled, and said, "Hey, sleepy head!"

"Hey, what are you doing?"

"Grilling. Can you believe it?"

He stepped outside. Dew had dampened the grass, saturating through his socks. Groaning, he bent over and pulled them off. "What's the occasion?"

"Not really an occasion. I just thought that maybe you'd worked yourself up quite the appetite after all the hard work you did today."

Surprisingly, he wasn't that hungry, even after smelling their father's old marinating recipe drenching the hunks of beef. His stomach felt full, though he hadn't eaten anything since the cold Pop-Tarts this morning. Lying, he said, "I sure am." From the size of her beaming smile, he was glad he'd said it.

"Well, this is my way of saying thank you. Breaking out Dad's old grill. He wouldn't be happy if we'd left it cooped up forever." She sighed. By the look on her face, it seemed painful remembering their dad's love for the grill. Any chance he had, he'd fire it up and rack on some meat. His favorite part of it all would be the two of them acting foolish in the yard while he and Mom observed. Joel yearned for those moments again. Much like he assumed Haley was doing. She'd mentioned the basement. That was his chance to interrogate her about what, if anything, she'd seen down there.

Also was a good way to change the subject. "So the grill was still down there?"

"Huh?" She glanced back at him. Her eyes were diluted. Could have been from the heat or smoke, but he doubted it. "Yeah, right where D…" She stopped, swallowed, and tried again. "Right where it was left."

"Oh?" She was having a hard time discussing it, but he had to know what she'd seen down there. "Where was it?"

"Up against the wall, right when you walk in." She took a deep breath. "We really need to go through that stuff down there. Maybe start this weekend, or something. There's a lot down there that we *both* need to decide what to do with. A lot of … Mom and Dad's stuff."

That was that. She hadn't seen Pillowface. Either the spot where he'd chosen to hide him was a really good one, or he was gone. One of the two, but for the moment, neither hardly seemed important. Haley was saying stuff that made sense for once. That *was* something they both had to work on. Something neither of them would enjoy, which was why it'd been put off for so long.

Joel wanted to cry. He was certain that Haley wanted to cry, too. Without realizing he was doing it, he went and hugged her. Stunned at first, she only stood there, but then her arms slowly wrapped around him, pulling him tighter against her.

It reminded Joel of the hugs he'd get from Mom, tight and full of love.

After a few moments passed, she said, "I'm afraid I'm going to burn the steaks."

"You better not," he said. "You know I like mine bloody."

"Me too." She patted him on the back and pulled away from the hug. She wiped her eyes with the side of her hand. "Thank you, Joel."

Smiling, he gave her a nod.

Turning back to the grill, Haley shouted. "They're done!"

And his stomach growled, finally allowing itself to be hungry.

(IV)

Using a biscuit, Pillowface sopped up what was left of the steak sauce on his plate. Joel had snuck him some food down around ten—a steak, potato, biscuit, and some sweet tea, and he couldn't have brought it at a better time. Although it killed him to move, and his wounds were piercing him with pain, his appetite was as strong as ever.

He guzzled down the rest of the sweet tea and belched. Finally, he felt full, and it was a good feeling. One he hadn't truly experienced in nearly five years. He liked it. He hoped to be spoiled even more tomorrow.

He stood up, stretched, then snuck over to the side door that led outside. He had to pee. Joel hadn't given him any suggestions on where he could take care of business, probably because the kid hadn't considered it, so he had decided to sneak off into the woods beside the house. It was out of sight from the neighbors, and he doubted that Haley would be able to hear him from upstairs in her room.

The dew-drenched grass whisked across his pants, leaving wet trails on his shins. Joel had left him a flashlight, but he didn't need it. His eyes had grown so accustomed to darkness he could see perfectly with only the moon as a light.

He entered the woods. Little green and yellow orbs flicked around him. Fireflies. He couldn't remember the last time he'd taken a moment to admire them. The crickets were loud out here, but not enough to drown out the frogs. He loved the combination, and during the winter months, missed their chorus.

After finding a spot behind a thicket of pine trees, he unzipped his pants, and released his penis. Relaxing, he let the urine come at its own leisure. It felt so good he shivered. The stream slowed to a trickle, then to a drip. He tapped a couple times, then put his member back in his pants.

Back in the yard, he glanced up at the house to where he figured Haley's room would be. The window was a pale-yellow square. She must have a lamp on, or perhaps she was burning some candles. He envisioned her lying in bed, on top of the blankets, and naked. A book was opened in front of her, one foot lightly gliding over the other leg, rubbing the velvety skin with a toe. She had a fingernail in her mouth, lightly gnawing its tip. Her eyes rose as she read over something on the page she wasn't expecting. He felt himself stirring inside. It wasn't quite the hatred he usually embraced This was different, a rumbling of something else.

Whatever it was, it was short-lived.

He turned away from the window, leaving his fantasy with it, and revisited his dwelling. He made sure he was quiet when he shut the door. On his way back to his hidden bed, his shoulder bumped a box, and knocked it loose from the others it was stacked on. Throwing his arms out in response, the box landed on his forearms like a present that was dropped from the sky. Something clanged inside when he shook it.

He placed the box on another stack that wasn't quite as high. It had been sealed by folding the corners under one another, so he was able to open it easily.

Inside was a variety of junk. Not much of interest. But as he sifted through the contents, his fingers slid across something cold and slick. Felt like a belt buckle. He tugged it out of the box to examine.

A back brace. Like the kind weightlifters would wear when doing squats. He remembered wearing his father's weight belt as a kid, turning it around so the rubber oval was in front, then pretending it was a wrestling championship belt. He would have make-believe matches with his stuffed animals where sometimes he won, and sometimes he didn't.

Why was he thinking about that? He hadn't thought about his childhood since before he joined the military. It was probably because of the kid. Being around him was bringing it all back. He wasn't sure if that was a good thing or not.

He closed the box back up and returned it to where it originally was. But he held onto the belt. As he looked around him, he noticed there was a city of stacked boxes running the length of the basement, more boxes than he could ever have imagined. And he was curious to see what had been hidden away inside the cardboard cubes. There was no way he'd ever make it through them all, but he wanted to at least make a dent in them tonight.

He spent an hour curiously digging through boxes and came across many interesting things. But he hadn't found anything he wanted to hold on to. Not until he discovered the hand saw. It was easily sixteen inches in length, with jagged teeth running along the bottom of its chrome-colored blade. The black handle was still clamped in cardboard which meant the saw hadn't been used.

He decided to hold onto that as well.

After putting the last box he'd scoured through back where it belonged, he was bushed. He plodded to his air mattress and lay down. He put the weight belt and hand saw above the pillow that Joel had given him from his room. Then he rested his head on it. Its feathery softness was comfortable, and he was asleep within seconds of closing his eyes.

CHAPTER NINE

(I)

"The sun's rising! Get up!" Buddy kicked Carp in the ass through the blanket. He jerked rigid, shooting his head up from underneath.

"What the hell!"

Buddy stood over him, hands settled on his hips. "He's not back. Get ready."

Carp sat up with a groan. The blanket was bunched around his legs and felt wonderful as a naked woman clinging to his waist and begging him not to go. But with a man like Buddy standing over your sleeping quarters telling you to get up, that was what you did. Promptly. "Are you sure?"

"What do I look like, an idiot?"

"Well, no ..."

"Don't you think I can tell if someone's bed is empty?"

"I'd hope so."

"You'd hope ...?" He shook his head. "Get your ass up!"

"I am!" Carp kicked the blankets off his legs and stood up. He was naked from the waist down. He looked around his cot for his pants, finding them heaped in a pile on the floor. His underwear sat on top. They were a soiled pair but would have to do for now. There was no time to find a clean set or to wash these in a creek.

"He's been gone for twenty-four hours. At least." Buddy tilted back his head, staring at the low hanging ceiling improvised from an old tarp. "It's not like him."

"I'm sure he's fine."

"I'm not."

"What's the big deal, even if he's not, then so what?"

"We need him, Carp, or have you forgotten?"

"I haven't."

"Good. Because, just like you, he has his own position on this team. As much as I despise you, I need you, too. Which is what has kept you in my good graces so far, but that can only last for so long."

"Wow, Buddy. Never knew you cared so much."

"We need to patrol the woods. Trace his steps. Make sure he didn't run into any trouble."

"What kind of trouble could someone like Face run into? Seriously, he's a fucking ox."

"I don't know. Forest Rangers, bears, cops. Could be anything, and it could be nothing. We have to find out for sure."

Carp hiked up his pants and looped the belt. When it was snug, he wrenched it taut, and buckled it. He scratched his head and felt oily hair under his nails. He realized he wasn't wearing his cap, so he combed the floor until he found it in the corner. Once that was on his head, he was ready. "Okay."

"Good to go?"

"Yep."

"Grab a tote bag. Stuff it with whatever you can bring, but just make sure it's light. I'm going to get my camera and mask."

Smiling, Carp said, "You think you might need it?" His crooked smirk probably was not the best thing to see this early in the morning. Actually, he knew it was nauseating. But the idea of Buddy bringing his mask meant only one thing—he'd planned on making some art, which really meant inflicting payback on some hapless chap. And that destined that Carp would get to play in front of the camera.

"Best to have it and not need it. Right?"

"Uh, sure."

94

Buddy stepped out of the tent, flinging the drooping flap behind him as if he were slamming a door. Carp followed. The sun had risen but wasn't exactly meting out the brightness of the day. It was early yet, and Carp assumed that Buddy had probably been up since before dawn, running around in a frantic mess because of Face's disappearance.

Disappearance? He'd probably fled.

Not as dumb as he looked if that was the case. But he doubted it to be true. He seriously couldn't see Face ever deserting Buddy for anything. Carp had never understood why the bond between those two had always been so strong. Their team was once larger by two people, and Buddy had hardly acknowledged them as being part of the group. When Junior and Slappy were killed, Buddy had barely seemed to notice. But Face missing for not a full day has him acting as if his favorite toy had been broken.

Maybe it was.

He looked across the hill to Buddy's tent. He was squatting in front of it like a catcher behind home plate. His green sack lay open in front of him. He slid something small and flat inside of it. *His mask?* Then he tossed in a couple of machetes and knives. No guns. That had been important to Buddy from the beginning. They do this, but without guns. Not only are they loud and can give away your location, but they also lack the boasting of a personal touch, as if each weapon had been garnered for a specific person.

Carp could appreciate that. He liked the feel of them dying, the look in their eyes. He was getting aroused just thinking about it. He felt at his hip and smiled when he felt the knife strapped to his belt.

Buddy packed the binoculars. *Great.* That meant their search was going to be a lengthy one.

Buddy wants to explore every inch of the forest until we come up with something.

And *that* would take a while.

"What a way to spend a day," he muttered.

Damn you, Face.

He stepped back inside his tent to fill up his own tote bag.

(11)

Joel waited in bed five more minutes after hearing Haley's car leave. When he was certain she wasn't coming back for any reason, he threw the sheets off him, and hopped out of bed. He'd slept in plaid lounge pants and a T-shirt with *Freddy Krueger* on the front. As he stretched, he admired the image of *Freddy* flashing his glove. He was fond of his T-shirt collection. He could go two weeks and not wear the same horror themed shirt more than once in that time span. Eventually, he'd be able to go a whole month without having to. His dream was to go a whole year and never be seen wearing the same T-shirt.

Can't wait.

He knew that wouldn't happen until he was older, had moved to California, and had multiple jobs on various horror projects as their special effects coordinator. It was his dream and had been since he was five years old and saw *Friday the 13th* for the first time. The ending where an adolescent *Jason Voorhees* leapt out of the lake and dragged the lady in the canoe down under the water with him had been stenciled in his mind as an iconic memory. It had stayed with him this long, and he imagined it always would.

Walking around his room, kicking a path through his dirty clothes, he looked for his Homer Simpson slippers. It might not be a bad idea to throw his clothes in the washer so Haley wouldn't have to do it. They'd had a good evening together last night, and he wanted to keep it like that for as long as possible. Maybe if he did some things around the house to help her out, she wouldn't feel so stressed, and in return, wouldn't be so mean. It was probably hard on her having to be the providing parent now when she was used to being the older sister that didn't have to spend much time with a kid.

Makes sense.

Joel caught a glimpse of a white oval with a small black dot in the middle peeking at him from under a pile of dirty clothes. As he neared the blank stare, he saw it was attached to a yellow head with stringy-thin hair. *There they are.* He scooped up some pants, tossed them on his bed, then slid his feet into the slippers. When he had both slippers on, he did a patrol of his room, gathering up every piece of laundry he could find. He wasn't surprised by the size of the mountain on his bed when he was finished. This pile would require two trips to the washing machine.

With his arms bowed under one load, he scurried downstairs, crossed through the kitchen and into the laundry room that was connected to the garage. Thankfully, Haley had left the door open after the last time she'd washed clothes, so he was able to just rush right in and drop the clothes into the machine.

He poured in a generous helping of detergent and set the dials where they needed to be. As he pushed *Start*, he remembered Pillowface's old clothes were still in a trash bag under his bed and needed to be thrown away. He figured just stuffing them down into the bottom of the trashcan outside would be enough.

What kind of a name is Pillowface?

Joel hated to admit that he was more than a little disappointed with the name, but he could live with it. A guy like Pillowface should be called something like *Psychoface*, or anything else that sounded menacing. If it had been up to Joel, he would have thought of something really cool he could have used as a name, something with franchise potential.

Maybe he'd ask him where the name had come from, or…maybe not.

(III)

After Joel had thrown the rest of his clothes into the washing machine, and—what he hoped—properly disposed of Pillowface's bloodied rags, he headed for the basement door around the side of the house. On his way, he noticed the shed's door was hanging open, lightly swaying back and forth. *I thought I closed it.* He was sure that he had after putting everything back inside yesterday when they had finished assaulting the lawn.

He took a detour, stopping in front of the yawning shed. Everything seemed in place upon first glance, but as he focused harder, he began to notice that all was not the way it should be. First thing he spotted was one of Dad's boxes lying tipped on its side on the shelf. Not the one he used for small parts, but one of the many that housed various leftover pieces to whatever his dad felt like tossing in.

Entering the shed, he was able to see the standing tool chest had two drawers that had been left open. He checked those, and the only thing he recognized being gone that was supposed to be in there was the welding torch. So, he checked the peg hooks beside the door, and confirmed the empty one in the middle was missing the welding helmet.

Pillowface.

He darted out of the shed, running all the way to the basement door. As he curled his fingers around the knob, he hesitated. Nervous. His stomach buzzed and popped. And because he was hungry, it made him feel nauseous. There was no doubt that Pillowface had taken the tools, but why had he done so? Did Joel really want to go in there and find out?

Sort of.

Maybe he'd go in there only to find Pillowface had fled in the night. There was relief in the thought, but also anger. If he had left, and taken his dad's tools with him, it would be hard for Joel not to go after him to get them back.

Whatever the case may be, he wasn't going to figure it out standing outside. He would have to go into the basement.

So, he did.

The basement was bathed in shadows. He heard a crackle, then piercing blue light inflated across the walls and ceiling. It hurt Joel's eyes, so he had to look away. But during the brief moment he was able to see, he'd located the light was at the other end of the basement. At least he knew Pillowface hadn't stolen the tools. He was just using them without permission.

Using his hand to shield his eyes like a visor, he stared at his feet while he walked through the basement. As he neared the back, the temperature steadily began to rise. Usually, it was cool and stuffy in the basement, even during the summer, but right now it felt hotter than outside. The sizzling sounds were much louder, and he could also smell something like heated metal.

"What's going on?" he shouted.

The sizzling sparks ceased. Joel lifted his eyes. He could see an orange dot floating in the darkness, but when his eyes adjusted, he realized it was actually the tip of the blow torch.

"Why did you take this stuff without asking?"

Pillowface stood up. He needed to cock his head to the side to avoid cracking his skull on the beams above him. Joel had forgotten how huge he was. He quickly dropped his accusatory tone.

"Sorry," he said. "What are you doing with the blowtorch?"

Stepping to the side, Pillowface pointed at an object on the floor. Joel had to get closer to actually see it. Whatever the thing really was it looked to be in the early stages of construction. He'd taken his dad's old back brace and had been welding skinny chains to it. He had probably taken those from the shed as well. There was a saw on the floor, but it hadn't been used from what Joel could tell.

"Uh-huh," said Joel, confused. He had no clue what his new friend was up to and decided not to pry. Pillowface would probably show him eventually. He could wait. But he was really puzzled by what he planned on doing with the saw. It seemed out of place with the work already done.

Pillowface sat the blowtorch on the floor, then brushed his hands on his pants.

"Wanna eat some cereal?"

He nodded.

"We've also got Pop-tarts if you'd rather have that."

Pillowface shook his head.

"Me neither. I'm not a fan."

Together, they left the basement. Joel hoped Pillowface liked *Lucky Charms* because that was all they had.

(IV)

The day had come and gone for Haley just as they usually would: dreadful and boring. Luckily, she and Carlee had managed to sneak out of the office for lunch before Jonesey had a chance to ask her for a second date, but she did have two awkward encounters afterward, and thankfully for her he'd been tied up in court for the remainder of the day.

Now, she was behind the wheel of her Dodge, and heading to Mario's Pizza and Sandwiches, Joel's favorite place. She wanted to do something fun for dinner to keep the momentum from last night going. They'd eaten together at the table, talked, and most importantly, they'd laughed. It had been months since they'd had so much fun together or had been able to spend an extended amount of time in the same room without fighting. She hoped that was a sign that things might be changing for them.

But the pizza was also a peace offering for a fight that hadn't happened yet. She was attending Alan's routine gathering at the bookstore tonight, and although Joel had never shown any sort of resentment for her going in the past, she wouldn't be shocked if tonight he did.

She was just waiting for something to happen that would damper what she felt was accomplished last night. Maybe it would all be fine. The jitters she was having were probably more about seeing Alan and finally making her move. And, of course, knowing Jonesey was planning to make an appearance meant that everything could get screwed up. These things were far worse than telling Joel she would be gone until late evening or early morning.

Bullshit.

As she steered the car into the small parking lot at Mario's, she knew without a doubt that her anxiety was from all the above reasons.

CHAPTER TEN

(I)

The doorbell's chimes clambered throughout the house. Joel tottered to the door at a sluggish pace thanks to a full stomach. He couldn't believe it was only nearing seven, but it felt so much later.

He opened the door to a smiling Carlee and felt his breath snag in his chest. Not that she ever looked bad, but he'd never seen her look *this* good. Her hair hung loosely around her neck. Her bronzed skin was glowing in the approaching night, but her smile was even brighter. The dress she'd chosen snuggled her breasts, projecting them above the top like two floats in a river. He glanced down quickly to keep from staring but met her legs. Tanned and smooth. Just the way he liked them.

He'd always thought Carlee was pretty, and tonight she set the standard. Joel wanted to speak but was afraid his voice would betray him. He suddenly felt nervous, awkward, which was odd, because he'd had many conversations with Carlee. She was normally the one that would sit and watch horror movies with him while Haley made fun of them or got too grossed out. Carlee was a good friend, a movie companion. On several occasions, she'd taken him to buy a lot of the monstrosities occupying his room.

"Joel?" she said.

Say something.

"Are you okay?"

He nodded. *Why aren't you saying anything?*

Laughing, she gnawed at her lip. "What's wrong? Can't you say something?" She almost appeared to be blushing.

"Y…" He lowered his head, giving up.

She laughed again. "Don't you like my outfit?"

Giving her another glance, he shrugged. "Yeah …"

Mocking him playfully, *"Yeah."* She squeezed his shoulder. He caught a whiff of her perfume. His pores seemed to come alive from its sweet aroma. The way it blended perfectly with the scent of her skin made his knees tremble.

"Are you going to let me in, or do you just want to keep me out here all night?"

"Oh, sorry." His cheeks were growing hot. His face was probably turning red. He hoped she hadn't noticed.

"Thank you, my boy." She said with a nod, entering.

"You look beautiful," he blurted, quickly slapping a hand over his mouth.

What have I done? Had he actually said that? He braced himself for the slap. But it never came.

Carlee was gaping. "What did you say?"

"You didn't hear me?" He did not want to repeat it.

"I think I did. I was just making sure I heard correctly."

"What do you think I said?" He realized he was speaking through a hand muzzle. Lowering his hand, his lips felt unusually dry, and his palm was drenched.

"Did you say I was beautiful?"

God, he *had* said that as she'd walked by.

He answered with a nod.

Then something happened that he didn't expect. It came fast, sudden. Carlee stepped over to him, leaned over, and gently grabbed him under the chin. Her thumb curved around one cheek with her fingers on the other.

"No one has ever called me that. *Ever.*"

He couldn't believe it. How could people be so blind? Her face was closer to him than it had ever been before and looked more gorgeous than ever. Her eyes were such a unique shade of brown and shaped in their own way. They curved at the tips and were portly wide. He could see himself floating inside their almond color.

Could feel the warm air from her lips tickling his before kissing him.

He flinched at the moist softness pressing against his mouth, just a small peck at first. Her lips tasted like strawberries. She raised her head, caught herself in his eyes and stopped. He was trembling, wondering what she had seen in his stare. Could it be that she caught him on the exact moment he fell in love in with her? His heart pounded against his chest so hard he expected it to burst through and ruin her pretty dress. His stomach twitched, popping like a dozen hand grenades exploding inside. A sudden weight like a thousand bricks plummeted on top of him.

Carlee's thick lips curved slightly. She sucked her bottom lip under her teeth and clamped down. Then she shook her head. She wasn't telling him "No." It was as if she was physically answering a mental question. As he began pondering what it could be, she leaned in and kissed him again. Parting her mouth, his lips stayed with hers and opened slightly. He tasted her warm, quivering breaths. Felt them on his tongue, swallowed them.

Then they heard footsteps descending the stairs, solid heels *thunking* on the wooden steps, the jingling of keys as Haley took them from her pocketbook. Carlee pulled away from him, placing a hand on her mouth. Her eyes were wide, shocked. Joel read it as astonishment mixed with worry. He suddenly felt guilty, not because of what they'd done, but wondering if he had done a good job. She seemed to have been enjoying it until Haley came.

Way to ruin it for me, sis.

Carlee gave herself a quick adjustment, straightened her dress, her hair. Though, he hadn't touched anything but her lips, they seemed to be the one place she wasn't concerned about. They were pretty close to the same height. He'd grown a lot this year. He remembered Carlee was a giant compared to him last summer.

Joel had recognized something in her eyes that he'd never seen before. Loneliness. His heart sank realizing that she was just as confused about life as he was. He wondered if he'd ever figure it out. Carlee was in her early twenties and apparently hadn't, so that left little hope for him.

He wanted to kiss her again.

Damn it, Haley.

"Hey ho," said Haley.

Carlee crunched her eyes shut, making a face. She quickly put on her regular mask and turned around beaming. "Hey, girl. You look great!"

"So do you. Stay away from Alan in that outfit. Looking like that, I think you might get him."

Carlee laughed abnormally loud. It sounded forced and fake. "Oh, please." She glanced at Joel quickly. "Besides, I got me a guy right here." She winked at him. He felt himself blushing again.

"Hands off my baby brother. Just because he's growing doesn't mean he's grown."

He was sweating. His shirt felt glued to his back. He needed to take a shower. He hadn't bathed all day.

How had Carlee been able to handle my smell?

He suddenly felt exhausted again.

"You okay?" asked Haley.

Wiping his brow with the back of his hand, he said, "Yeah, fine."

She made a face at him, not totally believing him. "Well, I'll be late getting home tonight. So, don't stay up for me."

"Trust me, I won't. I'm beat."

"Don't get too bored."

"I'll keep myself busy somehow."

Carlee nudged him, "Watch some gory movies, then tell me all about them."

Blushing again he said, "You got it."

When Haley looked down to zip her pocketbook, he caught Carlee quickly giving him a wink. He winked back, feeling excited, yet stressed that the two of them had their own shared secret. He wondered if anything else would be shared between them. Doubtful.

I'm just a kid. Probably a onetime thing and they'd never mention it again. Yet, he couldn't stop from being hopeful that it would eventually lead to something more.

Throwing her pocketbook over her shoulder, Haley adjusted it so it wasn't tugging her shirt so hard. "You sure you're okay?"

"I'm *fine*," he said, enunciating the last part to make his point.

"All *right*," she mimicked. "Sorry for being concerned."

Carlee opened the front door and stepped outside to wait. Haley stopped in the doorway. She looked over her shoulder at him. "You be careful, okay?"

Her sudden forewarning stunned him. "Okay?"

"I mean it. Don't do anything stupid."

Why was she saying this to him? "I won't."

"All right, that's enough motherly type heeds, wouldn't you say?"

"I'd scream."

Laughing, "I bet. Suits you better."

Carlee tapped her foot. It made clacking sounds on the concrete. "Come on Haley, all the good snacks are going to be gone and the coffee'll be cold!"

"I'm coming, jeez!! Don't get your panties all twisted."

"I'm not wearing any!!"

A tremor of excitement fluttered in Joel's crotch. He shifted his stance to his left foot, taking pressure off his penis. It helped.

"Nice talk! In front of my brother, no less."

"He's a big boy. Probably heard worse in movies."

He had, but it was different coming from someone he knew. Someone like Carlee. He wished he could drop down and take a peek up that skirt to see if what she had said was true.

Haley rolled her eyes, shook her head. "I'm out of here before she pollutes your mind even more."

Too late, he thought, but said, "Good idea."

"Bye. Call me if you need anything."

"I will." He shut the door after she'd walked out. He was glad she was gone, but already felt terribly alone. The house was uncomfortably quieter than usual. The constant ticking from the clock in the den droned through the house like a heavy thing. The faint sound of Carlee's car leaving came from outside.

He *was* alone.

He wondered if he should go to the basement and check on Pillowface but decided to leave him be. He would leave him some pizza on a plate outside the basement door. It was easier, and he wasn't anxious to discover Pillowface had *borrowed* more of his dad's tools. Plus, he was very tired, and wanted to do nothing more than shower and go to bed. That sounded like a plan. A great one. Slouched over, he stomped upstairs to the bathroom.

He could still taste Carlee on his lips.

(II)

He was back in the darkened room, and had been here for several days, maybe even weeks. The strong stench of old urine and feces clung to him like a parasite. He flexed his hands, feeling sharp stings of pain in his wrists. They had been bound to the arms of a chair with barbwire. The piercing points burrowed into his flesh, causing fresh blood to trickle over the scabs of his previous wounds.

Back in the Torture Chair.

He'd been subjected to what he'd given the moniker of *The Torture Chair* a few times already. He'd been beaten, punched, kicked, even sliced a few times, but had yet to be broken. His tolerance for pain was immeasurable.

There was only one out of all his captors that could speak some kind of English. He'd asked him questions about the invasion, his unit, basic interrogation stuff. He'd been a prisoner before and was accustomed to the drill. Didn't matter where in the world he was, all terrorists were the same.

Droids.

Something banged from outside. A channel of light flickered through the room. He looked away, squinting. He could hear their voices. The indistinct chatter of his captors, speaking in a native tongue that he couldn't understand. Why hadn't he been trained to speak the

Afghani language? Sending all these Americans to furtive lands and not teaching them to speak or to understand the local babble was absurd.

The six-inch-thick metal door opened with a rusted screech. A fresh breeze that reeked of dirt and molded rock quickly rushed in. *Cave funk.* Looking up, he saw the usual suspects entering. Four of them, their faces covered with black masks, thin, and nearly transparent, but thick enough to hide their features. The one that he could actually understand stood in the door frame, the lower portion of his face disguised by a checkered turban.

He only stood there, staring.

The others spread out through the room. Equally stretched, they stood with their arms crossed and soundless.

They've come in here to kill me.

As if hearing the thought, Turbanface began to laugh. It was a dark, ominous chortle that rippled his arms with gooseflesh. Then he disappeared around the other side of the door. He returned shortly, but not alone. Dragged by a chain around his neck was another American from his section, the director guy who'd joined the army to earn tuition money for film school. He couldn't remember his *real* name, but they'd nicknamed him *Buddy* from all of the interviews he'd conducted with the Afghanis. Each person, while on camera, had constantly referred to him as *buddy* when re-telling their horrible stories of suffering and woe. It was their way of trying to connect with the average American. Calling them buddy, meaning pal, friend, or companion.

He'd hoped to use the documentary footage someday, showing their true experiences in war. Not, as Buddy would say, the bubble gum version you saw on the nightly news, or what the president was spoon-feeding to a starving, American public.

Why *was* Buddy here?

Buddy's mouth, gagged with a hanky and duct tape, pleaded muffled syllables as he was dragged into the room. His hands were coupled together with the same kind of barbwire that had been used to bind Face to the chair. Turbanface stopped long enough to shut the door. The air became instantly dry and thick. He turned to the masked men and yelled something in their language. The second one to his left nodded, turned around, and handed him something from the back of his pants.

At first, he couldn't tell what it was. Then Turbanface turned to Buddy and forced him to take the object. In Buddy's hands it was decipherable.

A camera.

And not the large, digital contraption Buddy had lugged around before they were all captured, this one was small, and had a longer, narrower lens. Buddy shook his head, pleaded more muffled babbles and was struck by Turbanface's fist for his efforts. He shut up after that. Under the camera's base was a pistol grip and trigger. With his wrists bundled together, he struggled to clasp his hand around the grip. Once he'd managed that, he used his index finger to press the trigger. The small device emitted a loud cranking sound as something thin and flimsy belted through it.

Film.

Turning to Face, scowling with twisted, black eyes, Turbanface said, "Your soldier, da one dey call Junior. Before I cut out his tongue, and removed his jaw, he told me." Smiling, he waved a finger at him. "I know you. You pretty boy. You Face." Bending his finger, he outlined his own masked brown face with an elongated fingernail. "Dey call you dat. Correct?"

He was but said nothing.

"It do be a handsome face." Reaching to the sheath wrapped around his brown trousers, he removed a large blade nearly the size of a machete, jagged along one side and tarnished under thick rust. It would be sharp enough to cut, but too dull to do it quickly.

Face knew where this was going.

"I tink I will take dat face. Maybe if I wear it, I get bunches of girls …?" He turned to Buddy. "Cut on de camera."

Reluctantly, Buddy obeyed. With a wince, he raised the camera to his eye as if it hurt him to do so. He pleaded Face's forgiveness with his wide stare. Face nodded, offering it, understanding this was nothing he could have prevented.

As Turbanface approached with the knife, he dragged Buddy behind him. Making sure he kept the camera focused on the upcoming action. Face swore he would not give them the benefit of screaming or displaying the obvious amount of pain he was about to endure. Bite his tongue off if he had to, but he would not scream, cry, or yell.

They didn't deserve to see his anguish.

He'd honored his promise almost all the way to the end. While the blade dug into his flesh, Turbanface used his jagged fingernails to pull the flapping skin. As if he was carving a Thanksgiving turkey, he cut and ripped and flayed. When the screams started coming, he did just what he swore he would. He'd clamped down on his darting tongue. Gritting his teeth, feeling the warmth of blood flooding his mouth, he tasted its copper flavor.

His silence angered Turbanface even more, so he dropped the knife on the dirt-cased ground and used both hands to tug what remained of his face away. Many times, Face nearly passed out, but he'd willed himself to stay coherent. He continued to stare back at the man, his gaze just as cold as the one he was receiving. By the end of the lurid ordeal, he'd noticed Buddy's scared, frantic expression had turned to one of anger and determination.

Buddy's sanity had slipped away behind the rolling lens.

Then he woke up.

No longer was he a captive in the improvised torture room, Pillowface now laid on a deflating air-mattress. Drenched in a veneer of frigid sweat, he could hear air hissing from his rubber bed. His back nudged the concrete floor. The support and comfort were gone. The bed was deflating. Somehow, he'd made it pop.

He sat up with a grunt.

Enraged.

His vision had reddened, his heart was hammering. His skull felt as if it were about to crack open. Every part of him tingled with perverse desires. He needed to hurt something, to punish something beautiful. Briefly, he considered Haley, but shook her out of his mind. Then he stood up and kicked the piece of shit bed. Behind it sat his creation. As much as he wanted to use it on something, it wasn't quite complete, not yet, but it would be soon, so it'd have to wait.

Through the thin window ledges atop the wall, he saw night had come. Where the moon sat and the stars twinkled, he guessed it was nearing ten. Out there, he'd find what was needed. Opening the side door, his boots trampled over slices of pizza that had been wrapped in plastic wrap and left for him, then ran into the night.

He had a good idea where he'd find what he was looking for.

CHAPTER ELEVEN

(I)

At the point of liberation, Tonya curled her toes, arched her feet, and moaned as the orgasm pumped all through her. Going into convulsions, her body violently quaked with a pounding release.

Finished, she lay breathless a moment before pulling the sodden, penis-shaped device out of her clasping heat. Its small, bunny-like ears vibrated, buzzing like a swarm of angry bees. She reached beside her on the bed, found the power box, and shut it off. The tiny motor died. Her slippery wet body could feel its lingering, pulsating effects.

She smiled, satisfied.

Her hair, mussed and knotted on the pillows, was saturated with sweat. Its condensation seeped down the nape of her neck. Tonya's nipples were bloated and sore from the pinching and twisting she'd wreaked upon them. She'd imagined it had been Ray's hands. Contorting, pulling them, and causing just enough pain in the pleasure. She'd even called out his name a few times, even though he hadn't physically been there to hear it. It would have been better had he been. But she wasn't ready to cave in and let him have her, not just yet.

That was the reasoning behind these quick releases, to prevent her from being seduced. He'd been so nice to her lately that she was afraid of ruining it by fucking him. He'd probably planned for it to happen tonight, but nope, she'd already taken care of it, and for the second time today. The first had been a quick rub-out this morning. This time, with her parents out for the evening, she'd taken her time. Stripped down to nothing, sprawled out on the bed, used one hand to hold the toy in place, and the other to explore her vulnerable body.

God how she had wished it were Ray.

Soon.

The impulses were coming more frequently. She'd relieved herself twice today and could already feel the inclination of an approaching third. Could she honestly have him come over knowing her parents would be gone for most of the night and *not* give in?

Maybe, but she doubted it.

She sat up, propping herself on her elbows. She felt the warm after-effects trickling out of her. She shivered. Her panties hugged her left ankle. She pulled them off, using the pink material to wipe herself dry. After drenching them in her moisture, she wadded them into a ball, and climbed off the bed. Her legs felt quivery, and it was difficult to walk. She decided to leave the jackrabbit where it was on the bed and worry about washing it later.

In the bathroom, she shut the door, and pushed the button on the knob inward to lock it.

(II)

lean and fresh and soap free, Tonya shut off the shower. She stepped out of the tub and stood on the carpeted bathmat, letting the droplets dribble off her. The steam puffed from her warm body. Refreshed, she took a deep breath through her nose and slowly exhaled through her mouth.

"Much better,' she muttered.

She grabbed a towel and began drying. Leaning over, she let her soaked hair droop over her face, and scrubbed it with the towel. Starting from the back, she worked her way to the tips. When she leaned up straight, she was dizzy for a moment. Then she chucked the wet towel in the hamper beside the toilet. Standing there naked, she brushed the tangles out of her hair.

Once she was finished, she opened the bathroom door letting the steam expel from the bathroom like a heavy fog as she exited. Turning the corner, she abruptly halted to a standstill.

Her bedroom door was shut.

Hadn't she left it open?

She retraced her steps. She'd used her panties to wipe up the after-cum on her inner thighs, she'd wadded them up, and thrown them in the hamper. She hadn't returned to the room at all until now. She was sure about that.

Well, that's solves that, but if I didn't, then who did?

Her skin crawled, pushing up goosebumps. Who *had* closed it? She crouched over, covering her breasts and groin. What could she use to hide her naked ass?

Fuck. Not enough hands. Maybe I should go back for a towel.

She decided against that. To get a towel, she'd have to go to the laundry room and take the clean ones out of the dryer since she'd used the last one. The idea of wrapping her clean body in a towel from the dirty hamper grossed her out.

If someone was in there, let them have a good show before she kicked their ass.

Could be Ray, she thought, uncovering her body. He'd shown up while she was in the shower, ringing the doorbell, but she never came to answer. He probably walked around the side of the house and saw the bathroom light on. Then he'd snuck in, the asshole.

Smiling, she was almost positive that was what happened. He'd let himself in. Sly bastard. But why hadn't he just surprised her in the shower? That seemed more likely than him going to her bedroom.

She pictured him sprawled across her bed, naked, with a smile stretched across his face. "Come on in," he would say. The image made her chuckle.

The Jackrabbit.

Approaching the door, she felt the heat of blush on her skin. She'd left it out, so he'd certainly seen it. *Oh well, that's what he gets.* As she was about to open the door, she stopped. Another thought struck her that wasn't so fun and enthralling.

What if Mom and Dad had come home early?

Her warming skin went cold and clammy. The scenario played out in her mind.

Mom and Dad coming upstairs to let her know they'd decided not to go to the Martin's cocktail party after the movie. Dad's indigestion had started acting up again. Then they'd opened her door and saw the sex toy proudly displayed on the bed. They were probably in there right now, waiting for her to come in.

Oh God, please don't let it be that. Anything but that.

A shadow of movement waved across the slit at the bottom of the door. Someone was in there all right. Grinding her teeth, she cracked the door open just enough for a peek through. She immediately found the bed. Where she'd left the Jackrabbit was empty. It had been moved, taken. Small splotches of wetness, probably from her release, were spattered across the sheet. But the toy that had brought it thunderously out of her was nowhere to be seen.

"What the …?" Was all she managed to say before the door slammed shut against her skull. The impact wedged her head between the door and frame. Then it whisked open, allowing her to stagger into the room, dazed. Her neck pounded furiously with pain. The currents traveled into her shoulders, making her arms feel useless. She tried raising them but couldn't get them to move at all.

She couldn't wrap her scattered mind around what was happening. There was a looming shape in the corner of her eye. Massive, much taller than her, and thicker. It lunged, and she saw the rubber penis for an instant. It looked ridiculous floating there.

But the humor quickly died in her throat when the cord tightened around it.

"No …" She felt pressure against her skin, hindering her words and her oxygen intake. Gagging, trying to inhale, she only rasped. Her eyes bulged. Then she was hoisted into the air, the coiled cord being used as a noose. Her feet kicked out, desperately searching for something level to stand on.

Tonya pawed at the constricting cord but couldn't slip her fingers behind it to grant her some slack. Before her eyes rolled back into her head and hemorrhaged, she saw a quick glimpse of burlap, and one meaty arm being all that held her in the air by the cable.

Her back arched as her lungs wadded like a paper bag. The cord sunk deeper into the thin flesh of her neck, forcing the veins to jut out like stems on cabbage leaves. Her right arm became too heavy to hold and dropped. The left instinctively stroked at the binding cable, becoming weaker by the second. Thick strips of snot dangled from her nose, saliva dripping from her mouth.

Her muscles suspended the body lifelessly, swaying stock-still from his clutched hand. Then her bladder and bowels released, drenching the floor in urine and excrement.

She felt a last inkling of humiliation before feeling nothing more.

CHAPTER TWELVE

(I)

Haley and Carlee had no trouble finding somewhere to park. From outside, the bookstore looked nearly deserted with many open parking spaces. But once they were inside the bookstore, they discovered it was much more claustrophobic. People roved all over, cramping and lining the walls, filling the seats of folding chairs, plus the reading couch Alan kept in the center of the store.

Haley was impressed by the size of the crowd.

More nights like this, he won't need that second job. And, he wouldn't have to put up with douche bags like Jonesey insulting him, either.

They stopped at the refreshment table. Carlee snatched a handful of butter cookies like someone who feared she'd never taste another. Haley raided the coffee dispenser. Filling her cup to the brim, she slopped in some creamer and sugar, using the provided thin red straw to stir it, then took a sip. She smacked her lips to relish the taste. Then she tilted the cup upward and gulped.

With a mouthful of cookies, Carlee laughed.

"What's so funny?" asked Haley between swallows.

"You."

She lowered her cup. Turning around with her eyes narrowed to thin slits, she put on her best impression of Joe Pesci from *Goodfellas*. "Funny, how? Like a clown?"

A dreadful effort, but Carlee enjoyed it. She nearly choked on her cookies as crumbs sprayed out of her mouth. Through a cough, she said, "You're like a kid at a school dance."

"Well, can you blame me?"

"Alan seems to really like you. I bet he won't even think twice about that asshole, Jonesey."

"Sure, say that now, but when I'm leaving here with my tail between my legs, you'll be singing a different tune."

Carlee laughed, shook her head. "You're so cute. I'll make sure you leave after having *something* tucked between your legs, but it definitely won't be a tail."

"Gee, thanks." She guzzled down the rest of her coffee and went back for a refill.

"Whoa, take it easy there, girl. You're going to fill your bladder *real* quick."

"I'll be fine." After the cup was full, she sat it down, and faced Carlee. She had to ask, "Am I that bad?"

"What?"

"A kid at a dance?"

"Oh, yeah. Absolutely."

"Seriously, am I?"

"Just relax. Be your normal, charming self."

"I'll take that as a yes."

Turning around and observing the crowd, Haley leaned against the table while stirring her coffee. Her eyes combed the room. Various people were engaged in conversations that she couldn't hear. Out of all the diversities, she didn't spot Alan among them. But she quickly caught sight of someone else that she knew. Someone that made her groan in revulsion just seeing him.

"What's the matter?" asked Carlee. Her back was aimed at Haley as she was now filling a cup of her own with coffee.

"Guess who's here."

Jokingly, "Jonesey."

"That's right."

Flinching, Carlee dropped her cup but saved it from spilling. "He seriously showed up?"

"Look for yourself."

Carlee turned around and looked in the direction Haley nodded. There he stood across the room at the buffet line, munching on cauliflower with his hair slicked down by a superfluous quantity of gel. He watched the other people talking amongst themselves. Though he probably didn't care, he acted as if he was enthused to be there. Smiling with each bite he took and closing his eyes as if savoring the vegetable tray. He poked his teeth with the tip of his tongue to lash out lingering food bits.

"Okay," said Carlee. "I agree with you. This is borderline stalking."

"Borderline?"

More like he hopped over the border and started moonwalking to gloat.

"What are you going to do?"

"What *can* I do? I just hope he doesn't see me."

Having said that, she realized it was already too late. He plopped the last bite into his mouth and chewed while smiling his loathsome grin. His eyes were fixed over the mass of patrons and onto Haley. Her stomach flipped, nearly pushing the coffee right back out. He started walking toward them.

"Shit," Carlee said.

They were completely helpless. Dodging customers, he strutted to that tune that only he could hear. Everything appeared to be moving in slow motion to Haley, except for Jonesey. He moved like the only one who wasn't.

"Helloooo ladies." He spun a circle, then clapped his hands together for his finisher.

"Mr. Jones," said Carlee, "This is a surprise."

"Yeah?" he said, bobbing his head to the side.

That was very odd. There was no music playing in the store, but he couldn't stop bouncing to a rhythm as if a DJ were mixing beats.

Does he have his own theme music that only he can hear?

"You seem really happy about something." She added.

"Should I *not* be? I'm at this interesting place, nibbling on free food, and enjoying conversations with regular folk. And, to top it all, books as far as I can see. What would I have to *not* be happy about? That's the real question."

Haley wanted to vomit. She could think of one reason not to be happy, and she was looking at him.

"How are my angels?" he asked.

"Good, we're good," answered Carlee.

Realizing that she hadn't said a word, Haley cleared her throat. "Perfect." Before she could finish speaking, her throat closed up, making the last *fect* a whisper.

Jonesey's smile faltered a bit. "Are *you* okay? Sounds like you might be coming down with something."

"Oh, it's something, all right. But I'm sure it'll pass."

"Hope so, need you alert and on your toes."

"I bet."

"So," clapping his hands into a wave, he then pointed at them with both index fingers. "Haven't seen you're pal, Aaron, around."

"Alan," corrected Haley. "I'm sure he's here somewhere."

"I'm sure he wouldn't want to miss *you*. Now that you're here, he'll make his grand appearance."

Carlee butted in before Haley could retort.

"Plan on buying any books, Mr. Jones?"

"Oh please, call me Geoffrey, or Geoff, even Geoff-a-rino. Just save that mister crap for the office."

Haley thought she would either die laughing or just die if he didn't go away.

Carlee shrugged. "Okay, if you insist."

"I do, it's your job." He flashed them that atrocious smile. "Girls will be girls, I suppose." With pursing lips, his face contorted. His nose angled down like a maw. Haley wished she had a human sized mousetrap to fill with cheese.

"Haley," said Carlee. "Why don't you run along and find Alan."

Bless her heart.

"I probably should," said Haley.

At the mere mentioning of his name, Jonesey looked as if he wanted to bite something. His face wrinkled into a snarl, baring his teeth.

"Well, go find him. I'm sure everyone wants to talk with him. Better go get in line." She patted her on the back, and gave her a gentle shove.

"I'll help you find him," said Jonesey. "I've got a great pair of peepers." Rapidly blinking his eyes, he pointed at the two tapered slits.

"Thanks anyway," she said, walking away. "I'm sure I'll be fine."

"Have fun," said Carlee, then gave her a look of: *You owe me.*

Then she was away from them.

She already felt better. Her jitters were diminishing. Haley's stomach was no longer agitated as if trying to crease itself into a ball and felt loose and relaxed. In the crowd, there were a few faces she recognized from previous gatherings. She nodded, smiled, and waved at them in passing, but didn't stop to chat. Before long she was near the register at the opposite side of the store. She expected to find him there, but he wasn't.

How the hell is he supposed to sell anything if no one is running the register?

She did a quick scan from the side of the store. Pouting her bottom lip out, she huffed a gust of air upward, rustling her bangs in defeat.

Her nervousness was gone, but in its place was disappointment.

I give up.

If it was meant to be, she would have spotted him by now.

Maybe he's hiding?

After what he'd gone through at the restaurant, she couldn't hold it against him, because if it was the other way around, and she'd spotted him coming into the store, she would have hidden, too.

Sighing, she turned around, ready to go home.

And then bumped into something hard. The sudden impact nearly knocked her over. She quickly realized she had actually collided with a person.

The young man was reaching for her and saying, "I'm so sorry, that was my fault."

Then she recognized who he was.

Alan!

His eyes lit up, a smile quickly replacing the shock on his face. "Haley! Oh, damn, I'm so sorry."

"It's all right, it was my fault. I didn't see you!"

"Obviously. You almost knocked me on my ass."

She struggled to keep the goofy grin off her face but failed.

He looked good tonight. His hair was neatly styled, and he'd replaced that horrible uniform she'd seen in him last with jeans and a t-shirt. He looked the way she adored him and smelled wonderful.

"Where've you been? I've been looking for you." She resisted the urge to grab and kiss him.

"I was in the back, making sure all the desserts were being—wait. Did you just say you've been looking for me?"

Her blush turned to a scorching flush. Casually, she said, "Well, yeah, you're the host. Thought it would be rude if I didn't say hi." Bullshit, but decently executed.

He smirked. "Oh, okay. Well, hi."

She laughed. "Not buying what I said, huh?"

"Nope, too expensive."

"Yeah, I've been accused of having ridiculous prices."

"If by ridiculous prices you mean being a terrible liar, then yeah, that's absolutely correct."

Her skin felt so hot, she wondered if it would ignite. "Yeah?"

Smiling, he nodded.

"Well, I wanted to find you and apologize about yesterday."

"For what?"

"My boss."

"It's all right, water under the bridge." He made a rippling motion with his hand.

"No, you don't understand, it's like…"

Throwing his arms up as if surrendering he said, "Look, what you do in your life is your business, not mine. You don't need to explain anything to me."

"What I do in my life?"

"Yeah, he seems pretty possessive, though. I don't like that."

Hearing what he was saying made her realize that he, like several in the office, thought her relationship with Jonesey was more than platonic. *Relationship?* Hardly, it felt like a forced marriage.

"Oh, God, Alan. No! You're wrong. I'm not *seeing* him, he's just my boss. That's all, honestly."

"Ah, I see."

"That's it, I swear."

"Just be careful how you handle it then, because he has his eyes on you."

"Why do you say that?"

"Because, he *really* has his eyes on you. He's hiding in the historical romance section, watching us."

"What?" She glanced over, catching a head ducking down behind the shelves. "No way." The head bopped back up like a groundhog coming out of its den to search for its shadow. When it spotted Haley, it ducked back down again.

Jonesey.

"That asshole," she mumbled.

"Tell you what," he said. "Let's head to the back, he can't bother us there."

"The back?"

"Yeah, my little private area. We'll be safe there."

"Thank you."

"Come on."

Taking her by the hand, he led her away. She didn't bother looking back to see if Jonesey was watching, because she didn't care one way or the other.

(II)

Joel lay on his side, fitfully in and out of sleep. Weird dreams plagued his mind that featured Rusky, the naked lady Pillowface had disposed of, and Carlee. Each moment he found himself drifting off to sleep, a flutter of images would erupt, jolting him awake. He wished it were like last night, where he'd been so drained nothing bothered him.

However, what had woken him this time was not a broken nightmare. It was footsteps, diminishing thuds heading away from him. They'd sounded so distant at first and yet so close. As his vigilance improved, he realized that they were in his room. Now he could hear them in the hall, then descending the stairs.

He rolled onto his back. The ceiling was a lake of gray above him. Shadows from outside skipped across. His eyes were itchy and felt crusted with sand. He wanted nothing more than to close them and go back to sleep, but he was afraid of what awaited him in dreamland.

Freddy would be better to face than my own nightmares.

He rolled onto his side, wondering if the footsteps had been a dream, also. Then he noticed a traced shape on his nightstand beside the lamp, rounded, and was the size of a melon, or ball. It hadn't been there before.

He gazed at it, filaments of frizzes spiraling from the top. As he reached for the lamp, his hand brushed across something soft, yet it was also dry and brittle. Stringy. Using his pinky to feel around, it slipped between the stringy substance and dried gunk. He tried dislodging his pinky, but it had become entwined. With his left hand occupied, he used the right to turn on the lamp. Light spewed from behind the shade, revealing an offering that had been left gift-wrapped in darkness.

He screamed seeing what his fingers were tangled in. *Hair.* Blond and matted in sticky clumps from dried blood. The face, staring back at him with bulged eyes and gaping mouth, was Tonya's. Tracks of congealed blood trailed over her face like a map leading to the various bruises and welts. He snatched back his hand, bringing the head with it. Joel felt the jagged points of her spine rubbing against his crotch, then he saw its white stem extending from the fleshy stump that was her neck. Doused in blood, it hung disheveled in vein-like cords that smelled like copper and raw beef. He collapsed back onto the bed. The hair ripped away from the scalp, a piece of flesh was affixed to the roots. There was a sodden *thunk* when the head struck his floor.

The bedroom became packed with a furor of screams.

His screams.

(III)

Alan escorted Haley to a small card table in the back room of his petite store. From the loudness on the sales floor, it seemed deathly quiet back here. "Want something to drink?" he asked while walking to a refrigerator in the corner of the room. Beside it was a wooden stand with a microwave, toaster, and towers of Styrofoam plates, cups, and bowls on top. A coffee maker sat on the roof of the microwave, and a level of filters was next to the cups.

"Sure," answered Haley. "What do you have?"

"Oh, the hard stuff. Coke, Pepsi, Dr. Pepper." He opened the fridge, awaiting her decision.

"Dr. Pepper?" He nodded. "Cherry or regular?"

He looked impressed. "Both, but more cherry than regular."

"Cherry."

"Ah, I knew it."

"I figured you did."

"You said a couple weeks back that was your favorite soft drink."

"Wow, you remembered that?"

"I have a great memory. It's a curse and a gift." He reached inside the fridge and returned with two cans of cherry Dr. Pepper. As he extended his hand, he popped the tab with his thumb. Some red-tinted cola fizzed out, but nothing exploded, which was good. "Here you go."

"Thanks," she said, taking the can. "I think a good memory is a blessing. I can hardly remember this morning."

He laughed, cracked open his own soda, and sipped. "People that don't have my memory say that, but trust me, they'd sing a different tune if they did."

Taking a swig, she felt the burbling of a belch in her chest. It never failed with soda. She slowly exhaled, keeping her mouth closed as it bubbled, then released. She turned her head, blowing the fumes of coffee and Dr. Pepper away from Alan. When she was certain none of it lingered in her mouth, she turned back to him, and said, "Why do you say that? If you have a great memory, you'll never forget birthdays, anniversaries, and holidays. I could go on and on." She took another sip and could already feel another belch coming.

"Yeah, that's the brighter side of it. But the dark side is also never being able to *forget* when someone's lied to you, or forgotten *your* birthday, made a promise and didn't keep it. It also makes it incredibly hard not to hold a grudge." He guzzled a few swallows, shook his head. "A lot of the time, I hate it."

A burp tore from Haley's mouth, startling Alan enough for him to drop his drink. Seeing his can hit the floor and eject soda like an erupting volcano almost made her cry. "I'm so sorry!" She twirled in a circle, not knowing what to do first. Get something to clean it up, let him handle it, or run out of the store screaming. Settling for neither, she cupped a hand over her eyes and plopped down in a chair by the table. She pressed the weight of her humiliation against her palm.

She could hear Alan snickering. Raising her head enough to see, she asked "What's so funny? The fact I burped or my reaction to making you spill your drink?"

"Well, both, but that's not why I'm laughing."

"Why *are* you laughing?"

"Because I'm *never* gonna forget this."

Groaning, she said, "Me neither."

CHAPTER THIRTEEN

(I)

"**Y**ou can't do that!" shrieked Joel.

In the basement, Pillowface sat in a chair like a kid in the principal's office. His head hung low. Fidgeting with his fingers, he listened to Joel freak out while pacing back and forth.

"She's my neighbor! What are we going to do now?"

It sounded so wrong and inexcusable hearing Joel put it like that. Yes, he had killed her, but it was a warranted execution. She'd sustained the urges and thoughts his dream had brought on. It had helped him to avoid unleashing his wrath on someone else, like Haley. He'd chosen to inflict his internal pain on the neighbor girl so she could understand just what he battled on the inside by turning her into a visual landscape of what he'd become—a monster.

Tonya was someone that didn't deserve the beauty she'd been blessed with. He remembered what Joel had said, how she'd let him fondle her just so he'd feel better about someone dying. She was partly responsible for the demeaning of the human race.

He'd done the world a favor.

She'd deserved it.

And he'd brought home a token. Just as always, he'd kept a piece of the body as a souvenir, a reminder. This time, he hadn't kept it for himself to disfigure like he would the others. He'd given it to Joel as a gift, a way to let him know that he appreciated all that he'd done for him. She was pretty to him, and Pillowface thought that Joel would have valued the gesture.

He'd been wrong.

Joel was just too young, too green to understand.

"You *did* hide the body, didn't you?" asked Joel, stopping his gaiting long enough to look at him.

Pillowface, lowering his head even more, used his movements to confess that he had not. Actually, he'd left her in the bedroom, strewn about here and there and everywhere.

"Great, just great. I bet it's a mess over there, isn't it?" Pillowface shrugged. "What are we going to do? They'll find you, take you away! I've got to think." He waved his finger at nothing particular and returned to pacing. Stepping a few feet one way, he'd stop, turn around, and come back only to repeat this process again and again and again…

After several laps, Joel finally turned around beaming. "I've got an idea. We'll head back over there and clean it up. Then we'll take the body and hide it in the woods." He seemed to be waiting for an ecstatic response but didn't get one. What he did get was a blank stare behind an inch of burlap. "Listen, I know you're used to just leaving them where you killed them. But this is the real world. Your rules don't apply here. You go by that slasher movie guidebook, kill 'em all, violently and gory. But here they have investigators, scientists, people that can examine these murder scenes and figure out who did it. They use technology to do it."

As Joel explained what the technology was, he began to wonder just who the hell he had confused him for. Pillowface was an ex-military sergeant, one that had fought all over the world, seen more in a day than this kid had experienced in his lifetime. Yet, he spoke to him like a hillbilly woodsman that didn't know his ass from a pussy patch. Or as if he weren't real, like something from a movie. For the first time since their introduction, Pillowface questioned Joel's sanity.

"What I'm saying is we've got to go next door. Do you agree?"

He nodded, but really, he wondered what the point was.

"I'll be right back, gonna get some stuff to clean it up with."

While Joel gathered the supplies, Pillowface waited outside, staring into the woods. He wondered how long it would be before Buddy and Carp found him. He was surprised it had taken them this long, but he doubted it would be much longer.

He heard the bumping and rattling of a bucket as Joel tottered out of the house, having trouble carrying all the shit he'd gathered. In one hand he held a mop with a bucket lagging behind him in the other. The plastic bucket whacked the backs of his legs with each clumsy step. Joel had placed an unopened pack of sponges, some soap, and two bags of rubber gloves inside the bucket with a few plastic booties and shower caps. Where he'd found all this, Pillowface had no clue, but at least the boy was prepared.

"I think I've got everything." He stopped in front of him, panting. Not only did he act tired, he looked it. Pillowface reached out and took the bucket, patting him on the back. Joel nearly collapsed against him from exhaustion. He put a hand against the boy's chest, helping him stay balanced. "I'm okay, just a little beat, and thirsty, but it can wait. We've got to get this done before someone comes home." Starting to walk towards the neighbors' house, he stopped to glance back at Pillowface. "No one was home when you did this, right?"

Headshake.

"Okay, thank God for that." Joel made a face, as if wincing that he'd brought God's name into this ghoulish scenario.

Joel, with the mop hanging over his shoulder, led the way. Walking alongside the fence, they circled around the back, and entered the yard through the rear gate. The same path Pillowface had ventured earlier.

While Joel waited at the side patio doors, Pillowface quietly pried the back door enough that the tongue pulled away from the mouth in the panel. With no deadbolt on the rear door, he was able to do this easier than the first time. No tools were required, only pure strength. He shimmied it back and forth until it popped. Then he slowly opened the door. The wood was splintering; if he did this again the frame would probably break.

Inside, the house was dark. What little light there was came from the moon outside, casting slashes of gray this way and that. Pillowface didn't need it. His own eyes would guide him through the oily blackness.

He crossed the entranceway, the living room, den, and the kitchen. Joel awaited him on the other side of the glass doors. This house's layout was very similar to Joel's; the only difference he'd noticed so far was the outside color. He had no trouble walking through it.

Joel waved as he approached. Pillowface unlocked the door, then stepped back as he opened it, giving him the room he needed to carry in the mop. The handle clanged against the frame, a metallic vibrating clamor resounded through the tranquil house.

"Whoops," whispered Joel. Once they were both inside, Pillowface slammed the door shut behind him. Its echo was much louder than the mop's.

Wincing, Joel said, "Trying to give me a heart attack?" He shook his head. "Sheesh. Let me have the bucket." As if treading on ice, Joel lightly stepped into the kitchen. He propped the mop against the doorway on his way in. As Pillowface entered, Joel was already standing at the sink filling the bucket with hot water.

After he finished, they headed upstairs. Joel, carrying the bucket, was careful not to spill a drop. They arrived at Tonya's closed bedroom door. Joel put down the bucket, resting a minute while waiting for Pillowface to catch up. Sticking his hand under his shirt, he used it as an improvised glove on the doorknob. While he turned the knob, Pillowface wished he could somehow warn him of what he would witness inside, prepare him for the canvas of brutality behind the door. Deep down he knew there was no real way of doing that and decided to just throw him in the water and see if he could swim.

Joel vomited when he saw what remained of Tonya: a mangled torso on the bed. Naked, legs spread. Headless, disemboweled, moors of intestines uncoiled and stretched across the room. Blood had splattered the sheets, the floor, and the walls, filtering the room's radiance in a red gloom like the inside of a dingy bar.

Her head, of course, was nowhere to be found. It sat back in Joel's room, on his nightstand. Its open mouth gawkily contorted, and the milk-like eyes creamy with no color.

Heaving, he wiped tears from his eyes, took another look, and threw up harder than before.

(II)

Alan finished wiping the spilled soda with the last of his paper towels. He raised the cardboard roll above his head and said, "Well, that took care of that. I need to get some more."

Haley was so red she wondered if traffic was stopping outside. "I'm sorry. God, at least let me pay for some new paper towels."

"Nah, I wouldn't dream of it." He stood up, tossing the cardboard cylinder into the trash. It bunked off the wall and went in. Holding his hands out, he turned around with a smirk.

"Good shot."

"And thank you very much for noticing." He glanced back at the floor. "See any that I missed?"

"Besides your shirt? No."

He looked down at his soda-speckled shirt. "Yeah, not much I can do about that. Do you think it'll stain?"

It most definitely would. She groaned. "I'm *so sorry.*" She kicked her feet at the floor. "I feel like such a dumbass."

He laughed. "Brains have nothing to do with it."

"Gee, thanks."

"You burped and it scared the shit out of me. I should feel like the dumbass."

"Oh, whatever. It was all my fault."

"Fine." He joined her at the table and took a seat. "If you must shoulder the blame, then I'll oblige." He sighed. "It's *all* your fault."

"Thank you." She looked at the cleaned area and frowned. "Not to be a wet blanket, but that's going to have to be mopped or it'll be sticky *and* attract ants. With it being summer, you'll get them for sure."

"Are you volunteering?"

"Please?"

"If you feel like you really have to. The stuff's in the cabinet under the microwave."

"Thank you." She hurried to the cabinet. Squatting, she sifted through it and rose with a bucket, Pine-Sol, and sponge. "Where's the mop?" He pointed behind her. She turned around, saw it leaning against the fridge. "Ah." She put the bucket in the sink, unscrewed the cap from the Pine-Sol, and emptied what was left inside.

"Okay," he said, "You're getting expensive."

She looked at him over her shoulder. "What?"

"Not only will I have to buy paper towels, I'll have to add Pine-Sol to the list."

Laughing, she said, "I volunteered to buy the paper towels, you declined."

"I'm beginning to regret my decision."

She laughed again, but suddenly stopped. "Hmm ..." After a moment, she shrugged her shoulders and went back to work.

"What was that?" asked Alan with an obvious frown in his voice.

"Huh?" she asked without looking back. The water had finally become warm enough to allow in the bucket. She tilted it back, letting it fill.

"That shrug of the shoulders just now."

"That what?"

"You shrugged your shoulders and went 'Hmm'."

"I did?"

"Yep."

"Oh, I must have done that thing where your body reacts to what you're thinking. You know, like when you think of a question and then accidentally answer it out loud."

"I know that all too well."

"Want to know what I was thinking?"

"If you want to tell me."

"Sure." She shut off the water, turned around, and crossed her arms. "It's weird. All night, my mind has been focused on you."

His eyes rounded.

She noticed his reaction and laughed. "Calm down big guy." She cocked her jaw to the side, clucked her tongue. "But, for some reason, I just thought about my brother."

"It happens. You've probably been thinking about him all night, but it just now registered."

"Could be."

"How's he doing?"

She shook her head. "Not too good. His dog died the other night."

"Oh, man, that sucks. I remember that feeling, it's rough."

"Yeah." She lowered her head. "It's been hard on the both of us. But it almost feels like we might be finally finding a way to cope with everything. I don't want to jinx anything, but I think we've passed the stage where we're angry at each other."

"That's good. As tragic as the dog's passing is, maybe it'll bring the two of you closer together in the long run."

She wanted to hug him. He'd said the perfect thing, and it felt good hearing it.

Alan continued. "I bet the dog's death was just another reminder of what happened to your parents."

"I'm sure it was. Hell, I think it was for the both of us. After they were killed, it was just the three of us left, you know? Haley, Joel, and Rusky. Now, we're down to two." She took the mop from beside the fridge. Then walked to the bucket and drowned its stringy head in the water. Turning it this way and that, she let it soak.

Her breath snagged. Her exhausted eyes burned as fresh tears formed.

"I don't get it." He said, shuffling in his seat.

"Get what?" Her voice was shaky, rising in pitch.

"The problem. Everything with you two seems all right, but that little gesture you did earlier made you seem like you were worried about something. What's the deal?"

"I don't know. I just suddenly started wondering what he was doing." She pulled the mop out of the bucket and slapped it on the floor. "I got the feeling he was up to something."

(III)

oel finished mopping up the coagulated blood. He'd waited until last to do that. When they'd first started cleaning, he'd retraced Pillowface's every step, swabbing up his evidence. Then he realized that they were just muddling right over his clean floor and decided to wait.

While he'd cleaned, Pillowface, with a handful of trash bags they'd stolen from under the sink, had draped the body and taken it outside. He was probably already back at home, gathering up her head and waiting for him. Joel really should be wrapping up and getting over there. It was certainly getting late, and they still had more work to do before calling it a night.

He took the mop to the sink and stuck the head under running water. The clear liquid turned murky as it swirled down the drain. When he was finished, he stuck the mop-head in the bucket, and washed his hands. He used some paper towels to dry them and stuck the sodden pieces in his pocket when he was through. He didn't want to risk someone finding them in the trash. Maybe he'd burn them or flush them down the toilet when he got home, anything but leave them here.

A faint slamming sound made his heart lurch. He hoped it was Pillowface coming to check on him, but when he heard it repeat, he realized that it was coming from somewhere outside the house.

The garage.

The twin noises had been car doors.

Tonya's parents had come home.

Snatching the bucket off the floor, he whispered, "Oh, shit on me ..." The mop handle whipped back and slapped him across the face. His cheek stung from the blow, hot bristles scurrying up to his scalp.

He ran to the side door, pressing the bucket against his hip to keep it from making a noise. He held the mop tightly with his other hand to prevent a repeated attack by the handle.

He stopped at the patio doors and listened. Faint voices came from outside. One male, one female. *Tonya's parents for sure.* And he was still inside the damn house. Why had he taken so long cleaning? He'd finished several minutes ago, save a few touch ups. The job shouldn't have taken too terribly long, but he'd spent a lot of time paying extra attention to the smaller details. One mistake could be one too many in an instance such as this.

The metallic scraping of a key searching for a lock pulled him from his scampering thoughts. *I've gotta get out of here.* He turned to open the door and froze. Through the black of night, the flood lights at the top of the power-poles cast enough illumination for him to see that just outside the second entrance of the garage Pillowface stood against the wall with the machete clinched, holding the blade like a penetrating baseball bat.

Pillowface was planning to ambush her parents.

Now, Joel really needed to move. Any second now Pillowface would charge in and start whacking. In a dash, he flung open the patio door, cracking his knee against its solid wood. The door vigorously trembled as it opened. It hurt like hell, but the noise had at least gotten Pillowface's attention.

When Joel's feet met the grass, he pitched his ear to the air, and stopped. Tonya's parents were talking, and from what they were saying, Pillowface hadn't been the only one to hear all the commotion.

"I didn't hear anything," said the female voice.

Another pause. Joel could feel his heart pounding in his throat. He looked at Pillowface, saw he was about to enact his plan of attack, so he shook his head, hoping he could see him in the shadows. He must have because he stopped moving and waited.

"Maybe you're right," said the male voice, finally.

Joel realized he'd been holding his breath all this time and exhaled slowly. His lungs unnaturally wheezed. After he heard the door to the den shut, he bolted, passing Pillowface and cutting back through the opening in the fence.

When they were back in his yard, he realized he'd forgotten to close the patio door.

He could feel tears coming as fast as the panic. He turned around, creeping back to the fence. Through a thin slit between the boards, he peeked through. When he'd left, the room had been shrouded in darkness, but now it was lit up vividly. Two shapes moved back and forth throughout. The man—Tonya's dad—stepped over to the opened door. He stood there, staring out into the yard.

He called, "Hello?"

Joel flinched at the intensity of his voice. It probably wasn't as loud as it had seemed, but to Joel it sounded fiery. Any second now, he anticipated the man would catch him hiding. Convinced the man might see the whites of his eyes through the narrow slits in the fence, he screwed them shut.

Tonya's mom must have joined him at the doorway. "Who are you talking to?" she asked.

"The door was open."

"Wide open?"

"Yes."

Oh, shit. Joel tried telling himself he'd done everything that needed to be done to cover their tracks. But he couldn't be certain. He knew any moment they'd find a speckle of blood.

"Well, Tonya was lying out in the sun earlier."

"Oh, that explains it," he said back.

Yes, he thought. *That's it, now just go back inside, shut the door, and go away. Please, before Pillowface decides to take matters into his own hands.*

Joel pictured the two of them looking out in the yard when suddenly Pillowface was on them, using the machete to hack away at them until there was nothing left.

Then he'd have two more messes to clean up.

The skin around his testicles seemed to be shrinking and his buttocks felt heavy like granite. When he felt a hand squeeze his shoulder, he yelped. His bladder suddenly filled to the brim.

Thankfully, it was Pillowface's hand.

And thank God Tonya's parents had already shut the door and continued about their business, so it was doubtful they'd heard him, but how long would it take them to realize something was wrong?

After a few deep breaths, Joel stood up straight. "You ready?"

Pillowface shook his head, then pointed back at his house. Joel noticed he didn't have the head. "All right, I'll go grab it." He spoke as if it were nothing more than a gallon of milk, or bread. He darted in the house, leaving Pillowface to guard the yard. For a second, he'd considered sending him to get the head, that way he could handle Tonya's body. Just to feel it one more time before burying her.

Two funerals in just as many days. Keep it up, and he'd be a pro.

Still, if he could just touch her.

Stop it. She's all torn up.

Not all of her was torn up, he realized.

She was torn up enough.

When he was nine, he'd watched his dad and grandfather string up a deer and gut it. They'd spent time taking care of the carcass, treating it delicately, disposing of the innards in a healthy clean way. Pillowface hadn't shared their delicacy.

At the top of the stairs, he jogged to his room. He reached in to turn on the light but stopped himself. If he turned it on, it'd ruin his night vision. Leaving the room dark, he teetered through to look for the head. It wasn't on the nightstand where he'd left it. He turned a circle, scanning the floor for it.

An image flashed in his mind of Tonya's head dragging itself across the floor by its tongue, a wet and ghoulish *bump* followed by a *scraping* sound as it sluggishly slid over his feet.

Instinctively, he jumped up on the bed and looked down.

Nothing was there.

Of course there isn't. Why would there be?

Feeling foolish, he climbed down, then stepped over to the nightstand and toed something solid. It rolled. *Found it.* Crouching, he felt around the floor until his fingers raked across the desiccated flesh of her face, brushing against a soggy lip that didn't move. His index finger snagged one of her teeth as he latched onto her chin, pulling the head to him.

He was shocked that it weighed so much. In the movies, madmen would carry severed heads by the hair in one hand, but if he was to try that, her hair would surely tear away from the scalp.

So carrying the head two-handed like a football, he left his room.

CHAPTER FOURTEEN

(I)

Haley finished cleaning the floor. There was a large wet circle where she'd been mopping. She rinsed the mop in the sink. When it was good and doused, she sat it back in the bucket to dry. She turned around and bumped into Alan.

She squealed, quickly cupping a hand over her mouth.

Alan laughed. "Sorry, I didn't mean to scare you."

"It's alright. I guess we're even." Her voice was flat behind her hand. She brought down her arm. Alan stood only inches from her and was taller. Haley needed to tilt her head back to look at him. His full eyes stared into hers. She found herself losing all concentration and only wanting to kiss him. She thought about giving it a try but was afraid of what he would think. She wasn't even completely sure he didn't have a girlfriend.

He's never mentioned one.

But that didn't mean there wasn't one.

His hand brushed a loose strand of hair back behind her ear, his mild touch sending tingles through her. She resisted the urge to shudder. Her stomach was rolling. She sucked in a trembling breath as he leaned down to her. Arching herself up on her tiptoes, she met him.

Haley brushed her lips against his, feeling the fullness of his mouth. They're lips connected. Soft and cold at first, they quickly warmed against hers. Her body weakened, her legs felt soft and rubbery. She fell into him. He caught her, holding her tightly against his chest, and looked at her, again. She lost herself in the puddles of his gaze. He smiled. Then he glided his hands up her back, massaging it. She closed her eyes as his hands explored her, rubbing and kneading the curve of her back, up to her neck. She felt his warm breath stronger and heavier against her face. Haley opened her eyes as he came in for another kiss.

She parted her lips. This time, they kissed with fervor, a hunger that was finally being satisfied. His tongue entered her mouth, casual and tender. She lifted hers to find his. They rolled around each other. His rubbing hands moved down her back, finding the bottom of her blouse, then went under it. His hands felt warm and sweaty on the small of her back. She flinched as his fingers tickled her, bringing up goose bumps like pebbles on her skin.

Haley writhed against him, lifted his shirt, and glided her hands across his abdomen. It felt hard and solid. She traced its shape to his navel. She pressed herself sternly against him, wiggling against the length of his body. Her breasts, barely contained in her blouse, squished against his chest. He exhaled a trembling breath into her mouth.

She grabbed his arms and slowly guided him backward, kissing along the way, and backtracking to the table. Alan's heels knocked against a chair. She gently pushed him down in the seat.

Then she squatted between his parted legs.

"Wuh-what are you doing?" he asked, his breath heavy.

"It's okay." She slowly skimmed her hands up his thighs to his crotch. She found the hardness in his pants. She fingered the zipper and leisurely pulled it down, freeing his penis. It fell out of his pants, nicking her arm on the way down, and continued to grow as if being trapped inside his pants had prohibited it to.

His penis was much larger than she'd expected, and her reaction showed her astonishment. She gasped at it. The massive tube looked as if it would never stop growing. She leaned over, unveiling her tongue, licking and flicking. He squirmed in the chair. Then she took him in her mouth, and he tensed up, held his breath. She had to stretch her lips around the head of his penis. The corners of her mouth felt as if they would rip. Her tongue hastily flicked the shaft.

"God," he whispered.

She pulled her mouth away, popping a sound as it exited her mouth. She looked up at him, grinning as her hand wrapped around him and began to stroke. Alan quivered. She knew she needed to stop before he exploded. She wasn't ready for him to.

She stood up, taking a couple of steps back.

"You're so beautiful," he managed to say.

"Thank you."

He probably thinks I'm a slut that does this sort of thing all the time.

She considered stopping but couldn't bring herself to do so. She was enjoying it too much. She slid her hands up her thighs, and under her skirt. She hooked her thumbs around the straps of her panties and slipped them down her legs. At the knees, she let them drop to the floor. Then she kicked her feet out of them.

"This isn't happening," he said.

"You don't mind, do you?"

He shook his head and gulped.

When she caught a glimpse of that pole between his legs, it was her turn to gulp. *How am I going to handle this?* She stepped out of her shoes. From where she'd mopped, the floor was damp under her feet. She walked to him, spreading her legs as she fixed a foot on each side of the chair. She gripped his shoulders and slowly squatted, impaling herself on top of him. He pushed into her, deep. She sucked in a breath, the gasp catching in her throat. It felt wonderful but hurt at the same time.

After a moment of adjusting to the pressure inside of her, she pushed with her hips, keeping her feet vaulted firmly on the floor. Moaning, she wrapped her arms around his neck and jerked him closer. His hands roamed her, pushing her blouse down, releasing her breasts. He tore the bra out of his way and began squeezing them.

She should have asked him if he had a condom.

I'm on the pill.

The pill only prevented pregnancy, and it didn't do that three percent of the time.

It's Alan, he doesn't have a disease. I saw his cock. It wasn't infested with sores. Neither is his mouth.

But …

She was about to ask him, but he sucked one of her rigid nipples into his mouth and nibbled at it. She moaned even louder, becoming even more aggressive with her drive.

(II)

hat cunt!

With his ear pressed firmly against the door, Geoffrey Jones could hear Haley making the kind of sounds he'd dreamed about. *He* should be the one causing them, not some five-figure making asshole that needed to work secondhand as a waiter just to make ends meet.

He'd begun panting so heavily that he needed to hold his breath to hear them. He listened to the screeching of a chair on concrete, and Haley's soft moans and gasps.

The worst sound though was the consistent slurp.

He knew what that slurp was.

Jonesey quickly looked around, making sure no one had seen him snoop over here. So far, so good. He expected any moment for Carlee's nosey ass to find him. It had been nearly impossible to pry from her, but he'd eventually succeeded.

As Haley's convulsive breaths continued to rise, so did Geoffrey's anger. When she held the pitch, nearly shrieking, he knew she was having an orgasm. Enraged, he punched the wall. He'd expected the wall to cave under the blow, but instead it held steady, cracking all four of his fingers. Of all the places to punch he'd picked the one area of the wall where the stud had been implanted. He wanted to cry out in pain but bit his lip and held it back.

"What was that?" asked Haley from inside, breathless.

"I-I don't know," said Alan, just as bushed. "I might need to check."

Shit!

With his right hand tucked against his stomach, he ran. The pain was severe, throbbing. He wasn't a doctor, but he'd bet it was broken.

(III)

Haley was hiking her panties up her thighs when the reality of what she'd done hit her like a slap to the face. She'd *used* Alan. In a way, yes, but that wasn't entirely true. They'd both wanted it, but it was her who had needed the embrace, the approval of someone. And she'd reverted back to her old Tonya-like ways to get it.

I like Alan, she told herself, *a lot. More than I've liked anyone in a long time.*

But that wouldn't change what had happened. Since meeting Alan a few months ago, she had ordered herself to take things slow, letting them unfold naturally, slowly growing more intimate until the night finally came when they would give in to each other. Now, she feared she'd already ruined it before things had truly had a chance to begin.

Just as she'd done with Nick. *Fuck Nick, to hell with him.* Nick hadn't been worth it, but she'd felt in order to show him that she desired him, she had to fuck him. So, she'd let him take her, three times, and each one felt emptier than the one before it. He'd tricked her, prayed on her insecurities of being abandoned by the one man that she had thought would never leave her.

Dad.

She thought her father never could have made her cry. But, he had, and more than anyone in her life ever had or ever could. Standing in the back room of Alan's store, while he checked to see what that banging had been, she realized what the dark cloud—the one that had been hovering around her for so long, the one that made her do stupid things like riding Alan's cock in a folding chair—actually was.

Hate.

Not only had her father made her crumble, but he'd also shattered her, leaving jagged shards behind of what Haley used to be. *He died.* She knew it wasn't fair to blame him, but it was easier than accepting she was the cause.

How could I be? I didn't leave anyone behind! I didn't go off and leave someone alone and frightened to fend for themselves, to try and figure out how much bullshit is associated with living your life, and not being there to offer my guidance and support along the way.

But she'd done just that to Joel. She felt tightness in her throat, dampness in her eyes.

I'm going to cry? What the hell for? I'm pissed off. He left me here, they both did, to raise Joel when I wasn't done being raised myself. How could they do this to me?

Her shoulders were bouncing, clucking up and down like a chicken looking for seed. She could feel the coldness of that familiar hollow ache drifting inside of her, encircling her heart, and clenching the love out of it. She'd come to understand that she actually hated her *parents* for dying. Not hating *that* they died, but actually putting all her anger *on them.* Why? And, why, in return for the hate she focused on them, was Joel focusing his on her?

"I didn't see anyone out there." Alan must have noticed she'd dressed. "Hey, don't I get my turn?" He laughed softly.

She glanced at him, then erupted into a whirl of tears. Unable to stand any longer, she dropped in the chair, sat forward, bent her elbows on her knees, and pressed her face into her hands.

"Hey...I was just kidding...Are you okay?" He ran to her and kneeled. His hands slipped over her back, rubbing small circles on her shirt, and asked, "What's wrong?"

She couldn't answer. She sobbed harder each time she attempted to speak.

"Did I do something?"

She shook her head. Then she wrapped her doused hands around him, pushing her face against his chest. The sogginess of her tears soaked through his shirt.

He slowly put his arms around her and held her.

CHAPTER FIFTEEN

(I)

Joel led the way through the woods, his flashlight cutting tunnels of light into the darkness, dragging the shovel behind him. The metal end glided smoothly across soggy leaves. Unlike autumn, when summer leaves fell to the ground, they wouldn't become brittle leftovers from the limbs. Somehow, they remained green and alive until the end of the season.

Pillowface trekked along in the rear with Tonya draped over his shoulder and her head inside the bucket.

Mother Nature produced her usual ambiance when they began their journey. Crickets cheeped, owls hooted, tweets from birds that should be asleep, and some random scuffles that Joel chalked off as deer. But, as they continued onward the noises became less and less regular, then they'd stopped all together. Joel wondered if it was because everything had stopped to watch them.

He glanced over his shoulder and grinned at Pillowface. He wondered if, behind the mask, he was smiling back.

He doubted it.

"You know," began Joel, "I've never met anyone like you before."

Pillowface raised his head, listening.

He continued, "I guess that's obvious. I don't know, I just never would have thought I could do something like this. You know. *This.*" He waved the flashlight around them. "But, here I am." Joel leaned forward, putting his weight into his step as he marched up an incline. "Right up here." He pointed with the light; it danced across the trees on top of the short hill.

Pillowface had figured this was where Joel would bring him. It was where he'd first spotted him with that same shovel. This was where he'd felt that connection, the invisible current from the boy to him. They had been sharing the woods, the earth, and the same air for that moment. Death surrounding them, both nowhere to be found in their minds. Confused, sad, and even a little frightened. They were oblivious to where they would end up, and unknowing they would end up together.

A team.

He was thankful the girl he was pursuing hadn't gotten Joel's attention. He might have killed the boy if that had happened. He wouldn't have gotten the chance to see Haley, either, and he was also thankful for that.

Thankful for a real friend.

"We're here," said Joel, tossing the shovel on the ground. He sluggishly dragged his feet to a tree stump, barely lifting them as he walked, and plopped down. Elbows on his knees, he hunched over, rubbing his hands together. "This has always been one of my places to go when I need to be alone."

Pillowface combed it over. It seemed fine, isolated enough. He jostled his shoulder up into Tonya's hip and heaved her over. She fell to the ground, landing with a sickening thud. Joel winced, pursed his lips, and exhaled a hissing breath.

Pillowface sat the bucket down. Then he arched his back, holding his arms out beside him, and stretched. His body popped and cracked all over.

"This is where I buried my dog." He sighed. "I expected to spend most of the week crying over him, but you know what? I haven't had time to even think about him." He laughed, shook his head. "Can you believe it?"

Pillowface walked to the flattened area of loose dirt. The soil was mucky from dew. He knelt, poking a finger into the sodden earth. When he pulled it back the tip was covered with slimy mud.

"Should be easy to dig, huh?"

He nodded.

Joel sighed, "I guess we better get started then. Haley could come home any minute."

He walked over to Joel and took the shovel, patted his shoulder, then walked to the grave.

"I can help, you know."

Pillowface shook his head.

"You sure?"

He nodded and began digging.

Joel observed in silence as the shovel prodded the dirt, scooped it up, and dumped it in a pile close by. Pillowface's muscular arms flexed and retracted with each stroke. His skin remained dry, as if it had the inability to perspire. He'd grown so used to doing this that the work hardly seemed to affect him anymore.

Each time the shovel stabbed into the earth, Joel would flinch. The digging wasn't loud at all, but in the hushed air, it seemed ridiculous.

Finally, he spoke. "My dog used to come out here with me all the time. Sometimes, I'd take these walks. Not really because I enjoyed it, even though I guess that's part of it. It was really just to collect my thoughts, or something." He shrugged. "I know that sounds really gay, but it was all I had sometimes." He scratched his head.

Digging, Pillowface continued to listen.

"Rusky was like my only *real* friend. I mean—I have two other friends, Paul and Ethan, and they're okay, and like my parents were cool, but I couldn't talk to them about *everything*, you know. I felt like no one really understood me. So, I wouldn't bother with trying to express myself to them, you know? I'd come out here, walk, and talk to Rusky. I think he could understand what I was saying. He'd tilt his head if I said something confusing, or he'd make this…this noise if I said something funny, then he'd pant in a weird way, almost like he was laughing."

Joel wiped his eyes. "I'm going to miss that guy. He was all I had left."

Knee deep in the ground, Pillowface stole a quick glance over his shoulder. Joel sat on the stump. His chin settled in the palm of his hand. His eyes focused inward. As if he were watching a visual play of his words projected on a screen. He continued digging. Joel continued talking. "My Dad was sort of like my best friend, too. I mean, my Mom was awesome but, Dad and I had this sort of bond that I can't explain. It had always been there for as long as I could remember. He and I would play games, throw baseballs in the backyard, go to the movies-- just the two of us—and eat a *lot* of popcorn. I don't think he had very many friends, either. That's why I think he could understand me more than Mom. In some way, all we had was each other. He loved my mom, a *lot*, anyone could tell you that, but it was like, he could *identify* with me more, you know."

He nodded, now waist deep in the hole. A little deeper and he'd be ready to throw her in. He didn't have the heart to let Joel know he'd already passed Rusky's corpse in the progression.

Joel didn't stop, "I think he just didn't know what to do with Haley sometimes. She could be pretty dramatic, especially about boys. God, I can remember my dad throwing one of her boyfriends through the screen door because he caught him sneaking through the *wrong* window. He was trying for Haley's room but was off by one. He ended up in our parents' room. They recognized who he was when his head popped up above the window." Laughing, he clapped his hands. "When he crawled through, they waited for him to stand up, and cut on the light." He could hardly breathe he was laughing so hard. He wiped his eyes with the tip of a finger. "Oh, man. I wish I could have seen that guy's face. I woke up to the sound of him being dragged downstairs. Mom didn't get the screen door open in time, so Dad just threw the guy through it." His laughter slowed, "Haley was pretty pissed, as you can imagine."

All he *could* do was imagine her and her dusky skin with its comforting smoothness. How her black velvet panties hugged her hips, her ass pushing out, the thong line vanishing between them. Her high breasts, supported by the bra, but not shaped by it. Their fullness and size and perk were all hers.

He had transcended into the earth up to his ribcage and figured that was plenty deep. Tonya deserved nothing more than a shallow grave. He'd given her more than he should have.

Pillowface planted his hands flat on the edge and heaved himself up. He dug his knee into the soil at the top of the hole and climbed out. Standing, he brushed his hands on the legs of his pants, leaving behind brown streaks that looked like chocolate across them.

"Done already?" asked Joel. His face was colorless and wet.

Joel sat up straight. Sweat had glued his shirt to his back. He pulled at it, pealing it from his skin. Holding a piece of the shirt between his finger and thumb, he fanned it back and forth. He wanted to get up and help, but his legs were killing him. Their annoying soreness had morphed into a drastic ache, a throbbing that felt like knife jabs in his thighs and calves. His feet hurt so bad they felt numb. He was useless as an assistant right now, best just to stay out of the way.

Pillowface latched a hand around Tonya's ankle and dragged her to the hole. He laid her straight, walked around her toes to the opposite side of her. The hole was a foot shorter than her. She wouldn't fit, entirely.

Why don't I feel bad about this?

Not the slightest bit of guilt had been shed since finding Tonya's head proudly displayed on his nightstand. He hoped his lack of sorrow was for the same reasons as Rusky. Though, he was torn inside, he'd been too busy to worry about it. And quite frankly, he hadn't even given himself a moment to actually think about it. As sick as it made him, it was the truth.

Sorry Rusky, sorry Tonya.

With the toe of his boot, Pillowface nudged Tonya's headless body into the hole. She rolled once, then disappeared into the opening. Landing on her back, she bent at the middle, her legs bowed back to her chest. The stump of her neck pointed up at the sky. Dirt was adhered to the white looking holes in the middle of her neck.

Bones?

Pillowface went back to the bucket and picked it up by the handle. He carried it to the hole, dumping the head in just as casually as Joel had dumped dirty water from it earlier. The severed cranium bounced and rolled across the body, settling at the bend in her hips.

Facedown.

Joel felt a tingle in his pants and wondered why that was exciting him.

Then Pillowface took the shovel and began filling in the hole.

(II)

"You know," said Carlee, behind the steering wheel. "It sounds like he really cares about you."

Haley groaned. Sitting in the passenger seat, face hidden behind a hand, she couldn't bring herself to look at Carlee. Bawling like that in front of Alan had been bad enough, but damn it, now Carlee was getting a demonstration as well.

"I'm serious."

"I know," said Haley, shaking her head. Her face made sloshing sounds against her palm. "That's what makes it so *bad.*"

Carlee frowned. "Why?"

Raising her head, Haley used the back of her hand to dry her eyes. "Because."

Carlee stayed quiet for a minute. "That's the best you can come up with?"

"For now. I'll think of something better, later."

She rolled her eyes. "Why?"

"*He's* not taking me home, is he?"

"Well, no, but that's because…"

"I blew it."

Laughing, "Him."

"Same thing," she muttered.

Carlee's frown returned. "I was joking." She sighed. "The reason he's not taking you home is because he has to run the store. And it's his duty to close it down when everyone leaves."

"He's the owner; surely he has someone that could do that for him."

"Maybe, maybe not. Have you ever seen anyone else working there other than him?"

She thought about it. Every time she'd ever been there, Alan had been running the counter. He kept a nice supply of Laymon books for her, even going out of his way to order the European editions. She smiled thinking about that. He'd always done special things for her. *I really did something special for him tonight. God.* "I guess not."

"Me neither. So, I'm guessing he doesn't."

That was it, she decided. Alan wasn't trying to just pass her off on Carlee because she'd made a fool of herself. Well, she *had* made a fool of herself, but that wasn't why Alan bailed on the car-ride. If he could have easily left the store, then surely, she'd be riding in his car right now, and not Carlee's. *Does he have a car?*

He owns a business; he has to own a car.

But he also works part time as waiter. He might not have one. Haley groaned, again. *I'm not going to drive him everywhere all the time. The hell with him if that's what he thinks this is about. He can forget about a free ride.*

Carlee glanced at her from the driver's seat. "Look, you can't keep beating yourself up over this. It's not healthy."

"I know."

"Then what are you going to do?"

"Hell with him," she said.

"You don't mean that."

"Sure, I do. He probably doesn't want anything to do with me now that he's had me."

"Stop it."

"Well, it's true."

"No, it's not, and you know it. You're just spoon-feeding yourself all this bullshit because it's easy to swallow."

Grimacing, Haley pictured herself sitting at a table, shoving spoonful after spoonful of shit into her mouth, wisps of grass clinging to it, small white mushrooms growing out the sides. She felt a burning liquid rising in the back of her throat. She needed to knock that image out of her head, and fast. She quickly thought about the backroom of the Second Chance Book Store, straddling Alan in the chair. The way he felt inside of her, hard and deep. She could still feel him, ghost intercourses. Though, the memory was great, it left her feeling empty inside, her chest heavy and tingly. A lump had suddenly formed in her throat. She wanted to be with him, again, and now.

"Now what's bothering you?"

"Just thinking about Alan," she mumbled.

"So, that means you miss him, and when you think about him, he makes you smile."

Bitch.

"Am I right?"

"Bitch," she said.

Laughing, Carlee held a handout as if accepting an award. "Thank you very much."

"That doesn't mean anything."

"It means you should stop worrying so damn much. He understands that you lost your parents and are battling with how to raise a boy on the verge of being a man."

"He's got a few more years before he's a man, Carlee."

"Not really. I watch the talk shows, I read the magazines. Kids are having sex so much earlier these days. Can you believe they actually teach teenage girls that it's just as fine to give oral sex as it is to give a goodnight kiss?"

Why is she telling me this?

Haley remembered seeing a book on that very subject in Alan's store. It had sickened her. Not only that, when she'd expressed her dislike of it, he went on to tell her that it was one of his bestsellers. "I have a hard time keeping it on the shelf," he'd said. Teenage girls buying it, parents buying it *for* them! That had bothered her. It was one of those things that after she'd learned of it, she wished she hadn't.

Girls like Tonya get a book like that, and it's all downhill.

She realized Carlee was waiting for a reply. "I was never that kind of girl growing up."

"Me neither."

"What happened to you?"

Carlee laughed, "Oh, you want to play that game?"

"Not really."

"I didn't think so, Ms. Backroom bull-rider." She threw her hand in the air, grinding her hips in the seat. "Come on, ride it! *Ride* it!"

Laughing, Haley said, "It was like riding a damn bull, he was hung like one."

Carlee gasped. "Really? I had always assumed him to be an *average* kind of guy."

"Hardly. And he's cut like a lion."

"Muscles?" Her eyes widened, face beaming.

"Plenty."

She whistled. "Wish I would have gone at him first, that could have been me tonight."

"Girl, I would have left you lying where I knocked you."

They laughed.

Though, she couldn't stop thinking about how embarrassing it was to go haywire like that in front of Alan, the ride back with Carlee had helped her to at least *feel* better.

Then, like a dying lightbulb flickering off and on in a darkened room, an image of Joel popped into her mind. It was fast, only briefly illuminated in the flash of light. He was reaching out to her, covered in blood. Then it was gone. Her skin went prickly, her bowels felt heavy.

Where did that come from?

She suddenly wondered what he had been doing all night, and then wondered why it mattered. Why all of a sudden?

What if...

But, as soon as the thought had processed, Carlee began singing *Pokerface* by Lady Gaga, and she didn't think about it again. Too busy laughing at how terrible of a singer Carlee was.

The car's headlights raked across the sign for Marble Lane, and she was relieved to almost be home.

As Carlee drove and sang, Haley listened, but her attention was diverted out the window. The few houses in her neighborhood were dark. A couple of them had their front porch lights on, as if expecting someone to show up, while others had no lights on at all. The rest of the strip had settled down for the night, probably had been sleeping long before Haley seduced a bookstore owner. She wondered momentarily about Jonesey and where he'd ended up. *Did he leave?* She didn't really care.

"Haley," he'd say, that disgusting smile on his face. "I'll take you home."

"Oh, no thanks, I'm going to ride with Carlee."

"It's no problem. I'll take care of that, and you. I'll dry those tears for you."

She shivered. *No thanks.* That was something she could do without. It was his damn fault why this had happened in the first place. If he wouldn't have shown up, and then stalked her throughout the store, Alan would have never suggested they go into the back. Then she would have never been in the situation and wouldn't have done what she did. She was angry at Jonesey, yet thankful at the same time.

Then she wondered about Alan. Why had he suggested they go into the back? Couldn't there have been other places to go? *Maybe.* Did he plan for this to happen? *Maybe some of it, but not the flipping out on him part.* She sighed. No way of knowing for sure, but it seemed strange that each point of the night led them to that backroom, to that chair.

To Alan inside of her.

They passed Tonya's house. The place was lit up like a doughnut shop. *Tonya must have let Clay Ray come over after all.* She gazed through Carlee's window, and sure enough spotted Ray's car parked by the house.

She's going to get busted.

In Haley's driveway, Carlee parked the car, but left the engine idling. "Want me to come in for a while?"

"Thanks, but that's all right. It's late enough already, and I imagine if you come in, a pot of coffee will be brewed, then we'll get to talking about how much of a fool I am, and we'll be up all night."

"We *have* been up all night," said Haley pointing at the digital clock. "It's going on four."

Haley frowned. "Great. I'm going to be a peach to work with in the morning."

"You and me, both. Poor Jonesey won't know what hit him."

"Good, maybe he'll finally take the hint and fuck off."

"I doubt it," said Carlee. "Probably just make him try harder."

That was wishful thinking, and she knew it. No matter how rude or blunt she could be to him, he'd never stop. *Might need to start looking for another job.* Why was she bothering to work at all? She had inherited half of the money. After splitting it with Joel, her part was still large enough that she needn't worry about working for several years. But she'd kept the job regardless, working as if nothing had happened.

Why?

It was too late in the night for such serious thoughts. "All right, well, I guess I'll see you at work."

Carlee scratched her head, "Okay. And remember what I said."

A hand on the door-latch, she gathered her purse with the free one. "Which part?"

"All of it."

Smiling, "You bet."

"I'm serious."

"We'll see."

"You can tell me I was right when it falls into place."

"Or, wrong."

"Whichever." She yawned. "Want me to pick you up in the morning?"

"Nah, you'll have to leave earlier to do that, get what rest you can."

"Okay. I'll bring some coffee."

"You're a doll."

"Don't I know it?"

They hugged, exchanged kisses on the cheek, and said their goodnights. Haley climbed out of the car and bumped the door shut with her hip. She threw the strap of her purse over her shoulder and walked to the front door. As she dug for her keys, she noticed Carlee flashing her lights, so she waved at her one last time over her shoulder.

Then Carlee was gone, leaving her to find her keys in the dark.

Should've left the damn porch light on.

Finding her keys, she flipped through the ring until locating the correct one for the front door. She unlocked it and went inside.

The house was just as dark inside as it was out, but it felt so much darker. Up ahead, the stairs were a gray line that drifted up into total blackness. The white walls were oblique patterns all around her. Joel hadn't bothered to leave her a light on so she could find her way back to her room without breaking her neck. Oh well, didn't really matter. Her eyes were already adjusted, so she really didn't need any.

On her way to the stairs, her shoes clacked loudly against the hardwood floor. Wincing, she stopped, leaned to the side, and raised a foot behind her to take off a shoe. When she placed her foot down, she stood uneven, and much shorter on the left side. Taking off the other one, she was level once again. The floor felt cool under her warm feet. She hung her purse on the banister, then slowly mounted the stairs. She wanted to shower but was too tired to fret with it tonight. She'd wait until morning, plus, she might wake Joel up, and she didn't want him knowing what time she'd snuck in.

At the top of the stairs, Haley turned, and slunk to her room. Once inside, she quietly eased the door shut. She walked to her bed, undressing along the way, and leaving a path of clothes behind her. Naked, she climbed into bed, set the alarm clock, and the alert application on her phone. She had three hours to get some sleep.

She pulled the blankets over her, sheathing herself in them like a cocoon.

While Haley drifted off to sleep, her brother's room sat empty and untouched, and next door, panic and all hell was breaking loose.

(III)

"**S**till nothing," said Ray, closing his cellphone.

Richard slapped his hands on the table. "So that's that."

Sharon approached him from the side, set a steaming cup of coffee in front of him, then took the seat next to her husband.

"Something's happened." Ray leaned against the island, his cell phone in one hand, his other hand tugging at his Black Label Society t-shirt under his leather jacket.

"Let's not jump to conclusions." Richard lifted the mug. Hot vapors of Hazelnut and caffeine coasted into his nostrils, licking his eyes. "She may have just gone out with some friends."

"Not likely," he said, nearly laughing. He reached into the inner pocket of his jacket, which Richard thought was too warm for him to be wearing and removed a pack of cigarettes. He was about to light one when Richard stopped him.

"Not in here, pal."

"Come on," he said.

Opening his mouth to repeat himself, but this time louder, he felt a gentle touch on his hand. He glanced over and saw his wife, just as lovely as the day he'd met her, staring back at him behind her large blue eyes. The same eyes that had persuaded him to do many things over the last twenty years that he never would have done on his own, crazy adventures such as skydiving, going to Mexico for an entire summer, letting his only daughter date scum like 'Clay' Ray Hanson. And much like those times, her eyes were just as successful this go round. "Fine," he said. "Just this once, because I can see you're worried about her."

"I am."

"And why are you convinced that something's amiss?" That was the English Professor in him talking. He doubted Ray even knew what a word like *amiss* meant.

"Huh?"

He was right. "Why do you think something's wrong?"

"Oh, because we were supposed to...get together...tonight."

"Maybe she had other plans."

"No, she didn't."

"How do you know?"

"Because she sent me this about an hour before I was supposed to get here." He flipped open his cell phone and thumbed some buttons. When he found what he was looking for, he passed it over to Richard. He held it in such a way that Sharon could look over his shoulder and read it, too. In a small, hardly legible font was a sentence: *Taking a shower, making myself pretty for you!*

Seeing words this personal and written by his own daughter made him boil inside. He could feel the back of his neck becoming hot and sweaty. "She sent this to you?"

"Yep," he answered through a cloud of smoke.

"Give me a reason why I shouldn't put this phone down your throat."

Ray's eyes bulged, obviously shocked.

"Richard," said Sharon. "Don't be nasty." She took the phone from him and offered it back to Ray. Reluctant to take it, he stepped forward, cautiously reaching across the table for it.

"I'm going to be nasty," he said. "My daughter," he felt a nudge, "Excuse me, *our* daughter doesn't need to be sending messages like this to *him.*"

"I know you hate me," he said, "but can't you see where I'm coming from?"

"Yes," said Sharon. "We can see that very much, but you have to understand, it's coming off more like jealousy."

"What?"

"You're acting as if you seem more worried about *what* she's doing than over what may have happened to her."

Scoffing, "That's not it at all."

"Whatever the case may be, you just need to express yourself better."

More reasons why he loved this woman, why he'd married, devoted his whole life to her, and fathered her child. She was worth all those dangerous trips and adventures.

Worth every damn one of them.

She'd hit the nail on the head with that last comment, and he was proud.

Then she turned to him. "And so do you, for that matter."

How could she betray him like this?

"What are you talking about, Sharon?"

"The way you're talking to Ray, you need to calm down. He's obviously upset, and so are you. But neither of you are expressing it properly. This should be a shared moment between you guys. Father and, pardon the lack of terminology here, lover, teaming up to uncover the reasoning behind Tonya's disappearance. Yet, you're not and are close to fighting and you know it."

Richard looked at Ray. They shared the same look of agreement. She was right.

"All right, Ray," said Richard, "I'll admit, it's odd that she might have just taken off. But did you ever consider that maybe she just blew you off for something else to do instead?"

"She wouldn't do that." He sounded certain.

"And why is that?"

He smiled, "Because, I'm Clay Ray. And *no one* does that to Clay Ray."

What small amount of pity he had felt toward this kid quickly evaporated. "Get the hell out of my house."

"What?" The same dumb, shocked expression popped up on his face.

Sharon leaned over. "Richard?"

He held a hand up to her before she could say anything else. "I don't want to hear any more about how I need to express myself better, Sharon. That's bullshit. I'm expressing myself just fine." He looked at Ray. "Right?"

He shrugged, the cigarette flopping from his mouth. The ash needed to be discarded before it dropped onto the floor. And God help Ray if he spilled ashes all over his expensive tile.

"I'm pissed off, and I think I'm expressing that *clearly*. I mean, there's no way he could misread what I'm directing here. So I'm going to say it one more time, get out or I'll throw you out."

He nodded. Curving his hand into the shape of a bowl, he took the cigarette out of his mouth, and flicked the ashes in his palm. "Do me a favor?"

"No."

He groaned. "Just please have her call me and at least let me know she's all right."

"If she wants to call you, she will. Are we clear?"

"Yes."

"Don't let the door hit you in the ass on the way out. God forbid a piece of our property damages the goods of Clay Ray."

Walking like a child being sent to his room without supper, he left. They sat in silence until hearing the muffled roar of his car as it drove away. After that, Sharon looked at Richard, pity showing on her face. "You were awfully rude, Richie."

"Oh, please. A kid like that needs a kick in the ass every now and then. Did you see how convinced he was?" Imitating Ray, he sat up straight, twisting his features to best match his. "No one does that to Clay Ray." He shook his head. "Please."

"Well, he's right. Have you ever known Tonya to stand him up?"

Surely, there had to have been at least one occasion where she had been smart enough to do so, but he couldn't think of any presently. Without an answer to offer her, he only shrugged. "I don't know."

"Does seem strange."

"Maybe she had an epiphany. Or someone better came along."

"Better than Clay Ray?" She asked, her smile reeking of sarcasm.

"God," he said. "She could only go downhill from there."

They shared a laugh at the kid's expense. "But seriously, what if he was *right?*" Don't you remember the side door being left open?" Sharon's sarcasm was gone, and all that showed was a mother's worry.

He sighed. "We agreed she probably left that door open herself after she was lying out in the sun." That explanation did nothing to falter Sharon's worry. "Look, if she's not home by noon, I'll call around to some of her friends. And, if that doesn't turn up anything, I'll go look for her myself."

"Not without me."

"That's fine." He raised his hand to her hair, combing a few loose strands away from her lovely face. Hardly a wrinkle or worry line.

Keep this up, and she'll be showing plenty.

He was angry at Tonya for making her mother worry like this, for making *him* worry like this, too. Though he wasn't showing it, he was scared to death that something was wrong.

What if she's hurt? Or was in an accident?

He found himself wanting to laugh. Sharon had been right all along. He didn't know how to express his *true* feelings.

Wouldn't do any good. Me flying off the deep end with Sharon, and not to mention Clay damn Ray, so close to teetering off the brink themselves.

"So," said Sharon. "For the time being, it looks like we have the house to ourselves."

He smiled. "It appears so."

A sheepish look on her face, she said, "Want to join me upstairs?"

"That's a dumb question. When do I *not* want to join you upstairs?"

She laughed. "That's an even dumber question," then stood up, untying the robe she'd been wearing. Opening it for him, she gave him a quick glance of her soft naked skin that was hidden behind the cloth. He saw the dark tuft of groomed pubic hair briefly before she closed the robe back. "Come on."

"I'll be right up, let me guzzle the rest of this coffee and put my cup away."

"Okay," she said. "Want me to break out the blindfold?"

"And restraints?"

She bit down on her bottom lip, excited. "Want me to?" She looked as if she had to pee very badly and was holding it.

"It's been a long time."

"All right. Don't keep me waiting, or I'll really make it hurt."

"That's how I like it."

She laughed. "Yes, you do. You're such a bad boy."

"You love it."

"Never said that I didn't." With a beaming grin, she pranced away from him on a path to the stairs.

He pictured her waiting for him, lying on her side in nothing but high heels, gently rubbing the blindfold over the slopes of her breasts, tickling the dark coins of her nipples.

Something stirred in his pajama pants.

Hello, old friend.

He grabbed his coffee and chugged the last little bit.

Damn that Ray. Coming over in the middle of the damn night, upset because Tonya had ditched him. That's all it was, she'd ditched him, and he wanted to get her back by getting us involved.

That had to be it. In a neighborhood like this, nothing bad happened. That was why they'd moved out in the country. Peace and quiet. They knew their neighbors and vice versa, a tight community of folks that watched your house for you when you went out of town.

That kid next door, though he has a weird taste for movies, is actually a trustworthy kid. His sister is nice, too.

When they'd leave on their adventures, the ones Sharon had convinced him to seize, he felt comfortable in knowing that he'd come home to an undisturbed house.

With them next door, there was no way someone could get in and take something, or someone.

Like Tonya. His scalp crawled. *Please let her be all right.*

Richard was sure that nothing had happened to her. That damned Clay Ray, putting these crazy thoughts in his head; he should be shot for it. He smiled at that. He hoped he might be the triggerman.

"*Richieeeee?*" Sharon called from upstairs, a needy whine in her voice.

She wanted him, desired for him to be upstairs right now. He liked it when she became pouty like that. *Clingy.* Meant she would unleash herself once he got up there.

Hope she doesn't leave many bruises like last time.

That had been rough. She'd gotten way out of hand and hurt him, *a lot.* It was tough trying to explain them to people that happened to see them, which was why it had been so long since he'd allowed her to tie him up. He figured this time would be twice as bad. It had been so long since she'd been able to let loose like this, and even though neither of them suspected anything bad had happened, the possibility that Tonya was in danger was still crossing both of their minds. So she'd be extremely aggressive and agonizingly slow with her punishment just to keep her mind off of where her daughter might be.

Or the shape she might be in.

He stood up from the table, took his mug to the sink, and placed it inside. She called out for him again, this time it sounded much more pitiful.

I'm really going to get it this time.

Although he enjoyed the torture, enjoyed letting her do whatever she could conjure up to him, he still needed to groom himself for her wrath. It was fun in the moment, but when it was done, she usually left him sore and drained, with the aftermath vividly displayed on his body.

Just don't let her make me bleed too much.

A little blood was fine if he wasn't gushing.

He headed for the stairs.

Always those gorgeous eyes.

CHAPTER SIXTEEN

(I)

As the sun began to climb, showering the black sky in orange and yellow, the perpetual night for Joel and Pillowface was finally ending.

They traveled in silence, and by this point Joel could hardly lift his feet. He'd overestimated where they should have exited. His plan was to come out right behind the house, but when they stepped out of the trees, he realized they were much farther up. And in this neighborhood, that meant they had quite a hike back.

"I messed up," he said, eyes narrowed from fatigue, the lids felt heavy and itchy. "We came down the wrong side of the hill. Shit." He was angry with himself. Walking back through the woods would add an extra fifteen minutes to their journey, and Haley might wake up and find that he wasn't home. *Maybe she'd believe I went for a walk?* He glanced down at his filthy clothes and knew right away that wouldn't work. She'd believe he went pig wrestling before taking a walk. Looking up and down Marble Lane, all appeared deserted. No joggers, cars, no one walking their dogs.

Where the sun was now positioned, it smeared the sky with a purple aura and sheet of red, but to Joel it looked as if the sky was bleeding. He looked back the way they'd come and shrugged. *I'm going to guess it's about five in the morning. We should be safe if we just keep going.*

"Come on," he said. He waved Pillowface forward and began walking. *Hope like hell no one sees us.*

The neighborhood at this hour, so different than it was during the night, yet so similar, seemed to be observing them with accusatory resolve as they traveled back to the house.

(II)

When the alarm clock buzzed Haley's first thought was she was running late. She sat up disoriented, whipping her head around the room. With the alarm pulsing behind her, she allowed her mind time to assess the situation.

In my bed. Alone. That's right, because Alan is at the bookstore. No, wait, that's not it, he's at home? That's where he should be, it's morning. It is morning, right?

She looked at her window and saw the early, gentle sparks of daylight. Then she faced the nightstand beside her. 7:30 am. She wasn't late at all, and actually was up earlier than normal. Since she hadn't slapped the snooze button three times, she had plenty of time.

She reached over and whacked her hand down on the clock. Now with that annoying beep gone, she could hear the constant clamoring of her cell phone's alarm, too. She reached behind her, found it on the pillow, and shut it off.

Her sore and stiff muscles informed her she wouldn't be jogging this morning. She felt uncomfortable at the thought, like she was letting her body down by skipping one lousy morning of exercise.

I really should at least jog up the road and back one time.

But even that felt unfeasible, so she decided against it.

Should just lie back down, sleep another hour, then call Jonesey and tell him I'm not coming in, and then sleep some more.

She liked *that* idea, especially after the night she'd had. But by doing that, it would appear as if she were hiding from him—she is—and that could make things even worse for her at work. Plus, it might entice Jonesey to visit her at home to see how she was doing. "Haley, I brought you some coffee. Let's make a toast. To us."

She shuddered.

Why don't I just quit that place?

That was twice she'd considered it in twenty-four hours.

Seriously though, why hadn't she quit? Was it because a part of her liked having *someone*, even as ghoulish as Jonesey, being infatuated with her? Shadowing her, following her around like a little troll, always needing to sniff the air she'd wafted through? Jonesey was a *stalker*, nothing more, plain and simple as it may be. Mostly just at work pestering, but that all changed last night when he'd brought his game to the store.

Haley threw the sheets back, exposing her naked body to the cool air blowing up from the vents. On warm mornings such as this one, it normally felt great opening herself up in such a way, but not this time. She felt gross and sticky, and even though she didn't smell anything, figured she stunk of sweat and old sex. Her groin felt sore and flaky: a regular feeling after a night of good sex. And, it had been good, for *her*, but not so great for Alan. Poor guy wasn't even granted an orgasm. She'd broken down into a ruin of tears before he'd gotten the chance.

This made her feel pretty crummy.

She checked her cell phone to see if he'd called. He hadn't. As much as she'd like to hear from him, she assumed her chances with Alan had been shot.

Might be for the better. After all I did last night; he probably takes me for a nut job.

She wondered if he were right.

At least there's not any missed phone calls from the creeper.

She sighed. What a life she led. A stalker at work, another weirdo calling her and pleasuring himself for her to hear, and the guy she actually cared about had probably been scared off. She was a wreck.

Haley climbed out of bed and marched to her closet to pick out her day's wardrobe. Feeling as lousy as she did, she decided she would keep it basic and plain—a short sleeved purple shirt and gray pants. She thought about wearing heels but chose sandals instead. Not flipflops, these were open-toed, but buckled in the back. The outfit could almost pass as professional, so no one should say anything.

She tossed them on the bed. Then went to the dresser and dug through her panty drawer.

Do I own anything other than thongs?

At the bottom, tucked far away from the rest, she finally discovered a couple pairs of full panties, wide in the back, and since she didn't want to be attractive today, these were perfect. In the other drawer, she grabbed a thick white, cotton bra, so the notion of having breasts would be hidden from any suspecting on-lookers.

Not today boys. Sorry.

She didn't want any part of her to seem as if it were welcoming a comment or stare from Jonesey, or from anyone at all.

With her clothes in hand, she headed for the bathroom.

Afther the room had been empty for a few minutes, something stirred from within the closet. The slabs of clothes suspended from hangers parted, and from behind them Pillowface emerged. After he and Joel had returned from the night's voyage, he'd given the boy ten minutes to get in bed and fall asleep before sneaking back into the house, and into Haley's room.

He hadn't been able to stop thinking about her and wanted so desperately to see her, so he'd peeled back her blankets and watched her sleeping for a while, the slow rise and fall of her bare chest. Lying on her back, her full breasts receded against her body like mounds. Her mouth was slightly parted, and she snored with a faint steady purr that he'd found adorable. He'd wanted nothing more than to climb into bed with her and cuddle, to pull her to him, and hold her. It'd been such a long time since he'd felt a woman sleeping beside him, the warmness of their breath on the back of his neck, the gentle squeeze of their arm if he happened to squirm against them.

Not since Amanda, and when she'd died from a sudden blood clot in her heart, he hadn't wanted to be with another woman, but when he became cognizant of Haley's existence that had all quickly changed.

Now he stood beside her bed. He took her pillow and raised it to the burlap sack where his stub of a nose was, then took a whiff. Even through the mask he could still smell her pleasant fragrance, clean as if she'd just came from the shower.

He heard the pipes groaning from inside the walls, water rushing through them. *The shower.* He pictured her under the spray, enveloped in suds and bubbles, her skin shiny and slippery. Blond hair plastered against her scalp and down the curve of her back; torrents of soapy water trickling over her hips, down between her buttocks, making her moan from the sheer pleasure that only an early morning shower could bring.

His chest felt heavy with a yearning that pulled the air from his lungs. *Was it love?* He didn't want to jeopardize it by putting a name to it. He was happy with just feeling something other than hate.

With Haley in the shower, and Joel sleeping, he figured it was safe to go back down to the basement. He was nearly finished constructing the device and wanted to finish. All that was left to do was attach the saw blade. He wasn't sure where the idea had stemmed from, but he liked it, and hoped one day he'd be able to use it.

He fled the room like a ghost, then the house, and returned to his dwelling below like a dragon protecting the lovely princess up above.

CHAPTER SEVENTEEN

(I)

The water shut off.

Haley stood in the tub, dripping, her hair clutched in her hands. She stared blankly at the wall, slowly ringing her hands through her soaked mane. Her mind had been everywhere except with her in the bathroom. The shower hadn't been relaxing or rejuvenating, it had barely been anything more than just something to pass the time while she dreaded going into work. *Just call in!* As much as she wanted to, she knew that she wouldn't and really had no reason as to why.

Finally, she grabbed the shower curtain and whisked it back in one quick motion, and gasped when she saw Joel standing there.

"*Whaaaa?!*" She leaped back against the wall, her hand drastically feeling for the curtain to throw it shut but couldn't reach it. She heard Joel yelp, followed by the quick padding of his footfalls through the hallway.

In the corner of the tub, Haley clung to the wall with her arm draped across her breasts. She could feel the vigorous drumming of her heartbeat against her arm. Her drenched hair hung in front of her face like a curtain.

Why hadn't he knocked? He had to have known I was in here.

Her breathing was out of control as she tried to calm herself, tried to *think*. She flicked her neck, throwing her hair out of her face. She looked around the bathroom. The door was still open, and she couldn't close it without exposing herself. The towel awaited her on the toilet seat, neatly folded where she'd left it. Haley couldn't reach it from where she was.

Her skin burned with embarrassment.

She carefully leaned up, stretching her neck to see out the door. The hallway looked deserted. She eased a foot over the edge of the tub and sat it down on the carpeted mat below. The rug's whiskers tickled the bottom of her foot. She leaned over, balancing herself and reached. The tips of her fingers swept across the door, nudging it farther away from her, but not closing it. *Shit!* Pushing against the front of her toes, she mimicked the best of the ballerinas with her position. A thrust of her elbow, she knocked the edge of the door. It pushed against the frame but didn't latch.

It was good enough.

Haley stepped out of the tub and eased the door all the way shut. She scurried to the commode, taking the towel, and began drying herself. She dressed in a hurry. Then, ignoring the awkward situation, she began her morning routine, which shouldn't take long this morning since she'd decided while showering, she wouldn't be wearing any makeup today.

Haley's guidebook to Repulsion 101: Homely is the key to warding off unwanted flirtation from the appearance-obsessed ghouls.

By the time Haley had finished getting ready for work, she still had plenty of time to kill, so she had the idea to assemble breakfast for her and Joel to share.

While the coffee brewed, she dug through the fridge for a pack of bacon that she knew was in there. For whatever reason, she wanted to fry it up, join it with some eggs over easy, maybe even some toast if she was feeling frisky.

The eggs were easy to find. She checked the date. They still had a week before needing to be tossed. With the breakfast materials held against her chest, she walked to the stove and sat them down. She returned to the fridge, snatching the loaf of bread from the top. She couldn't wait to see the look of surprise that would surely be on Joel's face when he saw what she had done.

So began the measures for the feast.

(II)

When the scent of bacon drifted into his room Joel pulled his head out from under his pillow. After seeing Haley ... indisposed, he'd run back to his room, and buried his head. He'd remained there until now.

She's cooking breakfast?

He couldn't believe it.

If she's downstairs cooking, then she's not mad.

He hoped that meant she wouldn't say anything about the bathroom incident. But if she did bring it up, he wouldn't be able to tell her the real reason he'd gone in there. Haley usually went jogging in the mornings. So, when he'd awakened to the sound of the shower, he wanted to check and make sure it wasn't Pillowface. He'd dreamed that he'd snuck into the house and attacked Haley. It had been a horrible nightmare. She was on the bed, kicking and screaming, while he slashed at her with the machete. Joel wanted to help, but his legs wouldn't move. It was as if his feet had been glued to the floor.

The only way to know for sure was by checking it out. Granted, he could have just tapped on the door and hollered to see if it were Haley, but at the time, he didn't think about it. He just needed to know whether Pillowface was breaking his promise and coming in the house while Haley was home.

He hadn't expected the shower curtain to whip open, nor to see his sister naked and screaming. He didn't stare, but he'd seen enough. He felt heat in his crotch and hated himself for it.

Don't think about her like that, she's your sister.

But he knew it wasn't because she was his sister that was causing that reaction. It was having seen his third naked woman over the course of a couple days, but the first that wasn't dead. He was twelve years old, and *any* kind of female nudity could get him aroused.

I'm a kid for Christ's sake.

Endless numbers of nights, he'd stayed up in his room watching adult movies on the after dark channel, keeping the volume down so low it was practically muted, with his chair scooted right up to the television so he could hear the sounds they made. That was his sex education. Sure, they taught it in school, but the teachers seemed uncomfortable explaining things to a group of kids that were watching them with wide eyes and snickering each time they said the words *penis* and *vagina*. Joel was one of those kids. So what they'd learned in school wasn't worth trying to remember, but what he saw on those movies at two in the morning on Friday nights would stay with him for a lifetime. He'd never forget seeing Marilyn Chambers being molested by her dentist while high on gas, only to come out of the haze and pull him on top of her. The way his hips were thrusting deep into her and she, though acting really high or drunk, moaned and tore her shirt open to play with her nipples.

That was *real* education. The kind his parents were too intimidated to discuss with him and the kind the school never wanted the students to know existed. Although, they'd been forced to read a book about oral sex during the course, Joel had never finished it. What that book accomplished was making him want to go out and find a girl that was willing to give him a good night kiss like the ones the book claimed were out there.

His friends at school swore by it.

Without any of them having consented to it, a silent race to see who would go the furthest and the quickest had commenced.

I won, thought Joel, sitting up.

I haven't touched a naked body, but I've seen them.

They were *dead* girls, but he didn't care. They still counted to him, but Haley did not. She was disqualified, and he hoped to never think of what he saw again.

"Joel? Breakfast!" She shouted from downstairs.

He wondered if Haley could read his mind.

Joel suddenly felt nervous. Could he look at her the same? Groaning, he got out of bed, dreading the meal that smelled so delicious.

Downstairs, Haley had already set the table. Two plates were on each end, decorated with bacon, eggs, and toast. She was pouring Joel a glass of orange juice when he came in.

"Good morning," she said.

He studied her. She didn't seem upset and that lifted a colossal load off his chest. He could suddenly breathe better, and his appetite was much stronger. "Good morning," he said back. His stomach growled in anticipation.

"Does this count for an astonishing breakfast?" She held her hands over the table, gently turning them like a model on *The Price is Right*. "It's not Pop Tarts, but what could compete, right?"

He laughed. "I don't know. I haven't tasted it, yet."

She smiled. "Did you get much sleep last night?"

"A little." Actually, he'd hardly slept at all.

"You've got bags under your eyes. Big ones."

"Really?" She nodded. "Well, I guess maybe I was up late writing, or drawing, or something."

"Scary stuff?" She arched her eyebrows.

You have no idea. "Yeah..."

"I'd expect nothing less from you." She smiled, poured herself a glass of orange juice, then walked back to the fridge to put it away.

Joel sat at his designated spot and looked around the kitchen. It seemed brighter in here than normal. It hurt his eyes to open them all the way. It was probably the lack of sleep, but to Joel it felt as if he were trying to stare at the sun. He glanced over to the spot where they would feed Rusky and saw that his bowl was full of dog food. For a brief second, he expected the dog to come running in and start eating. That was stupid to think, and he knew it. Of course, he wasn't coming. He'd been buried yesterday, and now shared his resting place with Tonya. Joel felt tight and sick inside as it all came back to him. The eggs on his plate suddenly smelled awful. He was losing his appetite, again.

He could guess why the food was there. *Haley.* She must have filled the bowl, not thinking about what she was doing. Along with Joel, Haley had fed him regularly for years, and that wouldn't be a habit quickly broken. After their parents had died, Joel expected his dad to walk in at five just as he normally would during the weekdays. Weeks went by before he'd been able to kick himself of that, but even now, there were still those moments when he'd find his eyes looking at the clock to see if it was time for Dad to come home.

"Aren't you going to eat?" she asked, sitting down across the table.

"What?"

She took a bite of her eggs, chewing slowly as if to show him how it was done.

He smiled, glanced back at Rusky's bowl, then back at her. "I don't think Rusky's going to be joining us for breakfast."

She frowned, confused. "What do you mean?"

He pointed at the bowl. "You set food out for him."

She looked at the bowl, concentrating, as if she hadn't the slightest clue what he was talking about. Then her face expanded as she realized what she'd done. "Oh my God."

"It's no big deal."

"Yes, it is." She dropped her fork and sat her elbows on the table. She tucked her eyes into her palms, rubbing her temples with her fingers. "My God, I'm so stupid."

This was *not* the reaction he'd wanted. He'd tried to inform her of the mistake in a jokingly manner, but she had taken it to heart. "No, you're not." Wanting to find the right words that she needed to hear, he combed his brain. He found endless blank pages without witty prose. "Haley?"

She looked up at him from behind her hands with wet eyes. Lines of tears had trickled down her face. A droplet hung on her chin for a moment before splashing on the table. He felt his throat tightening, becoming awfully hard to swallow. Haley sniffed, wiping her nose with her hand. "What?"

"You okay?"

She laughed, cold and humorless. "Far from it."

"I was just kidding about the food, please don't be upset."

"It's not you," she said, smiling. He saw hints of sincerity somewhere in it. "It's just everything that's happened the last couple of days."

"It's been tough on me too."

"You seem to be handling it better than me. What's your secret?"

The color drained from his face. "I don't have any secrets."

"*I* was joking."

"Oh."

She shook her head. "I'm sorry you saw this. I'm probably freaking you out pretty good."

"It's fine." He swayed his hand as if her actions were a pesky bug buzzing around him. "I understand."

"I'm also sorry you saw..." Then she stopped. Joel was grateful she hadn't said anything else. "Well, I guess I better run off to work."

"Right," he said. "It's close to that time, huh?"

"Yeah, sort of. Will you be all right alone?"

"I always am." He smiled.

"Yeah..." She slid the chair back and stood up. She patted her hands on the table. "Want me to leave this for you?" She pointed at her plate.

Thinking of Pillowface, he nodded, "Sure, I'll finish it off for you."

"Thanks. Wouldn't want it to go to waste."

It won't. He sighed. "Look, I'm sorry if I upset you with what I said about Rusky. I was just trying to be funny about it."

"It's okay, that wasn't because of you." She took a deep breath, puffing her cheeks as she let it waft out. "Have a good day. Call me if you need anything." She walked to the counter, retrieved her purse, and threw it over her shoulder.

"I will."

"And no calls about madmen bleeding to death in the backyard, deal?"

Joel nearly pissed himself when she'd said that. It took him a moment to remember that he had done just that only Monday morning, but it felt like it had been months ago. "I won't."

She smiled. "All right, see ya."

"Bye."

Then she was gone. The house felt sad and empty without her. This was the first time—if there had been others he couldn't remember them—that he didn't want her to go. He knew the day was going to be long, and he wished she didn't have to leave. That was odd to him, any other day he'd have been pushing her out the door, but this time he found himself wanting to wrap around her leg and beg her to stay. *Should've asked her to stay home, she probably would have.* Scratch that, he *knew* she would have. But there was just one big problem with that: *Pillowface.*

What am I going to do with him on the weekends she's off?

He couldn't worry about that now. That was a bridge he had yet to come to, and he'd worry about crossing it later.

He really wanted to eat the breakfast Haley had made, even though his appetite had been shot. She'd worked very hard on it, so it would be rude to just throw it away. And he was certain Pillowface was probably starving. So he left the plates on the table and went out the back door to fetch him.

After one call, he emerged from the side door.

"Hungry?"

Nodding, he followed Joel into the house and joined him for a quiet breakfast at the table, eating bacon, fried eggs, and guzzling orange juice.

It was the best meal he'd had in five years.

CHAPTER EIGHTEEN

(I)

Haley sluggishly made her way into the Jones & Jones Law firm building ten minutes before she was due. *What can I do for ten minutes?* There wasn't much to choose from: chatting with the other early birds—Jonesey was normally one of them, so she already dreaded that encounter, or hide in a restroom stall until eight. She *could* sneak into the breakroom, grab a hot cup of coffee, and lock herself in her office.

Jackpot!

Carlee's ETA was no earlier than five after eight. She used the five-minute flex time to her advantage on a regular basis. Most would call it abuse, but Carlee called it, humanitarian.

Someone's got to put that rule to good use, she'd said, more often than not.

She made her way to the lobby. No one stood at the elevators.

So far, so good.

She reached over, rung the second floor, and waited. Standing there, she wondered what to do about her life. She'd screwed it up so badly and hoped she could repair the damage. Then for the first time since her parents died, she considered going to see a shrink. Maybe she needed some happy meds to settle her mind, clear her thoughts.

The elevator dinged, startling her. The doors opened with a *whoosh*, inviting her inside. She obliged. She slumped against the wall as the elevator began to rise. It dinged again on her floor. When the doors opened, she imagined Jonesey lurking on the other side. "Oh, Haley, fancy meeting you here."

He wasn't there.

Thank you, God. She hurried out of there, quickly scanned the upstairs foyer, then headed for the breakroom.

Why is it so damn far away?

She'd have to pass right in front of Jonesey's office on her way there. It was unavoidable.

Maybe I can sneak by.

There was no real way of doing that. How the building was designed and structured there wasn't a rear hall she could take to bypass his office. His sat in a direct line to the breakroom. As she approached it, she shrank inside, and contemplated crawling under the windows to avoid being seen. She might have tried it, but the sudden call from behind her stopped her flat.

"Hey, Haley!"

She jumped, stifling a scream, and slowly turned around. Eyes wide and pale face, she imagined she must look as if she were just busted taking money from someone's wallet while they were sleeping.

Cutting the corner farther back was Ashley Thompson, the receptionist. Because of her thick glasses and corpulent smile, she looked like teeth and eyes bobbing on the thin frame of a woman. She wore a sweater much too thick for summer and a long, tight skirt.

"Are you okay?" she asked, her falcate smile retracting.

Haley forced a smile and said, "Yes, I'm fine, Ashley. How are you?"

"Jolly."

"That's good." Brushing her bangs out of her eyes, her forehead was damp and sticky.

Ashley stopped in front of her, frowning. She scanned her up and down, her glare budding larger. "Are you *sure* you're all right?"

177

"Yeah, why do you ask?"

"Well, you look so…"

"Plain?"

"Uh…sure?"

"I'm not wearing any makeup."

"I see."

"And you scared me, sneaking up on me like that."

"Oh, I'm sorry, that was an accident. Sometimes I can be so loud." Her smile returned. Haley needed to squint at the brightness of her bulky teeth.

"Well, it's been fun talking to you…" She stopped as an idea shaped. "Want to join me for coffee in the breakroom? No one can mix creamer and coffee like I can." She lightly chuckled, hoping Ashley wouldn't detect her true motivations for the invite. Haley hoped to use Ashley as a buffer to ward off Jonesey.

Ashley politely smiled but declined.

Haley wasn't giving up. "Come on, real quick. It'll be fun."

"No. Thank you. I really need to get going. Plus, I don't think Mr. Jones would appreciate us hanging out in the breakroom when we should be working."

"He'll be fine with it…"

"I seriously doubt he'd say something to *you*, but he'd reprimand *me*."

Ashley's accusing tone wasn't appreciated, and Haley wanted to slap the smirk she was receiving right off her face. "And what do you mean by that?" She crossed her arms, feeling heat rush up the back of her neck. She felt droplets of sweat beading under her arms.

Holding up a hand as if about to swat a fly, she said, "Oh, nothing at all. Heavens, no. I wasn't implying … never mind. What I'm saying is that Mr. Jones isn't here yet, and I wouldn't want him coming in and finding us chit-chatting instead of working."

Could I be so lucky? "What?"

"Yep, see for yourself." She pointed at his office.

Disbelief masking her face, Haley turned her back to Ashley and crept a few steps up the hall. She could see the door, the plaque at the top that read: Geoffrey Jones, Attorney at law. The blinds were drawn, but a small slit remained at the bottom of the window. Inside, the office was black.

It's true! She whipped around at Ashley. "That's fantastic!"

Ashley looked puzzled by her statement. "Yuh-Yeah, it sure is. While the cat's away, you know what I'm saying?" She snorted.

"Right," said Haley, wanting to have been done with this conversation five minutes ago. "I'll see you later."

"Sounds good, I'm going to go take my place at grand central station." She laughed, snorted again, and disappeared in the direction Haley had just traveled.

She couldn't believe Ashley.

I seriously doubt he'd say anything to you.

As she walked past Jonesey's office she checked one more time to be sure he wasn't there. The light was out, and the door closed. He wasn't there. She was tempted to click her heels together in joy.

I seriously doubt you'd get in trouble for that, she heard Ashley's voice telling her.

She'd worried that people thought there was something going on between her and Jonesey, and the way Ashley had spoken to her proved it. Haley couldn't blame them for wondering, because she knew it didn't look right. If she were on the outside looking in like the rest of them, she'd be wondering the same thing.

The lunch date, always stopping by her office, and she was sure that they'd all seen him staring at her; hell, she had, and it was creepy, so it was no wonder Ashley was baffled by how she'd acted overjoyed by his absence. *Probably thinks there's trouble in paradise, a little spat between the lovebirds.*

"Gross," she said, entering the breakroom.

(II)

oel should have known by now that when it rained shit, it poured in heavy gloppy clumps. The doorbell rang at nine on the nose.

In the living room, Joel sat in the recliner, lightly dozing while the TV played, ignored, in front him. All he'd seen was flickering images of Chuck Norris trying to sell him exercise equipment while he was in and out of sleep.

Pillowface sat on the couch, flipping through the current issue of HorrorHound, a magazine devoted to all of Joel's favorite things—horror.

When the bells chimed, Joel's heart sank. A flutter rose in his chest, turning into an acidic gulp in the back of his throat. He leaped out of the chair and was on his feet in less than a second. Joel looked at the door. He tried to swallow, but the burning knot was too thick and wasn't going down. "Shit, I wonder who it is." He scratched his head, leaving red marks on his scalp. "Pillowface, can you ...?"

He glanced at the couch and found it empty. "...hide?"

Just like in the movies, one moment they were there, and the next, gone. *He's going to have to teach me how he does that.* The doorbell clamored a third time. Joel jumped at the noise. He could ignore it, and hope that they went away, but if his suspicions were correct, he knew who was out there, and also knew they would not go away.

On his way to the door, it felt as if he was treading across cotton. He'd never been high before but figured a bad trip must feel something like the way he felt now. He stood against the door, with his fingers folded around the knob. It felt as if it had been in the freezer for an hour. He took a deep breath and slowly opened the door to not one, but two visitors outside.

Paul and Ethan.

He was correct. The guys he considered friends. Both were a year older than him and would be going to high school at the end of the summer while Joel had to stay in middle school for the eighth grade. He dreaded being in that place without them.

Ethan lived at the other end of Marble Lane with his parents and younger brother, Jesse. At one point in life, he'd been a jock, and in love with sports and collecting baseball cards. But, after becoming friends with Joel, he began a torrid affair with splatter films. Soon after, he walked out on sports and moved in with gore. Like Joel, he collected toys, but unlike Joel, he wouldn't play with them. Instead, he'd leave them in the packages only to hang them on his wall. The ones he *did* open were placed on a shelf in his room. It wouldn't be so bad if he didn't own a few figures that Joel needed to complete his collections.

Paul was the exact opposite of Joel and Ethan, but just like them in every way. He was overweight, and had a body shaped like an albino Hershey kiss. His hair, strictly parted on the side, was slicked across his head with an abundance of hairspray and gel. He was a spitting image of his mother, even the breasts. Joel figured seeing Paul with his shirt off was like seeing a younger version of his mother. He didn't live on Marble Lane like Joel and Ethan, but instead he and his mother had a house on Shorebrick—a small road that cut between Crescent and Highway 52—with his grandmother living beside them. His dad had left them at the start of the school year to move in with another woman. Though it had happened in September, the guys didn't find out until winter. Paul had kept it a secret from them, and still wouldn't talk about it much. Joel couldn't believe the man he'd seen outside throwing a football with Paul in the mornings while waiting for the bus could run off and distance himself from his son like that. Joel had assumed, but kept quiet about it, that was the reason Paul had gained so much weight this year. He'd always been husky, but after the fall, the fat just seemed to pack on at a hasty rate.

There was pure hatred inside of Paul, and not just for his dad, but anyone. Luckily, he acted all right around Joel and Ethan. Joel could tell they were all he had, and vice versa.

"What brings you by so early?" Joel was out of breath, but he didn't know why.

They shared a puzzled look.

Ethan said, "What do you mean?"

"It's like nine."

"Yeah, but its Wednesday."

It still wasn't registering with Joel.

Paul rolled his eyes. "We're supposed to walk to the pool." His voice, much higher-pitched and three degrees more southern than theirs, sounded damn near feminine, especially when he got excited.

It all came back to Joel so fast his head spun. "Oh, shit..." He noticed both of them had a rolled-up towel hanging around their necks and Ethan had his book bag strapped to his back.

Probably filled with snacks.

"You forgot?" asked Ethan.

"Yeah...I guess I did." The pool–Blue Waves Pool–a public swimming spot off Highway 52, was within walking distance of Joel's house. They could get there by taking a trail they'd imaginatively christened Blue Waves Trail in the woods adjacent to Joel's backyard. Luckily, it was to the left of where Joel's secrets lay. The hike wasn't a short distance, either. It normally took them a little over an hour to get there. And by that time, they were more than ready to dive in and cool off.

Of course, Paul would keep his shirt on.

"How could you forget?" shrilled Paul. "We all agreed on the bus Friday that we'd do this."

"Yeah, but I thought Ethan had band camp this week."

"No," said Ethan. "It was canceled, remember? We talked about this. Mr. Safrit got fired for statutory rape. They called the whole thing off."

Joel *did* know that. He never took band, but he was well aware of Mr. Safrit. He'd noticed the way he stared at the girls in the lunchroom; something about his roaming eyes had always made Joel feel weird. Though he'd never met the man, he didn't trust him. "I forgot all about it guys."

"Doesn't seem like you to forget that," said Paul. "Everything all right with you?"

"Yeah..."

"Great," said Ethan. "Glad to hear you're not coming down with anything." He pushed his way past Joel, inviting himself in. "Because I wouldn't want to catch it." He laughed.

"Asshole," Joel muttered. He glanced at Paul who stood on the stoop, waiting to be invited in like a vampire. "I guess you can come in, too."

"Thank you, my good man," said Paul, smiling.

Joel stepped back to give him some room. After Paul was inside, he gave the yard one quick look-over for any other visitors, then shut the door. He walked into the living room. Ethan sat where Pillowface had been; looking at the Horrhound he'd left behind. Paul, naturally, had taken Joel's seat in the recliner. "Sorry, again, I ruined you guys' morning."

"It's okay," said Ethan, not looking up from the magazine. "We're still going."

"Oh?"

"Yep. And so are *you.*"

He'd expected this. "I can't. I wish I could, but as you can see, I'd forgotten all about it, and I've got a lot of shit to do around here."

Paul laughed. "Please. Like what?"

"Clean out the basement."

"That can wait," said Paul. "Shit, it's not like we're going to be there all day."

"That's right," agreed Ethan.

"Listen, I *really* want to go." That part was true. He'd love to go swimming with the guys. "I just can't."

His friends stared at him in silence a moment, then traded expressions, then looked at him again. Ethan tossed the magazine on the coffee table. The slap it made when it landed was awfully loud in the quiet room. "Sounds tough."

"What does?"

"Coming up with a whopper like that on such short notice."

"A whop...no, I'm not lying."

Not...not really.

With his eyes on the TV, Paul shook his head. He raised the remote and started flipping the channels.

Ethan continued laying on the guilt, "Look man, if you don't want to go, just say 'I don't want to go.' Don't waste our time with *that* shit."

Ethan's less than subtle way of trying to make him feel bad was working. Joel felt smaller than a cricket on the moon. "It's not that I *don't* want to go…"

"Then what's stopping you?"

Paul snickered. Joel glanced at him. "Oh, not you," he said, pointing at the TV. "Blue's Clues is so gay."

Joel rolled his eyes, "I don't know, Ethan, I've got some deep shit going on here."

"I can tell that much."

"The kind of stuff that's just *nuts.*"

Ethan raised his eyebrows, obviously intrigued.

Joel took a deep breath. "Rusky died the other night."

Ethan frowned. "Damn, I'm sorry. That sucks."

"Yeah," Paul agreed. "He was a cool dog."

"He was," said Ethan.

"What happened?" asked Paul.

"I don't know, really. I guess it was just his age."

"Is that *everything?*" asked Ethan, expecting more gossip than that.

Joel felt a pang of anger. He'd just told him his best friend in the world had died, and he wanted more?

What the hell? Fucking savage. "What do you mean?"

"You said you were in some *shit,* and the tragic passing of Rusky just doesn't seem like it's all."

"Well …"

Ethan threw a hand up, "You don't have to explain anything if you don't want to."

Oh, but he *did.* He wanted nothing more than to tell them what he'd been up to. He was *dying* to tell them. A secret this huge was too much for a boy his age to sit on, and he *needed* to tell someone about it, and soon.

But now wasn't the time, especially with the possibility that Pillowface was eavesdropping on the conversation. Joel knew that

Ethan would keep prying until he finally broke if they kept this up much longer. He needed to divert the conversation and knew just how to do it. "All right, let me go get my trunks."

"All right!" Paul shouted, folding down the footrest and standing.

"You're going?" asked Ethan.

"Yeah. Just give me a minute."

"You got it. We'll wait outside."

"See you in a few," said Joel.

He waited until they were outside, then snuck to the door and quietly locked it.

Don't want to take any chances of them sneaking back in.

He raced upstairs and into his room. He found Pillowface behind his door, just as he'd been when they'd first met.

"I've got to go out for a while," said Joel. Through the mask, it looked as if he was frowning at the announcement. "Just for a little while. I have a...obligation that I can't get out of."

He was right; he *couldn't* get out of it, not really. He'd tried, but it just hadn't worked. He actually really liked those guys even though certain things they did bothered him, and yet for some reason they made him miss his parents more whenever they were around. Could be from the sleepovers they used to have, when his dad would get pizza for them all, or just the summers spent in the backyard playing with water guns while his parents watched. Or, it could be, which Joel would much rather reject, that he was jealous of his friends, and he hated that they still had their parents to go home to while he had no one. Now with Rusky gone, he was only left with Haley, who wasn't even home most of the time.

Just me and a big empty house. Well, not exactly. He looked at his new friend and smiled. *Now, I have him.* Not that Paul's dad would win any awards for being an outstanding father, but at least he was still alive. Ethan was the real lucky one now; he had a mom and a stepdad. His own father had passed away when he was just a baby. He'd gotten off easy; he didn't remember him being alive.

But neither of them had Pillowface. He was Joel's alone.

Joel felt a touch of pride in that.

Pillowface sat at the edge of Joel's bed as Joel dashed from his dresser to his closet and back, moving quickly and grabbing what he needed, but forgetting everything he should take. In a drawer he found his swimming trunks, and in the closet were his sandals. He grabbed his over-night bag, threw in the gear, and zipped it up. Then he stood up and exhaled long and hard. He was sweating.

"That ought to do it." He looked at Pillowface who was watching him with poignant eyes. "It's okay, bud. I'll be back in a little while. I'll fake a stomach cramp or something and get back home as soon as I can."

He nodded, the burlap-bunny ears flapping. Joel put a hand on his shoulder and squeezed. "You going to be all right by yourself?" He shrugged. "Don't do anything that you're not supposed to, okay?" He raised his head; they looked at each other eye to eye. "Promise me you won't get into any trouble." He raised his hand, extended his pinky. "Swear to it."

Nodding, Pillowface bowed his pinky around Joel's, and they shook. "That makes it legit." He patted his shoulder. "I've got to get out there before they wonder what's taking me so long. Give us a few minutes to get gone, then go back down to the basement, but be sure to lock the back door on your way out." He walked to the door and turned back before leaving. "See you in a little bit, okay?"

Pillowface nodded, again. Times like these Joel wished he could talk. Would sure make it easier to know what was on his mind if he could just tell him. After a quick wave, Joel was off.

He descended the stairs two at a time and didn't stop his momentum once his feet slapped the floor. He whipped into the kitchen and took his set of house keys from the rack. Then he exited through the back door, circling around to the front where he found Ethan and Paul sitting on the steps waiting for him.

"There you are," said Paul. "We were beginning to think you weren't coming."

"Had to get my stuff. Ready to split?"

"Yep," said Ethan. "Let's go." He stood up, brushing off the seat of his pants. "It's already hot as hell out here. That water's sure going to feel good."

"I can't wait," said Paul.

Ethan's voice bounced to a serious tone, "You know you'd really like it a lot more if you took your shirt off in the water."

"Whatever, you know I have sensitive skin." That was Paul's excuse to keep his pudgy figure hidden under his shirt. He'd never had a problem with sunlight until he'd gained all the weight.

Joel and Ethan laughed.

"Right," said Joel.

Walking in a group, they traveled back around the house. As they approached the woods, Joel stopped and looked back at his bedroom window. He pictured Pillowface sitting on his bed, fiddling with his thumbs, and lonely. He felt bad about leaving him. He wondered if he purposely didn't try as hard to cancel this trip as he should just so he *could* get away.

"You coming?" asked Ethan.

Ethan and Paul looked at him curiously, and Joel realized he'd been staring at the window for the better part of a minute. He forced a smile that he knew probably came across more as a goofy smirk. "Yeah."

They were waiting for Joel at the start of the trail, and as he joined them, he hoped like hell Haley wouldn't come home and find his hidden guest. *If she does come home, he'll hide. He's good at that.* He wasn't fully convinced things would be all right, but what choice did he have now? He was already with the guys, trekking along the Blue Wave's Trail.

Neither of them knew who *actually* owned the land (other than the two acres the Olsen's owned on the other side), but they'd declared all of it as theirs. All the woods were their own private playground, their kingdom. To them, no one else had the right to be on their tramping grounds. They were the knights of the Blue Waves Trail, and everyone else were trolls, hobgoblins, and ogres that they must eradicate. The few instances they had actually come across other humans (hikers or cyclists), they had felt as if their privacy had been invaded by trespassers. It rarely happened, but it had before, and Joel figured it probably would again.

As the guys marched forward, talking about horror movies and music, someone trailed them at a safe distance, waiting for the right moment to make a move. The lanky figure moved in stealth, listening to their conversation and hating every bit of it.

But behind him, someone else was stalking.

(III)

The toilet flushed.

Richard tapped his penis once and had to stop. The tugging pain stunned him like a kick in the balls. He was *sore*. Peeing had been terribly difficult. Though his bladder was full, the urine oozed out of him as if it was yellow jam from the pit of a volcano. Much as he'd expected, Sharon had not been lenient with him last night; in fact, she'd acted as if an unhealthy hostility had possessed her: writhing atop him like a cowgirl trying to tame a wild horse. Screaming the recited dialogue from the infamous crucifix scene in The Exorcist. Slapping. Pinching. She'd even used hot candle wax to burn him, something he detested, but he had allowed her to use it, nonetheless.

He regretted it now.

Looking at himself in the mirror, what he found gazing back at him was a pitiful excuse for a zombie. The candlewax had left small red burns in a speckled pallet across his chest and neck. He noticed Sharon's purple teeth-prints under his Adam's apple like indentions in a coffee drinker's Styrofoam cup. There was no point in trying to cover those up. He tapped the welts tenderly with a finger and winced. The pain was ridiculous. When he used to be a smoker, on more than one occasion he'd accidentally dropped burning ash on his skin, and these were worse, a searing ache that wouldn't quit.

He glanced at them one more time under the bright fluorescent lights above the mirrored medicine cabinet. "You've looked better, Richie boy," he muttered. Then he shut off the light and stepped out into the hall.

On his way up the hall, he poked his head in their bedroom to find Sharon still sleeping naked on top of the covers. With her bronze-colored skin, she looked like an adult movie star trophy. She lay on her back, fully exposed, with her left leg bent at the knee, the bottom of her foot lightly brushing her calf. Her left arm was sprawled out next to her, while her right graced her chest with her fingers against her throat as if someone had just said something shocking and she was reacting to it. Her mussed hair was a knotted heap of tumbleweed against the pillow. Richard couldn't help but chuckle at what he saw. Even like that, she was the most beautiful creation he'd ever been fortunate enough to catch sight of. He was thankful today, much like every day, that he had her as his wife.

He needed to check on another beautiful creation. This one's loveliness surprised him the most because she wasn't just her mother's doing, she was his, too. He'd helped produce something so spectacular. Which, having just seen himself in the mirror, was an odd and not to mention, surprising feat.

He quietly drifted away from the doorway and treaded softly to Tonya's room. The door was closed. He felt a cramp of grief in his stomach and took in a deep breath. He leaned his head against the door, placing his ear flat against it. The door was cold and sent a dull ache into the inner canal. He lightly tapped a knuckle across the door. "Tonya?" A few moments passed, then he repeated the tap, but louder this time. He also raised his voice, "Tonya?" He waited some more, and still nothing. The grieving pull returned in his bowels. He could feel a good cry wanting to get the better of him, but he wouldn't allow it. "Are you home?" His voice was near its normal volume, but the pitch was all wrong. Higher, with too much worry and fear.

He sighed. *Might as well just open the door and see for sure.* He dreaded doing that for two reasons: One, he didn't want to risk barging in and finding her either dressing or sleeping a bit too comfortably on the bed like her mother. He'd made the mistake of catching her like that more than once and certainly didn't care for it to happen again. Two, he didn't want solid proof to confirm that the dirty little shit known as Clay Ray had been right. *Damn him,* he thought. Though he had nothing to support this theory, he would be willing to bet that somehow, if they were to trace this whole thing back to its root, Clay Ray would be discovered as the seed that had started it all. But, truthfully, none of that really mattered right now. Sooner or later, he'd have to open the door and find out for sure. He wrapped a trembling hand around the knob. "I'm coming in, Tonya. I hope you're decent."

I hope you're in there at all.

He opened the door and found her room just the way it was when they'd come home last night. Empty, unusually clean, and the bed made. There was no evidence that she'd slept in it or had even come home during the early hours of morning.

His world shattered around him. He wanted to cry but bit his thumb to hold it back. Now he knew, without any doubt, that something was wrong.

Something had happened to his daughter.

CHAPTER NINETEEN

(I)

The body, bloated and soggy like dough, was wedged in a dam of sticks and mud. Its skin was a pasty white and dark purple blend.

It was hard for Carp to believe that this decomposing piece of excrement had once been a beautiful woman.

The lovely girl's corpse had taken in water, expanding like a pool float.

Buddy nudged it with a boot. "That's her?" He obviously needed a confirmation from Carp because she looked nothing like the way they remembered her. He got it with a nod. "What the hell is she doing out here?"

Carp shrugged. For the first time that he could remember, he was at a loss for words. "I-I don't know. Maybe she ..." He trailed off.

Maybe she what, exactly?

"Yeah," said Buddy.

Confused, Carp just nodded, again.

"Well, here's the girl, but where's our boy?" Buddy nudged her again, this time harder. "Where is he, huh? Huh, bitch?!" He kicked her in the ribs; a sound like a thick branch snapping came from underneath her waterlogged skin.

The atrocious sound caused Carp to feel an ache in his own ribs. It was awful, but not so bad that Buddy was starting to lose control.

Buddy slouched, his backpack sliding off his shoulders, and squatted in front of it. He opened it, sifted around the inside until his fingers clinked on something metal. Carp knew what it was he was doing, but he didn't understand the reasoning.

"Why her?"

"Why not?"

"Well, it's not our M.O."

"Yes, it is and no it isn't." He removed his rusting 8mm film camera. A small, pistol-gripped entity that Buddy held closer to him than most would a child. Though it was miniscule in size and width, the interior gears were thunderous, earsplitting as the film fed through, photographing images up to eighteen frames-per-second.

"You're not making any sense," said Carp, burrowing his hand into his front shirt pocket, and removing a cigarette from the crinkled pouch. He pressed it between his parched lips and lighted it. The smoke entered his lungs like an invited friend.

Buddy stood up. "You just worry about doing what I say, and less about what I do, got me?"

Though he was lying, he said, "Completely."

Buddy stepped back to the stream's edge and balanced himself on a slab of mud and jutting rock. He raised the camera to his eye, squeezing the trigger as if firing a gun. The piercing sounds of the motor shot through the mostly tranquil woods. A small flock of birds, startled by the noise, flew out of their seclusion in the tall grass nearby. Carp watched them flapping through the sky, getting as far away as possible.

And for a moment, Carp wished he could join them.

(II)

"The *real* Jason Voorhees, not the one from the remake, could kick Pumpkinhead's ass." Ethan said this, looking back at Joel and Paul from the front of the line.

They marched single file through a tapered section on the trail. A chorus of birds chirped all around them, an airplane hummed in the sky. The trees were much heavier and thicker in the grove to their left,

mostly pine, but there were others scattered through. To their right was George Sifford's old meadow, once inhabited with cattle, it had long been deserted since George filed bankruptcy. The boys enjoyed having the woods all to themselves, and being able to play in the pasture, but Joel found himself from time to time missing the cows. Sometimes, when he was bored, he and Rusky would come out here and watch them graze. It was relaxing and he'd conjure up great story ideas for his monsters.

"Bullshit," Paul disagreed. "Pumpkinhead is a powerful demon; Jason is just a momma's boy that don't know how to die."

"Then how can Pumpkinhead kill him?" asked Ethan.

"Easily. Rip him apart."

"Yeah, right. Jason will go back together, just like the werewolf in Monster Squad."

"Whatever! He's never done that before in any movie." Paul's voice was becoming squeakier, girl-like.

"Well," said Ethan, thinking about it. "You're right, but he could just find another body like in *Goes to Hell*."

Paul pointed at him. "You said we couldn't count that one as part of the series."

"I didn't say that, Joel did."

Joel heard his name mentioned and focused on their argument more intently. His mind was still drifting to the pasture, and memories of him and Rusky. "Said what?"

"That we couldn't count *Jason goes to Hell* as part of the series."

"That's right, and *Jason X,* either."

"Whatever." Paul shook his head, chuckling.

"Well, give us *your* opinion," said Ethan. "Who'd win in a fight? Pumpkinhead or Jason Voorhees?"

"The *original* Jason Voorhees," added Paul for fairness.

"Yeah."

Good question. Joel thought about it as they approached the opening fork in the trail. They spread out with Joel in the middle, Paul on his right and Ethan on his left. Joel hated walking in the middle; he preferred one of the edges so he could stare into the woods without having to look past one of his friends to do it.

"Well?" asked Ethan.

"I'm going to say that's not a fair fight."

The guys hollered and laughed. Paul said, "And, why the hell not?"

"Because the only way of stopping Pumpkinhead is if he completes what he's been summoned to do, and if he'd been summoned to fight Jason, another deathless creature, then no one would win. It'd be like when Grey Hulk fought the Green Hulk."

"Yeah, but that doesn't count," said Ethan. "That only happened in David Banner's mind."

"Bruce Banner's mind," corrected Joel. "David was his name on the TV show. Anyway, I think they'd get tired of fighting and just go their separate ways."

"Or team up?" asked Paul.

"Maybe."

They grew silent for a minute. Then Ethan added, "That'd be a kickass team, if you think about it."

They all agreed on that one.

Then they heard Clay Ray's voice behind them say, "You faggots sure do talk about the *dumbest* shit."

All of them jumped, but only Paul let out a small squeal as they turned around. Clay Ray was stepping out of the woods to their left. *Asshole must have been following us,* thought Joel. But, he wondered, as Clay Ray walked over to them with a wicked grin on his face, why would he have done that?

"Hey, Ray," said Paul, as if they were old friends.

"Shut up, tubby." He had an unlit cigarette between his lips. It bounced as he talked. "What are you three fuckle-heads doing out here?"

"Going to Blue Waves Pool," answered Ethan.

"Oh, really?" Ray didn't sound like he truly cared.

"Yeah," said Paul.

Joel studied Ray's movements nervously. He knew this couldn't be good. Ray wouldn't have stopped them unless he wanted trouble. He was never one to hassle Ethan, and very rarely did Paul suffer his abuse. For reasons Joel never understood, he only inflicted his torture upon him. This time was different. However, all their other run-ins had happened in public or at Tonya's, never had Joel been so unfortunate to encounter him in the seclusion of the woods, and this deep out, too. There would be no one within miles that could hear what happened.

Hear us scream.

"So, you three fags are just walking through these woods to go to the pool, huh?" He lighted the cigarette. "I don't buy it. Why would you choose to walk all that way when you could have one of your parents take you instead?"

None of them answered.

"Oh, wait," said Ray. "That's right, not all of you *have* parents."

Joel knew he shouldn't let Ray's insults bother him, but they did. He couldn't help it. A burning rage was ignited inside of him. He felt the heat moving from his gut, up his back, and over his neck. He became light-headed as his vision blurred.

"That's not cool," said Ethan.

Ray glanced at him, "Shut up before I start on you. I've never had a problem with you except that you hang out with dumbasses like these two, so don't do anything to change that."

Ethan nodded, and Joel found himself losing respect for Ethan thanks to his spinelessness.

Clay Ray turned back to Joel. "Aw, did my comment about Mommy and Daddy hurt your *wittle feelwings?*"

Joel's hands, hanging by his sides, clenched into fists. "If I had parents like yours, I'd rather them be dead."

Paul gasped an exaggerated sigh of dread. One that said: *Damn it Joel, why'd you say that?*

Ray's mouth twitched as he exhaled a patch of smoke. "Nice. It's about time you said something. I've been getting tired of beating on someone that doesn't fight back. You're making it fun again."

"Fuck you." Joel could faintly hear himself through the bubbles in his ears telling himself to stop while he still had teeth in his mouth. But the lack of sleep, sudden loss of a friend, then the quick gaining of a new one, and also the kiss he'd received from Carlee, had changed him. In this small group of people, he felt the oldest and most mature of them all. He was worried about what Clay Ray might do to him, but he wasn't scared.

Instead of pounding him, Clay Ray only cocked his head back and bellowed a laugh that puffed out clots of smoke like a dying exhaust pipe. He looked at Joel. "That's good." He wiped a tear with his index finger and flicked it. "Now, are you speaking like this to me at your own will or because of your friend?"

Joel's suit of bravery began to shrink tight against his body. "What?" he asked, his voice betraying him and going shaky.

Ethan straightened his shoulders. "You told me to stay out of it."

"I'm not talking about you, asshole," said Ray. He nodded toward Joel. "He knows who I'm talking about."

How? How could he know?

"I don't ..."

"Here's the part where he tries to lie his way out of it. Just like all those times when he tries lying his way out of an ass kicking."

Ethan and Paul were confused.

Ray could obviously read it by their expressions. "Oh? He hasn't let you in on his little secret?"

"What's he talking about, Joel?" asked Paul, accusing him with his eyes, a shrewd look on his face.

"Nothing," muttered Joel.

Ray walked over to Joel. He stood maybe two feet from him. "I *saw* you."

Joel's skin went cold and crawly.

"This morning, walking back to your house. I was hiding in my car right off the curve."

Behind the field. We walked right by him.

"I was waiting for Tonya to come home. She's missing, but you probably already know that."

"Missing?" asked Ethan. "Since when?"

"Since yesterday," said Ray. "Now, shut up!"

"I didn't," Joel tried to say, but Ray grabbed his shirt and jerked him over, close enough to smell his aftershave, and the stale odor of cigarette smoke on his breath.

"What did you do to her?"

"Nothing."

"Liar," he shook him. Joel's head wobbled like an infant's. "Tell me! Who was that guy with you? The one in the mask! Why were you carrying a shovel and covered in dirt?"

Paul and Ethan didn't do or say anything. Only watched and presumably wondered themselves just what the hell Ray was talking about.

Joel kicked at Ray, aiming for his nuts, but pegged him in the thigh. He let go of him and called out. Joel turned around and had run just a few feet before Ray tackled him from behind. Joel landed hard on his chest, blasting the air from his lungs. The bubbles in his ears popped and started ringing. With tears in eyes, everything looked as if he was viewing it through the bottom of a drinking glass.

Then he felt the kick. The impact pushed Haley's breakfast up instantly.

"Last chance," said Ray. "You're a dipshit, and I *don't* want to kill you, but I *will*. I so fucking will if you don't tell me what the hell happened to Tonya."

Joel coughed and spat some blood into the dirt, crying. His sobs rained tears on the loose soil, turning it to mud.

Then, as if answering his distress call, another sound reverberated through the glade.

A chainsaw!

It erupted adjacent to them with such explosive force that the ground trembled. He quickly realized that it wasn't the ground shaking, but Ray's body quivering against him. The bulge of Ray's penis on the nape of his neck retracted as if pulling itself inward. Then he felt a warm sensation drizzling over him.

Ray was pissing *his* pants.

Paul and Ethan watched in disarray, mouths agape.

Pillowface seemed to appear out of nowhere, the chainsaw wielded high above his head, his body thrusting side to side as he revved the motor. Lines of exhaust hurled out from the saw's yellow frame, spreading them in a layer of gas-fumed fog. Joel had never been happier to see anyone in all his life, yet at the same time he was terrified of what would happen next.

Ray stood up on wobbly legs. He waved the knife. "It's you. You're the one, aren't you?! *You* killed Tonya!"

Blind fear that Ray had probably confused for confidence grew inside of him like an inflating balloon. He flicked his wrist at Pillowface, brandishing the blade, but the massive hulk of a man didn't even flinch. He stood his ground, which seemed to amuse Ray rather than frighten him. Laughing like a woodchuck on helium, he leapt over Joel's fallen shape, landing in front of his adversary.

"You think you scare me with that thing? You're wrong! *Dead* wrong!"

Scared enough that you pissed yourself, Joel thought.

He lunged. Again, Pillowface didn't move, which allowed Ray to plant the blade to the hilt below his sternum. As if this had no effect on him, he swung the saw, but Ray dodged it and landed a punch on the cheek of the mask. Pillowface swayed, but his feet remained firmly rooted to the ground. Tucked over, arms bent and fists clenched, Ray danced like a man in the ring. He leaned into Pillowface, pounding him with a rapid series of rights and lefts to his midsection. Joel swore he heard his friend call out in pain over the roar of the saw.

He dropped the massive machine two inches from Joel's rounded eyes.

He has a high tolerance for pain, but he's not inhuman. And Ray's hitting him where he was already wounded!

Pillowface doubled over, both arms hugging his abdomen. A wet spot was quickly spreading across the dark shirt.

He's bleeding!

Laughing again, Ray threw his leg up, kneeing him in the chin. Joel's fear for Ray's life was swapping for Pillowface's. He'd thought this would have ended by now, with Ray's bloodied body left to dispose of. He pushed himself up on his hands as if about to perform push-ups, flinging his soaked bangs out of his eyes.

Ray was spinning circles with his arms held high, laughing, twirling, looking merry and maniacally satisfied. Pillowface needed help. Joel figured he might just be able to take Ray by surprise. He rose to a squat, his knees popping, and grabbed the saw. He tried to stand up, but it was nearly impossible with the chainsaw's added weight. Joel could have been trying to lift a car. He gritted his teeth and strained with his back to heft it up.

Finally, he did.

Wobbling, he staggered toward the two men.

As Ray pulled an arm back, setting Pillowface up for another blow, he looked at Joel. "Say bye to ..." was all he got out before noticing what was about to happen.

Joel revved, charged.

Ray sidestepped the spinning chain, narrowly avoiding a split torso. His body evaded the attack completely, but his long hair did not. The blade seized up his lengthy mane in one quick swoop, jerking his head back. His locks tangled in the chain, choking the engine, and killing it. Joel dropped the saw and Ray went down with it.

Now on the ground, Ray was still trying to escape. He'd managed to get into a crawling position before the dead-load of the chainsaw had tugged his scalp. Ray was in tears and screaming with each effort he made to untangle himself from the saw. Seeing him like that, Joel felt a stir of pity, but not enough for it to matter. He sort of enjoyed seeing the guy who'd tormented him for the past two years at *his* feet for once, crying.

"Huh-help me!"

Ethan was on his feet, Paul only his knees. Both of them watched Ray, only flicking their eyes back to Joel every so often. Pillowface, bowed over, yanked Ray's knife from his midsection. A trail of blood followed the blade.

Then he threw an arm around Joel.

"You all right?" Joel asked, getting a nod for an answer. He took the knife from him and retracted the blade.

Another bout of silence fell on them as Ray continued to sob. Ethan was the first one to break it by saying, "We can't just leave him here."

Paul made a face. "Says who?" His nose had stopped bleeding, but now he had two drying tracks of red cascading to his top lip.

"That's fucked up and you know it."

"He had a knife. He was going to kill us."

"No, he was ..." Ethan shut up then.

Joel shot him a look. "What were you going to say? That he was just going to kill *me*? You did a whole lot to prevent that, didn't you?"

"He told me to stay out of it, so I did. Fuck you, man. I was scared!" He took a deep, shaky breath. "Was he right about Tonya? Did you do something to her?"

"What does it matter now, anyway?" asked Joel.

"Just cut my hair," said Ray from below. "I don't care. Just cut it so I can go."

Ethan threw his hands about madly, his eyes misting over. "Come on, Joel! I just want to go home! Let him go, then *I* can go. Okay?"

Joel shook his head.

"Please?" It was Ethan who now sobbed. "I don't want any part of this. I just want to go home, please Joel. I just want to go home."

Joel looked down at Ray. He lay on his stomach, his right arm reaching over his shoulder and pawing madly at his hair. The saw sat on the ground diagonally from his ear, stretching his scalp out so much that it looked like a small, pitched tent on top of his head.

Wincing, Joel felt a stinging pain in his gut just looking at it.

"Who *is* that guy?" asked Paul, speaking to Joel as if they were the only two there.

Joel answered him just the same, "I don't know his real name, but he goes by Pillowface."

Paul nodded, as if knowing. Now, he spoke to Pillowface. "Thank you."

If Pillowface heard him, he gave no indication of it.

"What do we do now?" asked Paul, groaning as he stood up. "Our trip to Blue Waves just went to shit."

Their plans had gone so far to shit they were swimming in it.

"I won't say anything," cried Ray. "I swear!"

"Me neither," said Ethan. "Please, Joel. I just want to go home and watch TV, maybe play some checkers on the computer. You know I won't rat you out."

"For what? For standing up for myself?"

"You're right," he said. "You had to. That's what we'll say. You had to!" Ethan slapped Paul on the shoulder, trying to get him to chime in.

Instead, he shook his head, and walked away from Ethan, leaving him alone on the other side of Ray.

"Does anyone know you're out here?" Paul asked Joel.

Joel thought about it. "No. Haley doesn't know, that's for sure."

"My mom wasn't at home for me to tell her I was coming out here today." He looked back at Ethan. "Did you tell your parents we were going to the pool?"

Eyes fixed on Ray, he said, "No, I told them I was going to your house."

"Perfect. We could just leave, and not worry about a thing." He slapped his hands together. "Right?"

It bothered Joel how quickly Paul had come up with this solution. Also, it worried him how much fun he seemed to be having. He'd often wondered if Paul had been slowly losing his mind since his dad left. Now, he was damn near convinced he had lost it completely. "I don't know. It *could* work."

"I won't tell ..." Ray repeated.

Over eager to please them, Ethan said, "Yeah, it would work for sure. We can walk back through the woods, taking the longer way back to Joel's."

"What for?" asked Paul.

"So we won't run into anyone. There won't be any trace of us out here."

"Wrong," said Joel. "Our footprints are all over the place, and so's my blood and puke, and Paul's blood. On *CSI* they always figure shit out with evidence like that."

Ethan shook his head. "Nope. You're talking to the guy who wants to be a cop, remember?"

"What are you getting at?" asked Paul, a red bubble popping in his left nostril.

"Walk back through the woods like I said, but we take a long branch with a lot of leaves on the end and anywhere in the dirt we see our tracks, we just stretch the limb onto the path, and use the leaves to wipe them away."

Joel was catching on, "Erasing our footprints?"

"Exactly."

Paul pointed at his blood drops on the trail. "But what about that?"

"It probably doesn't go down that far; we'll just scoop up the dried chunks and get rid of them."

"How?"

"I don't know; throw them in the creek or something."

"Carry them?"

Ethan nodded sternly, but the look on his face wasn't convinced. "It's all I can think of on short notice."

"Do you have a plastic bag in your backpack?" asked Joel.

Thinking about it, Ethan nodded, "Yeah. Actually, I do."

"Good, we'll dump the dried dirt in the bag, carry it to the creek and dump it."

"Perfect," said Paul, his face glowing with excitement. "Put our minds together and there's no telling what we can accomplish."

Ignoring him, Joel turned to Pillowface. "You okay?"

He nodded as he stood upright on his own. He patted Joel on the shoulder, again. The comfort felt good. For a short moment, it felt as if they were the only two out there, being friends, hanging out, and going on their own adventure.

But Paul's voice killed that illusion. "Let's get this going, guys."

Joel sighed. "Okay."

Ethan pulled off his backpack and squatted. He laid the bag across his thighs. He sifted inside for a moment, then pulled his hand out. Sagging between his fingers was a white plastic bag. "Here it is."

Joel took it from him. While Ethan found a lengthy stick that was bushy on one end, Joel and Paul gathered up their messes and dropped them in the bag. Joel nearly vomited again while cleaning up the drying puddle of puke. The thick summer heat had made the smell unbearable, like old milk that had spoiled to putty. When they were finished, Joel tied the bag in a knot and stood up.

They looked at each other quietly, catching their breath. Finally, Ethan said, "What do we do about *him*?" He pointed at Ray.

"We ..." started Joel but stopped. He looked up at Pillowface. "We have to get your saw out of his hair."

Nonchalantly, Pillowface strode over to Ray's prone body. With one immense tug, he wrenched his saw free with a wet rip that sounded like scored cabbage. Dangling from the chain was Ray's ponytail; his bloodied scalp had come with it.

The question had been answered. Ray was quiet after that. He didn't even seem to be breathing.

CHAPTER TWENTY

(I)

It was nearly lunch time and Jonesey still hadn't made an appearance. Could Haley be so lucky? Was he so embarrassed over his behavior last night that he couldn't come in and face her? She seriously doubted it.

Probably just out somewhere being Jonesey.

But it was still strange that he was *this* late.

Maybe something happened to him.

She couldn't ask Jonesey's father and partner at the firm, Ronald Jones, if he'd heard from him, because he was never at the office, and Jeff Lamberson, their office manager, hadn't heard anything, either.

Sitting behind her desk, she skimmed over the final pages of *Demon Seed* but barely read a single word. Finally, she closed the book, promising to go back to it later. She glanced at the phone on the desk and contemplated calling Alan, but quickly talked herself out of it.

Why hasn't he called me?

She snatched a pencil off the desk, tapping the eraser's end nervously against the keyboard on her desk. She'd dumped guys for less than this.

That's fine. He doesn't want to talk, so I'll just stay away. Show him what it's like not having Haley Olsen around.

Carlee poked her head in. "Hey, just got a second, but I wanted to see where you wanted to go for lunch today."

"Doesn't matter."

"Okay, I'll be right back after I fax that letter for you. Anything you in the mood for?"

"Books."

"Huh?"

"I want to go to the bookstore."

Smiling, Carlee said, "You got it." She disappeared behind the door.

Haley tossed her pencil across the office. "So much for that plan," she muttered.

(II)

Geoffrey Jones parked his car a mile from Haley's house. Leaving it on the side of the road, he stuck a white t-shirt in the door and shut it, hoping to give the impression that it was stranded. He thought about leaving a note saying *please don't tow me*, but it would have been too hard to write with the cast on.

The mile hike would be hard in his expensive shoes, but worth it.

He glanced at his car one last time, beaming over the spot he'd pre-selected to park his car. Last week on a long lunch, he'd driven out here to find Haley's house, and had concocted a plan. He'd learned right away the dog would be a problem, so he'd returned on Sunday and fed it a poisoned hamburger patty. The risk was mind shattering, because Haley was at home when he'd done it, but it must have paid off. Word around the office was the dog was dead. He hadn't planned on putting his plan into motion so soon, but oh well, shit happens.

As he started away, he heard his cell phone ringing from inside the car. Ignoring it, he assumed it was either Margie or someone at the office wanting to know where he was and why hadn't he come in yet.

I can come in whenever the hell I feel like it!

Margie was a different matter though, but she could easily be handled later. If she showed any signs of resentment at him for not coming home last night, he'd just have to remind her of how much money he put in the bank account each week. That usually shut her up pretty damn quick.

He decided to use the woods for shelter as he walked. The damp grass whipped at his pants leaving lashes. As he entered through a shaded area, his right foot came down in some fresh mud, swallowing his shoe. "Shit!" He pulled his foot out, but the shoe remained stuck. His black sock now had a tear in it. *Great, a perfectly good sock ruined!* He found a dry spot on the ground and crouched low. He stretched his arms, trying to get the shoe, but it was just out of reach. He could see the tongue of his loafer protruding from the mud like a hand reaching for help. "Two hundred bucks going to putt!" He should have gone home first and changed clothes, maybe into a sweat suit and some sneakers, but that would have taken even more time, and he was already running behind.

The bookstore had held him up longer than he'd anticipated.

He found a stick in the grass and using his left hand, poked it into the mud like he was stoking a fire. He held his right hand in the air, trying not to get any mud on the cast. That would be hard to explain. He already had enough to explain away as it was.

After a few jabs the shoe was loose enough to grab.

The damn thing was caked in mud; all but the interior of the shoe was filthy. He slid his foot inside.

A branch snapped.

He gasped, and quickly shot around, only to find a rabbit hopping away from him. He slowly exhaled through his tightened lips. "Damn rabbit." He adjusted his suit–the same one he wore to the book sale— fixed his tie, and marched onward.

Haley's house was the destination he had in mind.

(III)

When Haley and Carlee arrived at the bookstore, they couldn't force themselves to leave the car. They stared in shock, neither of them speaking a word. A single tear spilled from Haley's eye. It was awful, absolutely horrible.

"What happened?" whispered Carlee, unable to raise her voice any higher.

The condition of the store should have been enough for Carlee to not have needed to ask at all. Its twisted features and charred-black boards, a shattered door hanging on a frame without a building behind it and opening to nothing but snaking plumes of smoke. Between two other shops that stood untouched from the flames, the bookstore was a broken cavity between two crowns. If the girls still weren't completely sure what had happened after all of this evidence, the dozen or so firemen shuffling through the ashes and rubble making two piles, one for salvageable books and another for not a chance in hell books, the not a chance pile was three times higher than the other, should have been the final clue they needed to solve this mystery.

Haley only shook her head, because saying it aloud made it true, and perhaps if she were to keep quiet, then it wouldn't have really happened.

Haley stepped out of the car, as if in a trance.

"Wait," said Carlee. "Where are you going?"

Haley drifted to where the debris met the sidewalk. She stopped in front of some firemen. The tallest one of the bunch, a man probably in his fifties, stopped what he was doing and looked at her.

"Don't come any further than that," he said. "Too much for you to hurt yourself on."

"How did this happen?" she said, her voice flat.

"Caught fire sometime early this morning; we think it was arson."

She couldn't swallow. "Was anyone…hurt?"

"No, and damn lucky, too."

She felt her stomach relax a bit. "Where's Alan?"

"The owner?" She nodded. "Over there." He pointed over her shoulder to the right. A bench next to a Dogwood was a good twenty yards away. Alan sat there, staring at nothing, his eyes glassy like a man coming down from a terrible high. Haley recognized it for what it was, the same way she and Joel had looked when they'd learned their parents had died.

"Are you a friend of his?" She looked back at the firefighter and nodded. His face was black with soot except around the eyes which made him look like a six-foot tall, albino raccoon. "He could probably use someone like you at a time like this."

The firefighter was right. "I'm going to check on him." She didn't know why she felt the need to inform the fireman of her plan, but his approving smile made her feel as if it was well deserved. Then she offered him a "Thank you."

"You're welcome." He turned back to the wreckage and shuffled about, kicking at some serrated pieces.

She neared the bench. Alan's attention was hooked elsewhere. She thought about placing a hand on his shoulder, giving him a tender squeeze, but was afraid of scaring him half to death. "Alan?" She spoke softly.

He glanced back at her. His eyes were brimming with tears. Black smudges were peppered across his face, wavy lines where tears had passed and dried cut between them. He attempted a smile, and it was a decent one, but not one of his best.

Lucky he can smile at all.

"Hey," he said.

"My God. Are you all right?"

He shrugged, turned away. "I don't know what I am."

She walked around the bench and sat right beside him, their hips touching. She put an arm around him. "I'm here." He smelled like a spent campfire of rotten wood, but she didn't care, she was happy to touch him again, hoped she could offer some sort of comfort.

He looked at her. "You have no idea how good it feels for you to be."

She smiled and felt her eyes starting to water. "I hope it helps somehow."

Nodding, "More than you realize." He laid his head on her shoulder. She cupped her hand over his face and began stroking his cheek. "It's gone, Haley, all of it. I lived in the loft upstairs, and I have nothing left!"

He began to cry. She'd never heard a man cry before and there was something extremely sad about it, such defeat and misery. After listening for a while, Haley joined him. She wished she had something to say that would help, but what could she offer him at a time like this? *Nothing.* It was just the same when the lawyers and the doctors tried convincing her life would be kosher without her parents. She'd actually believed them, but they'd been wrong, so very, very wrong. How could anyone make such a specious promise? She wouldn't do that now, because she couldn't guarantee him that anything would ever be fine again.

CHAPTER TWENTY-ONE

(I)

"**F**resh?"

On one knee beside the loose soil, Carp nodded. "Yeah, the dirt hasn't even dried up yet." He patted the dirt. "Soft like a tilled garden."

"So something *was* buried here."

"Judging by the layout, I'd say that's a pretty good assumption." The area was six foot in length, and four in width—the perfect size and location under the hanging branches of an oak tree for a shallow grave.

Carp looked up at Buddy through squinted eyes. He could see the vague appearance of worry, and possibly even fear on his leader's face. That was unnatural for Buddy given *any* circumstance.

"Looks too small to be Face, though," added Carp.

"I don't know, unless he was dismembered."

Carp grimaced. "Chopped up?"

"Exactly, shit for brains. You act like that could never happen. How many have *we* done? Thirty? More?"

"I'd say more, easily."

"That's right, so I wouldn't put it past someone else to do the same." Buddy began to investigate the area, moving about quickly and alert. He looked at the trees, the *grave*, and the ground around it. He circled the site twice before crouching across the way from Carp. "Found something."

"What is it?"

"Tracks."

"No shit?" Carp sprang to his feet, darting over the sinking dirt to join Buddy. Over his shoulder, he saw the perfect imprint of a size nine sneaker. "Looks like a kid's."

Buddy smiled, "Yep. I'd say Converse."

"I doubt someone this size could have gotten the drop on Pillowface."

"I told you to stop calling him that."

"It's what he *wants* to be called."

"He punishes himself with that name."

Carp studied the prints. "Those tracks probably belong to a little boy."

"Not necessarily. These days, girls dress just like boys and the boys dress like the girls. Sometimes it's hard to tell the difference."

Wrong Buddy, there's one easy way to tell a difference. You make them take off their pants.

Carp looked to the right and spotted something else just as interesting. Another kind of print, and much, much larger. A fifteen boot, Army-issued. "Buddy, look at that." He pointed to a newborn tree that had most likely been working its way above ground for years. It was a thin piece, a couple of tiny branches developing with maybe three leaves sprouting on each. The print was at its base.

Buddy kicked the tree over as he settled in front of the other footprints. "Now, these definitely belong to Face."

Carp studied a tight path from the tree and found more. "Looks like they're walking together."

"What do you mean?"

"Well, I see two sets, one small and one big, but both appear to be walking next to each other right up this way." A hill careened down to a thinner section of the forest.

"Makes no sense," Buddy said.

"Should we dig up this hole?"

Buddy stood up. "You better believe it."

They went to their bags and found their shovels. Small, easy to carry, but depending on how deep this grave was they'd be a bitch to use. Plus, the handles were metal and would be shit on their hands.

Down on their knees, they each picked a side and began digging, tossing the dirt wildly behind them. They weren't planning to refill it when they were done, so the requirement to make a pile was absent. After fifteen minutes, Buddy found the body. Slower and more vigilant, they unearthed the remains of a female body. They stopped digging once they exposed her legs.

"Looks like she might have been a pretty girl," said Carp, gliding his fingers in over the gelid skin of her thigh.

"Was."

"She still is. Could be useful in a pinch." Laughing, he patted her leg.

"A pinch only your sick fucking mind could enjoy." Buddy shook his head.

"Check this out," said Carp. He spread her legs to show Buddy the furry body underneath. "A dog."

"Maybe she was killed with her dog."

"I've never known Face to kill an animal."

Buddy shouted, stabbing his shovel into the ground. "None of this makes any goddamn sense, and I'm a fucking wizard when it comes to abnormal." Carp only nodded. "I mean, look at this. Some woman buried with a dog. Two sets of tracks. One obviously Face's, but the other is some kid, or a very small adult leaving the scene together. It's all fucked up!"

"Big time," he agreed.

"Put your shovel up. We're going to find out where these tracks go. Maybe it'll lead us to Face."

"You got it."

They packed up in less than a minute and quickly got out of sight, because what they heard off in the distance were voices.

Kid's voices.

(ll)

The boys, along with Pillowface, wandered up on the opened grave. Ethan was the first to notice the pair of legs poking out of the shallow hole like roots. "What the hell is that?" He froze, the color draining from his already insipid face, making him look even sicklier.

Somehow, Joel knew even before he saw that Ethan had discovered Tonya. He wasn't as worried about what his friends would say and do as much as he was terrified over how the hole had been opened. There weren't any kind of animals big enough to dig it up…or were there? Actually, Joel wasn't sure what kind of animals were in these woods. He'd never come across anything bigger than a fox, but that didn't mean there wasn't anything bigger than that.

Paul stopped walking. Using his hand as a visor, he placed it on his brow to shield his eyes from the sun. "A hole or something."

"I can see that, but what's *in* it?"

"How am I supposed to know that?"

Joel kept quiet as they approached. He and Pillowface shared fretful looks, both wondering what to do when the guys realized it was Tonya's body in the pit. Ethan stepped onto the loose soil, caught one look at the lower half of the naked body, and turned away to vomit. Body heaving, the contents of his stomach splattered at his feet. He glanced at Paul for a moment, and then fainted in his puddle.

They grimaced. Not just at Ethan's unfortunate landing spot, but also the smell of the puke and decomposing body melding in the scorching heat. Joel had been sweating profusely the entire hike, but now, he was shivering. His spine felt as if it were being strummed with icy fingers. His testicles retracted against his abdomen.

"It's Tonya, isn't it?" asked Paul.

Joel nodded.

Sighing, Paul stepped over Ethan like he was just a rock and walked around to the other side of the hole, then got on his knees. He sifted through the dirt with his hands, eagerly pushing it away to see what was underneath. When he finished, he leaned back on his knees, and placed both hands on his hips. "I knew she had tits, but damn I didn't think they were *that* big."

Joel stared at Paul, repulsed.

Paul shrugged his shoulders. "Cut off her head, huh? Well, you had to do what you had to do." He sighed like a man talking about the weather. "Remember all those nights we spent at your fence, watching her bedroom with binoculars?"

Of course Joel remembered. It was exciting, the thrill of being caught, the possibility of seeing her *naked*. They'd never succeeded, but one time Joel was blessed with seeing Mrs. Cantrell practically naked.

Late one Friday night, Joel and Paul were taking turns spying on the house through the binoculars when the back door suddenly opened. Afraid of being caught, Paul had quickly ducked down, but Joel risked being caught and was thankful that he had. Tonya's mother had stepped outside to smoke a cigarette naked, well not completely, she was still wearing pieces of a nightgown or something. It looked as if it had been shredded, and sections of her skin showed through the holes. She'd seemed bushed, out of breath, her skin slick with sweat. Joel had always thought Tonya was the gorgeous one, but after that night, he knew he'd been wrong.

Joel noticed the wicked grin on Paul's face. The morbid wheels of Paul's mind were turning. He leaned forward and reached into the hole. Before Joel could ask what he was doing, Paul had cupped a breast in his hand. "Wow. It's still soft."

Disgust churned through him, but somewhere else, he also felt the heat of jealousy. Paul had tramped on his grounds.

Don't think like that. It's wrong, it's sick!!

He cleared his throat. "Stop it."

"Why? It's not like it's bothering her."

"It's sick."

"Oh, sure, and what did *you* do with her before putting her here?"

"I didn't do anything to her."

"Right." He slid his hand down her stomach, flicked away some ants, and fingered her navel. "I wonder…" He rubbed her groin.

"Stop it!"

Paul laughed, then abruptly stopped as Pillowface moved towards him. He stood up, holding out his hands. "Sorry, I'm sorry!"

Joel reached out as if his arm could stretch like Mr. Fantastic's from the Fantastic Four. "No, Pillowface!!"

He grabbed Paul by the shoulders and slung him against a tree. There was a vicious cracking sound when he hit. He ricocheted off the tree, landing in the brush, his feet sticking out from underneath it. Joel thought for sure he was dead. He realized he was holding his breath, so he exhaled. Everything around him was teetering. He wondered if he was going to faint.

Joel ran on flimsy legs to where Paul lay. He got down on his knees and examined him. Paul's feet stirred, twitched. He was breathing. *Thank God.* With tears in his eyes, he looked at Pillowface. "Why'd you do that? Huh?!! He's just a kid!!"

Pillowface lowered his head, shamefully staring at the ground.

Joel looked up at the tree Paul had struck and saw that bark had split and some chunks were missing. *Broke the damn tree.* He crawled out from under the bushes.

Pillowface put his shoulder against a tree to sustain his weight, his chest rising and falling profoundly.

Joel watched him worriedly.

He's losing a lot of blood. He might die.

He looked at his friends. One was passed out in his own puke, and the other unconscious. He got down on all fours by the hole and began scooping dirt back in. As he worked, he tried to think of something to do about them but couldn't get his mind to stop focusing on Pillowface.

The hole was only halfway full when he stopped. He went to Pillowface and pulled an arm over his shoulder. He decided to leave Paul and Ethan there for now, then come back and check on them in a little while. If he could at least get Pillowface inside and cleaned up, Joel could return to the woods while he patched himself up again. He felt guilty about it, but it was all he knew to do. He was exhausted and scared, but not enough that he couldn't recognize he wasn't thinking clearly.

"Come on." Joel and Pillowface moved on, going much slower than they already had been.

Pillowface glanced back at the bush, ignoring Paul and Ethan, because of the footprints he'd spied around the exhumed grave. Two sets of army-issued boots, size ten and eleven. *Buddy and Carp.* He looked at Joel, wanting to warn him that hell was coming in a pair.

Buddy and Carp came out of hiding, both surprised. Sure enough, Face was courting around with a kid. Carp watched them leave, wondering why Buddy had stopped him from confronting the duo. "I don't understand why we just didn't rush out …"

"We need to assess the situation, Carp. You of all people should understand that."

Carp looked back at the grave.

Buddy was already trying to wake up the kids they'd left behind. "I'm sure we'll find out plenty from one of these little bastards."

When the fat one flinched, Carp grinned. He was ready for some fun.

(III)

Jonesey took a used pair of Haley's panties from the hamper and sniffed them. His eyes fluttered, savoring the aroma of her natural juices. He thought about licking them but didn't. That would just be weird.

He felt jittery and couldn't stop shaking. There was a constant drone in his ears as if he'd been at a very loud concert. His throat clucked loudly, but not from fright. *Adrenaline.* The rush of being somewhere he shouldn't be, in a house with no one at home, and all of Haley's possessions for him to play with.

Should've been here a long time ago.

He stuffed the dirty panties in his pocket, then left the bathroom.

It didn't take him long to find her room.

The bed was a mess of bundled covers and crooked pillows. This was where she slept, her body had caused this. He pictured her laying on her back, nude, her long sunny hair draped across the pillow beside her. Rose petals spread out, a rose stem clenched in her teeth.

Then he thought back to last night, and how she'd disappeared into the back of the bookstore with that guy, *Alan*, and the noises the two of them had made, sounds that should have been saved for him and Haley to share. Out of anger, he'd punched a wall, and then spent three hours in the ER getting a cast put on his hand. *Broke the bone in two places!* Afterward, half high on pain meds and his rage flaring, he'd snuck back to the bookstore, broken in, and torched it. He'd seen Alan in the upstairs loft sleeping and had been tempted to smother him with a pillow.

But he didn't.

Let him burn.

Kicking off his shoes as he walked, he went to the bed and sat on its edge, laughing at what he'd done to the bookstore. He'd watched it go up from his car, windows shattering, the flames lashing from inside. An old building, parched books inside, the store had disintegrated quickly to a heap. He pitched his head back on her pillow and laughed so hard he felt a squeeze in his gut.

A strong scent of sugary soap and perfume breathed on him from the pillow. *Her scent.* The hum of Haley's fragrance killed his laughter, hitching it tight in his throat. A deep void opened in his chest, making it hurt to breath. Just thinking about her made him crazy, made him do things he never thought he could do, or would do again.

Arson.

The bookstore was his first time.

Breaking and entering.

Not his first time, but it had been several years since he last had.

Getting a hard on, calling Haley so she can hear me, and I can hear her, while jerking off.

A month ago, he'd never even thought it possible to *consider* such things, let alone committing them. What had she done to him? To his mind?

But he'd learned in the past that breaking into the store and the house wouldn't be as hard as it should have been. Having defended some of the scummiest crooks this side of the state had to offer, he'd picked up a thing or two from their testimonies, confessions, and police reports. Taking it all to his brain blender and thumping spin, he had a dangerous mixture and vast knowledge of their secrets and tricks. He could have written a book on how to get into a place without consent. He wondered why other lawyers didn't try this.

He reached into his pocket, tugging Haley's black thong-panties out by the band. He raised them to his nose, sniffed, and let out a slow, aching moan. The thick-sweet smell of Haley's sex licked his nose and brought tears to his eyes. "Oh Haley," he whispered. "Haley..." As if in a trance, he pushed his pants down to his knees, releasing his erect penis. Uncircumcised and fleshy, it looked like an earthworm the length and girth of a minute snake. He'd had a complex about it his whole life, but here and now he couldn't care less. He held Haley's panties like a napkin and wrapped the fabric around his shaft, making his own version of an uncut hot dog in an underwear bun.

Then he began stroking while moaning Haley's name.

(IV)

Buddy slapped the fat kid again, leaving a red handprint on the kid's cheek. "Where are they going!?!"

The tub of pre-teen strangled a sob. His lip quivered so vigorously that it was a wonder it didn't lift him into the air like a propeller. "Huh-who?"

This would have been fun for Carp to watch if it wasn't so damn sad. The other kid, the shorter and much thinner one, hadn't lasted long before Buddy ordered Carp to slit his throat. He just wouldn't stop that damn screaming. Buddy tried to tell him, tried warning him that if he didn't shut up what would happen, but the kid just couldn't control himself.

Now, *that* had been fun.

"Face and the kid," said Buddy, saliva shooting from his mouth onto the kid's face.

"Pr-Probably to his house…"

"Where is it?!!"

"Through the woods, but there's probably people there…"

"I don't give a good goddamn; I want to know where this house is and why the hell our man is there!"

"I don't know why, I just met him today…Joel knows him, knows him real good, kept calling him his friend…"

Buddy sighed, then screwed his eyes shut for a moment to think. While he zoned out, disappearing to that part of his mind that made the calls, drew up the blueprints, and relinquished strategy, he didn't dare let go of Paul's hair. Keeping a good handful of it intertwined in his fingers, he was able to hold the kid's head close and the knife closer to his throat. When he came back to reality, he said, "All right, here's how this is going to work, I have to get to this kid's house and take my friend. But I can't do that until I have taken a full assessment of their position. Do you understand this?"

"Yuh-yes…I can help you!"

Laughing, Buddy looked at Carp. "Do you believe this?"

Carp laughed.

"No, seriously, I can help you. I'll take you to the house, show it to you, then you can just let me go home. I'll go and you won't have to worry about anything from me, I swear!"

This time, Buddy didn't laugh. Carp admired that Buddy had the best bullshit detector there was, and he must have sensed the sincerity in the kid's offerings. "Good. We can use you. You do what I say and when I say it, you may live to go home and jack off on your favorite pillow after all." Nodding, snot and blood dripped from the kid's chin. "You've just become the ace up our sleeve boy, you should be proud."

The kid looked to be anything but proud.

CHAPTER TWENTY-TWO

(I)

The doorbell rang.

Sharon, having just come from the shower, was about to join Richard at the kitchen table. He was looking through Tonya's cell phone for more friends of hers to call. It looked as if he had three more to go, and if nothing was resolved with them, the police would be next.

He'd finally decided to search her room and had nearly cried when he found her cell phone sitting on her dresser with several missed calls, mostly from him, but some from Ray and girlfriends. If she had left of her own will, she would have taken the phone. Tonya never went anywhere without it.

Sharon stopped at the table on her way to the living room and looked at him, the kind of look that a wife gave a husband when she wanted him to be frank with her and avoid all the bullshit.

In her stare, she asked: *Did she come home?*

Although she spoke nothing, Richard had heard her and only shook his head. Her throat constricted and pulled. Call it a parent's instinct, call it what you want, but the fact of the matter was their baby girl, their only child was missing. Didn't matter if it had been two days, or two hours, she wasn't home, and no one seemed to know where she was.

The doorbell chimed again before Sharon could ask another question without speaking. She looked at the door, then back to her husband, feeling the same pang of dread, scared of who may be at the front door and the news they'd be bringing.

"Want me to get it?" he said.

Shaking her head, she answered, "No, I will."

"Maybe I should come with you."

"No, it's fine."

They shared another look before Sharon pried herself away. She left Richard and walked to the front door.

Without checking the peephole, she shot the door open, making the heavy kid standing outside jump. He gasped when he saw her; and she returned the expression, only louder. This kid was a mess. Bleeding and swollen, his hair were stiff and muddled with bruises dotting up his neck and face like purple freckles. A red mark on his cheek, the size and layout of a hand, seemed to shimmer in the sunlight.

"My God. Are you all right?"

"No, you've got to help me. I barely escaped them. They'll be here soon."

"Who?"

Upon hearing the commotion out front, Richard came to the living room. "Honey, what's wr …?" He stopped when he saw the kid and darted across the room to the front door. "Paul?"

Sharon put a hand on his shoulder. He flinched at her touch. "Who did this?"

"Two guys have Tonya. You've gotta help me!"

Their minds were speaking to each other again. He'd mentioned a name, their daughter, and someone's coming.

Get him inside. Phone the police right away.

"Get in," said Sharon. She stepped aside so Paul could stagger through.

The kid collapsed against Richard. Even though Richard was much taller and stronger, he struggled to hold the burden of Paul Lancaster.

Sharon raised a hand to her throat, reflexively tugging at her necklace. In her tank-top, the necklace hung above her breasts like a golden smile. "How long do you think it will be before they're here?"

She was shutting the door as she asked, but it stopped rigid when she heard, "Oh, I'd say a lot sooner than expected."

Sharon screamed, trying to push the door closed, but the owner of the voice was much too strong for her. He slammed the door back against her, knocking her sideways into the wall. She reflected off it and crashed onto the floor.

Then he calmly let himself, plus a guest, into their house.

Before Richard could act, he felt a clout of doughy skin hitting him hard in the crotch. His stomach went to his throat, making it difficult to breath. He couldn't counter the assault. The chubby kid had already crippled him with a low blow. As he fell to the floor, a man in a white t-shirt with spiky hair closed the door. The other man, dressed in green fatigues and a hat, was dropping shoulder bags on the floor. Whatever was inside rattled and clanked, shaking the floorboards when they landed. Richard could feel the vibrations against his cheek. He looked at Sharon hugging her knees to her chest. The skin across her chest, normally the tint of melted butter, showed the early signs of a straight-lined bruise from the door. She looked at him, again asking a question with her eyes.

Are you going to let them do this?

Then, as the man in the white T-shirt began putting on a clear plastic theatrical mask with makeup painted on the face, of the type you could get at any drug store during the Halloween season for a buck, Richard answered her back with *I have no choice.*

Sharon started to cry.

He heard an indistinct giggle coming from behind him. He rolled onto his back and was surprised to see that it was Paul who was laughing like a kid that caught sight of boobies for the first time. Richard glanced back at his wife, who was staring at the floor, her eyes bulging. He hoped she was slipping into some kind of catatonic state, one that would prevent her from being vigilant through what was to come.

The man hiked the mask up on his head, making it look like he had another face growing from the top of his skull. "This will all be over before you know it. We're just borrowing your place so we can scope out the house next door, all right? Play your cards right, and you won't even know we're here."

Confused, Richard shook his head. "Next door?"

"Yes," he answered bluntly. "You have a house next door and we're going to scope it out from here, incognito if you catch my drift. I'm Buddy and this is my comrade, Carp."

Nodding a greeting, Carp added, "Much obliged."

"We'll be out of your hair before you know it."

One thing Richard took pride in, but also considered to be a curse, was his ability to decipher bullshit from legit shit. And this man—Buddy—was handing him the dankest bullshit by the bucket full. He had no desire to let them live and why should he? After all, they'd seen their faces and he'd read enough crime novels to know that the witnesses were always the first to be dispatched.

No loose ends. My God, Sharon and I have become loose ends. What about Tonya? Was Paul telling some kind of truth about them having come in contact with Tonya?

He had to know. "What about my daughter?"

The one called Carp ignored him as he paced around the living room, observing their framed pictures, plaques, and diplomas.

Buddy peeked out the window, then back to Richard over his shoulder. "What about her?"

"What did you do to her?"

Buddy rolled his eyes up as if searching for the answer somewhere on the ceiling. It was apparent he had no idea what Richard was talking about. He only shrugged, and then looked back out the window.

"Wouldn't happen to be this sweet thing, would it?" Carp had taken the picture of Tonya in her track uniform from where it hung on the wall. His fingers were rubbing her glimmering bare legs through the glass.

"Yes, that's her," said Richard. "Have you seen her?"

"Oh yeah I've seen her. Sure have. I'd recognize a nice pair of legs like these anywhere. Check this out, Buddy." He tossed the frame across the room. Richard expected to see it crashing to the floor, but Buddy was quick with his reflexes and caught it.

His face stretched, nodding with approval as if finding something on a menu he liked to eat. "Yep, that's her all right."

"You know her?" demanded Richard.

"Where's my baby?" hollered Sharon.

Buddy tapped a finger to his tightened lips, motioning her to shush. She immediately obeyed. "Now, I don't how to break this to you, but we found her in the woods."

"You what?"

"We found her in the woods, just a bit ago, same time we found fatty over there."

On cue, Paul reentered the room with half of a cold hot dog in his hand; the rest was in his mouth as he chewed. No one had noticed he'd left. "She's dead." With his mouth full, it sounded more like: *"Shesh deadsh."*

Sharon shook her head, her reaction slowly building. The pain in Richard's groin went away completely, as if the ache in his heart sucked all feeling from everywhere else in his body.

"To put it bluntly," said Buddy, "yeah."

"No no no no no," shrieked Sharon, pounding her fists down on her knees, her head violently shaking back and forth like a broken sprinkler. Her yellow hair whipped and lashed ferociously enough to cut someone.

Buddy listened to this for about two seconds before ordering, "Carp, shut her up!!"

A wicked grin on his face, "Gladly," he walked over to her, playing with his belt.

Richard could see by the bulge in his crotch that whatever he planned to do to shut her up, he was looking forward to it.

"Stay away from her!" Richard shouted, jumping to his feet. Buddy stood by the fireplace but had already turned his back to them so he could throw his attention out the window. The fireplace pokers stood in a tin square right next to the hearth like soldiers in flank. Richard had two guns upstairs, but they might as well have been in Nebraska, and the pokers were much closer.

He went for them.

Carp grabbed Sharon by the shoulders and shook her, hard, then knelt down to her. "Guess what I like to use to gag little screamers like you?" His question seemed to suck all the answers, all the sounds right out of her mouth. She held her breath, terror frozen on her face.

Without turning around from the window, Buddy said, "Carp, don't tease the poor lady. Just get her out of here. But if I catch you doing something I don't approve of, you'll have to answer to me."

"You hear that, little lady? You're coming with me."

She shook her head, her eyes becoming wide enough to rip.

Paul had caught Richard sneaking to the fireplace, hunched over like a cartoon character trying to sneak through a haunted house. He'd gasped to warn the others but accidentally sucked what he was chewing on down his throat where it had lodged. At first, he couldn't make a sound, but he managed to swallow some chunks which opened his airway enough to wheeze. Like a breathless old man bobbing to his oxygen tank, Paul skulked to Richard who was quietly removing one of the pokers from the liner. By this time, Buddy had heard Paul's winded attempts at getting his attention and turned around just in time to see Richard assail.

The poker came down on the top of Paul's head and didn't stop carving a gully down his skull until it reached his brow with a splattering crunch. The look on his face was one without pain, save complete surprise. Paul's legs buckled, pulling him down to the floor. As he fell, Richard yanked the poker from his head. Stringy filaments of gore flapped from the tip. He turned around as Buddy lunged, sidestepping him, and swinging the poker like a ball bat. The iron rod whacked Buddy across the chest.

Doubling over, he hugged his chest and dropped to a knee.

Richard raised the poker to finish him, but heard Sharon shout a warning. He was too late to counter. Carp punched his knife's blade into Richard's throat up to the handle, twisted it in three circles, and wrenched it back out with a stream of red behind it. He was turned and checking on Buddy before Richard hit the floor.

"I'm fine, I'm fine! Finish off that bitch! Enough of these games!"

"You got it," said Carp. He glanced back at Richard grinning. This time it wasn't just wicked, it was maniacal. "You really fucked up, you know that? Killing the fat kid ruined our plans."

"Do it, Carp!" Buddy winced as if it hurt to shout, as if it hurt to breathe. His voice was muffled behind the plastic mask, but the point had been clear.

"Yes, sir." Carp stood up, unhooked his belt, and stalked toward Sharon who was already scooting away on her rump and hands like a crab.

The last thing Richard saw before his life drained out on his expensive floor was Carp ripping her tank top down the middle, cupping handfuls of her springy breasts.

Sharon looked at Richard, and in their silent communication begged with her eyes to be rescued, pleaded for him to get up and get this man away from her.

As Carp shredded into her shorts, ripping her panties like paper, Richard was too weak to reply.

(II)

Geoffrey Jones knew that he wasn't just fortunate, but he was perversely blessed with the luck of the devil, because they hadn't discovered him yet, but they might, so he needed to get the hell out of here, and promptly. *Quick and quiet.* A kid, presumably Haley's little-shit brother and someone else, was in the house. He was still hiding in Haley's room, checking his watch, and counting the minutes. They'd only been here for twenty, but it felt like hours. Whoever was with the kid had gotten hurt, and listening to what was being said, he'd gathered they'd come home to bandage him up. He wondered who was with him. *Haley?* Flurries that felt like a horde of spiders scurried up his back. His bowels felt like lead.

Maybe she left work early, surely she's heard about the bookstore by now.

He checked the time again, saw it was nearly four.

Damn wfe's probably been calling every damn body looking for me, probably called the police and filed a missing person's report.

Before squirting his orgasm in the pad of Haley's panties, he hadn't been thinking about these things, nothing had mattered to the perpetual Mr. Jones, but now that he'd spent his load, he was seeing everything with his *own* eyes again. He couldn't believe what had come over him, but he was glad that it had come out of him with his gluey explosion of white inside Haley's panties. He had planned to dump them back into her hamper when he was done, or smearing the glop all over her pillow, but now that he was thinking clearly again, he realized that wasn't a good idea. So he wadded them up into a ball, making sure the wet spot was on the inside, and stuffed them down his pocket. He might toss them out the window on his way home, but then again, he might just keep them as a souvenir.

I'd rather have Haley.

Damn it. He was here, in her room. He *could* have her.

Not yet ... not yet.

He slunk to the door. Thankfully, the floor was heavily carpeted, so his tread was silent, but there was still the fear his steps would make something in the house pop. Houses, no matter their age, were always settling and screeching and popping when someone walked. He prayed that wouldn't happen now.

As he stepped up to the door, he heard the kid tell the other he'd be right back and then listened to his retreating footsteps becoming faint as they went down the stairs to the house's main floor. *Fuck!* His plan had been to tiptoe downstairs and bolt through the door, but that had changed.

Haley's door hung half-open, giving him a good two feet to peer through. He lowered his head to the door and peeked around the side. To the right was the bathroom, its door opened. A mat of light shimmered across the hall from inside the bathroom. A dark shadow raked across. Someone was in there. He was stuck like a rat in a trap, and not one of those spring-levered traps either, the round ones with a welcoming entrance that lured them inside, then snapped shut and kept them there until they died.

"What now," he muttered.

The person in the bathroom stilled, blocking the light and giving him a view of their outline. Gargantuan. An ogre-like shape stood solid in the bathroom. He'd heard Geoff speak. Even though he had barely articulated his concern above a whisper, he'd heard him. *Shit, oh shit.* But instead of drawing back like he should, Geoffrey Jones only stood frozen at the door, unable to tear himself away so he could hide. Then he saw a thick arm, muscular and filthy reach out. A burlap sacked head poked out like a bear coming out of its cave after hibernation.

A scream snagged in his throat.

Backtracking, he stumbled over his feet and tripped over the bed, doing a reversed somersault onto the floor. The carpet may have been able to silence his footsteps, but it did nothing to mute his landing. In fact, it sounded like a mini avalanche in the still morning hours of winter. *Fuck me sideways and backwards,* he thought as he leaped to his feet.

Clunking footsteps resonated from the hall.

"What was that?" shouted the kid from downstairs.

He looked around the room, hoping to find either a place to hide or a way out. He had two options: the window, or the closet. He might as well just call the cops himself if he hid in there. The window was his only logical option, though it wasn't a rational one. He was two stories up and would have to jump. He might survive the fall, but he wouldn't escape it unscathed. A few broken bones, probably some busted ribs, might as well add even more casts to match the one on his hand that was already causing a deep itch he couldn't reach if he tried.

He ran to the window, flipped the hinge-lock to the right, and raised it with his left hand. It was still cramping from the masturbatory act he'd performed earlier. There was a screen, but it could be opened also by two latches on each side that needed to be pushed concurrently. How in the hell was he going to deal with this?

When the door opened and the hulk from the bathroom stepped in, he no longer worried about how to maneuver the screen. In fact, it became the farthest thing from his mind. "Oh my God!" he shouted, his legs folding under him.

The giant was fuming through the heavy burlap. He raised his hands like the Frankenstein monster and charged for him.

Geoff didn't stop to think about what he did next. Turning around, he stepped back and punted the screen, sending it soaring. He was already halfway through the window when he felt hands pawing and grabbing at him as he set his foot down on the landing outside. He launched his other foot through, knocking his balance off, and much like the screen; he teetered over the edge. He held his breath the entire way down. Cold instinct kept his arms windmilling out to his sides in search of something to grab.

They finally found it when he struck ground.

Joel charged into Haley's room, finding Pillowface looking through where the window had been, both hands resting on the sill. "What happened? Was someone here?"

He looked back at the boy and nodded. Then he stepped back and pointed. Joel rushed past him, leaning out and scanning the yard. The screen lay busted on the ground. He combed the yard from one side to the other but found no one. The grass was compressed where someone had landed, but there wasn't a body to match the impression.

What he didn't know was the man who'd thrown himself through the window had managed to slide under the bushes by the house, injured and frightened.

"There's no one there, now. What'd he look like?" Pillowface had no way of answering, and even though he could write it down, Joel didn't consider it for a moment's sake. All he worried about now was how they would fix the window before Haley came home.

(III)

The mask was different, but the body was the same size and shape it had always been. No one else had a build like *that*.

It was him, for sure.

Buddy had been watching through the binoculars, and now he scanned the bushes where the man was cowering. He lay on his stomach and appeared to be crying. Buddy laughed at the idiot but was also wondering just what the hell was going on in that house.

CHAPTER TWENTY-THREE

(I)

Joel handed the bandages, twine, and needle to Pillowface, then left him alone in the bathroom and went outside. He found the screen from Haley's window, took it to the woods, and chucked it. He hoped with Haley's window closed and the drapes lowered, she wouldn't notice the missing screen. She never opened the stupid window anyway, but if for some reason she did, he'd play dumb.

Haley, I have no idea. Why would I do something to the screen?

He took a seat on the steps and buried his face in his hands. A moment later he was crying, soon after that, he was sobbing hysterically.

It was bearing down on him—Pillowface and all the *quirks* associated with him were getting the best—scratch that—the worst of him. He didn't like the thoughts that had crossed his mind the past couple of days, or the things he'd been tempted to do.

But he *had* found a friend, hadn't he?

He guessed they were friends.

Why me?

Joel could wonder that a million times and never find the answer. He could ask Pillowface, and even if the man *could* talk, Joel doubted he even had an answer. He looked beyond the grove of trees at the edge of his yard and wondered about Ethan and Paul. He hoped they'd gone home and forgotten all of this had happened. He doubted it, though. He figured more trouble was bound to come once they woke up, if they hadn't already.

(II)

Jonesy still hadn't reported to work when Haley and Carlee got back to the law firm, and that meant there wasn't going to be much to do at the office. With that in mind, Haley packed up her things, and told Carlee she was going back to the bookstore to spend some time with Alan. She also invited her to dinner at her house tonight, figuring it would be something nice to remind Alan he still had friends that cared. She told the office manager to deduct the hours from her personal time since there were *personal* matters she needed to deal with. She'd spent the next couple of hours at the remnants of the bookstore, and now that the afternoon was in its later hours, and the firemen had all cleared out, she was finally on her way home.

Glancing at Alan in the passenger seat, she saw that he seemed to be genuinely smiling. He probably thought he'd never be able to again, but Haley had that effect on people, and could usually bring out a smile even in the worst of situations. Not always, of course, but it was something at which she was moderately good.

Thinking back to what had put Alan in her car, and why he was accompanying her to the house, she wanted to smile, but couldn't rightfully do so because he might take that as her being grateful the bookstore had burned down. She was by no means happy about that, but she couldn't lie and say she wasn't hopeful for what might come from it.

"… could always stay with me," she'd said.

"I couldn't do that," Alan had said, patting her leg. "It's a sweet gesture, but I couldn't."

"Why not?"

"I would be imposing on you, and I can probably just stay with my sister."

"You wouldn't be imposing on me at all. I promise. I don't want

232

you to feel *obligated* because of last night or anything, but I'll say it again—you're more than welcome to stay at my house for as long as you like."

He'd thought about it for another moment and said, "What about your brother?"

She hadn't considered Joel's feelings on the matter. In fact, she was so consumed with Alan that she'd almost forgotten he existed entirely. "I-I don't think he'd mind." It was a lie, but if Alan had caught wind of it, he hadn't let on.

"Well, maybe just tonight. I don't really feel up to explaining everything to my sister yet, anyway. Plus, I'd need somewhere to sit down and contact the insurance companies and all that ..." He groaned, then turned around on the bench, looking at what little remained of his home, and his store. The firefighters had finished hauling everything off, but an investigator stayed behind to sort through the ruins with a long stick, looking for clues as to what had caused this disaster in the first place. Then Alan faced Haley again. "You sure your brother wouldn't mind?"

"Positive." Joel would probably *more* than mind. He'd freak. Maybe even cause a scene, but she hoped not. "It would mean a lot to *me* if you did stay the night."

That was what had settled it.

She was so proud of herself that she only half noticed the car hidden amongst the trees on the shoulder of Marble Lane. It was vaguely familiar, but she hardly cared enough to acknowledge it. Before she had driven much further, the car was already forgotten.

(III)

With Pillowface stitched up again and back in the basement, Joel used this rare moment alone to sneak back to the woods. Ethan and Paul never came back to the house, and he wanted to find out if they were still out there. But if they weren't then where had they gone? That also worried him. He wouldn't be surprised if Ethan had gone straight home and told his parents about what had happened. On the other hand, there was Paul. He seriously doubted he would tell anyone, but since he hadn't come waddling to the house, sore and bruised, had him just as confused.

He grabbed the shovel leaning against the side of the house, planning to finish filling the grave properly while he was out there. The plate was caked with two days' worth of dried dirt from burials. As he entered the woods, he considered hiking back to Clay Ray and burying him too. If he went there first, he could take care of Tonya on the way back. *Forget it.* Going back wasn't worth the time it would take to do it. Clay Ray was dead. They'd dragged him off the trail and left him under the pine trees.

What if he's not dead? What if he's waiting for me somewhere in the woods?

Joel knew that he was still where they'd left him. The top layer of his head had been attached to Pillowface's chainsaw until he'd torn it from the grooves and chucked it into the creek.

Would probably take weeks for someone to find him. If ever.

Joel felt hollow inside for what he'd done to his friends, and how he'd left them behind. Summer was ruined, for himself, his friends, and probably would be soon for Haley, too. The last few weeks he'd looked forward to summer vacation as impatiently as he used to for Christmas when he was little.

He'd mapped out his whole break, which consisted of horror movies until his eyes burned. He'd bought three paperbacks and planned to have them read by August, and he was going to make a puppet of Herschel, a little alien he'd sketched out in Algebra class.

Keep it up like this, and I won't ever get to.

That depressed him. To think that he wouldn't be able to enjoy his time away from school because he was too busy hiding bodies that his new *friend* kept dispatching.

Maybe I should ask him to leave.

That was an appealing idea that lingered longer than he'd expected it to. How would Pillowface react if he was to suggest it? *It's not like I'm ending our friendship, just telling him he can't stay at the house. He can come and visit whenever he likes.* Would he want him to? *Why wouldn't I?* Walking up the steep incline, he began to seriously ponder the idea of telling Pillowface to leave.

But the more he thought about it, the more he didn't want to do it.

They liked each other, and it was kind of cool having someone like that on your side. Still, *something* had to be done. Couldn't keep going like this. Maybe he could train him or teach him to be less brutal. Show him that he doesn't always have to kill.

Joel stopped dead in his tracks. He'd arrived at the spot, but what he found was not what he had left. Paul was gone, and Ethan now lay on his stomach, face down in the dirt.

What happened here?

(IV)

Geoffrey Jones needed to make his move. He hurt all over, which was only being made worse by staying cooped up under the bushes. *Can't stay here forever.* But that was exactly what he wanted to do so he wouldn't have to go home and face the wife, the kids, or go to work and tell everyone a hoaxed tale about what happened to his hand, and on top of that, whatever extra bones he'd broken in the fall. The hospital was going to love him before it was over with, but his insurance company was going to be livid.

Can't wait to make that phone call.

He wiggled his toes first. There was no pain in doing that, so his feet seemed fine, along with his ankles and shins. However, when he tried bending his leg, scorching explosions popped in a chain reaction of liquid ice up into his thighs and hips. He opened his mouth to cry out, but only managed a gasping squeal. His left knee was swollen. There was no mistaking it from the bulge under his posh pants. The right seemed okay enough, even though it throbbed with a dull ache. He could handle that, but the left knee was out of business.

How am I going to do this without being seen?

He rolled over to his side and scoped what he could see of the backyard. There was a wooden fence running up the side of the house, but it was open in the back with an outlet to the woods. If he went the other way, he'd have to cross straight over the backyard. At the rate he'd be moving, he'd be spotted for sure. That left him only one choice. Since one leg was busted, he would need something to support him. The fence could do that, plus it may also offer support by means of shelter. From the neighbors, mostly, but he'd still be wide open to the Olsen house. He was willing to risk it to get to the woods. From there, he could walk at his leisure back to the car.

Geoff Jones stretched out an arm on the grass. It had recently been mowed and was hard to grab. A couple attempts later, he got a firm hold. He stuffed his tie in his mouth and bit down to keep from screaming as he dragged his aching stone of a body into the yard. A pain like burning grease singed his left knee. Grabbing, tugging, and pulling, he slid out from under the bush as if he were the survivor of a plane crash crawling to salvation. His brow was glossy with sweat. His hair, normally slicked back and shiny, hung over his forehead like Shemp from *The Three Stooges*.

Now he needed to stand up. It seemed impossible. He pushed his right knee forward, planting it into the ground. Cringing, he shuffled his left out to the side, keeping it fully extended. He shivered in pain, his teeth chattering. He hurt deep into his gut, churning his stomach. He sniffed, sucked down the phlegm and hocked it back up.

Then, with what gusto he had left, he forced himself to stand.

Surprisingly, it wasn't as difficult as he'd anticipated. He stood there a moment, composing himself, letting his breath settle. His vision was hazy. *I did it. I fucking did it.* After a few short moments, he stumbled to the fence, dragging his left leg behind him like a dead weight. He collapsed against it. The unforgiving wood punished his already sore hip, but he didn't care. He'd made it this far and wasn't about to let a little more pain stop him. Putting his arm without the cast above him, he grappled the top of the fence. Hanging on, he guided himself back through the yard, the fence as his stanchion. It was hard with his damaged leg pushed forward, but he made it work. Any moment he expected to see that man again, or Haley's brother, but no one came. As he loomed toward the end of the fence, he assumed he was home free.

Then a man dressed head to toe in green stepped out from the other side of the fence. His smile was triangle-shaped, and his eyes beamed menacingly, spiteful, and wicked.

"Going somewhere?" he asked.

Geoff's eyes did a quick scan of the man's body and locked on the knife clutched in his hand.

"I hope this isn't a bad time, but I'm going to have to ask you to stay."

Spitting while he spoke, Geoff Jones said, "Who are you?"

Unflinching, he raised a hand to his face and wiped the spittle away. "No time for that now." He sighed, putting the knife away. "Now, are you going to cooperate on your own or do I have to make you?"

He didn't answer. Instead, he hobbled closer to the man, allowing him to escort him where he was requested.

The man smiled, "Good. This way."

Once they were around the fence, Geoff Jones was pushed against it and held there. He could feel the knife's cool blade against his throat. "My name's Carp...this guy behind me is Buddy."

"Glad you could make it." The other voice was muffled, as if it was being spoken from behind something.

A different man, wearing a plastic mask and holding what looked to him like a squeaky camera, looked him over, surveying him like a section of land.

He released the trigger and the camera silenced. As he lowered the camera from his eye, he said "What's your business with that house?"

"What is this?" he asked through the sobs. He realized he was crying, and as sad as it was, he didn't feel the least bit ashamed by it. He'd had a horrible day. Of course, it would end like this.

The one called Buddy pushed his mask to the top of his head. "I'm asking the questions..."

"Oh God, just let me go...All I did was play with her panties!! That's all!"

Carp laughed, clapped his hands. "Man after my own heart."

"What do you want from me? Money? I can pay you, just please let me go."

Buddy rolled his eyes. "This will go a lot quicker if you'd just answer my questions."

"O-O ..." He took a couple deep breaths. "Okay ..."

"I take it you don't live there?"

"At Haley's house? No-no, I don't live there..."

"If you don't live there, why were you there?"

The man called Carp cleared his throat. "I believe it was to play with some panties..."

Geoff's tears turned to bawling, and he choked on his own slobber.

"Oh, sweet Jesus," said Buddy. "This is getting us nowhere. Carp, kill him."

Geoff Jones grabbed Buddy's arm. "No, no please. Don't kill me."

Jerking his arm away, he said, "Then stop your goddamn crying!"

"Yes...yessir."

Carp laughed. "He called you sir. That's hilarious."

"You could learn something from that," said Buddy.

"Please. I call you sir."

"Yeah, but he meant it." Buddy returned his wild-eyed stare to Geoff. "Do you know the people that live there?"

"Yes..."

"How many are there?"

Geoff took a deep breath, trying to calm down. "Just two. Haley works for me...and she has a little brother..."

"How old is Haley?"

"Early twenties. Twenty-two or twenty-three, I think."

"Okay. And the brother? He's what? Twelve?"

"I don't know ..." He felt as if he was about to burst into uncontrollable sobs again but fought with all he had to keep them back. Then he remembered the monster that had chased him out the window. "But ... there's ... I don't know how to describe him..."

Carp did it for him. "A huge beast of a man?"

"Exactly. Huge! His arms were like ..." He tried to show them the size by holding his hand several inches above his own bicep.

"He's the one we're looking for," said Buddy. He glanced at Carp, who shrugged, then looked back to Geoff. "Here's the deal I'm offering you, and I want you to seriously consider it before you answer."

"Anything."

Buddy sighed. "You haven't even heard my offer yet. I could have said I'm either going to have Carp here slit your throat or cut off your balls and you would have just agreed that either one would have been all right."

"Please don't ..."

Buddy put his hand on Geoff's lips, then pinched them together. "Don't say another fucking word until I finish saying what I have to say. Got me?"

"Better do what he says," added Carp.

Geoff couldn't talk with his lips smeared together, so he nodded.

Buddy kept his hold as he started to talk. "The kid snuck out to the woods about twenty minutes ago and I need you to go out there and bring him back to the house. If you do this for us, I will let you live. I know you won't say anything to anyone because you weren't supposed to be there either, but if I send you out there and you don't come back?"

He nodded towards Carp who raised his hand, showing Geoff that something was gripped between his fingers and thumb. It was square, made of leather, and looked very familiar.

My wallet?

It *was* his wallet. That Carp guy had picked his pocket.

Geoff's fear started to succumb to anger, but it quickly retreated when Carp removed his license from the pouch, then he almost cried again when Carp recited his address back to him. He was tempted to lie and say he'd moved and hadn't updated the card yet, but figured it wasn't worth it.

Buddy continued. "So if you don't come back on your own and decide to make a break for your house, we'll be there shortly after and slaughter everyone inside and if you think you can pack them up and go hide for a while, we'll just make ourselves comfortable until you get back."

With a grimace, Buddy removed his hand and wiped his slobber-covered fingers on Geoff's expensive jacket.

"I-I-I don't know if I *can* get the kid. My knee …"

"You better think of a way. Because we'll kill you right here."

"The neighbors would see."

Carp laughed, then pointed at the house behind them. "Who them? We already took care of them. They won't see nothing."

He was stuck going after this damn kid. "Why do you want me to go get him? Can't one of you?"

Buddy grabbed the lapels of Geoff's jacket and jerked him close. "Do you need an explanation other than we'll fucking kill you if you don't?"

Carp pointed his knife at Geoff. "Just let me kill him."

"No," said Buddy. "I guess it's fair that he knows why. I mean, we're asking him to do a lot but not saying why."

"I liked your first reason," said Carp.

"Basically, Carp and I have to handle what's going on *in* Haley's house, and we don't need the kid sneaking back without us realizing it. What would happen if he were to come home and stumble upon something? Now, him being twelve or whatever fucking age he is, I doubt he'd try to be a hero, but I *bet* he'd run off to one of these other houses and get one of them to call the police. It's true that we could go from house to house and kill everyone living in them …"

"We have before," added Carp.

"But we just don't have the *time* to do that. We really need to get moving."

Geoff felt as if he might pass out. His legs felt as flimsy as dental floss.

"Do you think you could help us out by getting the kid?"

Geoff slowly nodded.

"That's great to know," said Buddy.

"What do I do when I get him back here?"

"Just get him inside, then you can go, and we'll handle the rest."

(V)

Pillowface used liquid weld to fuse the saw blade to the back support on the weight belt. He held it there, giving it time to dry. While he waited, he sat on the floor in the basement, enjoying his moment alone. Constructing odd weapons such as this had become as therapeutic to him as building birdhouses might to a normal person. It relaxed him, helped take his mind off current frustrations. And it was very, very fun.

He was allowing himself to slip into one of those rare moments of serenity when he thought he heard the approach of a car. A car that sounded like Haley's, and not only that, she was also about an hour early and Joel hadn't gotten back yet.

Nervousness fizzed in his stomach. He set down the weight belt and got to his feet. Listening. If it was Haley, he might get to sneak back upstairs and watch her again.

With Joel not being back from the woods, he just might attempt more. Not much, just a swipe of his finger on her skin. He imagined it would feel like fine silk.

And maybe ... he could do even more.

CHAPTER TWENTY-FOUR

(I)

Haley pulled into the garage and killed the engine. Even from just sitting in her car, she could feel the house's silence, and not the peaceful kind that she enjoyed. Morgue silence. She never wanted to experience that awful hush again like she had when she went down into the morgue to identify her father. It was like a frozen stillness, one that wasn't welcomed.

The garage door hit the concrete, rattling; its sudden noise startled her.

Alan slowly exhaled from the passenger seat. They looked at each other. Alan seemed anxious, worried.

"Nervous?" she said.

"Yeah, actually. I don't want your brother to hate me."

"Why would he hate you? He's always liked you."

"That was when I was getting scary books for him at the store. Now, I'm in his house, on his turf."

Haley laughed. "His turf? Are you two in rival gangs?"

"Might be after he finds out I'm crashing on his couch."

Hardly his couch. My bed.

"It'll be fine."

"Famous last words."

(II)

"This is a *really* nice place you got here," said Alan, looking around, impressed.

Blushing, Haley smiled. "Thanks, my parents thought so, too."

"Did you grow up here?"

"For the most part. I was really young when we moved here, like four or something. But Joel did." She pursed her bottom lip. "Speaking of, where is he? I figured he'd be sprawled out on the couch watching *Georgia Hammer Massacre* or something."

They walked into the living room. The TV was on, but no one was there to watch it. Haley was really confused, now.

Alan pointed at the TV, "Someone's been watching."

"Yeah …" She glanced up to the ceiling. "Joel? You up there?" They waited a moment in silence. There was an audible clucking in Haley's throat as she listened for a response that never came. "I guess he's not here."

Alan nodded. They stared at each other another moment before simultaneously moving toward each other and embracing. Their lips pressed together, tongues flapping and sliding across the tender, plushy mounds.

"This time," Haley said between their kisses, "let's go to my bed."

"Sounds great…"

They continued to kiss as Haley walked backwards, guiding him toward the stairs. She pulled back, and anxiously climbed them, pulling him along by his hand. He followed her, just as eager.

At the top of the stairs, they embraced again, their mouths finding each other, their tongues darting through their lips as they smacked with heavy breaths. The sound was thunderous in the quiet hall, reverberating off the walls around them.

"Where's your room?" he managed to ask.

Haley pulled away from him, bending at the waist and walking backwards. She motioned for him to follow her. "Right this way…"

Alan smiled. Haley took a moment to treasure it. She hadn't seen him so happy all day. Her rump bumped against her door and flung it open. She kept moving into her room.

Alan jogged to catch up.

And without slowing down, he lifted her off the floor and held her up as his lips folded on her neck. She felt his teeth lightly nibbling. A current sizzled through her body. Putting her feet back on the floor, Alan moved his lips back to hers. As they kissed, Haley found his pants, unbuttoned them, and began pushing them down his legs while Alan worked at kicking off his shoes. They seemed to be giving him some trouble, but eventually he conquered them.

Haley's shoes were much easier and all she had to do was step out of them. She felt Alan's hands roaming her back, working their way down to her buttocks. When they reached the top of her pants, his fingers slid under them and found her panties.

They froze.

"Wha ...?" Alan pulled his head back, a confused look on his face. Obviously, he'd felt something he wasn't intending to find.

At first, Haley didn't understand what the problem was, but then she remembered her choice of panties for the day. She felt the heat of a blush warming her cheeks. "Whoops. I forgot I put on big girl panties. Didn't feel like being pretty today."

Alan shook his head. "Well, you failed."

She sucked in her bottom lip, flushing even darker as he leaned forward. They began kissing again. Alan's hands pulled out of her pants, found the waistline, then proceeded to slide them and her panties down in one swoop. She assisted him. Alan finished the work on his own pants, getting them to the floor, and kicked them out of the way. At the front of his boxers was a tent from his jutting erection.

Haley grabbed the bottom of her shirt and pulled it off, then reached behind her back, finding the clasps of her bra. She had it off and with her other discarded clothing before a full second had passed.

Then she pressed her naked body against Alan, writhing against him. She felt the hardness between his legs poking against her belly. Haley tried to help him down to her bed, but he quickly twirled her around, and helped her instead. She sat down on the edge, then pushed with her hands, wiggling her way backward. Before she'd gotten too far, Alan grabbed her by the ankles and scooted her back down to the bed's edge.

She watched him, nervous and anxious, while he pulled his shirt over his head. She took her time studying his chest, his lined abdomen. But it dropped out of her view when he got on his knees.

Her breathing intensified as he slid his arms under her thighs and angled her toward him. His mouth was only inches from her. She could feel the pant of his breath puffing against her moist, swollen lips. She knew what he was about to do and wanted him to so badly that she began to tremor.

Finally, he gave her what she wanted, snuggling his face between her thighs. Before he'd even introduced his tongue, she was moaning. When she felt the narrow tip flicking her, she screamed. Her release was already imminent, but she fought it, not wanting to give in just yet.

And thankfully, Alan didn't spend much more time down there or she would have. He stood up, using his thumbs to push his boxers down his legs. When she caught site of his penis, she gasped as loudly as she had the night before. Although she remembered its size, it still shocked her to see it again.

He approached her, putting his hands on each side of her. Now she could wiggle backwards to her pillows, and she did so with Alan crawling above her, matching each move. When they were at the top of the bed, he planted his elbows on each side of her head, angled his hips, and slowly eased himself inside of her.

Tears trickled down her eyes as he went all the way in, expanding her, making room for himself. He'd been invited, so it wasn't hard for her to oblige his arrival. He lowered his head as she leaned hers up and connected their lips once again. As they kissed with an intense hunger for one another, he began to thrust, pounding her deep, and Haley loved every second of it.

"When I…Well…" He stopped, taking a moment before trying again. "Where do you want me to…you know…"

She understood right away what he was asking. "I'm on the pill," she whispered, her voice already blown from the screams.

With her permission to just let himself go, he began to pump faster, his need to reach orgasm consuming him. She began thrusting with him, matching his tempo, so that each time he delved, she was coming up to accept him.

A few moments later, Alan began to tense up, his thrusts becoming heavy jabs, then she felt him spurting inside of her, filling her up with his warmth. It triggered her own release, shaking her all over as he drained himself dry.

When they were both spent, Alan collapsed on top of her.

She wrapped her arms around his neck, and her legs around his hips, holding him there so he couldn't pull out.

(III)

Ethan was sprawled face down in the dirt and didn't look to be breathing. Joel stood frozen, holding his own breath, trying to see if Ethan's back was rising and falling.

It wasn't.

He's dead.

Ethan's skin, usually a dusky shade, was abnormally pasty, the color of school glue with a hint of indigo. The ground around his body was sodden. Not quite muddy, but wet and dark. A murky liquid had spilled into the dirt.

Joel walked slow and stilted to the opening, stopping just shy of Ethan's head. The mushy effect on the ground was caused by a dark liquid, all right. *Blood.* A slow pool had spread from under Ethan's chin. Joel took in a shaky breath. His bowels felt like hollow ice. Slowly, he squatted next to his friend. He set the shovel down, avoiding the soppy spot. Reaching out, his hands hovered just above Ethan's shoulders.

The woods held its breath in anticipation. Finally, Joel forced himself to grab Ethan's shoulders. He felt a chilliness seeping through his friend's shirt. Rolling him over, he was greeted with a blank stare from vacant eyes. Ethan's mouth was stationed in a sideways smirk. There was a deep trench in the center of his throat. He saw tendons, brown and red and gooey. Joel looked away and heaved. Other than phlegm, nothing spewed out, but that didn't stop his stomach from trying. After four attempts, it finally gave up. His eyes stung with hot tears. Loud shrieks and clamors hammered his ears. As it all began to fade back to normal, the habitat of the woods slowly came to life again. *Just a dead boy*, they seemed to be saying and going about their business.

Giving his head some time to clear, Joel began wondering things. Such as: *Who did this? When did it happen? Where's Paul?* That seemed to be the logical direction he should take this. He could sit here feeling guilt and sorrow all day, but it'd get him nowhere. So he stood up. The trees were bending and flexing this way and that. He could feel cold runnels of sweat on his searing skin. He'd felt like this before when he'd had the flu, but this was something totally different. This was his body trying to succumb to shock, and his mind struggling to resist it.

He did a quick and sloppy search of the nearby area. When he didn't find Paul anywhere, he came back and flopped down on his butt. He took slow, deep breaths and rested his head against a tree. It was rough against the back of his skull. He could smell the souring stench of rot intensifying around him but didn't care. Was he getting used to those smells?

Is this where I should give up and call the police? Or Haley?

In a way, Joel found it odd that he wasn't reacting more harshly to the sight of his friend's demise. It was as if over the past couple of days, he'd become desensitized to dead bodies and bloodshed. Sure, he felt bad, but he wasn't as deeply affected as he should have been. He also knew that he wouldn't call the police or let Haley know what was going on. This was his mess. He'd deal with it.

He pushed himself up, walked back to where he'd left the shovel, and grabbed it. His hand was sweaty, making the top of the handle slippery and moist. He looked down in the hole. Tonya looked as if she was simply lying in a bath of dirt. Ants had already made their way up her thighs, burrowing themselves into her groin. Grimacing, he turned away, but was met by Ethan. The sight there wasn't any better. He groaned, shook his head. Was he really going to do this?

Yes.

Was he really going to add his best friend to the body pit? *Yes, again.* Was he going to cover it up and go about as if nothing had happened? *Yes, times three.* He ran a hand through his dripping hair and wiped the sweat on his shirt sleeve.

His mind drifted again to thoughts of who could have done this. *Pillowface? No way. He's been at the house with me. Could he have snuck back?* Joel tried imagining that in his head but couldn't. There was no way he could have gotten back here and back to the house without Joel noticing him being gone.

Paul?

His mind absorbed that one for a moment. It seemed highly doubtful, but at the same time, utterly possible. Paul had been acting weird. *And the way he seemed to be enjoying what was happening.* Joel couldn't hold that against him, though, because he'd felt the same joy deep down as well. *Yeah, but I wasn't giddy and excited. Paul looked as if he wanted to do it again.* Is that what happened? Did Paul kill Ethan? Was he coming after Joel next? *No way. And even if he tried, he'd have to get through Pillowface, first. Like to see him try and do that.*

Then he remembered Pillowface wasn't out here. Joel was alone in the woods, so if Paul came at him now, he'd have to fight him solo. After a quick scan around, he convinced himself that Paul wasn't lurking nearby and got to work.

He pressed the shovel against Ethan and gently nudged him. His body seemed happy where it was and didn't move. Joel pushed down, digging the shovel under Ethan's back. Then, poking his tongue through the side of his lips, he placed his foot on the spade, heaving with everything he had. Ethan rolled into the hole, settling on top of Tonya. His waist nestled between her legs, his face down in the dirt. It looked as if Joel had wandered upon them doing something dirty in the woods.

He stood up straight with an ache in his lower back. He rubbed the tender spot. It was *really* sore. *Did I pull something?* That was all he needed on top of everything else. He imagined his back going out, and being unable to walk back to the house, and having to lie with the dead bodies until dark. What if that happened and Haley came looking for him? She'd not only find him but would also uncover all of his secrets.

A twig snapped off in the distance. Then another. Joel whipped his head around, prepared to catch Paul sneaking up on him with his face twisted into a demented leer, but found no one. Just trees and plenty of them. *Paul's not going to ambush me. My back isn't going to give out. Get over all that and get this shit done.*

Ignoring the sounds of the woods, he went back to work.

(IV)

eoffrey Jones watched the kid pitch a body into a hole and using the head of a shovel to do it. Then he began scraping dirt that had gathered around the edges on top of it to cover it up. *That must be Haley's brother.* He studied the kid, his features, and determined that he was definitely her brother. They had the same jaw line and blue eyes. His hair was a little darker though, but there was no mistaking that the two were siblings.

Whatever the kid was mixed up in, he seriously doubted Haley knew about it. Here he was *burying* a body with a monster man back at the house. At least, he hoped he was back at the house. He did a quick scan of the woods and decided that he was. And for whatever reason, this same kid had two other sickos wanting to kill him.

Do they want to kill Haley?

Of course they did. They would probably kill her soon after he delivered the kid. It was the kid they really wanted, why would they hurt Haley? *Maybe I can use the kid as a negotiation, offer them a trade.* Or he could just ask them to let him take Haley. If they did, he knew the perfect place to take her.

The cabin.

He owned a cabin on the other side of the mountain in Bear Hill. It was secluded, and his bitch of a wife never went out there. He could take Haley there, then take a week off work, but tell the wife he was going out of town and spend seven days and nights doing whatever he wanted to Haley.

But even with a cast on his leg? Surely he would get a cast put on his leg once he went to the hospital. It must be broken. There was no way it wasn't.

He'd make it work one way or another.

The kid began scraping loose dirt that was around the hole into it.

Geoff checked his watch and cringed. It was nearing six. He wouldn't be surprised if his wife had the police out looking for him.

How should he approach the kid? Not only would it be odd seeing a man dressed as he was in the woods, he wasn't so sure the kid hadn't spotted him leaping through Haley's window.

Geoff watched a few more moments. The kid stopped working, leaned the shovel against a tree, and sat down on the ground across from it. He was probably taking a break, and this gave him the perfect opening to make his move.

(V)

Joel didn't know if it was the overindulgence of concealing bodies, or the lack of sleep, but he was drained. Not just drained, but sick. Exhausted. For the first time, he truly knew how it felt to be so tired. He felt guilty for the hard times he used to give his Dad for not wanting to do something Joel wanted because he was *tired*. He used to get so furious with his father. But he didn't understand. How different would things have been if he had understood?

More thoughts he didn't need to dwell on right now; more thoughts that would just bring him down farther than he already was. He needed to finish...

Don't want to...

He leaned his head against the tree. It felt good letting it take the burden of holding up his head away from his neck. He could already feel his eyes wanting to shut, and he didn't mind letting them. With his eyes closed, his body suddenly felt weightless. A tingling current started in his toes and moved up to his thighs. All over he felt relaxed. He promised he wouldn't fall asleep, swore to it, but could already sense the oncoming images of a dream.

Can't be asleep. I'm just thinking. Was he? Or was it a dream? It felt as if he were above himself, looking down at a sleeping soon to be thirteen-year-old boy that had suffered through more in less than a year than most would in several.

He was thinking about all these things when he heard the sudden exodus of a flock of crows. *A murder of crows.* He'd always liked that expression. He listened to their cawing and shrieking as they lifted into the air. Their wings flapping like a raised flag in the wind.

He opened his eyes. And saw why they'd taken flight.

A man in a suit was creeping amongst the trees. His pointed face was aimed at Joel, and his narrowed eyes focused intently on him. The growing fear pushed away his drowsiness. He tried to scoot back, but the tree kept him there. Not only did the man not look friendly, but he was also walking with a severe limp. The kind of injury falling from a second story window could make. He checked his hands and didn't find a weapon, but not seeing one didn't make him feel any better.

"You're Joel, right? Joel with a J?"

He knew his name. How in the hell did he know that? But instead of asking those questions, Joel only nodded.

An eerie smile stretched across the man's face. "Thought so. I'm Geoffrey Jones. With a G."

Joel knew he should recognize that name, but his brain seemed to be on pause.

Geoffrey with a G Jones rounded the trees to Joel's side, bypassing the incline so he could keep his eyes locked on him. "Your sister works for me."

That was why he should know him. Because he *did* know him. He'd met him a few times and had always thought of him as a very creepy guy. Not the fun kind of creepy he liked to watch in movies, but the bad kind. The *real* kind. Joel's eyes focused on his torn clothes, and his shamble of a walk.

Why is he out here in the woods?

Geoffrey with a G looked down at his legs, then back at Joel as if he'd forgotten about the limp, but when he raised his head, a shifty smile was arching his lips. "Wondering why I have this limp?"

Joel shook his head. He wasn't wondering because he already knew why. He was the person inside Haley's room, the one who'd broken the screen.

"You seem like a smart kid. You've probably got it all figured out."

"What do you want with me?"

The man named Geoffrey laughed, his nose sputtering with each giggle. "You have to come with me."

Joel shook his head.

"It's not your choice to make," he told Joel. "It's not my choice, either. Unfortunately."

"Get away from me."

"People will die."

Joel's throat tightened. "What do you mean? Who will die?"

"Me for one. And Haley."

Joel was confused. How did he know all this? "I don't ..." Joel didn't know what to say.

"Two men snagged me and said if I didn't bring you back to the house, they would kill me. And Haley too."

"What two men?"

"How the hell should I know? Two men said they were looking for the big guy."

"Pillowface?"

"Pillow ...?" He looked as if he wanted to laugh. "Whatever his name is. The two that told me to come get you were going to your house, and they wanted me to take you there."

Joel wasn't going anywhere with him.

"Now come on. Let's go."

"No."

He leaned back as if Joel's answer had taken a swing at him. "What did you say?"

"*No.*"

He checked his pants again, then nodded. He pointed at his knee. "It's this, isn't it? You won't come back with me because of my limp. So you probably know I was in Haley's room, don't you?"

Joel didn't respond.

"You also probably know I have her panties in my pocket. Don't you?"

"What?"

"See?" He crammed his hand into his pocket and tugged out a damp pair of black panties. "These were between your sister's legs, hugging her ..."

Joel felt sick. "Did you do anything to Haley?"

"I wish." He shook his head as if it were a shame, took a savoring breath, and exhaled. Then he stuffed the panties back into his pocket. "Haley. Probably the most gorgeous thing I have ever seen in this shitball of a world. But of course, you already know that, huh?" Now he stood at Joel's feet. "She has my mind so messed up right now..." He laughed a nervous, maniacal laugh. "Bet you've spied on her lying out in the sun, or in the shower a time or two, haven't you?"

Remembering the incident from this morning, Joel winced, shook his head.

"Come on. You can tell me. I'll keep quiet about it. In fact, I'll let you in on a little secret of my own. I used to peek on my own sister when she showered. But hell, that was different. She knew I was doing it and didn't mind. There would be times when she'd really put on a show for me." He laughed. "She was a looker too, but nothing like Haley. I think I might be in love." He took a moment to breathe before continuing. "But they'll kill her if I don't take you back to the house. I don't give a shit what they do to you, but Haley can't die until I've at least fucked her."

Joel was shaking, and not entirely from fear. The more Geoffrey Jones talked, the more he found himself wishing he had something to stab him with. This asshole was talking about his *sister* in a way Joel didn't approve of. No one got that benefit, including Ethan and Paul. The few times they'd spoken of her derogatively, they'd paid for it with either a punch to the face or gut. Don't cross that line if you know what's good for you. Obviously, this piece of trash hadn't learned what was good for him, yet. Joel planned to teach him.

With the toe of his mud-caked leather shoe, he nudged the bottom of Joel's shoe. "What's the matter? Did I say something to upset you?" He laughed, again, but the unnatural grin he wore looked too fake and sick to be real. "I bet you've even jerked off to her before, haven't you?"

Joel's hands clenched to fists. Geoffrey with a G noticed.

"Uh-oh. Looks like you're aiming to use those little dick swatters as weapons." His grin diminished. "Don't even try it. Just because I'm wearing a suit doesn't mean I can't kick the shit out of a spoiled brat like you. I wouldn't even break a sweat."

Joel knew just by looking at him he was lying about not breaking a sweat, because he was drenched in a layer so thick it looked like his skin was secreting it. He also knew he didn't stand a chance against fighting this guy.

No way in hell.

But knowing that still wasn't going to stop him from trying.

Geoffrey with a G's foot nudge turned into a kick the second time. "Now get up so we can get this over with."

Nodding, Joel shifted his weight against the tree and pushed himself up with his feet. *How am I going to do this?* The man wasn't big, or ripped, but he was stronger, which was a lot more than Joel surely had going for him.

Joel's intentions must have been written across his face.

"You want to hit me?"

Hesitating a moment, Joel shook his head.

"Didn't think so. It's time to go, so come on."

Joel tried shoving his unwilling body into motion, but it just wouldn't cooperate. *Work legs, damn it, move!* They wouldn't listen, nor would his feet. Apparently, they were just happy where they were.

"All right, you're pissing me off."

"F-F-Fuck you." In his mind, Joel pictured it would have sounded threatening. It was nothing close. His voice had betrayed him. He shut his eyes and sighed.

Geoffrey Jones tilted back his head and really cut a laugh. When he looked back at Joel, he was wiping tears from his eyes and holding his side. Joel had never made anyone laugh so hard before, and this time he hadn't tried. "Good one. Oh shit. You're a pretty witty kid. Know that?" He sniggered some more.

Joel used this moment to survey his situation. The temptation to attack the man was unbearable. He *must* try for it. He saw the shovel still leaning against the tree where he'd left it. If he was going to do any kind of damage, he would have to use it. How long would it take to grab the shovel, raise it, and bring it down on his skull? Would he be quick enough before Geoffrey noticed it was coming?

Only one way to find out.

He sprung for it, passing Geoffrey Jones as he leapt through the air. He landed inches from the shovel, rolled, and snatched it up. The handle nearly slid through his sweaty hands.

The humor drained from Geoffrey Jones's face.

Joel acted quickly, much quicker than he thought he could.

He brought the shovel up and down with a ferocious speed unparalleled for most twelve-year-olds.

Maybe if he'd swung a second sooner ...

Geoffrey Jones caught the shovel under its base, stopping the plunge in mid-swing. "You dirty little shit," he said between gritted teeth.

He jerked the shovel in his direction, bringing Joel with it. Then pushed the handle back, cracking the wooden staff across Joel's forehead. Everything went black for a moment, then turned fuzzy. Joel lost all his momentum and sagged to his knees. He felt his stomach turning.

"Trying to get me by surprise?" He seemed appalled by such an act.

Joel coughed, gagged. He'd failed. He felt pathetic.

Geoffrey Jones shook his head. "I should bust your fucking skull for what you just did." He slammed the metal end of the shovel into the ground. It stuck, protruding like a shaft sowed there. "I think I'll just kick the shit out of you instead. Then drag you back to the damn house by your little pecker."

Joel knew it would hurt and braced himself. He was right. The first kick caught him in the chest, knocking the wind out of him. He fell on his back, an acorn or rock digging into his spine.

His muscles and lungs acted confused over what to do. Spasms raked his body while his lungs desperately tried to inhale. It hurt to do either. He swore his chest had caved in. He screamed with the second kick on his side. It felt that whatever organ was in there had not just popped but exploded.

He was crying now. Bawling.

Geoffrey Jones struggled to stand upright on his bad knee. "Not such a tough little shit now, are you? Want to hit me with that shovel still?" Joel's answer was a convulsion of sobs. This seemed to please him. "Didn't think so. But you know what? I'm not done proving my point. I can hold a grudge for a long fucking time!" Laughing, he leaned over and grabbed Joel under the arms like an infant, then hoisted him up, putting him in some kind of bear hug.

Now, Joel really couldn't breathe. His lungs were pleading, but Joel was helpless to give them what they wanted. The pressure was intense, paralyzing. He knew he could probably kick him, but doubted it would do much other than angering him even more.

I'm going to die…

Joel was slipping into a void, a sort of tranquil state where the pain wasn't so bad. And he knew Geoffrey Jones wasn't going to stop until he realized the error of his ways *after* he'd killed him. He needed to fight. By some means, whatever he could muster, he *had* to fight.

He began to squirm.

"Be still. If you'd just calm down we can get moving and all this will be over. If you keep moving it's just going to hurt that much worse until you finally pass out."

Or until he died. Joel wondered how long it would be before his back snapped. Either asphyxiation or a broken spine would get him out of this situation. But his vote lay in the third choice, the one where he came out unscathed.

Squirming like the wind!

Wriggling, twisting like a worm about to be hooked, he managed to free his right arm. This allowed Geoffrey Jones to compress even harder. Like a boa constrictor, he tightened, slowly applying more strain. Joel's arm was free, but he couldn't do a damn thing with it. He was hurting too bad to think straight. His arm just drooped about like a loose piece of grass.

"You ready to give up?" asked Geoffrey with G.

Joel stopped struggling.

Geoffrey Jones was calmer, "That's a good boy. Now when we get back to the house, I want you to convince those guys that I should take Haley. Because I'm not going to give you to them until they agree. If I don't hurry up and do something about this infatuation for her, there's no telling what I'll do next. I mean, I've broken into her room, jacked off in her panties, burned down a bookstore, killed her dog, and now I'm get between her legs."

Killed Rusky?

Joel began to bubble inside.

"Maybe …yeah …maybe your death will bring us closer together."

Joel's arm suddenly felt rejuvenated. On its own whim, it shot his hand up, thumb extended, and jabbed into Geoffrey Jones' left eye. He pushed inward with ease. Inside the socket was warm and squishy like poking a finger into a fresh jelly donut.

Geoffrey trembled as Joel pushed his thumb in as far as it would go. Finally, he was dropped. His thumb ripped out of the socket with a slippery pop. On the ground, he heaved for air that wouldn't come fast enough.

Geoffrey hunched over, cupping a hand over his eye. Blood and another mixture like white paint leaked through the cracks between his fingers.

"My *eye!*" He pulled his hand away. Where his eye had been a few moments ago was now a deep cavity. The left side of his face was coated in blood. He looked like a distraught Viking Warrior. He reared back his head and howled like one.

Joel couldn't relish the victory a moment longer. He crawled over to the shovel, curving his hands around the wooden pole, and using it as leverage, hauled himself up. He was woozy, but he didn't have the time to find his balance.

"You little bastard! I'm going to tear you apart!"

Joel stood to the side as if stepping up to the mound on a baseball diamond. The one sport he had ever been good at was baseball. He'd played a few years for his dad's team when he was younger. He hiked the shovel over his shoulder like a bat and swung the way the pros did it.

Dad would have been proud.

The metal base cuffed Geoffrey with a G's face with a loud twang. The drive lifted him in the air, launching him a few feet away. He landed on his back and didn't move a twitch.

Motionless.

Joel hoped he was dead. Walking around the side of Geoffrey with a G's body, he kept the shovel ready, expecting any moment for a hand to snatch at his ankle.

One never did.

But that didn't stop Joel from whacking him again for good measure.

And again.

Another time.

One more, gone.

CHAPTER TWENTY-FIVE

(I)

Alan rolled over. Haley clenched her legs tighter to keep him inside of her.

"Where do you think you're going, mister?"

Alan smiled. "Felt like I was crushing you."

"Not at all…" She rubbed her hand through his hair, then watched it droop right back into his eyes. "Feel better?"

He laughed softly. "A lot."

"I'm glad I could help."

"You're amazing," he said. "Did you know that?"

"Amazing?" She pretended to mull over it. "I assumed outstanding, but amazing? Wow."

"Did I say amazing?"

"You can't take it back. You said it, no take backs."

He put his fingers against her side and tickled. She squirmed and squealed.

"Stop," she shrieked behind her laughs.

He did. "Sorry, just couldn't resist." He kissed her on the forehead.

Haley didn't want this moment to end, just the two of them, caressing each other as if nothing else mattered. It was a false realism, but one that she enjoyed. She sat her head up and looked toward her

door that they'd left wide open while exploring each other. A chill of
fear snagged her belly. "I wonder if Joel came home while we were …"

Alan's eyes widened. "Do you think so?"

"Well…I didn't hear him, but that doesn't mean anything…"

"Yeah, we were being a little too loud to notice."

Her skin went prickly. "A *little* loud?"

"Well, *I* was being a little loud, but you?" He shook his head.

"Stop it," she said, laughing. "You're so mean to me."

"Want me to make it up to you?"

"You better."

He put his hand on the side of her cheek and held it there. Then he
gently kissed her. It developed into heavy smacks, but Alan pulled away
before it went much farther.

"Why'd you stop?"

"Sorry," he said. "But I really have to use the bathroom, and now
that you've mentioned the possibility of Joel having come home, I feel
too weird about lying naked on top of your bed with the door open."

She glanced at the doorway again. "Yeah, I see your point. Close it
on your way back in?"

"Absolutely."

He sat up, shifted his hips, and pulled out. Haley already missed
him being there. "Hurry back."

Smiling, he sat at the edge of the bed, putting on his boxers. "I
would pee out the window so I wouldn't have to leave if I knew you
wouldn't think differently of me in the morning."

Haley laughed. "If you peed on *me* then we might have a problem."

"Well…the temptation would be there…"

She laughed again. Alan had always had a profound sense of humor.
She was glad it was back, and he'd been able to abandon his sadness
with the rubble of the store.

*It's like they say—sometimes in tragedy, happiness is always there
waiting to be found, again.* She wasn't exactly sure if anyone had ever
said that before, but they should. It was a good line.

Pulling his shirt on, Alan walked to the doorway. He peeked his
head out. Then he glanced back at Haley. "I don't see anything."

"Hurry up." She bounced on the bed anxiously.

"I will!" He stepped into the hall, pulling the door shut behind him.

Haley laid her head back on the pillow. She was tempted to get under the blankets but decided not to. They'd just get in the way when he came back.

How long had it been since she'd had sex? Not counting last night, of course. She thought about it. *Maybe a month after the funeral...* Yes, that was it. She and Carlee had gone out with strict intentions of picking up a guy for each of them, taking them back to Carlee's apartment, and screwing them. They'd succeeded. Carlee took her choice to her bedroom, and Haley accompanied hers in the guest room.

The guy, Eric or Mike, or whatever, was a decent enough looking guy, but awkward and quick on the release in the sack. She could tell when they had finished that he was embarrassed about his uninspiring performance by how he'd acted so over-sexual afterward. She was polite and went along with it, but her eyes wouldn't stop gawking at the digital wall clock across the room. She nearly jumped with joy when she heard Carlee and her date in the living room talking.

She was so thankful when the guys finally left. Apparently, Carlee's bedroom adventure hadn't thrived any better.

Haley stretched, relaxing her arm across her eyes, and smiled. She planned to see where this relationship with Alan took her. It was obvious he felt the same way about her, and she intended to be there for him through his difficult time. It was something she wished she'd had several months ago. He wouldn't be going through all of this alone.

He'd probably want to go apartment or house rental shopping in the next day or so, once he talked with his insurance company. She would take him. *Probably need to take him back to the parking lot in the morning to get his car.* Worry about that later.

Was she already falling in love with him?

The sound of the doorknob engaging silenced her fluctuating thoughts. She wiggled her toes, excited to have him back in the room with her. "Get it all flushed out?"

He didn't answer, nor did he shut the door behind him like he'd promised. Actually, the aura in the room now felt off balance. Not as it had been before Alan left. The new presence with her didn't feel at all like Alan.

Was it Joel?

She moved her arm away from her eyes. The brightness of the room shocked her, so she rapidly blinked to soften it. She started to sit up. "Alan, what's going …?"

Her voice hitched.

Fear blasted her so quick and sudden that she couldn't move, couldn't speak, nor could she blink. All she could do was stare. Stare at the hideous looking man that had entered her bedroom. He was gargantuan in size, his exposed arms reminding her of the superheroes from Joel's comics. They were so ripped that they didn't seem real. No way could someone in real life have that much muscle.

The ogre of a man approached her on the bed, cautiously reaching his hand out to her as if she were a snake that might strike. She wished she were something that *could* strike. And even if she could move and stop squeaking when she tried to scream, she doubted she could do much harm to him.

Her eyes fixed on his mask, some kind of hood, and recognition kicked in.

It was Joel's. He'd made it.

Why was this guy wearing it?

His hand trembled as it reached for her calf. When it touched her, his eyes fluttered closed as if his sensations were being overloaded. She could hear his wheezy, fervent breaths behind the burlap hood.

As scary as this situation was, and as horrifying as it should be, Haley didn't feel as if she was in any real danger from this man. There was a hint of bashfulness in his movements, in his approach. Like a virgin about to have to sex with a porn star.

Bad analogy.

Haley could feel the roughness of his calloused hands as he massaged her calf, moving up to the back of her thigh. She let him, knowing it was pointless trying to stop him. Plus, she couldn't move. Her body seemed to be locked up like a computer screen.

He stroked her a few more times before being interrupted.

"So, *this* is why you've been incognito all week?"

The man in the hood jumped. Haley joined him in looking at the man standing in her bedroom doorway, lightly tapping the side of his face with an object that might have been a camera. Another man, possibly dressed in camouflage, stood outside the room. It was hard to tell exactly because her view of him was blocked.

Haley should be hysterical at this point, should be lashing and kicking, fighting her way through these three men, but she couldn't bring herself to do anything.

The one with the camera looked at Haley, cold and stern. "Get dressed."

Finally, she was able to move, scampering around the bedroom while trying to keep herself covered as she gathered her clothes. With all of them watching, she dressed herself in the clothes she'd been wearing. She made herself ask him what was on her mind. "Where's Alan?"

"Who?"

"My ..." She debated what to call him, then decided on, "Boyfriend."

"If you're talking about the guy lying halfway out of the bathroom over here, I'd say in a world of pain."

Haley began to cry.

(II)

When Haley was almost to the bottom of the stairs, she felt a shove at her back. Trying to keep her balance, her feet tousled together and pitched her forward. She missed the remaining stairs and fell straight to the floor. Hard. Her breasts felt as if they'd been jammed through her back.

She slowly rolled over.

The guy she thought was called Buddy grabbed the one in the green shirt by the shoulder. "What the hell was that, Carp?"

"She tripped."

"Tripped my ass. Did you push her?"

"Nope."

Haley wanted to tattle, wanted to say, "Yes he did push me!" but knew it was best she kept her mouth shut. Besides, even if she tried to say anything, there was no way she could actually do it through her wheezing.

Buddy, who wore a mask on top of his head like a hat, turned to the one who'd been feeling her up before they were interrupted. He stood at the back with Alan draped around his shoulders the way snobby rich women wore mink wraps. "Face. Did you see anything?"

The oval shape of burlap shook from side to side.

"You're on thin ice with me, Carp. Don't let it happen, again."

Carp nodded. But when he turned around, Haley could see the cocky sneer on his face. She knew he was going to make it his duty to torment her. He'd already done a good job, so far. Her chest felt as if it had fissured and cracked.

"Go get the bags from next door," said Buddy. We can start getting set up while we wait for What's his name to bring back the kid."

The one in burlap whipped his head around.

Buddy leered at him. "Is that *concern* I sense, Face? Worried about the kid?" Face stood motionless as if he'd been planted there.

Haley was also worried about the kid. Where was Joel? Who had they sent out there to fetch him?

"Put that guy down," ordered Buddy.

Alan's limp body plummeted to the floor with a heavy clunk. Haley had feared he might be dead, but he started to groan, and it was the most wonderful sound she ever thought she could hear.

Putting his hands on his hips, Buddy turned away from the one he'd called Face, and stared at the floor. His bottom lip was clamped between his teeth. His wild blue eyes were forming tears.

Carp had been on his way out, but he'd come back to join Buddy, sharing the disappointment.

Haley glanced at Alan. She wanted to help him up, hug him, but all she could do was watch this awkward confrontation.

Buddy looked Face over. "Got new threads, I see. And you've bathed recently. A new mask too? Looks good. Did you do that yourself?"

Face shook his head.

"They were gifts?" A nod. "From that kid?" Another nod. "Well, that was nice of him, huh? Guess that explains why you haven't come back. Been busy getting your ass *spoiled* here."

He's speaking like an upset parent.

Face's wide shoulders slumped as if his posture had suddenly gone bad. His heavy feet towed him reluctantly closer to Buddy while his fingers fretfully clicked across his thumbnail.

"We thought you were either locked up somewhere or fucking dead. Did you not think we would be worried? Or confused?"

Face was now standing directly before Buddy, towering over him. Buddy had to lean up on the tips of his boots to smack him across the burlap. Haley flinched as if she'd been the one hit. She expected to see Face strike back, but he did nothing. Just stood there and took it. He also took the much harder second slap as well.

Haley sat up, propping herself up on her elbows to watch.

"What were you *thinking*, Face? You're not stupid! I can't even begin to imagine what the hell you've been up to with this kid. Playing with matchbox cars? Going one on one on some video games? Did the two of you stay up all night eating pizza and swapping funny stories about summer camp? The kind of shit that I *hate!* The shit that *you* swore you hated just as much! This American waste of decency!" His eyes were relentless, feral as a lion in the jungle.

"You need to help me understand, Face. Three days ago, you left to dispatch that whore we found camping up in the hills and never came back. We found her floating down stream and you've been here cozying around with a goddamn kid! Have you been teaching him to do what you do? Showing him the ropes? Giving him pointers on how to kill? To hunt?"

Face shook his head.

"We saw that body pit you two left out in the woods. The one with that whore from next door. We had to kill her fucking parents earlier today, and all because of you and your new pal. You know how I feel about suburban assaults. It's too damn risky and here we are in the middle of our second in just one day."

Haley's weight gave out on her, and it took all she had to stay balanced on her elbows. She had no idea how Face felt about this verbal outpour, but she was about to shut down. She wondered if it wasn't a bad idea to drop her skull back on the floor hard enough to make it crack open. From what he was saying, her brother had been up to some very disturbing activities in her absence. And the craziest part of all this was that she blamed herself. To her, Joel was totally innocent, and it was as if she were the one that had done the things Buddy was saying.

"So why didn't you come back to camp after dispatching the whore?" asked Carp.

Buddy slapped him across the chest. "I'm asking the questions here, and you're supposed to be getting our shit from the neighbor's house."

"I want to hear this."

"I bet you do. I'll allow it." He looked back at Face. "Answer his question."

Face grabbed his shirt and jerked it open as if flashing the room. His abdomen and chest were a map of stitched lines. It disgusted Haley as much as it would have had he been disgorging his entrails. Something about those kinds of tight stitched patterns had always grossed Haley out. She could handle the blood better than the patchwork.

"You were hurt bad," said Buddy. "Did the kid do this?"

Face shook his head.

"The whore?" Face nodded. "With what?"

Face tapped the elongated blade strapped to his thigh.

Carp chuckled. "She got you with your own machete?"

Buddy stepped closer, bending at the hips to study the wounds. "Yeah, she got you good. Damn lucky you're alive."

Face nodded in agreement.

"So you hung out here to heal?"

Another nod.

"The kid let you?"

Another nod still.

Buddy grabbed the back of his neck and squeezed as if this was making him tense. Haley could relate. She was so tense it felt like she had concrete under her skin.

"This was on Monday. Correct? You got hacked up on Monday?"

Face nodded, but cautiously.

"So after you got stitched up why didn't you come back to camp? We gave you until sunrise on Tuesday morning to make it back. Then Carp and I hiked through those fucking woods, sleeping under the stars on damp ground, and found your other mess in the woods. Then we teamed up with some fat kid to get into the neighbor's house, but went and got killed, which fucked up our plans of having him get uh-uh …"

"Joel," Carp added.

Haley wondered if Buddy was talking about Paul.

"The fat kid's death ruined getting Joel for us, who we had planned on using to lure you next door. So after killing the people who lived there, we had to invade *this* house."

Haley jumped to her feet, unable to listen to another word. "Stop it! All of you just shut the fuck up!" Haley leaned over, her chest above her thighs. "I can't take this anymore! You bastards are talking about my brother like he's some kind of maniac. And if you say *anything else* like that, I'm going to gouge your fucking eyes out!"

Carp shoved past Buddy and planted his shoulder between her breasts. She lifted off her feet, her back striking the top of the couch. Her limbs slapped the wall, and then she rolled back, bouncing off the cushions, and crashing to the floor beside the couch.

She made an *oomph* noise.

Face moved at Carp as if he were about to attack but suddenly stopped.

Carp slowly stood up straight. Messing with the waist of his pants, he looked at Face. "Got a problem with the way I'm handling the lady?"

Face didn't move, but his stare remained fixed on Carp, like a dog about to attack.

Buddy looked back and forth from Face to Haley. She watched them from the floor, her arm clutched to her belly.

"Carp asks an interesting question, Face. *Do* you have a problem with the way he's handling the lady? I mean, you know I never approve of pointless violence against women, but you've never seemed to care either way. Something about this one that's got you changing your mind?"

Face looked at Haley. For the first time, she actually saw his eyes and could almost see into them, to the anger and pain behind them. It only lasted a second, but Haley learned a lot about him just in that glimpse. He was hurting, and not just physically, there was great pain in his heart. He was a lonely person who used his sorrow to express his hate.

What made him this way?

She looked at the other two and wondered the same thing about them.

"So, that's it then?" asked Buddy. "She's the reason, huh? You stayed here because of her."

Face lowered his head.

"A woman ..." Buddy shook his head. A single tear spilled from his eye and trickled down his cheek. He wiped it away with the back of his hand. "Never have I once questioned your loyalty to the group, or to the mission. You were the one who understood what we are meant to do from the beginning. My number one guy, the one I always knew would have my back ..."

"Well, he totally fucked you. Didn't he?" asked Carp, amusement in his voice.

"Yes, he did Carp. And for a goddamn woman."

Buddy slugged Face where a stitched line snaked down from his chest to his belly button, making the large man stoop down with a groan. Haley felt sympathy for him, but the anger she held for Buddy was much stronger.

Pushing Face back up straight, Buddy pressed against him with rage boiling in his eyes. "Don't you remember the stories I told you about Amy? The woman I was going to marry? And all the shit she did to me? How she fucked with my mind the entire time I was over in Iraq, only to dump me two days after we get back?" He slapped Face somewhere around the same spot he'd punched him, inducing another bellow of pain from the big man. "That's what women do, Face. That's what they do."

He snatched the collar of Face's shirt, the same shirt that looked an awful lot like the shirt Haley's father would wear when working on the cars and lugged him to where she lay on the floor.

"Look at her. She's gorgeous, isn't she?"

"Damn right she is," agreed Carp.

Buddy whipped his head around. "Go get the shit from next door!"

"Can't it wait? I'm enjoying the hell out of this."

Fuming, Buddy turned his back on Carp to focus on Haley. "Look at her close. Look at those legs. You like her legs, don't you?"

Face hadn't moved from his hitched over position. Dabs of blood dripped from between the stitches and onto the floor. His eyes were squinting. Haley could tell he was in some serious pain.

"Yeah," continued Buddy. "You like her legs? You were playing with them when we found you. Think back to that moment when you held her smooth leg in your hand. Do you have the image?"

Face didn't acknowledge the question.

"I'm sure you do. Concentrate *real* hard on that moment. Now, take your eyes away from her delicate legs and look at her face. Remember the look on her face? Was it a pleasurable look?" Buddy tapped him on the shoulder. "Did it look like *she* was having a good time?"

Face took a couple deep breaths, then finally shook his head.

"No, it didn't. You're absolutely right. She was grimacing, wasn't she? Looking at you just as that little girl did. Remember the little girl? Remember how she looked at you?" Buddy frowned as if the memory hurt even him. "You got off the bus. Your face covered with bandages, except for your eyes."

Face stood up straight. His eyes that had looked so helpless only moments ago now scorched with rage.

Buddy didn't let up. "Remember what she *said* to you?"

As if on a prompt that only they could hear, Buddy and Carp began to chant together. "Pillowface. Pillowface. Look Mama! He's got a pillow face."

Carp stopped, but Buddy kept talking. "Oh, how she laughed and laughed...oh how she laughed at your scars...laughed at your ugliness. But you weren't always ugly...you were *made* ugly...and that little girl thought your injuries were hysterical..."

Face shoved Buddy so hard his feet left the floor. By the time he landed, Face was throwing his fists around, hitting whatever he could, and smashing anything he could find. As his blatant rage consumed him, Buddy hooted from the floor, egging him on, cheering for him.

Haley watched as Face scooped Alan off the floor and chucked him through the sliding glass door in one swoop. Carp leaped out of the way, just missing Alan's body folding and contorting awkwardly as it crashed through the thick glass. He landed on the brick patio outside in a shower of broken shards.

Alan was too far away to see if he was all right, but Haley doubted that he was. Her eyes welled up, and her chest pinched tight. She fought to hold back the sobs, because she knew that was what Buddy wanted to see, and she wasn't going to allow herself to cry.

A few minutes later, when Face was spent and on his knees on the floor, panting heavily from behind the mask, Buddy finally turned to Carp.

"Go get the shit from next door or I'll let him do that to *you* next." He pointed at Alan.

This time Carp didn't argue. He walked to the shattered doors, and carefully stepped through the large jagged breach made by Alan's body. Glass crunched under his boots as he walked away, avoiding Alan's fallen form.

Haley crawled as far away from Face as the room would allow. She nestled in the space between the couch and the wall, hugging her knees to her chest. She had still managed to keep her sobs at bay, but she didn't know if she could much longer.

"If that guy's not back with the kid in twenty minutes, I want you to go get him so we can finish this."

Face nodded.

Haley quickly looked away as tears began to leak from her eyes. From this side of the couch, she had a great view of the far wall. A clock hung from a nail in the center of the wall between some artificial floras.

6:51 p.m.

Her crying spell stopped cold in her chest. It was almost seven, and she remembered what she had planned for that time. *Dinner.* Not just any dinner, but a special meal that was going to be shared with Alan, Joel, and...

Carlee.

CHAPTER TWENTY-SIX

(I)

By the time Joel had reached Marble Lane, the blazing sun had surrendered to the softer shades of dusk. The sky was an orange and red flush. Choruses of crickets were just beginning the opening bars of their concerts.

An owl hooted, scaring Joel so badly that he jumped. For a split-second Joel thought someone had called his name.

He'd decided to take the same way back he and Pillowface had before to avoid being spotted. He dragged the shovel behind him, stepping onto the gruff-coated blacktop, and panting. He'd never been so out of breath. Stopping in the road, he bent over, resting his head against the rod. He spotted chunks of Geoffrey Jones' skull flaked across the flat base. He should be appalled but seeing the gore was like a sadistic proof of victory for him.

Looks like it does in the movies—a crunchy shell with some gooey delights thrown in for effect.

He was so enthralled by his observation that he didn't notice the headlights until his body was illuminated in their glow. He gasped as the car whipped around the curve, opened his mouth to scream, but tensed up, helping him to understand how a deer could do the same.

The car's brakes locked. He could hear the tires crunching over small pieces of gravel as it swerved to the shoulder.

It came to an abrupt halt a foot short of plowing him over.

He nearly crapped his pants. Of all he'd been through, it took almost being run down to make him feel human again. It was like a kick in the head by how jarred he felt coming back to reality. His body shook all over. His fingers stiffened, making it impossible to hold the shovel. It fell to the road, clanging when it hit.

He heard a door open and looked up to see someone stepping out of the car. Bathed in the shadows, he couldn't interpret who they were. Not at first, but the voice was incredibly comforting to hear. "Joel?"

Carlee?

"My God. Is that you?" The shape ran around the car and into the flush of the headlights, revealing her to be who he'd suspected, and looking better than he could have predicted. *Carlee.* Though it was only last night, it felt like months since he'd seen her last. She kneeled in front of him, looking up into his eyes. He was tall for his age, but still not taller than her, so seeing Carlee below him, and where he could gaze down at her, was an incredible feeling. It almost made him forget that he probably looked like Michael Myers from the opening of the original *Halloween.*

And he stunk. Reeked. An odor reminiscent of a sewer, or a leaking septic tank on a summer day.

None of that seemed like it mattered to Carlee. If she'd noticed the aroma or his appearance, she hadn't given it a second thought. Grabbing his arms, she wrenched him against her pleasing chest and hugged him. "What *happened* to you? Were you attacked? Did someone do this to you?"

At first, he resisted the urge to tell her what was going on.

But it didn't last.

He began unveiling the sinister tale through a muffled voice obscured between her breasts. She didn't bother moving him or adjusting. She only waited, listening. Surprisingly, he found it easy to confess his actions over the past few days to her. Of course, he'd left out the parts where he'd fantasized about molesting the dead girl. He felt Carlee could do without that fact.

When he'd finished coming clean, he felt sick, because in his mind it hadn't seemed that bad, almost like a movie he'd cut together in his imagination with people he knew as the cast of characters. The monsters were supposed to be fake. Make believe. But hearing it aloud, and from his own voice, it had finally become extremely authentic.

He couldn't believe all he'd done. All he'd allowed Pillowface to do.

And yet, considering all of that, he still couldn't hate him for it.

"Jonesey did this to you?"

He nodded. When he'd told her the boss that she and Haley shared had demanded to bring him to the house, she had seemed appalled, but not surprised. They agreed that he probably wasn't involved with the others, but he wasn't entirely innocent either. His role in all this was very confusing. When Joel confessed to killing him in self-defense, Carlee didn't even blink an eye.

"And Haley's with these people now, but we don't know what they look like?"

He nodded. It was impressive that she'd believed everything he'd said without the slightest hesitation. That was when he knew he truly loved her.

"We should call the police," she said.

"No," he said. His voice was raspy, as if he'd been at a concert screaming all the lyrics. "If they see the cops coming, they'll kill her for sure. They're holding out for me to get there before they do anything, and I don't know what they've done with Pillowface, but he may not be able to stop them."

"Shit." She looked at the darkening sky as if the answers were aligned amongst the stars. Joel wished they were. Then she brought her pitiful expression back to him. "We can't go get her out of there. They'll kill her and *us* at the drop of a hat. We're totally fucked."

"I don't know …"

"What? Do you have a plan?"

"Not really, but maybe we can come up with something together?"

"We should really call the police. Maybe get them to meet us at the end of the road. They can infiltrate the house, raid it. Get her out of there."

"Right and shoot everyone in the house." Carlee looked distressed.

She chewed at her lip as if it were gum. "I want to save Pillowface, too, and get him out of there and on his way before the cops show up."

"Even after what he did to Tonya? You still think he's a good person?"

Knowing that Carlee would find it hard to understand what he was about to say, he tried to quickly organize it in his head. "Something about him is a lot like me."

"Don't say that."

"It's true. I'm not saying I could do the things he's done, and I'm sure what I don't know about is just as bad, if not worse. But there's a connection. I know he's good at heart, but somewhere along the way, he lost it."

"And you think you've helped him find it?"

"I think we've helped each other."

"Because you're alike?"

He nodded. "Yeah. I accepted him, and he accepted me. No judgment, no discrimination. Just two friends, trying to adapt to what the other person is."

She smiled. "You're pretty slick, you know that? I always knew you were something special."

He blushed. A rush of heat ignited the back of his neck. He felt extremely proud of the fact he'd caused her to say that.

Carlee was quiet a moment. Then she said, "Okay, if we do this, we have to construct a *solid* plan. It's crucial that we stick to it, no matter what."

"I agree."

"All right. Let's talk this out. Quickly. Because I doubt we have much time left."

He agreed with that, too, but had a strong feeling they were already too late.

(II)

The barbwire hurt, but not as bad as it should. Maybe she'd become so numb that she couldn't feel it, or possibly she was already dead and could no longer feel pain. She guessed the real reason the barbwire didn't poke her that bad was because Face had been the one to bind her wrists to the chair before disappearing to a corner of the room where it was hard to see him.

Simple as that.

He liked her. She could tell that even if he hadn't confessed it, but so could everyone else, which was why they'd been so hateful to him. She also knew it was why they were going to torture her and Joel severely, just to prove a hellacious point to Face for coming here in the first place.

Why *had* he come here? That was the million-dollar question. She thought back to Joel's erratic phone call the other day. He'd called her and told her about the maniac in the backyard, and she hadn't believed him. If only she would have. He'd been asking her for help, but she had ignored him and told him to handle it, and this was how he'd handled it.

It was all her fault. She should have taken him seriously. *He's a kid for Christ's sake. He pulls shit like this all the time.* She glanced around the room again. Yes, if she would have at least *listened* to what he had to say that morning there was a good chance that none of this would have happened.

She tried to avoid looking at the broken glass where Alan was still lying but couldn't help herself. Gazing at his crumpled body, she felt as if her heart had been smashed with a hammer. His death was her fault too. She wasn't even going to be optimistic about it. He was dead. There was no possibility he'd survived such a brutal throw.

When Carp had returned with the bags, Buddy ordered Face to strap her down. She was glad it had been him. Because he'd been so gentle with her, but she despised him most of all because of how much he'd tainted her brother's innocence, and also because he'd been the one who'd killed Alan.

If she got the chance, she would kill Face first.

Buddy stepped out from the kitchen, running a wet hand through his hair. It looked as if he'd been running water in his hands and splashing his face. His camera sat on the end table, the mask on top. He took them, walked to the center of the living room, and positioned the mask back on top of his head, the plastic face aimed at the ceiling. He twirled around. The camera was nestled under his arm, his hands out in front of him. With each hand he extended his thumb but kept the four fingers tightly together. Then, matching up their poses to form a square, he held them straight out, squinting one eye as he observed the layout of the room through the small opening he'd made.

My god, she thought. *He's setting up the shot.*

As if approving, he lifted his eyebrows and nodded. "Not too shabby. The room's layout is perfect. Flat walls on each side, a good solid foundation in the middle, and plenty of room to work with."

He looked at Haley. She quickly glanced in the other direction, but knew he'd already caught her staring.

"Were you wondering what I was doing with my hands just then?" He repeated the motion.

"Not really," she said.

Ignoring her answer, he responded as if she'd invited him to explain. "See, these old cameras only film in four-by-three. Full frame. So, I have to frame up the angles like that just to make sure everything I want to shoot will fit on the screen. Make sense?"

"Perfect," she said, but couldn't care less.

Carp stuck his head into the room from the patio. "There're some gas cans half full in their shed. Want me to take one of them next door and douse the place?"

Buddy seemed to think on it a moment, then nodded. "Yeah, but don't light it, if the neighbors see smoke before we're gone it'll be trouble."

"All right. You got it."

Then he was gone just as quickly as he'd arrived.

Finally, Haley had to ask. "What do you plan on doing to us?"

Buddy gazed at her from over his shoulder, his wicked grin prophetic to the madness behind it.

"Why are you doing this to us? We didn't do anything to you!" As pathetic and hopeless as she sounded, what she'd said was the truth. They *hadn't* done a damn thing to them, yet here they were, enacting punishment as if they had.

Buddy whipped around so quickly, Haley gasped. "Those are just hollow sentences because *you* have done more to us than others. While we were overseas, fighting a pointless war over oil prices, you sat here, in this luscious house with air conditioning, three large meals a day, working a goddamn overpaying nine-to-five job while people that worked harder than you could ever imagine protecting you had to sleep in holes dug in the sand with the constant risk of being pricked by scorpions.

"And while we're killing ourselves for you, you sit here in luxury, complaining about how prices are going up on milk. Whining about how it's a little hot and humid out today or my expensive car just doesn't have the padded seats like I wanted!" Foamy spit fired from his mouth as he unloaded on her.

Face somberly appeared from the shadows as if he were curious.

"*We* marched through sandstorms with temperatures in the hundreds. Our *padded* seats were broken crates in the back of a Jeep. We had no cereal and milk to complain about. Just dehydrated meat, old bread, and tepid water to drink."

"I'm sorry! Okay? I knew it was bad over there—"

Buddy stopped her right there. "*Bad* over there?" He laughed as if revolted. "You didn't just honestly say it was *bad* over there."

She had, but now wished she'd kept her fucking mouth shut.

He looked at Face. "Did you hear that?"

Pillowface nodded once, folding his arms over his chest, across his torn open shirt.

"She said it was *bad* over there." Buddy nearly collapsed with insane laughter. It stopped abruptly, his mood returning to the frenzied state it had been. "I was promised I'd be a big hero to my country if I went over there. Hell, we were all promised that." Face nodded again. "Those promises were shit, just words." His voice allayed, becoming a husky whisper. "Lucky for me, I was a filmmaker, so I got to experience the true horrors of war through the lens of a camera. Which made it like make believe, surreal." He smiled. "Safe. But, now that we're back at home, there are no more empty promises, no more fairytales."

"Wuh-what are you talking about?" she asked.

Motioning to himself, then to Face, he said, "A world where *normal* people are trained to execute men, women, and children on sight, at the drop of a hat." His voice was rising again, "And we're not supposed to feel a goddamn thing about it, because we're told to leave our conscience at the door, to stifle all human emotions and feelings." He laughed. "And we did. We were damn good at it, too. Then when we had to come home, our new president flashed his money around and gave us a payoff to walk away. We took it but were sickened with ourselves for doing so. Now we have our own ways of making people see, making them understand."

He took a deep breath. "This is no longer your America. This is my holocaust." He walked to her chair, leaned over, and put his face directly in hers. "A killer they made me. A killer I shall be."

She held his stare, not daring to look away. She was too afraid of what would happen next. He'd been on the border of a massive collapse into violence for the last several minutes. This close to his eyes, she could see the abandonment on the other side of them. A pure hatred boiled inside of him so severely that she could feel its heat through her clothes.

He was forsaken.

And he had others that agreed with his twisted ideology. She didn't know how many members of this cult there were, but she didn't doubt for a second that Buddy couldn't find more who suffered from the same illness he did. The inability to shut it off. She'd heard about this sort of thing before. Shellshock. Kill-mode. Becoming so entrapped, they didn't know how to find their way back to normalcy. She couldn't help feeling a tinge of pity for them.

But when she looked at her wrists, pricked and bleeding from the barbwire, and knowing they'd set her up as their next victim, that pity quickly took a hike.

CHAPTER TWENTY-SEVEN

(I)

Carlee let Joel out of the car in front of Tonya's house.

"Wait," she said, rolling down the window.

He walked back, leaning into the car through the window. He held the shovel away from the car to avoid scratching its paint. He was suddenly just inches from her lovely face.

"Take this." She leaned over, lined her lips with his, and kissed him. Joel tensed up. She ran her hand along the back of his head, and through his hair. His skin lit up with gooseflesh. Then she slowly pulled away. "Good luck."

Nodding, he groaned some kind of response.

She smiled. "You really are something, I hope you know that and never forget it."

"So ... so are you."

It was her turn to blush. "Thank you. I know you mean it, too."

He did, with all his heart.

Able to speak rationally, he added, "Be careful."

"I will. You too."

For the first time since its conception, Joel felt that their plan wasn't going to work. He wanted to put an end to it, to tell Carlee she was right in wanting to call the police, but she had already driven away by the time his tongue could pronounce the words. He watched her taillights flash red, then disappear around a pine tree as the car turned onto the driveway.

Too late now.

He had to go through with his part. He stood on the road another moment before he could will himself to move further.

He ran alongside the fence, around the back of Tonya's yard, and circled around to his own. From there, he listened. He heard the faint thump of Carlee's car door shutting. Unease flapped in his stomach.

Gotta do this. Can't be a pussy. I need to be a man for Haley and for Carlee.

He bolted across the yard to the side door of the basement. He was inside quickly and silently, being careful not to let the tongue on the door click as he eased it shut. He didn't slow down his pace until reaching Pillowface's sleeping area. All looked fine. The deflated mattress was where it should be. In fact, nothing looked out of place except for the man who should be down there.

Joel had expected as much.

Leaning the shovel against the wall, he wished he could hold on to it. He'd bonded with it, and it had helped save his life. But the shovel was much too big to take with him, so he had to leave it behind.

He looked around. Spotting the chainsaw on the floor, he decided against taking it for the same reason as the shovel. They were too heavy to carry up the side of the house. But the machete would do fine. A feeble grin formed on his face as he searched for it. After a minute of quick hunting, he gave up on trying to find it. Then he spotted the weapon Pillowface had devised while spending his time in the basement. It sat on an old rag and now had the handsaw blade attached to the back support.

What is this thing?

He didn't have time to ponder its possibilities. He ran over to it, snatched it up, and checked the density of the blade. It was sturdy, but thin enough that he should be able to use it.

Then Joel backtracked out of the basement, circling around to the other side of the house. He looked up at Haley's window. A part of him expected to find the window had been boarded up like in *Night of the Living Dead*, but it was still as he'd left it. Earlier, he'd been terrified over the broken screen. And now he was thankful. It was his way in. Otherwise, he'd have been out of luck.

He checked the saw, again. It should be able to slide under the window so he could pry it open. He hoped so. He'd only have one hand to do it with since the other would be holding him up and keeping him from falling.

He took a deep breath, draped the looped strap of chain over his shoulder, and began climbing up the gutter.

(11)

Buddy ducked down as if under fire from the sudden chimes. His wide eyes became even wider. But this time, there was fear in them.

"What was that?"

"The doorbell," said Haley matter-of-factly.

"Shut the fuck up. I'll be getting to you in a second."

"I can't hardly wait," she muttered.

Ignoring her, Buddy looked at Face. "Do you think Carp would pull some shit and ring the doorbell?"

Face shrugged.

"Me neither." He turned back to Haley. "Who are you expecting, girl?"

She could probably guess who it was. Instead of informing Buddy of this, she only mimicked Face's response and shrugged.

He could see right through it. "You're lying. Who's out there?"

"I *don't* know."

"Lie!"

The doorbell rang, again.

Face unsheathed the machete from his leg strap, and proceeded to go to the door, but Buddy was quick to stop him.

"I'll go check it out. Keep an eye on her." He pointed to Haley. "Don't let her try any stupid shit like saying she'll love you if you let her go. All right?"

Face nodded.

Buddy bolted from the room, but not before removing his mask and handing it to Face for him to hold.

Haley prayed to God that Carlee wasn't at that door, but she knew without a doubt that she was.

Waiting for the door to open, Carlee held her breath. When it suddenly did, the breath forced its way out in a gasp.

The man on the other side of the door smiled. His hair was damp, his face glossy with a coating of water or sweat.

Had he just come out of the shower?

He kept his right arm concealed behind the door, but his left was in plain sight. "Hello. May I help you?" Though a little winded, his voice was very pleasant.

This had to be one of the men Joel told her about. Since he wasn't wearing a burlap sack on his head, Carlee assumed he wasn't Pillowface. She flexed a bogus smile for the man. She'd become quite talented in this field from having to deal with frequent herds of scum at the firm.

"Hi. I'm Carlee."

"Hello, Carlee. I'm Buddy. What can I do for you?"

"I was coming by to pick up Haley. We're supposed to go to the movies?"

His smile receded, but he quickly put on another one. "Oh?"

"Yeah. Are you a friend of hers?"

He nodded. "Sure. A friend of Haley's. That's right."

"Oh, okay. Is she ready? If we don't hurry up, I'll miss the coming attractions. And I can't *stand* it when that happens. It's just as important as the actual movie, if you ask me."

Buddy looked as if he struggled to hold back his joy at what she said. "So true. I was the same way."

"Was?"

"Well, I imagine I still would be But I never go to the movies anymore."

"Aw. Why's that?"

"Let's just say I never have the time."

"That's too bad. You're missing out on some great ones."

"I'm sure I am. It's not that I don't *want* to go. It just never works out that I *get* to go. You know what I mean?"

She knew he'd been lured by her charm and fallen right into her trap. He was talking more than he'd probably bargained for.

"So I hate to ask again. But *is* she ready?"

"No. Sorry. She's not here."

"What?"

"Yeah. She took off with some other guy. Thin, kind of nerdy looking."

"Alan?"

"Alan. Yeah that's right. I'm just here, hanging out."

"Well then, this is your lucky day."

His smile coiled. "I'm sorry?"

"You get to go to the movies with *me*."

"How do you figure?"

Carlee threw another grin at him and swayed her hip. "Since Haley has blown me off, then you get to accompany me to the show."

Buddy appeared to be legitimately delighted by the idea. "You're asking me to the movies?"

"Yeah. You sound surprised."

"Well, I am. You don't know me. What if I'm some kind of psychopath?"

"Oh, I doubt that. You seem like a pussycat."

He laughed.

Look at that smile. Very warm and charming.

"I appreciate the offer, but I've got too much to do."

"Like what?"

He sighed. "Too much. I'm sorry, Carlee, but I have to close the door on you now."

"Aw. Really?"

"I'm afraid so. Again, I appreciate the offer, but I just can't."

"That's too bad."

He attempted to close the door, but she managed to stick her foot in to block it. He glanced down at the dusky leg glowing with perfection from the shorts she was wearing. Her delicate calf was turned to the side, flaunting the curve at him.

Carlee immediately regretted doing it. She was being too pushy and a guy like this would surely suspect something before too long.

Hurry up, Joel. This is going to get bad.

"What are you doing?" he asked.

"I-I don't know."

"You just stopped me from closing the door. Didn't you hear what I said? I've got things to do."

"I heard you, but I just didn't like it."

Smirking, he appeared to be growing tired of her act. "Look, I don't know what you're up to, but I want you to leave. I'll let Haley know that you stopped by. I'm being *very* generous here."

Oh, I know that.

She was still alive, and he'd given her multiple chances to leave, and she'd taken none of them. His courteous offer would expire soon.

"Okay, if you *really* don't want to come with me."

"I do, but I *can't*." At the end, his voice rose in pitch.

"All right, I won't keep you any longer." She reached into her purse hanging from her shoulder.

"Thank you for being understanding."

"I know how hectic things can get."

Nodding, he added, "I'm sure you do."

"One more thing, really quick."

"What is it?"

Her fingers curved around the aluminum canister in her purse. It was cold and slick in her hand. "Could you give her this?" She wrenched her hand free of the purse, aiming the mace at his eyes. She squeezed the nozzle and waited for the spray to splash him, temporarily blinding him so she could run inside. Hopefully Joel would be coming down the stairs about that time. Then they could get Haley and assuming Alan was in there, get him too, and get the fuck away from here.

There was just one slight problem with her plan. One pivotal point that she'd completely neglected in all of this.

She hadn't removed the safety block from the mace after purchasing it. Instead of misting his eyes with a scorching liquid, it only hissed at him.

He wasn't amused.

Carlee looked at the can and realized her mistake. "Oh, shit."

Then he decked her in the mouth, splitting both her lips up and down the middle. Her head rocked back. She felt vertebrae popping at the back of her neck. Before she could fall, Buddy had scooped her up and hoisted her over his shoulder. He gave a quick look around.

No porch lights were clicking on. Carlee didn't detect any neighbors running to her rescue, so apparently, he hadn't been spotted.

He was inside with the door shut and locked before the colorful splotches began exploding through Carlee's vision.

Running back into the living room, Buddy shouted, "Face?"

He dropped Carlee on the wooden floor. It jarred her body, flashing pain from her toes to her eyes.

"This is getting fucked. We've got to get this wrapped up and out of here. I'm sure more will be popping up before too long."

Haley looked down at her friend. Poor Carlee had no idea what the hell was going on here.

What she was walking into.

More tears spilled from her scratchy, red eyes.

Buddy glanced down at Carlee, shaking his head. "I told you to leave. Gave you ample opportunities to walk, but you wouldn't. Do you think I like being rough with women? Well, I don't." He looked over at Haley. "Who is she? What was she doing here? How did she know something was going on?"

Haley shook her head, sobbing. She had no idea why he would think she knew anything.

"Tell me who she is, or I'll stomp her throat in!"

"Carlee! My friend ..."

He looked down at Carlee, his hands on his hips like someone who'd just watched a bad football play. "This is really bad for Carlee. She forced her way into this. Now she can't leave."

Face lowered the machete, the tip pointing at the floor. He looked from Haley to Carlee with evident regret in his eyes.

Haley figured he was dreading the order to kill them that would surely come soon.

"Carp should be back any second now. He can handle Carlee. But Haley?"

She looked up at him, her bottom lip quivering and flinching from the torrents of snot streaming over it.

"I'm taking care of you, myself."

Haley felt some sort of relief in hearing that because that meant it would soon be over.

(III)

The saw had worked perfectly as a wedge. Pushing it under the window, he'd angled it down on his side, and the window shot upward with a quick *shwoomp*. He tensed, expecting at any moment for the intruders to barge in and see him clinging helplessly to a gutter outside.

They never came.

He tossed the saw apparatus into the room and used his left hand to raise the window high enough for him to squeeze through. Once inside, he didn't bother closing it back. He scooped up the saw and walked to the closed door. Gently, he eased it open. The muffled sounds became clearer and more audible. From downstairs he heard a man declaring he would take care of Haley himself.

His heart lurched.

No!

He needed to act now. No holding back.

Pushing back the tears that wanted to shed, he took in a deep breath as a stellar image materialized in front of him as if it were real. Its chrome body eased Joel's fear, but only a little.

Dad's gun.

A six-cylinder .41 magnum revolver that his mom had detested from the day it was purchased at a gun show.

It had been Joel's idea to sneak in through Haley's window, get the keys to their parents' room, and go to the closet where the gun had sat in its wooden box since the one and only time they'd gone into the woods to shoot it. Mom had *really* freaked then.

But wasn't the box locked with a padlock?

I'll break the fucker open.

But Carlee had convinced him he would need a distraction to help conceal what he was doing. He'd protested, but she'd eventually won him over.

He spun on his heels and hurried to Haley's dresser, opened the jewelry box, then snatched the key. With it dangling from his fingers, he went to the door, poking his head out through the tight space he'd allotted himself. Things sounded as if they'd somewhat settled downstairs. He could hear the perceptible tones of voices but couldn't understand what was being said.

Keeping the saw close so the chains wouldn't jingle, he darted across the hall, ducking down as he came to the railing over the living room. In the corner of his eye, he detected some people down there, and one of them for sure was Pillowface. It was hard to miss someone of his build. He was just standing off to the side, doing nothing.

Why wasn't he helping them?

He stopped at the bedroom door and pushed the key into the lock. His trembling hand gave him trouble with the key. After a couple attempts, he succeeded with turning it. The knob clicked and he twisted it open. The door slowly swayed inward. He didn't hesitate as he dashed through the darkened room, heading straight for the closet. He was inside before taking another breath and fumbling at the string hanging from the overhead light bulb. He found it, pulled it down, and the light switched on. It was a soft yellow glow. The bulb would probably burn out soon. That depressed him. He could remember when Dad had put that bulb in. He wasn't looking forward to replacing it with another one.

He found the box centered on the top shelf. Bringing it down to the floor, he knelt in front of it as if it were the lost ark. As he'd suspected, it was locked tight. Dad was extra careful with how he stored it. Joel raised the saw above his head with the flat end pointed down like he was about to sacrifice the box to a mythical god. He brought the blade down, splitting the box in the middle. The wood splintered and cracked. Then he punched it, putting the final say on its existence.

Joel pulled back the broken pieces. The gun, untouched in years, still shined as if it were brand new in the carpet-comforted case. It was loaded. Another round-clip with six bullets was nestled into another compartment above it. He grabbed the magazine, stuffing it down one of his pockets. He curled his fingers around the handle of the magnum and lifted it out of the box. It felt cold and slick in his hand. An orb of light glimmered off the barrel. He felt much stronger, powerful. Strange, how a mean weapon such as this could do that to a person, even one as young as Joel.

If he hadn't been so mesmerized by the pistol, he probably would have heard the approach of footsteps. He'd wasted so much time already, and the gun had distracted him even more.

"That's a pretty piece you got there. Won't Daddy get pissed if he finds out you been playing in his toolbox?"

Joel jumped at the deep voice full of a staggering rage that came off as nearly pleasant.

Looking behind him, he saw the voice's owner. A slim man, dressed in green, with a hat on his head. He stood near his parents' bed with his arms folded over his chest. His smile stretched the corners of his mouth.

"I take it that Jones guy didn't find you."

"He found me ..."

The man scanned Joel's clothes and nodded. "I see. Is that his blood on you?"

Joel nodded.

"I'll bite. I'm impressed kid. You killed the man sent to kill you. I'll be damned. But you fucked up in the meantime. Want to know how?"

Joel did want to know but had suddenly forgotten how to speak.

The man continued. "You haven't shot me yet."

Remembering the gun clutched in his sweaty hands, Joel tried to quickly aim it at the man's chest. But before he could even focus his line of sight, the man had snatched the pistol from his fingers and slapped him across the face with his other hand. Joel's eyes welled with tears as stinging tendrils of pain coursed through his head.

The man stepped back, putting the gun behind his back, then he reached down and picked up the saw. The belt dangled from behind it like two tails.

"This is odd looking. Did you make this?"

Joel held his cheek, sobbing. He tried to speak but couldn't slow his breathing down enough to do it, so he only shook his head.

"I didn't think so. This looks like Face's work."

Just like the movies. I should have expected this. I've written stuff like this. Just when you're about to win something out of the blue happens.

He'd been careless and slow. Stupid. Letting his guard down instead of being on alert like a *real* man would have been.

Sorry Haley. Sorry Carlee. I let you down.

His eyes were still streaming with tears as the man reached for him

CHAPTER TWENTY-EIGHT

(I)

This wasn't how it was supposed to happen.

In the movies, the central characters always won in the end by beating the bad guys, slaying the maniac in a gory demise, or succeeding in sending the demons back to hell. One problem Joel never took into consideration until now was: This wasn't a damn movie!

By a handful of his hair, Joel was being dragged. He struggled to keep up, and when he wasn't moving fast enough, he felt it on his scalp. As they reached the bottom of the stairs, the man began yelling.

"Here's the little shit!!"

Another man turned. "Carp? Where the hell have you been?"

"I was on my way back from the neighbor's and saw this little shit sneaking around the house, so I followed him in."

"Where's the guy we sent after him?"

Carp shoved Joel forward but didn't release his hair. "Who, Jones? Look at the blood all over him."

The one with the plastic mask on his head looked surprised. "He *killed* him?"

"Yep."

"Wow kid."

"Guess you know now that you should have sent me, Buddy. This would have been over a long time ago."

"Don't start with me."

Haley screamed when she saw Joel. Carlee lay on the floor, moving, but barely. She was bleeding pretty heavily from the mouth. She'd failed, but that was all right, so had Joel. The plan that they'd thought was so brilliant had turned out to be a catastrophe.

A man was splayed awkwardly on the patio, the glass door shattered. Joel guessed he'd been thrown through the door and probably sliced to ribbons by the glass. It was obvious the man was dead. Joel had seen enough dead bodies in recent days to recognize the blue cast of skin as a bad sign. He also recognized the guy as Alan from the bookstore, which hurt Joel even more. How many people were going to die because of him? He'd already lost so many.

"Toss him down there next to his sister."

Nodding, Carp flung Joel by the hair. He crashed against Haley's legs. She quickly lifted them and wrapped them around his shoulders. He supposed it was her way of trying to hold him close to her. As awkward as it was, it was great to have. He hugged one of her legs and didn't want to ever let go.

Carp held up the gun. "The kid snuck in through a window and had gotten this. I guess he was going to go all *Death Wish* and start shooting everybody." He turned around and planted his boot firmly in Joel's stomach.

Joel's cries pulled Pillowface from the kitchen. He charged into the room and spotted Joel on the floor by Carp. Buddy had that look in his eye. The one that normally meant hell was on the verge of breaking loose. Haley sat in the chair, crying and screaming. All her beauty was practically gone. Her strength had been replaced by panic and collapse. Buddy was good at that. Bringing people down to their lowest rung before letting them drop.

The order for everyone's death was coming. Any minute now, he and Carp would be put to work.

Pillowface was being pulled in two directions. To Buddy, who he'd been loyal to for a few years now. And to Joel, the one who made him remember what it was like to be innocent, and that everyone could be cursed by abandonment. This kid was a lot like them actually. He'd watched his happiness and dreams get pushed to the wayside while life dealt him a cruel, bitter hand from the reality deck of cards.

He didn't deserve to die.

Joel saw Pillowface. A small spark of hope flickered in his eyes.

"Pillowface? Help me!"

Buddy laughed hysterically.

"You can stop this, Pillowface. You can stop this!" As if they weren't laughing hard enough at the poor kid, he began to cry. Then he added for fits, "You're my friend!"

Buddy had tears in his eyes, laughing so hard.

Carp yanked back on Joel's hair. "If he was your friend, kid, would he be letting me do this?"

He pulled Joel away from Haley's legs and onto his knees, then slammed an elbow against the back of his head, knocking him forward to the floor. He landed near the other girl. She reached out to him and stroked his face. Her touch looked to calm him some. But the back of his skull had to be pulsating like someone was hammering a spike back there.

He'd witnessed Carp perform unnecessary acts of violence to people before, but this was the first time it had angered Pillowface enough that he was tempted to snap the man's neck.

Buddy looked at Face. "You friends with this snot or what?"

Pillowface couldn't take his eyes off Joel.

Buddy's smile began to fade. "Tell me you weren't *hanging out* with this kid."

Pillowface still didn't answer, just continued gaping at Joel who was crying really hard now.

Through sniffles Joel whined, "Pillowface …?"

Buddy didn't give him a chance to respond. "Let me tell you who the *real* Pillowface is. The one we call *Face*. He's a killer, and he loves it. A fucking assassin. He's the best at what he does. The best there ever was or will be."

Normally when Buddy stroked his ego, Pillowface felt as if he were some kind of God among men, an artist painting on a sadistic pallet. Everything Buddy had said was true. He did take some form of pride in his work. But after seeing the undeniable hurt in Joel's eyes, he began to remember there was another side to his work, one he didn't usually see.

Their side. The kid had had a hard enough life as it was, and he'd made it even harder by becoming his friend.

Pillowface's pride had turned to shame.

Buddy's patience was worn out. He stomped his foot. "Face? Answer me, goddammit! Are you friends with this kid?"

He nodded.

"Un-*fucking*-believable." He looked at Carp. "Did you see that?"

"Sure did."

Buddy obviously couldn't believe what he'd heard.

"You son of a bitch. You fucking traitor!"

He slapped a hand across the front side of the burlap. Pillowface shot his head around. Buddy jumped back when he saw the rage bubbling in his eyes.

"Don't look at me like that. This is *your* fuckup. You're the one that brought *us* to *them*. You call that kid your friend, but what about Carp? He's been there for you a lot longer than that twerp."

Agreeing, Carp said, "Goddamn right."

"So, to prove yourself to us once again, you're going to have to take a test."

Pillowface tilted his head. He should have known it would come to this.

"Grab the kid, Carp."

"My pleasure."

Screaming, Haley kicked at Carp as he leaned over to lift Joel. He still had the gun in one hand, so he reached for Joel with the other and grappled a nest of his hair. Haley continued to lash out but didn't come close to connecting. From the floor, Carlee swung her fists, but missed as well.

Carlee began to scream high-pitched wails that couldn't be understood.

Haley tugged against the barbwire, looking at Face with hatred in her eyes that he hadn't seen so severely other than his own. "Leave him alone! He's just a kid!" She looked at Carp. "You're going to kill a kid?"

"No." Slapping a hand on Pillowface's back, Buddy said, "He is."

Writing and squirming, Joel hammered on Carp's chest. This did nothing to save him. With each attempt at striking him, Carp tugged his hair harder until finally Joel gave up. An hour ago, he wouldn't have thought Pillowface might actually kill him. But now he wasn't so sure. He'd never once truly feared him in the short time they'd been together.

Now, he was terrified of him.

The girls screamed and begged from behind Joel. He couldn't tell them apart. Sounding more like disarranged shrieks, their words were hardly understandable. At last, Carp had forcefully escorted him to Pillowface. They faced each other.

Carp released his hair and jostled Joel against the towering build of Pillowface's body. The feel of it, its firmness was familiar, but nothing was comforting about it anymore. Everything had changed in such a short amount of time.

The screams behind him lightened. He made himself look up at Pillowface. Their eyes locked. Staring for a moment, Joel saw a tear break away from his eye and soak into the burlap.

Simultaneously, Buddy and Carp began a chant. Slow at first, it steadily increased to a drum. *"Face! Face! Face!"*

The chant continued as Joel felt Pillowface's brawny hands find his throat. He hoped his eyes, ample and full of fear, asked him to make it quick, because he was begging for it in his mind.

Pillowface glanced at Haley. Her mouth hung open as if she were screaming but had been put on mute. Though he knew it could never have happened, he'd fantasized some kind of life with her and Joel in this house. But he should have known better. He had kissed those dreams goodbye.

All he'd brought them was pain and torment.

One quick spin of the wrists would snap Joel's neck, ending it all. The agony, distress, the loneliness. A quick crack and he'd be free.

The perceptible chant was thunderous as if they were waiting for him to kick a field goal.

And his mind was made up. Joel shall be set free. It ends now with a mercy kill.

(II)

With everyone's attention diverted, Haley began working at the bounded wire on her wrists. Being able to gulp down scorching hot coffee without having it touch the back of her throat wasn't her only talent.

She was also very flexible.

And she had been for as long as she could remember.

Leaning over, she sucked in a breath to make her stomach even flatter than the paper elevation it naturally was. This allowed her to contort herself so her mouth could touch her wrist. She gnashed her teeth to a snarl and bit down on the rusting wire. Her mouth lit up with a flurry of stings like crunching aluminum foil.

But she didn't stop. She continued like a mouse caught in a trap, gnawing and chewing. Her lips formed around the rudimentary knot. She felt her canine tooth penetrate its fold, permitting her to lock down. Her rows of enamel met, then she tugged with all the strength in her neck.

The knot came free. The wire drooped around the chair.

(III)

The pressure didn't come right away in one quick squeeze.
Pillowface slowly applied it as if he were undecided to do so. Joel
could still breathe, but it was hard. When he tried to swallow, his
spit became lodged behind his Adams apple. If Pillowface squeezed any
harder Joel realized his throat would be crushed.

Joel wished he'd go on and do it. Dragging it out like this was
torture. He wanted it to be over and done, so that way he would no
longer have to live with knowing what he'd done to so many people.
Sure, it hadn't been *his* hands that had murdered Tonya, her parents,
or Ethan. But it might as well have been. He hadn't been the one to
tear Clay Ray's scalp from his head, but he'd been the one to put the
chainsaw in his hair so Pillowface could do it.

It was his fault. He should have never allowed Pillowface to come
into his life.

Another tear spilled from Face's eye as the pressure increased.

Here it comes.

The chanting stopped. Instead of hoots and cheers, he now heard
grunting. A shriek of rage that sounded like it could have come from
Haley tore through the tight room.

Pillowface released Joel's throat and together they turned towards
Buddy and Carp.

Carp held his hand away from him at neck level, struggling with
some kind of wire or something that was trying to coil around his
throat. He turned to the side, revealing Haley behind him with the
barbwire she had been tied with now wrapped around each of her
hands and trying to strangle Carp with it.

As Buddy moved in to assist Carp, Carlee speared him in a nearly
perfect tackle. He hit the coffee table and smashed through it to the
floor. Carlee rolled across him. On the floor, she reeled back and forth,
apparently also stunned from the impact.

Joel looked at Pillowface who in return looked at him. Much like
Joel, Pillowface probably didn't know what to do. Joel should help his

sister, and Pillowface should be helping Carp, but neither of them could budge from this spot.

Holding his stomach, Buddy got to his knees. "Face … for fucksake, help him!"

Pillowface glanced at Joel one more time before charging.

But so did Joel.

He went straight for the gun still clutched in Carp's hand. It wasn't going to be as easy to dislodge it as he'd thought it would be. Carp had a firm grip, and even worse, his finger was inching closer to the trigger. With the barrel pointing directly at his face, Joel fought to pull the gun away from him.

Face ignored Joel to walk around behind Carp where Haley was and yanked her back. The barbwire slid across Carp's hand, ripping it open. Blood secreted from the gash in thick spurts.

He finally let go of the gun.

Joel caught it before it hit the floor. Then he staggered back, thumbing back the hammer, and aiming.

He wanted to shoot Carp, but Pillowface was too close and since he was struggling with Haley as she slapped him with fists layered in barbwire, he was afraid he might hit either one of them, or both.

"Damn it, Face!" yelled Carp. "Look what you made her do to my hand!"

There was a swoosh of movement to Joel's left. He turned as Buddy sprung at him. Joel quickly pointed the gun and fired. Explosions shot up his right arm to his shoulder and back down to his fingers, locking them up. Screaming, he dropped the gun. He pulled his hand close. It dangled loosely at the wrist, flopping this way and that.

It had been snapped completely.

He could vomit from the pain.

Buddy was also screaming. His hand was clutched to his ear as blood jetted down his forearm. When he pulled his hand away, Joel saw he hadn't shot his entire ear off, but only the top half.

It would do. Seeing Buddy injured in any fashion brought a smile to his face.

Carlee ran to Joel, swiping the gun off the floor on her way. She wrapped an arm around his shoulders and pulled him tightly against her. Holding him close, she aimed the gun at Buddy and cocked the hammer with her free hand.

"Leave Haley alone!"

Pillowface was holding her by the wrists, but he wasn't trying to harm her, only subdue her by the looks of it. If he wanted to kill her, he could have done so three times already. Joel had witnessed displays of the man's strength enough times to know that Haley posed no real threat to him.

"Kill her, Face!" shouted Buddy.

"You do it, and I'll blow a hole straight through your leader here!"

Carlee's tone sounded serious, but it was hard to be afraid of her from how her swollen lips made it almost impossible to pronounce the words she was trying to say.

Carp approached Buddy but was slapped repeatedly for doing so.

"Ow! Shit! What was that for?!"

"Get them!" He pointed at Carlee and Joel.

"Fuck that."

"She can't shoot all three of us at once."

Carp was doubtful. "No, but she'll get one of us for sure."

"Then so be it."

Joel saw Haley step away from Pillowface and kick, planting her foot squarely between his legs. He moaned nearly as loud as he had in the woods when fighting Clay Ray. It was a low blow, and even after all this, he still felt bad for Pillowface.

Haley managed to pull her hands away from him as he dropped to his knees and ran past Carp to join up with Carlee and Joel.

Buddy began to laugh. "You two are completely ridiculous. Do I have to do everything?" Still holding his ear with one hand, he used the other to reach behind his back, and when he brought it back, he was brandishing a white canister.

It looked like the can of pepper spray that Carlee showed Joel back in the car.

Before Carlee could even react, Buddy had used his thumb to flick the plastic stopper off the top and pushed the button down. A stream shot across the room, lapping Carlee's eyes. Her shrieks murdered Joel's ears. She pawed at her eyes, swiping them with her fingers as if she could pull the burning out.

Buddy and Carp lunged.

Carlee didn't even notice, nor did she try to shoot.

Haley yanked Joel away from Carlee so fast his toes slid across the floor a couple feet before finding traction again. The last thing he saw before being hauled outside was Carp punching his knife deep into Carlee's stomach three quick times.

CHAPTER TWENTY-NINE

(I)

Haley pulled Joel behind the shed. She leaned over, looking past him and around the side of the building. Through the windows she could see Carlee being slashed repeatedly by Carp. No way was she still alive. She was being punished extra brutally.

Buddy stood near Alan, gazing directly at her, but she doubted he could see her.

"I know you're out there," he said. "We'll be along shortly." Then he went back inside.

"What's happening?" Joel asked.

"Don't look," she said. Thankfully, he listened. "We can't get to the cars, or they'll nab us on the way. We have to go through the woods, make our way up the road that way. Get to someone's house and have them call the police."

Joel nodded, but Haley doubted he'd comprehended anything she had said.

"We have to move quick. They'll be coming after us."

Joel didn't say anything.

"Joel?"

He looked at her. His eyes were two white spheres in the dark.

"Are you going to make it?"

"Yuh-yeah. I'll be all right … I think."

"How's your hand?"

He looked down at it. From where it was broken it made his right arm look slightly longer than the left. "I can't hardly feel it anymore."

That wasn't good. Shock was probably setting in, making him numb to everything. Haley needed to keep him moving before he became completely catatonic.

"Let's go before they come after us."

"Pillowface. He … didn't kill me."

"Come on!"

She grabbed his left hand and tugged him along. Together they ran to the trail directly behind the house. If Haley remembered correctly when they got to the fork in the trail, they needed to take a right and it would lead them up to the bend on Marble Lane. Even if it didn't, it would still lead them away from here.

The darkness enveloped them when they entered the woods.

"He didn't kill me, Haley."

"I know, Joel. Come on!" He was lagging and it felt like she was about to rip his arm off. With an already broken wrist, she didn't want to add a dislocated shoulder to his injuries. "We need to move faster!"

"You don't understand."

"You're right. I don't." She sighed through her huffing breaths. "Come on!"

He jogged with her, but not fast enough. They stumbled over rocks and roots. Haley's bare feet were being poked and pricked by acorns and jagged sticks, and though it hurt, she was not going to let it slow her down. That responsibility was Joel's, and he was doing a damn fine job of it.

"We *are* friends," added Joel. "He didn't kill me because we *are* friends!"

"That's wonderful, Joel. But he killed Alan and God knows who else."

"Tonya."

"He killed Tonya?" Her legs went rubbery. "And you *knew* this?"

"Not until afterward!"

He spoke as if that was a perfectly logical argument.

"Joel, if we get out of this, you and I need to have some serious discussions about your wellbeing."

She might be able to save him physically but feared that mentally he was already dead.

(II)

She's dead, Carp. You sick bastard, that's enough!"

Carlee lay on her back while Carp was knelt over her with his knife to the hilt in her belly. He twisted the knife so the sharp edge of the blade faced her breasts, then heaved it up to her ribcage. Finally, he pulled the blade out, syrupy dark strings of blood seeping off. There were at least a dozen stab wounds on her front side and Buddy had lost count of those on her back. She'd been mangled beyond recognition, which was a shame because she had been so pretty. Buddy actually liked her and had hoped to let her live, but when she got hold of the gun, everything changed.

He put the piece of gauze he'd taken from their first-aid kit to his ear and tore the tape across it to hold the square of white mesh in place. Carp would need his hand bandaged, but the idiot could wait. "Carp, get next door and set it ablaze, posthaste."

Carp wiped the blood from his knife on the one spot of Carlee's shirt that had remained unsoiled, so now it matched the rest. "What about the two runners?"

"Face is going to get them."

Face, who'd been fretfully pacing the floor, stopped and gawked at Buddy. Buddy wasn't sure if he liked the new look, but assumed he'd warm up to it eventually.

"You heard me, old friend." Buddy stood up, grabbing his camera and mask as he got to his feet. "I'm going to pack up here. Carp's going to torch the neighbor's place, then come over and torch this one. We'll meet up at the creek in one hour."

"That doesn't give us much time," said Carp.

303

"Time is something we don't have. Not anymore. I'm sure the neighbors have heard that gunshot and are probably wondering what the hell's going on. So, we need to get this in gear."

Carp nodded. "I'm gone." He walked to the broken door, stopped at the dead body, and dragged him inside by the ankles. "I'll be back in five minutes." Then he took off.

Buddy looked back to Face, who hadn't moved. "And I don't want you going in those woods and wandering around for a while, then come back and tell me you killed them. I want proof. Bring me something. Not a finger or a toe or some bullshit like that. I want one of their heads. Got me?"

Face didn't move still.

"Face?" He raised his head to look at him. "Got me?" Finally, he nodded. "Good. Get going."

Face walked towards the door.

"Oh, Face?" He turned back. "Do you want me to pack this?" He held up the saw that had been welded or glued to a weight belt with chains adorning the sides. Face waited a moment, then nodded. "All right. They're in the woods, because it's the only place for them to go. Make it fast and don't be late getting to the creek."

Face disappeared into the shadows.

Face kicked the basement door open and marched straight to where he'd left his chainsaw. He picked it up. It felt good being in his hands again. A wonderful reunion.

He exited the basement, then walked to the edge of the yard. He could smell Haley's perfume. It would lead him straight to them like a vaporous finger beckoning him in the right direction.

He entered the woods unwillingly.

CHAPTER THIRTY

(I)

Carp stood shivering and naked in the creek, scrubbing his skin with leaves to get off the blood. It had dried and was now tacky, but he was still managing to clean himself just fine.

The gash across his hand burned like hell. Getting some antibiotic cream on it wouldn't be a bad idea once he was finished washing it. He hoped infection wasn't already setting in. That barbwire was old, rusted, and filthy, and it had been ten years since he'd had a tetanus shot, but his jaws didn't feel like they were wanting to lock up, so that was good.

Buddy slowly walked back and forth atop the slanted mound, his hands behind his back, and his eyes focused on the ground. Pillowface wasn't late yet, but there were only a couple minutes left before he would be.

Carp wondered if Buddy would stick with what he'd said. On their way to the creek, he'd declared that if Pillowface wasn't on time, they would leave him behind.

Did he mean it?

He wasn't anxious to see Face gone from the group, but he also knew they would do just fine without him. It would be tough for a while, but they'd get new members and be a strong unit yet again.

Smoke from the burning houses had corkscrewed its way through the trees and now lingered above the woods like a blanket. But from where they were at it seemed to spread around them like fog. They'd heard the faraway sirens from all the fire trucks reverberating through the trees several minutes ago. It would take them a long time to get those fires under control. He doubted the police would even realize anything was truly awry before they were long gone.

The sound of snapping twigs pulled Carp's attention to the woods. Buddy had stopped walking and was listening as well. The crackle became louder as Face emerged from the thicket of trees, carrying his chainsaw with one hand, and something else with the other.

When he stepped into the clearing, the gray light of the moon exposed the mystery item.

A head.

"Holy shit," said Carp.

It was Haley's head. Even in the darkness he could see the long blond hair twisting around Face's fingers, the stump of her neck and track of spine protruding from the bottom of it. Her eyes had been gouged out, and most of her face was torn away. In fact, if it weren't for the hair, he'd have had no idea it used to be attached to Haley's body.

I wonder how much it fucked him up to kill her and the kid.

Face would probably never recover from it. He'd seemed to really like those two. He agreed with Buddy that Face was jeopardizing everything they'd set out to do by shacking up with them, but he also thought Buddy was a son of a bitch for making Face be the one to kill them. Carp would have gladly volunteered to save him the agony.

Seeing Face stalking over the hill with the moon casting a net of murky light behind him, the saw and severed head on each side of him, spooked Carp more than he wanted to admit.

Buddy met Face by the tree stump where they'd set their bags. "I knew it." He lightly clapped his hands. "I knew you wouldn't let me down."

Face held the head up so Buddy could see. He nodded his approval. Then Face chucked the head at the creek for Carp to see. It splashed in the water like a heavy rock. Carp shouted in revulsion, hopping about the water as if a snake were nipping at his heels. He leaped out of the creek, a cold chill shuddering up his spine.

"Damn it, Face!" Carp hugged himself. "I was fucking taking a bath in there! You don't just throw a fucking head in someone's bath water!"

Buddy laughed.

"Glad *you* got a kick out of it," said Carp, stomping to his clothes. He shoved his legs into his pants.

"I am very pleased. It was a mess there for a bit, but we pulled through. This was a huge steppingstone in the plan."

Carp pulled his shirt over his head. "Glad you're happy." He hoped the sarcastic tone in his voice didn't go unnoticed.

"I am *very* happy."

Carp could see Buddy's appreciative smile glowing in the night. He wouldn't mind shoving his fist through that grill of teeth. "What's the plan from this point on, boss?"

"We need to move on. Pack up our camp, load up the van, and drive."

"To where?"

"Somewhere I've been trying to avoid going since getting out of the army."

"And where's that?"

"Home."

"No shit?"

Buddy nodded. "Yep. Since Face has proved to me that he could do what needed to be done to secure our future, I need to prove to the two of you the same. And going back home to Wisconsin will do that."

"The cheese state." Carp laughed.

"I figure we can set up a new camp and start over. In the town of Doverton, a place I used to go to as a kid. Whisper Lake."

"Sounds boring."

"Not much is out there, so it's the perfect place for us to prepare."

Pillowface waited for Buddy and Carp to finish getting the bags. Going to the Midwest was a good idea. He needed to be as far away from here as he could get and relocating to Wisconsin would ensure that.

When they were ready, Pillowface followed Buddy and Carp deeper into the woods. He looked at the blood on his hands and sighed.

He already missed the kid.

He'd never forget him.

(11)

Iridescent flames crackled and snapped behind the scorched-twisted planks of their house by the time Haley and Joel made it back. The roof had collapsed into the upper level. What remained of the overall structure was a jagged J shape.

Firefighters and police officers had raided the yard, darting back and forth in frantic dashes and shouts. The fence that ran between their house and the Cantrell's had been knocked down so the firefighters could battle both the fires simultaneously. Both looked to be under control, but massive damage had been done.

Haley's throat tightened with the swelling of her eyes. All their stuff, their memories. Mom and Dad's room, their belongings, were all gone now, burnt to crispy flakes that were now soggy clumps of ashes from all the water that had been used to douse the flames.

She looked down at Joel. Tears streamed down his blood-smeared cheeks, cutting wet lines through the dark red. He would never recover from this. His mental health had already been deteriorating after Mom and Dad's deaths, but after all this, she was certain he'd spend some time in an institution.

Please, God. Let him get back to normal someday.

Maybe Joel would take some kind of comfort in knowing he'd been right about Pillowface, and that they were indeed *friends*.

When they had fled into the woods, they'd stumbled upon a trodden body with a crushed head. For obvious reasons the face was unrecognizable, but the suit dressing the body was very familiar.

Jonesey.

She'd asked Joel about it. More like grabbed him by the shoulders and violently shook it out of him. But he finally said Jonesey had made some kind of deal with the killers, and they'd let him go in return for bringing Joel to them. He and Pillowface had found him slinking around her room earlier today and he'd escaped by jumping out the window. When he told her about the panties in his pocket, and how he'd admitted to killing Rusky, it felt as if she'd been stabbed in the back with an icy dagger.

She also believed he was the one who'd been calling her and masturbating into the phone. It all made sense in a weird, sick kind of way.

And that was when Pillowface had found them.

He lowered the chainsaw he was carrying down to the ground. There was no confrontation as he went to a spot near Jonesey and began digging into the soil with his hands. Once his arms were in the earth elbow deep, he sifted around for a couple minutes before extracting a severed head. *Tonya's* head. She had recognized her, even with the frozen face of death. Then he produced a machete and began cutting at the face, scaling the skin off like a fish. When he was finished with that, he used his thumbs to push her eyes back into her skull. The sloshing sounds her eyes made as they were imbedded into her brain were terrible.

Mercifully, he finally finished.

Joel walked over to him. Haley thought in hindsight that she should have grabbed him, but he was out of reach by the time it had occurred to her. When he approached the giant of a man, they hugged. And it was actually nice to see. Somehow, it had felt right to her knowing their friendship hadn't been affected.

She also understood his plan. Tonya had the same color of hair as hers and mauling the skin like that was his way of making it so the other guys wouldn't be able to tell it wasn't her. Why he'd had to do it, she wasn't sure, but he was going to attempt tricking them into believing Haley was dead.

They finally separated from the hug.

Joel then ran back to Haley as Pillowface hunched over and picked up his chainsaw and the severed head. Before leaving, he nodded a single nod of goodbye, then turned around and vanished into the woods as a tumult of sirens descended from the roads.

Joel hadn't spoken a word since.

Back at the edge of the yard, Haley curled her arm around her brother's shoulders and led him toward the multitude of firefighters. They spotted them coming and ran to greet them.

The one at the front, the same firefighter she'd met at the bookstore, already had a blanket and was throwing it around them. If he recognized her, he gave no indication. "What happened to you?" He cringed when he saw all the blood. "Were you attacked?"

She nodded. "Help my brother. His wrist is broken."

"Medic!" The man hastily waved his arm in their direction. Two paramedics darted towards them, medical kits bouncing off their legs. "This kid needs medical attention right away."

"What about her?" the dark-haired paramedic asked.

"I'm sure she does, but just a second on her."

He nodded, then eased Joel away from Haley's hold. They led him to an ambulance that had been backed up into the yard on the other side of the house.

"What happened to you?" the firefighter repeated.

He was escorting her to a pair of police officers. She felt nervous as they joined them at the nearest fire truck.

"She and her brother were attacked," the firefighters told the police officers.

"Do you live in one of these houses?" asked the first police officer.

"Yuh-yeah."

"This one?" He threw his thumb over his shoulder, referring to the wreckage that used to be her home.

She nodded. "I'm Haley Olsen. My brother's name is Joel."

"Tell me what happened."

She took a deep breath. "It was Geoffrey Jones. He went crazy."

"The lawyer?"

She nodded again. "Yes. His body's in the woods. My brother killed him in self-defense."

The police officer gaped at her a moment before turning to the firefighter. "Get her to the medics and see if she needs to go to the hospital right away."

"You got it." The firefighter eased her into his arms and adjusted the blanket so it fit snugly around her. "Let's get you taken care of."

Someone taking care of her sounded lovely.

As she walked with the firefighter away from the police officers, she could hear orders being barked for a unit to search the woods behind her. It was hard not to smile knowing that Jonesey would be blamed for all of this.

Bastard.

Served him right.

She wasn't exactly sure why she'd neglected to notify the police of Buddy, Carp, and Pillowface. Surely, once the rubble of both houses was searched through and dead bodies were recovered, questions would develop. She could most likely pin Carlee's regrettable death on Jonesey, but she wasn't sure about any of the others. She'd just play dumb about everything else and hoped they'd believe her.

The medic who'd taken Joel met them. "The kid's in bad shape. His wrist is badly broken and he's in shock. We need to get him to the ER."

"All right This is his sister. She needs medical assistance as well."

"We'll take her too."

"Good luck to you both," said the firefighter.

She watched him rush back to the chaos that was her backyard. She realized why she felt so comfortable around him. Something about him reminded her of her father.

She smiled.

The ambulance floored it as they pulled away from the house.

Maybe it was for the best that it had burned. They could start a new life, a new beginning. She looked at Joel, and seeing the blank expression on his face, she understood that she would probably start this new life alone.

PILLOWFACE RETURNS!

HELL DEPARTED: PILLOWFACE VS. THE LURKERS

Now Available!

They've lived in the woods and cornfields for too long. Now they're out, killing anyone that crosses their paths. The town of Doverton has been nearly wiped out, due to the army of small, humanoid creatures with sharp teeth and bloodthirsty appetites. Those who have yet to be added to the creatures' menu live in fear and seclusion.

But that is about to change with the arrival of three psychopaths on the run from a bloodbath they left behind in North Carolina. Pillowface, Buddy, and Carp are looking for a quiet place to hide, a place to recharge and heal so they can kill again. Little do they know, another form of monster is waiting for them, ready to give them their biggest challenge to date. Though they are an army of three, the tribe of ancient creatures known as the Haunchies, have never faced such a deadly threat.

The fight will be bloody. Many will die. And those caught in the middle of this war will be lucky to survive.

The Skin Show

The Skin Show has existed all over the south for generations–hidden clubs offering their patrons a location to be whoever they desire, in a playground with free reign to do whatever they want without judgment or castigation. There is no cover charge, the drinks are free, and rules do not exist within the walls of The Skin Show. However, once you've entered, you'll never leave, for what exists underneath each club is something of fairytales.

Danny Raab was drawn into The Skin Show's inescapable clutch, and he never returned. Now, Andy Raab is in the midst of a desperate search for his brother. Accompanied by Karen, Danny's probation officer, they will infiltrate The Skin Show's living nightmares of debauchery, only to learn they have been on the guest list all along.

The Lurkers

They've lived in the woods and cornfields for as long as anyone can remember. Small, humanoid creatures with sharp teeth and grasping hands. The people in what's left of the small town Doverton live in fear. They've learned that if they let the creatures take what they want, they won't be attacked. An uneasy peace has reigned. But no more. The leader of the creatures has decided his kind will be dormant no longer. To survive, they must kill. They will satisfy their unholy hunger with their favorite prey—humans.

But some humans—females—will be kept alive in captivity…to breed.

The Lurking Season

People have whispered about the tiny humanoid creatures in the woods and cornfields of Doverton, Wisconsin for decades. Three years ago, a wildfire devoured much of the rural village, but as the ashes were cleared, more questions were uncovered—including abandoned houses, missing people and dead bodies. Since the fire seemed to wipe out most of the town's woodland acres, the murmurs about the creatures have gone quiet. The remaining residents have begun to rebuild their lives, trying to forget about the tragedy that nearly killed them all. Yet the mysteries remained unsolved.

Now a group of people will go there with good intentions, venturing into the dead heart of Doverton, thinking it's safe. But they will find out that the legend was only sleeping. Now it's awake. And ready to kill again.

Something Violent

Ron McClure, a cherished marriage counselor, has helped many couples through matrimonial turmoil. His latest accomplishment was the complete restoration of a popular Hollywood couple, once notorious for the public slandering of their spouses. The garnered notoriety has attracted the attention of publishers, magazines, and countless talk shows. It has also attracted the attention of a couple who've not only lost the thrill in their marriage…but also the thrill to kill together. Fearing they're at the tragic end of their relationship, the couple kidnap Ron in a bizarre attempt at the restoration of a shattered, twisted love now on the brink of a terrifying metamorphosis.

Bigfoot Beach

A bizarre, brutal murder. A missing woman. And a giant footprint in the sand. Now, the dying beach community known as Seashell Cove finally has a hook to attract the tourists—a Bigfoot on the beach! As the summer season winds down, the tourists go home, and the town begins preparing for the colder months.

Soon, more strange footprints are found, other mysterious sightings are reported. Then the deaths begin. Could there really be a Bigfoot running loose in Seashell Cove?

Kristopher Rufty

A tracker with a personal agenda, the local sheriff, a hero whose fifteen minutes of fame expired a long time ago, and a female reporter looking for a scoop will team up to find out for sure.

Jagger
Other than the trailer park left to her by her deceased daddy, Amy's favorite treasure is Jagger, her 180-pound bullmastiff. One day while she is away, Clayton, her best friend's scumbag boyfriend sneaks into her yard and takes the dog. His prize fighting pit bull was killed during its last match, costing a lot of bad people a lot of money. To make up for his dog's losses, and to save his own life, Clayton enlists the help of a medical student dropout to turn Jagger into a killing machine by pumping him full of experimental drugs and muscle enhancers. Now Jagger is a monster, a beast that can't feel pain, with an unquenchable thirst for blood. He quickly breaks out of his pen and starts making his way home, tearing apart anyone in his path on his way to the one he feels has betrayed him the most—Amy.

Prank Night
The onslaught starts with the brutal murder of a woman. The following night, cars are vandalized, stranding the residents, rendering them vulnerable to the looming chaos. With no chance of escape, the town becomes a battleground as, one by one, the residents fall prey to Prank Night.

Terror will flow through the quaint village, flooding the streets with blood.

A Dark Autumn
He's a writer seeking solitude. They are four women on vacation looking for fun and relaxation. But when they meet they will find only terror. An appalling crime will lead to an unthinkable, gruesome revenge. In the deep woods of Mountain Rock, no one will hear the screams, the agony, the mayhem.

No one will hear them die.

Anathema

Hunter Jensen always dreamed of a big family house in the country. Thanks to the success of his latest novel, he's finally able to make his dreams a reality in the tranquil town of Hargrave, North Carolina. Life is beautiful until his daughter Crystal tells him about the girl who lives in her closet. Her imaginary friendship is only the first of many disconcerting events that threaten to fracture his dream of country living into a nightmare straight out of his novels.

Does an invisible girl truly conjure the sobs that haunt the hallways at night? Is she to blame for the bizarre noises in the darkness? Or has his daughter's vivid imagination simply crept into his own?

As Hunter seeks to uncover the secrets long buried in the town's shadows, he begins to fear a force more sinister than anything he's ever imagined is drawing him and his family toward their demise.

ABOUT THE AUTHOR

KRISTOPHER RUFTY lives in North Carolina with his three children and pets. He's written numerous books, including *All Will Die, The Devoured and the Dead, The Lurkers, Pillowface, Desolation*, and more. When he's not writing, he's obsessing over gardening and growing food.

For more about Kristopher Rufty, please visit his website: www.kristopherrufty.com

He can be found on Facebook, Instagram, and Twitter as well.

Made in the USA
Las Vegas, NV
13 July 2023

74690207R00194